JORGE AMADO is "Latin America's most widely read writer" (*Washington Post Book World*). The son of a cocoa planter, he was born in 1912 in Ilhéus, the provincial capital of the state of Bahia, Brazil, whose society he portrays in such acclaimed novels as GABRIELA, CLOVE AND CINNAMON; DONA FLOR AND HER TWO HUSBANDS (basis of the highly successful film and Broadway musical); and TEREZA BATISTA: HOME FROM THE WARS. The theme of class struggle dominates his novels of the 30s and 40s, but with the 50s and GABRIELA, CLOVE AND CINNAMON, the political emphasis gives way to a lighter, more novelistic approach. Other novels translated into English and published in Avon Bard editions include: HOME IS THE SAILOR; SHEPHERDS OF THE NIGHT; TENT OF MIRACLES; TIETA; TWO DEATHS OF QUINCAS WATERYELL; THE VIOLENT LAND; and SEA OF DEATH.

Other Avon Bard Books by
Jorge Amado

DONA FLOR AND HER TWO HUSBANDS
GABRIELA, CLOVE AND CINNAMON
HOME IS THE SAILOR
SEA OF DEATH
SHEPHERDS OF THE NIGHT
TENT OF MIRACLES
TEREZA BATISTA: HOME FROM THE WARS
TIETA
TWO DEATHS OF QUINCAS WATERYELL
THE VIOLENT LAND

JUBIABÁ

JORGE AMADO

Translated by
Margaret A. Neves

A BARD BOOK/PUBLISHED BY AVON BOOKS

JUBIABÁ is an original publication of Avon Books. This work has never before appeared in book form in English. This work is a novel. Any similarity to actual persons or events is purely coincidental.

AVON BOOKS
A division of
The Hearst Corporation
1790 Broadway
New York, New York 10019

Published by arrangement with the author
Library of Congress Catalog Card Number: 84-91139
ISBN: 0-380-88567-0

First Bard Printing, October, 1984

Printed in the U.S.A.

OPB 10 9 8 7 6 5 4 3 2

JUBIABÁ

PART I

CHAPTER 1
Boxing Match

The crowd stood up as if it were all one person. There was silence. The referee counted: "Six . . ."

But before he could count seven, the blond man forced himself up on one arm, and gathering all his strength, got to his feet. Then the crowd sat down again and started to shout. The black man attacked him furiously, and the fighters grappled with each other in the middle of the ring. The crowd screamed, "Knock him down! Knock him down!"

Largo da Sé Square had been drenched by a downpour that night. The men were squeezed together on the benches, sweaty, their eyes pinned on the ring where Antônio Balduíno was fighting Ergin, the German. The Holy Virgin of the centuries-old church gazed down on the men. Sparse light bulbs illuminated the raised platform that served as a boxing ring. Soldiers, stevedores, workers, students, men who wore only a shirt and pants, anxiously followed the fight. Blacks, whites, and mulattoes cheered for Antônio Balduíno, who had already knocked down his adversary twice.

The second time it had looked like the white man wouldn't get up again. But before the referee could count to seven, he rose and kept on fighting. There were words of admiration from the audience. Someone murmured, "That German's some man, all right."

Even so, they continued to cheer for the tall black man who was the Bahian heavyweight champion. They screamed without stopping now, wishing the fight would come to an end and that that end would be with Ergin stretched out on the floor.

A skinny little man with a dried-up face chewed a dead cigarette butt. A short Negro marked the rhythm of the crowd's yelling by slapping his knees.

"Knock-him-down! Knock-him-down!"

And they shifted restlessly, shouting so loud you could hear them down in Castro Alves Square.

But in the next round, the white man came at the Negro angrily and drove him onto the ropes. The crowd didn't mind very much, expecting the black man to retaliate. And Balduíno really wanted to pound the German's bloody face. But Ergin didn't give him time, punching him violently, making the Negro's eye into a well of blood. The German grew bigger suddenly and hid the black man, who was now taking blows in the face, chest, and belly. Balduíno again went on the ropes, held onto them, and remained there passively without reacting. He gripped the ropes hard, concentrating only on not falling down. In front of him the German seemed like a demon hammering his face to a pulp. Blood streamed from Balduíno's nose, his right eye was shut, and there was a deep cut below his earlobe. Confusedly, he saw the white man jumping in front of him, and from far away he could hear the roaring of the crowd. They were booing him. Their hero had fallen. They yelled, "Get 'im, black man!"

But only at first. Little by little the crowd grew silent, discouraged, watching the black man lose the fight. When they started shouting again, it was to boo him.

"Female nigger! Woman in pants! Go, blondie, get 'im!"

They were angry because the black man was losing. They had paid three mil-reis to see the Bahian champion finish off the white man, who said he was the "Champion of Central Europe." And now what they were seeing was the Negro losing the fight. They weren't happy, moving restlessly, and at times cheering the white man, at times booing him. When the gong sounded to end the round, they gave a sigh of relief.

Antônio Balduíno staggered to the corner of the ring, holding himself up on the ropes. There the thin man who was chewing the useless cigarette spat and called, "Where's Antônio Balduíno, the black man who always beats the white guys?"

Antônio Balduíno heard him. He took a gulp of rum from the bottle that Gordo offered him and turned toward the audience, looking for the owner of the voice. It came again, metallic: "Where's the man who can beat the white guys?"

This time part of the crowd accompanied the little man, crying in chorus, "Where is he? Where is he?"

That hurt Balduíno more than the lash of a whip. He didn't feel his bruises from the white boxer, but he could feel the censure of his fans. He motioned to Gordo.

"When I leave here, I'm gonna work that guy over. Keep an eye on him."

And when the signal sounded to resume the fight, the black man threw himself at Ergin. He landed a blow on the German's mouth and then another in his stomach. The crowd recognized its champion once more and roared, "Yay, Antônio Balduíno! Yay, Baldo! Knock him down!"

The short Negro went back to slapping his knees in rhythm. The thin man smiled.

The black man continued to fight, a great fury in him.

It was when the German came at him, wanting to hit his other eye, that Balduíno dodged him with a rapid movement, and like a mechanical spring uncoiling, caught Ergin under the chin. The body of the Central European Champion described a curve and fell flat.

The crowd, hoarse, applauded in chorus.

"Baldo! Bal-do! *Bal-do!*"

The referee counted.

"Six . . . seven . . . eight . . ."

With satisfaction, Antônio Balduíno viewed the white man stretched at his feet. Then he surveyed the audience where the catcalls had come from, looking for the man who had said Balduíno couldn't beat white guys anymore. He smiled at Gordo as if he hadn't found the man. The referee was counting.

"Nine . . . ten!"

He raised Balduíno's arm. The crowd bellowed, but the Negro heard only the metallic voice of the man with the dead cigarette.

"There, black man, you can still beat the white guys."

Some of the spectators went out through the wide, rusty gate. But the majority ran toward the square of light where the ring was and carried Antônio Balduíno on their shoulders. A stevedore and a student held one of his legs, and two mulattoes the other. They carried him to the public urinal in the square where the boxers changed their clothes.

Antônio Balduíno put on his blue outfit, took a gulp of rum, received the hundred mil-reis to which he had the right, and told his admirers, "The white man was a weakling . . . white guys can't stand up to Antônio Balduíno . . . right here's the man."

He smiled, stuffed the money into his pants pocket, and went off toward Zara's boardinghouse, where Zefa lived. Zefa was a crossbred girl with filed teeth who came from the state of Maranhão.

CHAPTER 2
Childhood

Antônio Balduíno would sit on top of the hill watching the row of lights that was the city below. Sounds of a guitar would wind about the hill as soon as the moon appeared, and sorrowful songs would be sung. The store-cum-bar of Lourenço the Spaniard would fill with men who stopped to talk and read the newspaper that the owner provided for his drinking customers.

Antônio Balduíno always wore an old cotton shirt. He would run through the muddy streets and alleys of the hill, playing with other boys his age.

In spite of being only eight, Antônio Balduíno was already the chief of the bands of kids who roamed through Capa-Negro Hill and adjacent neighborhoods. But when night fell, there was no game that could tear him away from contemplating the lights that came on in the city, so close and yet so distant. He would sit on the same embankment when twilight came and wait with a lover's anxiousness for the streets to light up. There was something voluptuous in that expectancy, like a man waiting for his woman. Antônio Balduíno's eyes would strain in the direction of the city, waiting. His heart beat faster as the darkness invaded the houses, covered the streets and hills, and sent up from the city a muted clamor of people going home, of men discussing the business of the day and the crime of the night before.

Antônio Balduíno, who had gone into the city only a few times, and on these occasions dragged hurriedly along behind his aunt, could feel all the life of the town at that twilight hour. The sounds rose from below. He would listen to the confused stir, the wave of noises that floated up the slippery streets of the hill. He could feel his nerves vibrating with each sound, each suggestion of life and struggle. He would imagine himself a grown man, living a man's hurried life, fighting each day's fight. His small eyes would sparkle, and more than once he felt a desire to run off down the hill and watch at close hand the spectacle of the city in those hours of dusk. He knew very well that he would miss his supper and get a thrashing when he returned. But that wasn't what kept him from investigating close-up the animation of the city returning from work; what he didn't want to miss was seeing the lights come on, a thing that for him was always new and beautiful, a revelation.

Thus the city would become almost completely enveloped in shadows.

Antônio Balduíno would watch until he couldn't make out anything more. A cool wind would rise with the darkness, but he would not feel it. He would luxuriate in the noises, the sound-mixture that gradually became louder and louder. He didn't miss a single element. He could distinguish the laughter, the shouts, the voices of the drunks, the conversations about politics, the trailing voices of the blind men begging for a hand-out for the love of God, the screech of the trolley cars loaded with people so full that they even hung on the outside. Slowly he would savor the life of the city.

One day he felt a stab of emotion so strong that it made him shiver all over. He even stood up, trembling with pleasure. It was because he distinguished somebody crying, a woman, and voices that consoled her. It rose with a confused rush inside him and swept him away, dizzy with enjoyment. Crying . . . somebody, a woman, was crying in the darkening city. Antônio Balduíno listened to the mournful sobs until they were extinguished in the shriek of a trolley scraping along its tracks. Antônio Balduíno held his breath, hoping to catch the sound again. But they must have taken the woman away from the street, because he couldn't hear her anymore. That evening he didn't want any supper, and he didn't run through the streets with his friends as usual. His aunt commented, "That boy saw something. He's sly as I don't know what. . . ."

Good days, too, were those when he heard the bell of the ambulance clanging below in the city. There was suffering down there, and Antônio Balduíno, a boy of eight, took pleasure in those bits of suffering as a man takes pleasure in a woman.

But the rows of lights that came on purified everything. Antônio Balduíno would lose himself in contemplating the rows of bulbs, his bright eyes submerged in their glow. He would want to be kind to the other little black children of Capa-Negro Hill. If anyone came up to him at that moment, he would undoubtedly caress them, instead of greeting them with his customary pinches and the curses he had mastered early. He would, likely as not, stroke the springy hair of his playmate and lean against his chest. And perhaps he would smile. But the other boys would be running about the hill, Antônio Balduíno forgotten. He watched the lights, distinguished passing figures. Perhaps they were couples out for a stroll. Behind him, on the hill, guitars plinked, black people conversed. Old Luísa would shout, "Baldo, come eat your supper! Impossible kid . . ."

His Aunt Luísa had been mother and father to him. Of his real father, Antônio Balduíno knew nothing except that he had been called Valentim, that he had been a follower of the revolutionary Antônio Conselheiro when he was a young man, that he loved the black girls he found on all sides, drank valiantly, and died under a streetcar one day when he was having an extra-big bash. These things he heard from his aunt when she discussed her dead brother with the neighbors. She would always conclude: "Now there was a black man handsome enough to make your mouth water. And the worst temper you ever saw. Biggest drinker, too."

Antônio Balduíno would listen, quiet, and would make his father into a hero. Certainly, he must have lived the life of the city at the time the lights went on. At times he would try to reconstruct his father's life with the pieces of adventures that old Luísa told him. His imagination was soon lost in heroic acts of courage. He would stare at the fire, thinking about what his father must have been like. Every time he heard about something grandiose and extravagant, he immediately imagined his father had done it, or something better. When he played cops and robbers with the other boys of the hill, they would ask him who he wanted to be. Antônio, who had never been to the movies, didn't want to be Eddie Polo, Elmo, or Maciste.

"I want to be my father."

The others always jeered.

"What did your father ever do?"

"Lots of things."

"He didn't pick up a car with one arm like Maciste."

"He picked up a truck."

"A truck?"

"Yeah. Loaded, too."

"Who saw him do it?"

"My aunt. Just ask her. And if you don't like it, say so and see what happens."

Various times he fought for the heroic memory of the father he had never known. In truth, he fought for the father he imagined, the father he would have loved had he known him.

Of his mother, Antônio Balduíno knew nothing at all.

He ran free over the hill, and so far, he neither loved nor hated. He was as innocent as an animal and had instinct as his only law. He chased up and down the streets of the hill in a mad rush; he played with broomstick horses. He talked little and smiled widely.

Very early he became the leader of the other boys on the hill, even those much older than he. He was imaginative and had more courage than anybody else. His aim with a slingshot was good, and his eyes would flash during fights. When he played cops and robbers he was always the chief. And often he would forget he was playing and fight in earnest. He knew all the dirty words there were and repeated them constantly.

He would help old Luísa to cook the *munguzá* and *mingau* that she sold every night in Terreio Square downtown. She would seat herself beside her small folding table on which the pots were placed and ladle out the food. Antônio Balduíno would bring her the grate and help her with the cooking equipment; the only thing he didn't know how to do was grate the coconut. At first the other boys made fun of him, saying he was the kitchen maid, but they stopped it when Antônio Balduíno threw a rock at Zebedeu and hit him on the head. His aunt whipped him, but he couldn't understand why. However, he always quickly forgave the old woman for the thrashings she gave him. Besides, not many of her lashes hit him since he was very agile, wriggling like a fish in his aunt's hands and dodging her blows. It was a game, an exercise from which he often came out laughing, the winner, having managed to avoid various attempts of Luísa's strap. In spite of all this she would say, "He's the man of the house."

The old woman was a talker, and interesting to listen to. The neighbors would come to chat and hear the stories she told, tales of ghosts and fairy godmothers and things that happened during slave days. Sometimes she would recite or read stories in verse. There was one that started like this:

Dear readers, come let us assemble,
A terrible tale I'll relate.
'Twill cause every person to tremble
A hair-raising story of hate.
For who could believe there existed
A being so filthy and vile
As to murder alone, unassisted,
Her parents, and she but a child?

It was the story of a daughter who was cursed, a murder case the newspapers had reported with big headlines. A popular poet, the author of ABC ballads and sambas, had made it into a long poem to sell for two hundred reis in the market.

Antônio Balduíno adored this story. He would ask the old woman to tell it over and over, and cry when she wouldn't. He also liked to hear the men tell stories about the outlaws Antônio Silvino and Lucas da Feira. On these nights he didn't go out to play.

Once they asked him, "What are you going to be when you grow up?"

He answered promptly, "A bandit."

He didn't know of a more beautiful or noble career, nor one that required more virtues, such as knowing how to shoot and to be brave.

"What you need is to go to school," they told him.

He asked himself what for. He had never heard that bandits needed to know how to read. Bosses knew how to read, and bosses were soft. He knew of Dr. Olímpio, a doctor with no patients, who from time to time would come up the hill in search of these nonexistent patients, and Dr. Olímpio was a skinny weakling who couldn't even take a well-aimed slap.

Moreover, his aunt could hardly read but was very much respected on the hill. Nobody bothered her, nobody gave her any back talk. Who was fool enough to talk to old Luísa when she was having one of her headache attacks? These headaches terrified Antônio Balduíno. Every so often his aunt would get one, and she would scream like a crazy woman. The neighbors would come to help, and she would throw them out, yelling that she didn't want anyone there, they could go to hell.

One day Antônio Balduíno heard two women neighbors talking when old Luísa was having one of her attacks.

The first one said, "Those headaches of hers are from carrying big pots of boiling-hot food on her head every night from here to the Terreio. The heat affects her head."

"Oh, go on, Rosa! That's a spirit, don't you see? A spirit and a powerful one at that. One of those that walks around lost, not knowing they're already dead. They wander up and down looking for a living body to house them. A spirit of the damned, Jesus forgive me."

The others agreed with her. In Antônio Balduíno's mind there was great doubt mixed with great fear. He was afraid of souls from the beyond, but he couldn't understand why they would come to inhabit his aunt's head.

On these days Jubiabá would come to his house. Antônio Balduíno would go to call him at Luísa's bidding. He would arrive at the small door of the low house and knock. A voice would come from within, asking who it was.

"Aunt Luísa's asking for pai Jubiabá to come over to our house 'cause she's having an attack. . . ."

And he would run off. He was scared silly of Jubiabá. He would hide behind the door and watch through the crack as the old medicine man came, leaning on a staff, walking slowly. His hair was white, his body bent and thin. Men would stop to greet him.

"Good day, pai Jubiabá."

"Our Lord give you a good day. . . ."

He would walk by, blessing people as he went. Even the

Spaniard from the bar would bow his head to receive the blessing. The children would disappear from the street when they saw the ancient figure of the voodoo priest. They would whisper, "Here comes Jubiabá!"

And they would run off to hide in the houses.

Jubiabá always carried a bunch of herbs that rustled in the wind, and muttered words in the African Nagô dialect. He would come along the street talking to himself and blessing people, his old cashmere trousers dragging, and above them, his embroidered shirt flapping like a flag according to the caprices of the wind. When Jubiabá went in to pray for old Luísa, Antônio Balduíno would run out into the street. But he knew the old woman's headache would go away.

Antônio Balduíno never knew what to expect from Jubiabá. He respected him, though with a respect different from that he had for the priest Silvino, his aunt Luísa, Lourenço the Spaniard, Zé Camarão, or even the legendary figures of Virgulino Lamipão and Eddie Polo. Stooped over, Jubiabá would make his way through the alleyways of the hill, receiving greetings from the men, who always treated him respectfully. Once in a while luxurious cars would stop before his door. One day a boy told Balduíno that Jubiabá could turn into a werewolf. Another affirmed that he had the devil corked up in a bottle.

On certain nights, the sound of strange music would come from Jubiabá's house. Antônio Balduíno would toss and turn restlessly on his straw mat. The music seemed to be calling him with rhythmic drumbeats, sounds of dancing, mysterious voices. Undoubtedly, Luísa was there with her red chintz skirt and wide petticoats. Antônio Balduíno didn't sleep on these nights. In his healthy and unfettered childhood, Jubiabá was the only mystery.

Nights on Capa-Negro Hill were lots of fun. Antônio Balduíno learned many things in the nights of his childhood, principally lots of stories. These were told by men and women gathered in front of their neighbors' doors in the long conversations of moonlit evenings. On Sunday nights when there was no voodoo ceremony at Jubiabá's house, many people would come and sit on the sidewalk outside old Luísa's house. Since it was a holy day, she didn't go to sell her *mingau.* At other doors, other groups would converse, sing to the guitar, and drink a gulp of the rum that was always brought out for company, but none of the groups was as large as that which gathered in front of Luísa's door. Even Jubiabá would appear occasionally, and he, too, would tell stories of things that happened many years ago, often using words in Nagô. He would give advice and cite proverbs. He was sort of a patriarch to that group of blacks and mulattoes who lived on Capa-Negro Hill in shoddily built dwellings covered with zinc. When he spoke, everyone listened attentively and nodded their assent in respectful silence. On these nights of conversation, Antônio Balduíno would abandon the races and games of his friends and sit down to listen. He would give his life to hear a story, and if it was told in verse form, better yet.

That was why he was so fond of Zé Camarão, a rowdy young man who was always out of work and even had a police record for vagrancy. Zé Camarão had two great virtues in Antônio Balduíno's eyes: He was brave, and he sang ballads of famous gunmen, accompanying himself on the guitar. He would play sad music, too, waltzes and songs, at parties in the shacks on Capa-Negro Hill and in other poor districts of the city, for at parties he was an indispensable element. He was a tall, yellowish mulatto, and was continually twisting his body. He had been famous ever since he disarmed two sailors by using *capoeira* fighting blows. There were those who didn't like him, who looked at him with hostile eyes, but Zé Camarão spent hours and hours teaching the boys of the hill *capoeira* technique. He had infinite patience. He would roll on the ground with the urchins, showing them how to strike a blow with the legs while turning a cartwheel, or how to grab the knife from a man's hand. He was loved by the boys, who looked on him as an idol. Antônio Balduíno liked to hang around him, listening to him tell of things that had happened to him. And since he was already the best *capoeira* student, he wanted to learn to play the guitar, too.

"Will you teach me, Zé Camarão?"

"Sure, I'll teach you."

He would take messages to Zé Camarão's girl friends and defend him when they spoke badly of him.

"He's my friend. Why don't you go repeat that in front of him? You're scared, that's why. . . ."

Zé Camarão was inevitably part of the conversations in front of Luísa's door. He would walk up, hips swinging in his swaggering manner, and squat down, dragging on a cheap cigarette. He would listen to the interesting cases, the stories, the discussions, without speaking. But when someone told a tale that impressed the audience, Zé Camarão would tuck his cigarette behind his ear and say, "Hmmm, that's nothing compared with what happened to me one time . . ."

And an adventure would unfold, a story so full of details that no one would doubt the truth of it. And when the mulatto saw a sign of doubt in the eyes of someone present, he wouldn't show the slightest discomfort.

"If you don't believe me, friend, ask Zé Fortunato; he was with me."

There was always somebody who had been with him. Always an eyewitness who wouldn't let him lie. And whenever there was a lot of noise over something in the city, Zé Camarão had been in the middle of it, by his own account. If they were talking about a crime, he would interrupt: "I was right nearby . . ."

And he would tell his version, in which he always had an outstanding role. But when he had to, he would fight for real. You could ask Lourenço the barman, who had two knife scars on his face. Hadn't he tried to throw Zé Camarão out of his bar, the dirty Spaniard? The dark-skinned girls who listened to the talk would stare at him. They liked his swaggering ways, his reputation for being brave, and the imaginative way he had of telling a story, making comparisons with them and their characteristics: the smile of one, the red lips of another. They especially liked to hear him sing with his full voice to the music of the guitar.

In the midst of the talk, when someone finished telling an incident and everybody fell silent, a girl would always remember, "Sing something for us, Zé."

"Oh, but the talk is so good—" He would pretend to be modest.

"Come on, Zé, sing!"

"But I left my guitar at home."

"It doesn't matter, Baldo'll go get it."

Antônio Balduíno would already be running toward the shack where Zé Camarão lived. But the latter would make them plead.

"Today my voice isn't so good. Excuse me, girls, but—"

Then they would all beg, "Sing, Zé Camarão, sing, please!"

"All right, just one song."

But he would sing many, *tiranas, cocos,* sambas, old-fashioned songs, sad songs that would fill one's eyes with tears, and adventurous ABC's that delighted Antônio Balduíno:

"Adios, Saco de Limão
The place where I was born,
They took me prisoner to Salvador
And now I am forlorn."

This was the ABC of the gunman Lucas da Feira, one of Antônio Balduíno's favorite heroes.

"Brave and bragging, I went my way,
I had everything you please,
From a princess to keep me company
To a snuffbox to make me sneeze.

"Carried me off to Salvador,
They thought they'd jeer and hoot,
But I rode on horseback into town
And the guards they went on foot."

They would comment in whispers.

"He was awful, that Lucas."

"They say he had an aim with a gun that was something cruel."

"But they say he was a good man . . ."

"Good!"

"He only robbed the rich people. To get their money and give it to the poor."

"What does a poor man have to steal?
I always let them be.
But rich men with padded wallets
Not a one escaped from me."

"Didn't I say?"
"A good man, for sure."

"Mulatto girls with long black hair,
White ladies fine to see,
Black girls when there was nothing else,
Not one escaped from me."

At this point, Zé Camarão would glance sweetly over the group of girls and smile his very best smile. They would be admiring him as if he were Lucas da Feira himself. The men would chuckle aloud. And then would come the part about the outlaw's boastful heroism and faithfulness to his word.

"No one will know my partner's name
I'd rather die than tell,
'Cause the man who turns his partner in
Deserves to fry in hell.

"Stories of my doings spread
Through town and countryside,
They used to call me captain,
A name I wore with pride."

But there was one part of the song in which Zé Camarão's voice was fuller and his eyes sweeter. It was when he sang the verse of the letter *U*.

"U is a vowel letter,
A-E-I-O, then U.
Good-bye Caldeirão da Feira
And good-bye to one I knew . . ."

He would look at his favorite girl, and in that instant he would be Lucas da Feira, outlaw and assassin, who nevertheless loved someone. He would finish the song to rounds of applause.

"Zero is what my life is worth,
I jeered at old and young,
But fate caught up with me at last,
And now my song is sung."

One more samba to finish up. Very nostalgic and romantic, sung in Zé Camarão's saddest voice:

"I'm leaving this land
Where the women are cruel,
I'm leaving this land
But I'll be longing for you . . ."

The girls and women loved it. "So pretty . . ."

"Sad enough to make you cry . . ."

A woman with a swollen belly, several months' pregnant, was soberly telling a friend her story.

"When I was still pretty, he liked me. There was nothing he wouldn't buy me. He even said he'd marry me, with a priest and a judge."

"With a priest and a judge?"

"That's right, honey . . . when men want to take advantage of you, they're worse than the devil. He promised me all sorts of things. And like a fool I believed him. We lived together for a while, and he fixed me up like this. I had to go to work and got all yellow; I lost my color. He left me for a half-breed tramp who was always flashing her teeth at him."

"Why don't you cast a spell on him so he'll come back?"

"What for? I'm carrying out my destiny. It's God who determines our destiny. . . ."

"But look: If I were you, I'd at least cast a spell so the creature who stole him would get sick, then maybe if some woman took my man, would I leave it like that, do nothing? No, honey, I'd get somebody to cast a spell on her; she'll get leprosy and he'll come back nice as anything. And pai Jubiabá can do it so well, his spells are so strong."

"What for? Destiny is something decided up there," and she pointed at the sky. "We each bring one with us into the world, and we have to carry it out. This one here"—she pointed at her enormous belly—"he's already got his all prepared."

Old Luísa supported her opinion.

"That's right, child. That's how it is."

The conversation turned to general matters.

"Say, do you know Gracinha, a dark-haired girl who lives in Guindaste dos Padres?"

One little woman knew her. "Isn't she the one with no teeth, ugly as a rattlesnake?"

"That's the one. Well, listen here, even with that face of hers, she stole Ricardina's boyfriend, Ricardina who's a real piece of woman. It was a powerful charm Jubiabá used."

"She had the charm in bed," a man said, laughing.

"They say Balbino died of a spell, too."

"No, he didn't. That one died from sheer rottenness. He was mean as a snake."

A fat old Negro who was scraping the sole of his foot with a jackknife said in a low voice, "You know what he did to old Zequiel? It was enough to make your hair stand on end. You all know the old man was a fine fellow, serious-minded as they come. I knew him real well, we worked together as bricklayers. An honest man. There wasn't another like him on earth. But one day he had the bad luck to run up against Balbino. That rotten so-and-so pretended to be friendly with the old man so he could get hold of his daughter. You all remember Rosa. *I* sure do . . . she was the most beautiful black gal I ever looked on with these mortal eyes. Well, Balbino took to courting her; all he talked about was getting married."

The pregnant woman said, "Exactly like what Roque did to me. . . ."

"They even had the date fixed. But wouldn't you know, one night old Zequiel went out to work. At that time he was working down on the docks. There was a ship they had to load. Balbino, being the fiancé, went inside the house and took Rosa in to show her his new clothes that were put away in the old man's room. He threw her down on the bed, and she said she yelled and wouldn't let him have his way. So he started in hitting her until she was all beat up, covered with blood just as if she had been murdered. And then he was even calm enough to open the old man's suitcase and get the money that was inside, his miserable fifty mil-reis that was to be for the wedding party. When the old man got home, he nearly went crazy. So Balbino, who was just a windbag and no man at all, got scared of the old man. He hid out until one day he got two more men together, and they jumped old Zequiel in the dark. They beat him up so bad he almost died. Didn't even go to jail. They say Balbino was being protected by high-up folks."

"That's what they say. One day a soldier arrested him and locked him up. You know what happened? Balbino got loose, and the soldier was put in the clink."

"They say he was always telling the police where the voodoo ceremonies were being held so they could come close them down."

Nobody had noticed Jubiabá's arrival. The magic man spoke:

"But he died an ugly death."

The men lowered their heads. They knew very well they couldn't tell Jubiabá anything; he was a pai-de-santo.

"He died an ugly death. The eye of mercy ran dry in him. Only the eye of wickedness was left. When he died, the eye of mercy opened again." He repeated, "The eye of mercy ran dry. Only the eye of wickedness was left."

Then a thickset Negro moved close to Jubiabá.

"How is that, pai Jubiabá?"

"Nobody should close the eye of mercy. It's bad to close the eye of mercy . . . it doesn't bring anything good."

Then he said something in Nagô, and when Jubiabá spoke Nagô, all of them trembled.

"Ôjú ànun fó ti iká, li ôkú."

Suddenly the thickset man threw himself at Jubiabá's feet and said, "I've closed the eye of mercy, folks; one day I closed the eye of mercy . . ."

Jubiabá looked at the Negro, his eyes like slits. The others, men and women alike, moved away.

"It was up in the high backlands one time. Everything was dry. Cattle were dying, people were dying, everything was dying. We decided to run away from the drought. There were lots of us at the beginning, but many people were left along the way. Finally, it was only me and João Janjão. One day he carried me on his back because I couldn't stand on my legs. He had the eye of mercy wide open, and our throats were dry. The sun was terrible, and where could you find water in that endless desert? Nobody knew. . . . One day we got a canteen of water at a ranch so we could continue our journey. João Janjão was carrying it; we had to ration what we drank. We were always thirsty. It was when we met another man, a white man who was almost dead from thirst. João Janjão wanted to give him some water, and I wouldn't let him. I swear there was only a few drops left, not even enough for me and him . . . and him wanting to give it to that white man. He had the eye of mercy wide open. But the thirst had dried mine up. Only the eye of badness was left. He wanted to give the man some water and I fought with him. And I killed him in my anger. He had carried me on his back. . . ."

The Negro stared into the blackness of the night. Countless stars sparkled in the sky. Jubiabá's eyes were closed.

"He had carried me on his back one whole day . . . he had the eye of mercy wide open. I want to make him disappear from in front of me, but I can't. He's there, right there in front of me, looking at me. . . ."

He rubbed his eyes, wanting to remove something. But he couldn't, so he kept staring.

"He carried me a whole day on his back. . . ."

Jubiabá repeated monotonously, "It's bad when the eye of mercy runs dry. It brings disgrace."

The man got up and went down the hill carrying his story.

Antônio Balduíno listened and learned. For him, these conversations were beneficial classes—the only school that he and the other children of the hill possessed. Thus they were educated and chose careers. Strange careers, those of the children of the hill, careers that didn't demand many lessons: vagabonds, rowdies, thieves. There was only one other type of career: the slavery of country labor or one of the proletarian trades.

Antônio Balduíno listened and learned.

One day a man arrived from a trip and lodged in the house of Dona Maria, a fat mulatto woman rumored to be getting rich at the expense of Jubiabá's clients. The man had come to consult Jubiabá about an old and agonizing pain in his right leg. The doctors had given up a long time ago. They recited complicated names and prescribed expensive medicines. And the man showed no improvement; his leg got steadily worse, and he was unable to work on account of the pain. So he decided to make the trip just to consult Jubiabá, the pai-de-santo who cured everything in his voodoo ceremony on Capa-Negro Hill.

The man came from Ilhéus, the rich cocoa city, and almost dethroned Zé Camarão from the place of honor he occupied in Antônio Balduíno's eyes. This was because the man, having been remarkably cured in two sessions at Jubiabá's house, came one Sunday to chat at old Luísa's door. Everyone treated him with great deference, since it was rumored he was a rich man who had made money in the south of the state of Bahia and had given Jubiabá a conto-de-reis. He wore good cashmere clothes; they had even taken him a letter that had come addressed to Ricardina. But he had said, "I can't read, ma'am."

The letter was from a brother of hers who was dying of hunger in the Amazon. The man from Ilhéus had given her one hundred mil-reis. So when he arrived at Luísa's door, the group that was chatting there fell silent.

"Make yourself at home, Mr. Jeremiah," said Luísa, offering him a rickety straw-bottomed chair.

"Thank you, ma'am."

And, as the silence continued, "You were talking about . . . ?"

"To tell you the truth," said Luiz the shoemaker, "we were just talking about the wealth where you come from. About the money a man can make in that zone . . ."

The man bowed his head, and only then did they notice that his hair was almost white and that there were deep wrinkles in his face.

"It isn't really like that. You work a lot and what you earn isn't much."

"But you're a man of property yourself."

"Not at all. Oh, I have a little piece of ground, but I've lived in that region for thirty years. I've been shot three times. There, nobody's free from treachery."

"Are the men brave there?" But nobody heard Antônio Balduíno.

"Because, you see, there were a lot of men here who were wanting to go back with you."

"Do the men there have a lot of courage?" insisted Antônio Balduíno.

The man stroked the black boy's stiff hair and addressed the others.

"It's a rough place I come from. A place of shooting and death."

Antônio Balduíno had his eyes fixed on the man, hoping he would tell things about that place.

"There are people who kill just to make bets in Ilhéus . . . the men bet on how a traveler will fall, whether he'll fall to the right side or the left. They put up their money and shoot a fellow just to see who'll win the bet."

He looked at the others, wanting to see the effect he was producing. Then he lowered his head and went on.

"There's a Negro there who's the devil in person. José Estique . . . brave a man as you'll ever see. Nobody could have more courage. But they don't come any meaner. A foul pest of a man."

"Bandit, is he?"

"He's not a bandit, because he's a rich rancher. Zé Estique has land that stretches for miles and miles. So many cocoa trees you can't count them. But the number of murders he's done is even bigger."

"Wasn't he ever arrested?"

The man looked up, blinking his small eyes.

"Arrested?" He smiled. "He's rich."

His smile was a sarcastic comment. The others exchanged wondering glances. But they understood at once and continued to listen in silence to the man from Ilhéus.

"You know what he does? He rides into Itabuna, and when he passes somebody important he dismounts and says, 'Open your pocket, I want to piss inside.' There isn't a man who doesn't do it. Zé Estique has truly good aim. One time he came into Itabuna and met a white girl, the city councilman's daughter. Know what he did? He said, 'Girl, come here because I want to piss.' And it was for the girl to hold his thing. . . ."

"And did she?" Zé Camarão asked, laughing loudly.

"What choice did she have, poor thing?"

Now all the men laughed and sided with Zé Estique. The girls looked down, embarrassed.

"He killed, he robbed, he ruined all kinds of girls. He had the courage of a madman."

"Is he still alive?"

"No, he died at the hand of a gringo weakling from around there."

"How was it?"

"This gringo turned up one time and started pruning his cocoa trees. Before he came, nobody ever pruned cocoa trees. He made money, bought a little land. Then he packed up and went back where he came from. He was going to get married. He came back with a white woman, so white she looked like one of those porcelain dolls. The gringo's farm was real close to José Estique's ranch. One day Estique went by and saw the woman hanging up washing on the clothesline. He grabbed her and said to Nicolau—"

"Who's Nicolau?"

"The gringo. He grabbed her and said to him, 'Leave this doll here, boy, tonight I'll be back to get her.' The gringo got very scared and went and told one of his other neighbors. The neighbor said either he had to leave her there or he'd die, because Zé Estique wasn't a man to go back on his word. If he said he was coming back, he'd come. There wasn't time to run away, and besides, where could he run? The gringo went home, unable to do a thing. He didn't want to give up his pretty wife who he'd brought all the way from his homeland. But if he fought for her, he would surely get killed and Zé Estique would get the woman, anyway. . . ."

"So what did he do?" The audience could hardly contain itself. Only Zé Camarão was smiling as if he knew a more impressive story than the one this man from Ilhéus was telling.

"That night Zé Estique came back. He jumped off his horse, and instead of finding the woman, he found the gringo behind a tree with a great big ax. He split that black man's head open right down the middle. An awful death . . ."

A woman murmured, "Good job. He deserved it."

Another crossed herself, terrified. And the man from Ilhéus stayed a long time, telling stories and more stories about deaths and shootings in his heroic region. When he left, cured, Antônio Balduíno felt the sadness of one who is separated from a sweetheart. It was because Antônio Balduíno listened and was learning in the moonlit conversations on Capa-Negro Hill. Before he was ten years old, he swore to himself that one day his story would be sung in an ABC, and his adventures would be related and listened to with admiration by other men on other hills.

Life on Capa-Negro Hill was harsh and difficult. All the men worked very hard, some at the docks, loading and unloading ships or carrying bags for travelers, others in distant factories and in poorly paid trades: shoemaker, tailor, barber. The black women sold rice pudding, *munguzá, sarapatel,* and *acarajé* in the twisting streets of the city; black women washed clothes; black women were cooks in rich houses in stylish neighborhoods. Many of the boys worked, too. They were bootblacks, messengers, newspaper vendors. A few went to handsome houses and were taken in to work for rich families in exchange for room and board. The rest sprawled over the streets of the hill in fights, races, and games. These were the smaller ones. They already knew their destiny from an early age: They would grow up and work at the docks where they would become bent under the weight of the bags of cocoa, or they would earn a living in the huge factories. And they were not resentful because for years and years it had been that way; the boys from the pretty, shaded streets would be doctors, lawyers, engineers, businessmen, rich bosses. And they would be the servants of these men. That was why the hill and those who lived there existed. This was something Antônio Balduíno learned very early from the day-to-day example of his elders. Just as in the well-to-do homes there was the tradition of the uncle, father, or grandfather who had been a celebrated engineer, successful speechmaker, or wise politician, so on the hill where so many black people and mulattoes lived, there was the tradition of slavery to the affluent white master. And that was the only tradition. Because they had long ago forgotten the tradition of freedom in the African forests; those who remembered it were rare, having been persecuted or exterminated. On the hill only Jubiabá preserved that tradition, but Antônio Balduíno did not yet realize this. Free men were rare on the hill: Jubiabá, Zé Camarão. But they were both persecuted, one because he was a voodoo priest, the other for his petty crimes. Antônio Balduíno learned much from the heroic stories that they told the people of the hill, and rejected the tradition of servitude. He resolved to be one of the free men, one who someday would have an ABC and ballads written about him and who would be an example to everyone—black, white, and mulatto alike—who was enslaved beyond hope. It was on Capa-Negro Hill that Antônio Balduíno decided to revolt. Everything he did later could be traced back to the stories he heard on moonlit nights at his aunt's doorstep. Those tales, those old songs had been made to show people the example of those who revolted. But people didn't understand, or else they were already very much enslaved. Still, some heard and understood. Antônio Balduíno was one.

Next door to Luísa lived a woman called Augusta Lacemaker. They called her Augusta Lacemaker because she spent the week making lace, which she would sell in the city on Saturdays. Though she often seemed to be staring at something in particular, her eyes were actually lost in the sky, gazing at something invisible. She was assiduous in her attendance of Jubiabá's voodoo ceremonies, and even if she wasn't exactly black, she enjoyed a great prestige in his eyes. She would give Antônio Balduíno pennies, which he spent on candy or saved up to buy a pack of cheap cigarettes, pooling his money with Zebedeu's.

They would invent stories about Augusta's life, for she had appeared one day on the hill without saying where she had come from, nor where she was going. She stayed. Nobody knew anything about her life. But since she had that lost gaze and a sad smile, they imagined things about her, stories of unhappy romance, sad adventures. She, herself, when asked about her life, would only say, "My life is a novel . . . it only needs to be written."

When she was selling laces (and she measured out the yards by a very rudimentary process: holding the lace in her right hand under her chin and stretching her left hand sideways), she frequently would get mixed up.

"One, two, three . . ." She would stop, angry and upset.

"What do you mean, twenty? I'm still at three."

She would look at her customer and explain, "He mixes me up so badly, ma'am, you can't imagine. I can be counting perfectly well, and he starts to count in my ear so fast it scares me. When I'm still at three he's already at twenty. I can't do anything with him."

And she would beg, "Go away, I want to sell my lace right. Go away!"

"But who is it, Miss Augusta?"

"Who is it, ha! And who should it be? It's this pest who follows me wherever I go. Even after he's dead he won't leave me alone."

Other times the spirit would decide to have some fun and would get Augusta's legs tangled up in her thread. She would stop in the middle of the street and with an immense patience begin to unwind the threads he had knotted around her legs.

"What are you doing, Miss Augusta?" people would ask.

"Can't you see? I'm untangling the threads that disgraceful pest wound around my legs so I won't be able to walk and sell my lace. He wants me to starve to death."

And she would keep on removing the invisible threads. But if they asked her anything about who the spirit had once been, Augusta wouldn't say a thing. She would stare away into space and smile her sad smile. And the women would say, "Augusta's nutty because she suffered so much."

"A sad life, hers."

"But what happened to her?"

"Hush up. Everybody ought to mind their own business."

Augusta Lacemaker was the first to see the werewolf that appeared on the hill. It was on a moonless night when darkness reigned in the muddy alleyways of the hill, and only an occasional lantern twinkled in the houses. A spooky night, a night for thieves and murderers. Augusta was coming along the hillside when she heard, coming from the underbrush, a snort that made her shudder. She looked around and saw the fiery eyes of the werewolf. She had never put much faith in stories of werewolves and headless mules, but this time she was seeing one with her own eyes. She dropped the basket full of lace and fled to Luísa's house where she told her news with wide gestures of alarm, her voice still choking, her eyes popping out, her legs weak from running.

"Have a drink of water," Luísa offered.

"Yes, it helps the shock to pass," she accepted.

Antônio Balduíno overheard everything and took charge of spreading the news. In a short time, the whole hill knew that a werewolf had appeared, and the next night three more people saw it: a cook coming home from work; Ricardo the cobbler; and Zé Camarão, who had thrown a dagger at the creature. It had let out a great peal of laughter and dived into the underbrush. On the nights that followed, other inhabitants of the hill saw the monster, which would laugh and run away. Fear took over the hill; doors were locked early and people didn't go out at night. Zé Camarão proposed that they form a hunting party and capture the thing, but few people had the courage. Only Antônio Balduíno was really exultant at the proposal and found some sharp stones for his slingshot. Reports of the werewolf continued: Luísa saw its shadow one day when she was coming home late; Pedro ran away from it. The hill was restless and talked of nothing else. A newspaperman even turned up and took some photographs. That afternoon an article came out, saying there wasn't any werewolf at all, that it was the invention of the people on Capa-Negro Hill. Lourenço the barkeeper bought the paper, but nobody believed what it said because they had seen the werewolf themselves, and besides, werewolves had always existed. Between games, the children commented on the happenings.

“Mama told me that bad kids turn into werewolves, kids who do bad things.”

“Yeah. Their fingernails grow, then they turn into a werewolf on the night of the full moon.”

Antônio Balduíno was most enthusiastic.

“Hey, let’s turn into werewolves.”

“You do it, if you want to go to hell.”

“You’re a dummy, you little turd.”

“So why don’t you turn into one?”

“All right, I will. How do you do it?”

There was one boy who knew, and he said, “You let your fingernails and hair grow, don’t take a bath anymore, and every night go out and look at the moon. Act real bad to your aunt. When you look at the moon, get down on all fours.”

“And call me when you’re on all fours. I’ll come and stick—”

“I’ll stick my fist in your mouth. Your mother’s home, why don’t you go stick it in her?”

The other boy got up.

Antônio Balduíno said, “You don’t like it, do something about it.”

“I will,” he said, punching Antônio Balduíno in the face.

They rolled on the ground. The band of children whooped. The other boy was stronger than Antônio Balduíno, but the latter was a better student of Zé Camarão’s and quickly knocked the other boy down. They only stopped fighting when Lourenço jumped over his counter and separated them.

“Stop it! No upbringing at all.”

The other boy went off into a corner, and Antônio Balduíno, his clothes torn, asked the boy who knew how you turned into a werewolf what he should do.

“Do you really have to walk on all fours?”

“Yeah, to get used to it.”

“And then what?”

“Then you start changing. You get hairy all over, and you start rearing up like a horse and digging the ground with your nails. And pretty soon, you’re a werewolf. Then you run all over the hill haunting people.”

Antônio Balduíno turned to the boy he had been fighting with.

"When I turn into a werewolf, the first person I'm going to go after is you."

He started to leave. But he stopped in mid-stride and went back to ask, "And to change back again, what do you do?"

"Oh, I don't know that part."

That afternoon, the boy who had fought with him came up and said, "Look, Baldo, you should start by going after Joaquim; he said you're the worst soccer player."

"Did he say that?"

"I swear it."

"Honest to God?"

"Honest to God."

"Then he'll pay."

The other gave Antônio Balduíno part of a cigarette, and they made peace.

Antônio Balduíno tried to turn into a werewolf. He acted terrible around old Luísa, got two good thrashings, and let his fingernails grow. He stopped cutting his hair. On moonlit nights he would go out in back of the house and get down on all fours, walking back and forth. But nothing happened. He was becoming disillusioned, tired of the jeers of the boys who would ask him every day when he was going to turn into a werewolf, when the thought came to him that he wasn't sufficiently bad. So he decided to do something really awful. He spent several days pondering what it would be when one afternoon he saw Joanna, a spoiled little black girl, playing with her dolls. Mr. Eleutério always brought them for her, and she had many of them: cloth ones, both black and white, and "witches" she named after people she knew. She would make dresses for them and spend the whole day playing in the doorway of her house. She held baptisms and weddings for all the dolls, and these were special occasions for the children of the hill. They could still remember the party Joanna had given when she baptized Iracema, a porcelain doll that her godfather had given her for her birthday.

Antônio Balduíno had already formulated a plan. He approached her, talking in a sweet, friendly voice.

"What're you doing, Joanna?"

"My doll has a boyfriend."

"She's pretty. Who is the boyfriend?"

The boyfriend was a poppet with crooked legs.

"Do you want to be the priest?"

What Antônio Balduíno wanted was to get hold of the boy doll. But Joanna said no and pursed her mouth, ready to cry.

"Don't touch him or I'll tell my mother. Go away!"

Antônio Balduíno made his voice sweeter, smiled, and lowered his eyes.

"Come on, Joanna, let me hold him."

"No, you want to break him." She clutched the doll tightly against her chest.

Antônio was as startled as a thief caught red-handed. How could she have guessed? He was frightened and wanted to go back. But Joanna pursed up her mouth again; the tears were ready to drop out of her eyes. He couldn't stand it. He went blind, throwing himself on the dolls like a madman and breaking as many as he could. Joanna made no move, crying softly. Her tears spilled from her eyes and ran down her face into her mouth. Antônio Balduíno glanced at her and stopped, thinking how pretty Joanna was with her eyes full of tears. Suddenly the little black girl looked at her broken dolls and began to scream at the top of her lungs. Antônio Balduíno, who seconds before had felt sorry and thought she was pretty, got angry. He leaned back, enjoying her screams. He could have run away and perhaps hidden in time to avoid a beating, because once old Luísa's anger was past, she would laugh instead of punishing him. But he sat still, enjoying in his anger Joanna's heartfelt screams. He only went away when they dragged him. He got whipped all the way from Joanna's door to Luísa's kitchen. That day he didn't even try to twist his body away from the strap. He still had the image of Joanna before his eyes, her tears running into her mouth. But later he was tied to the table leg, and little by little the pleasure left him. Since he had nothing to do, he amused himself by killing ants. A neighbor said, "Jew boy! That one will end up a criminal."

He didn't turn into a werewolf. However, he was obliged to fight with two boys and break a third one's head in order to retain his prestige among the kids on the hill. This prestige had been seriously undermined by his failure to become a monster. Also, the original werewolf disappeared after Jubiabá, accompanied by almost all the neighborhood people, held a powerful magic session on top of the hill at the height of the full moon. He chanted as he held a bunch of leaves in his hand and ordered the creature to go away. Then he threw the leaves in the direction the werewolf had last been seen. The monster went back where it came from and left the people of Capa-Negro Hill in peace. It never appeared again, but to this day it is talked about on the hill.

Nobody knew how many years Jubiabá carried on his back, but he had lived on Capa-Negro Hill long before there were any other inhabitants, and he explained the story of the werewolf.

"He's appeared various times before. I've made him go away a whole lot of times. But he comes back, and he has to keep coming back until he pays for the crimes he committed here below. He'll have to come back many times, yet . . ."

"Who is he, pai Jubiabá?"

"Ah! You wouldn't know. He's a white master who was the owner of a big farm. This was in the olden times, the times when black people were slaves. His farm used to be right here where we live now. Right here. Don't you know why this hill is called Capa-Negro Hill? Ah! You don't know . . . well, it's because this hill was part of this master's farm. And he was an awful man. He liked when the Negroes made babies inside the black women for him to have more slaves. And when a Negro didn't make any babies, he would order him castrated. He castrated lots of Negroes. An awful white man . . . that's why this hill is called Capa-Negro Hill and has a werewolf on it. The werewolf is the white master. He didn't die, he was too bad for that. One night he turned into a werewolf and went out across the hill scaring people. Now he's still looking for the place where his house used to be, here on the hill. He still wants to castrate black men. . . ."

"God preserve us!"

"If he comes wanting to castrate me, he'll have his hands full," laughed Zé Camarão.

"The Negroes he castrated were our grandfathers, our great-grandfathers. He goes after us, thinking we're still his slaves."

"But black people aren't slaves anymore."

"Black people are still slaves and white people, too," interrupted a thin man who worked in the docks. "All poor men are slaves. Slavery isn't over yet. . . ."

The black men, mulattoes, and whites lowered their heads. Only Antônio Balduíno held his head high. He wasn't going to be a slave.

Antônio Balduíno wasn't very popular on the hill. Not that he was any worse than the other boys; he played soccer with them, kicking a ball made from a cow's bladder, spied on the black girls urinating in the sandhill behind the Baixa dos Sapateiros, stole fruit from street vendors, smoked cheap cigarettes, and swore horrendously. But it wasn't because of any of these things that he was disliked. It was because he was behind all the trouble the boys got into on the hill; all the ideas for unusual pranks, for unconfessable mischief, came out of his head.

Hadn't it been his idea for all the kids on the hill to go and watch the Bonfim fiesta? They had left about three in the afternoon and hadn't come back until three the next morning. The anguished mothers were running from house to house, some in tears; the fathers were going out to search. For the boys, it was a remarkable adventure; they went all over the city, reveled in the fiesta to the very end, played all they wanted, and only remembered to go back when they got so sleepy they couldn't stand up. They had stolen homemade candy from the stands of black women, pinched a lot of girls' behinds, and gotten into brawls. When they went home at the break of dawn they were terrified at the thought of getting thrashed. And they told their parents, "It was Balduíno who made me go along."

But this time old Luísa didn't whip Balduíno. She patted her nephew's head, saying, "They went because they wanted to, didn't they, son?"

Jubiabá also liked Antônio Balduíno. He would speak to him as if he were an adult. The black boy gradually became friends with the medicine man. He respected him because he knew everything and solved all the problems among the people of the hill. He cured their diseases and made strong charms and was free; he didn't have a boss or any time he had to be at work.

Once, in the middle of the night, painful cries for help shattered the peace of the hill. Houses were thrown open; men and women ran out into the streets with their eyes still half-closed in sleep. The screams had come from Leopoldo's house. But they had already given way to low moans. Everyone ran in that direction. The packing-crate door was open, its lock broken, and inside was Leopoldo, floundering in a widening pool of blood. There were two knife wounds in his chest. He raised himself up and then collapsed, never to get up again. A stream of blood gushed out of his mouth, and someone put a lighted candle into his hand. They spoke in hushed voices. A woman started to say a prayer for the dying. Little by little the house filled with people.

It was the first time anyone had ever gone inside Leopoldo's house. He didn't like anyone coming there. A man of few acquaintances, he wasn't close to anyone. In the time he had lived on the hill, he had never gone to visit his neighbors. Only once had he gone to Jubiabá's house and spent several hours there. But nobody knew what he had said to the medicine man. He worked as a carpenter and drank a lot. When he drank in Lourenço's bar, he would get even surlier and pound the counter with his fist for no reason. Antônio Balduíno was afraid of him. And he was even more afraid when he saw him dead, stabbed through the chest in two places. They never discovered who the murderer was. However, a year later, Balduíno was running down the hill one day when a sick-looking man in torn pants and a battered old hat came up to him and asked, "Say, boy, does a fellow named Leopoldo live around here? A tall black man, serious . . ."

"I know. He doesn't live here anymore."

"Has he moved?"

"No. He died."

"Died? Of what?"

"Stabbed."

"Murdered?"

"Yes, that's right." He looked at the man. "Are you a relative of his?"

"Who knows? Tell me, which way do I go to get downtown?"

"Don't you want to go up there and find out anything more?

My aunt could tell you. I'll show you the house where Mr. Leopoldo used to live. It belongs to Mr. Zeca now."

The man took fifty reis from his ragged trousers and gave them to Balduíno.

"Look here, boy, if he wasn't already dead, he would have died today." And he walked off down the hill without waiting for an answer. Antônio Balduíno went running after him. "Don't you want to know how to get downtown?"

But the man didn't even look back. This encounter frightened Antônio Balduíno so much that he never told anyone about it. And in his dreams, the image of the man with the battered hat pursued him for a long time. It seemed he had come from far away and was tired. Antônio Balduíno thought that the eye of mercy had run dry in that man.

One, two, three years went by in the life of the hill. The people were the same, the life was the same. Nothing changed, except that Luísa's headaches worsened. By now they were almost daily, coming upon her as soon as she returned from selling *munguzá* and *mingau.* She would start shouting and throwing the neighbors out; Jubiabá would come and every time take a little longer to cure Luísa's pain. The old woman was getting strange; she would arrive home furious, yelling, angry about everything. She would beat Balduíno for any little thing he did; then, after the headache went away, she would hug her nephew, hold him on her lap, smooth his kinky hair, cry softly, and ask forgiveness.

Antônio Balduíno went around in confusion, not understanding. He found his aunt's excesses of anger and kindness incomprehensible. Sometimes, as he played, he would stop and think about her and the headaches that were killing her. He sensed that he would lose her shortly, and this feeling oppressed his small heart, already so full of love and hatred.

It had been a somber afternoon, full of black clouds. With nightfall came a thick, heavy wind that clutched at men's throats and whistled through the alleys. Before lamplighting time, the wind dominated the city, ran with the urchins over the hills, visited the women in the Beco das Flores and the Beco de Maria Paz. It stirred up clouds of dust, invaded houses, and broke clay water pots. When the lights came on, a violent rain fell, a storm such as there hadn't been for some time. Lanterns were blown out; no voices were heard inside the houses. The hill closed itself into the shacks. Luísa was getting ready to go out. Antônio Balduíno was killing ants in a corner of the room. His aunt said to him, "Give me a hand here, Baldo."

He helped her to place a large pot on top of her folding wooden table, which in turn she lifted up and placed on her head. She stroked Antônio Balduíno's face and went toward the door. But before opening the latch, she dashed table, pots, and all to the floor with a furious gesture and screamed, "I'm not going!"

Antônio Balduíno was dumb with astonishment.

"Ah, ah, I'm not going anymore, whoever wants to go, let them! Ah, ah!"

"What is it, aunt?"

The *munguzá* was running over the tiled floor. Luísa grew calmer, but instead of answering, she began to tell a very long story about a woman who had three sons, one a carpenter, another a bricklayer, and the third a stevedore. Then the woman went into a convent, and Luísa started telling the story of the three sons. But Balduíno couldn't make head nor tail of it. Even so, he couldn't help laughing at one point when the carpenter asked the devil, "Where are your horns?"

And the devil answered, "I put them on your father's head!"

It was then that Luísa, who was at the best part of the mixed-up story, looked at the pans of *munguzá* and *mingau*. She jumped up and caroled, "I'm not going again, ever again, ever again."

Then Antônio Balduíno grew frightened once more and asked her if she had a headache. She looked at her nephew with such a strange expression in her eyes that Antônio Balduíno drew back behind the table.

"Who are you? You want to steal my *mingau*, you no-good ragamuffin! I'll teach you!"

She ran after Balduíno, who dashed out into the street and didn't stop running until he got to Jubiabá's house. The door was only closed, not locked, and he pushed it open and entered. Jubiabá was reading an old book as he burst in.

"What is it, Baldo?"

"Pai Jubiabá, pai Jubiabá . . ."

He couldn't speak. When he caught his breath, he began to cry.

"What is it, son?"

"Aunt Luísa's having an attack."

The storm raged outside. The rain was falling in enormous drops. But Balduíno didn't hear anything; he only heard his aunt's voice asking who he was and saw her strange eyes, eyes he had never seen in anyone before. They ran beneath the storm, the rain falling, the wind howling. They were silent.

When they arrived, the house was already full of neighbors. One woman was saying to Augusta Lacemaker, "This is on account of her carrying those heavy pots on her head. I knew of another woman who went crazy, too, because of that."

Antônio Balduíno began to cry again. Augusta disagreed with the neighbor woman.

"No, it isn't. What she has is a spirit, and a strong one. Jubiabá will get rid of it in no time, you'll see."

Luísa was singing in a high voice, chuckling, and Zé Camarão was agreeing with everything she said. Jubiabá began to chant over her. They took Antônio Balduíno to Augusta's house. But he didn't sleep, and in the midst of the storm, above the noise of the wind and rain, he could hear the screams and laughter of his aunt. He sobbed out loud.

The next day a car came from the public asylum, and two men took the old woman away. Antônio Balduíno clutched at her, not wanting to let them take her. He tried to explain. "It's nothing, it's nothing. It's just her headache she always gets. But pai Jubiabá can cure it. Don't take her."

Luísa caroled happily, indifferent to everything.

Balduíno bit the attendant's hand and wouldn't let go of Luísa. They had to bring him by force to Augusta's house. And then everyone was very nice to him. Zé Camarão came to talk to him about guitars and *capoeira,* Lourenço the barman gave him caramels, Miss Augusta kept saying, "Poor little thing, poor little thing." Jubiabá came, too, and hung an amulet in the form of a clenched fist, called a *figa,* around Antônio Balduíno's neck.

"This is so you will be strong and brave. I like you."

Balduíno stayed for a few days in Augusta's house. One morning, however, she dressed him up in his best clothes and took him by the hand. He asked where they were going.

"You're going to live in a nice house now. Councillor Pereira's house. He's going to raise you."

Antônio Balduíno didn't say anything, but he thought at once of running away. When they got close to the hillside, they met Jubiabá. Antônio Balduíno kissed the medicine man's hand.

Jubiabá said, "When you grow up, come back to see me. When you're a man."

The boys were all standing in the street, watching. Balduíno waved a sad good-bye. They went down the hill.

From down below he could still see the silhouette of Jubiabá seated on a wooden bench, his shirt fluttering in the wind, a bunch of herbs in his hand.

CHAPTER 3
Zumbi dos Palmares Street

The dirty houses and low, uncertain-colored buildings of the old street stood in a straight, undeviating row. Only the sidewalk in front of the houses was uneven, now higher, now lower, now advancing toward the middle of the street, now fearful of moving away from the doorsteps. A poorly paved street of rough cobblestones, overgrown with grass.

A stagnant stillness permeated everything. It seemed to come from the distant sea, from the hills far behind the unlighted houses, from the occasional lamp posts, even from the people. It came from the very air, enveloping the street and the creatures on it. Night seemed to fall earlier on Zumbi dos Palmares Street than on the rest of the city.

Not even the sea that beat on the faraway rocks could awaken that street from its sleep. It was like an old maid waiting for her fiancé, who had gone off to the distant capital and lost himself in the confusion of hurrying men. It was a melancholy street, a dying byway. Its calmness was heavy, moribund. Everything seemed to be dying: the houses, the hill, the lights. The silence was harsh; it made one uncomfortable. Zumbi dos Palmares Street was dying.

How unkempt the pavement was with its loose stones, and how old the houses were! As old as the ancient Negress who lived in the dingiest house of all. With maternal gestures she would give the urchins pennies to buy candy. She spent the day puffing on an old clay pipe and muttering words nobody understood.

The street bent its back downhill, and the houses became

more decayed. The silence was deathly, oozing down the slope, rising from the stones.

Zumbi dos Palmares Street was dying. Once a newlywed couple came to see a house that was for rent. It was comfortable and quiet. But the bride said, "No . . . no, I don't like it. This street is like a cemetery."

On the corner, facing each other, were a pair of two-story houses. The rest of the street was made up of cramped, dark dwellings and one or two other low, colorless buildings in which lived hordes of working men.

The two-story houses on the corner, though quite old, were nevertheless large and gracious. In the one on the right lived a family that had suffered a great tragedy: the loss of a son who had been murdered. They lived a retired life, never appearing at the eternally shuttered windows, and always wore mourning. When, on rare occasions, a window was opened, one could see into the visitors' parlor where there was an enormous portrait of a blond young man in uniform, a lieutenant. He was wearing a provocative smile on his lips and holding a flower in his pale hand. This house had a balcony on which a blond girl dressed in black often sat. She would read a book with a yellow cover and throw coins to Antônio Balduíno.

Every afternoon a handsome young man would come and walk the length of the street. He would whistle softly until the girl saw him. Then she would get up, come to the railing of the balcony, and stand there smiling. The elegant young man would pass by various times, bow to her, and smile. Before leaving he would take a carnation from his lapel, and after kissing it, throw it onto the balcony. The girl would grab it quickly, a smile on her lips, her face hidden in her free hand. She would put the red carnation into her book of poetry and wave good-bye to him. The man would go away and come back the next day. The girl would toss a coin to the black boy who was there below, the only witness to this love.

Facing this house was that of the Comendador. Geese promenaded in the flower garden, and mango trees grew by the drive that ran alongside the house. The Comendador had bought the house cheap back in the good old days. "A real bargain," he would say on Sundays after taking a stroll through the garden and stretching out for a nap in the orchard at the back. He had lived there for many years, ever since he had begun to prosper, and liked the old house with its numerous bedrooms in the quiet street.

Antônio Balduíno was amazed at the size of the house. He had never seen anything like it. The houses of Capa-Negro Hill were tiny, with floors of beaten clay, packing-crate doors, and zinc roofs. They had only two rooms: the dining room and the room where people slept. But not the Comendador's mansion. How big it was, how many rooms there were! Some were never even used. There was a guest room always furnished and ready, though no one ever arrived; enormous salons; a handsome kitchen; a better latrine than any house on the hill had.

It was lunchtime in the Comendador's household when Augusta Lacemaker and the black boy arrived, both tired after their long walk from Capa-Negro Hill to Zumbi dos Palmares Street. There was an aroma of food seasoned in the Portuguese style. Senhor Pereira, in his shirt sleeves, presided over the family's midday meal. When Augusta came in, holding the boy by the hand, Antônio Balduíno raised his eyes, and the first thing he saw was Lindinalva.

At the head of the table was the Comendador, a Portuguese of wide mustaches and generous forkfuls. Beside him was his wife, almost as large and fat as he. And Lindinalva, seated at her mother's right, very thin and freckled, with her red hair and small mouth, made the most ridiculous contrast to them in the world. But Antônio Balduíno, accustomed to the dirty little black girls of the hill, thought Lindinalva looked like the figures on the calendars Mr. Lourenço distributed among his customers at Christmas.

She was a little taller than the boy, for she was three years his senior. Antônio Balduíno lowered his eyes and studied the complicated parquet design of the varnished floor.

Dona Maria, the wife, invited, "Sit down, Miss Augusta."

"Oh, I'm fine, Dona Maria."

"Have you had your lunch?"

"No, not yet."

"Then help yourself."

"No, I'll eat in the kitchen later." Augusta knew her place and how much sheer politeness was contained in the invitation.

When the Comendador had finished chewing the food he had in his mouth, he laid his knife and fork down on his empty plate and yelled toward the kitchen, "Amelia, bring the dessert!"

He turned to Augusta as he waited.

"So, Augusta?"

"I brought the boy I was telling you about, sir."

The Comendador, his wife, and daughter all looked at Antônio Balduíno.

"Oh, that's him! Come here, boy," called the Comendador. "What's your name?"

"My name is Antônio Balduíno."

"That's an awfully big name. From now on you'll be called Baldo."

"That was my nickname on the hill."

Lindinalva laughed. "Baldo sounds like bald."

Augusta spoke to Senhor Pereira.

"So, will you take him to raise, sir, and keep him?"

"Yes, I will."

"It's such a great charity you're doing, sir. The poor little thing has neither father nor mother. He had only one relative, his aunt. She went crazy, poor thing."

"Why?"

"I think it was an evil spirit got into her . . . a real bad one. He won't let her go. I know a lot about this business of spirits."

Antônio Balduíno's mouth puckered up as though he were going to cry. The Comendador stroked his kinky hair and said, "Don't be scared, nobody's going to eat you."

Dona Maria asked Augusta, "Speaking of spirits, how's yours these days?"

"Ah, Dona Maria, don't talk to me about him. He persecutes me worse all the time. Lately he's taken to getting drunk and falling on top of my shoulders. It's such a weight I can hardly stand it. I'm always tired."

"Why don't you go to a session and get rid of him?"

"Oh, I do. Every Saturday. Pai Jubiabá takes him away, but he comes back again. He always was stubborn."

"But that's only *macumba.* You should go to a real spiritist session. Over on São Miguel Hill there's a good one."

"Oh, no, Dona Maria. If pai Jubiabá can't get rid of him, who can? And I really don't mind much. It's just that he bothers me. And now he's started drinking. Just look at me, I'm so tired you can't imagine, ma'am. He's riding on my back, fearful heavy . . ."

She turned to the Comendador.

"God repay you, sir, for this charity you're offering the boy. God repay everyone in this house with good health."

"Thank you, Miss Augusta. Now take the boy to the kitchen and tell Amelia to give him some food." And Senhor Pereira attacked his dessert of cashew-fruit compote. Dona Maria added, "You, too, Augusta, have something to eat."

In the kitchen Amelia served them heaping plates. The three ate their lunch as Augusta movingly recounted the history of Antônio Balduíno's life to the cook. The latter wiped tears from her eyes with her apron, and Antônio Balduíno, when he heard them mention his aunt's madness, stopped eating and sobbed.

After selling some of her laces, Augusta said good-bye to Antônio Balduíno.

"Sometimes I'll come to see you."

Only then did the boy understand that he was separated from the hill, that they had torn him away from the place where he had been born and raised and learned so many things, and put him, the freest of the hill urchins, in the house of a master.

This time he didn't cry. He looked over the house, thinking about how to run away. But Lindinalva called him to play with her, and he forgot about running away. He built a house for the angora cat, which was Lindinalva's passion; ran through the orchard with her; jumped up and climbed to the highest branch of the guava tree to get guavas for her since she said she liked them. They became friends on that first day.

Later the trouble started. He was caught smoking and got a beating from the cook. He was outraged. He didn't mind his aunt thrashing him, but the cook, no! And when he cursed, which happened every other minute, Amelia would smack him on the mouth as hard as she could. He started to hate the Portuguese woman with her long hair, which she made into two long braids and then admired in the mirror. Whenever her back was turned, he would stick out his tongue at her.

Still, the Comendador was good to him. He even enrolled Balduíno in a public school in the Largo de Nazaré where a froglike little woman taught with a stick in her hand. That year Antônio Balduíno took charge of the students' mischiefmaking. Soon he was labeled incorrigible, and expelled. Amelia said to Dona Maria, "Niggers are a race that's only fit to be slaves. They weren't born to know anything."

But Antônio Balduíno already knew enough. He could read perfectly the ABC of any of the celebrated outlaws and the crimes that were reported in the papers. And when he was on good terms with Amelia, it was he who read at night, from the newspapers, the stories of the crimes that were happening in the world.

And so his life went by, divided between games with Lindinalva, whom he admired more and more, and fights with Amelia, who complained daily to Dona Maria of the "mischief of that dirty nigger," and hidden from the others, beat him unmercifully.

He would get news from the hill through Augusta, who every month would come to sell lace to Dona Maria. He missed the free and easy life of the hill and went back to thinking about running away.

One Sunday Jubiabá came to the Comendador's house. They conversed in the parlor and ordered Antônio Balduíno to put on his best clothes. He went out with Jubiabá, and they took a streetcar. Once again the boy saw the city and breathed in the air of the streets, enjoying his liberty. He didn't even remember to ask Jubiabá where they were going. Besides, he thoroughly trusted the pai-de-santo, who on that Sunday was dressed in an old frock coat and was wearing a ridiculous hat on top of his kinky hair. Finally, they got off the streetcar, went down a wide, airy street, and turned in at a large gate guarded by a man in uniform. Antônio Balduíno thought he was going to be a soldier and laughed. He would like to be a soldier, wear a uniform, promenade with mulatto girls through the parks. But he was disillusioned at once. He didn't see any soldiers on the patio of the large grayish house, which had bars on the windows like a jail. What he saw were men and women, all wearing the same kind of clothes, walking absently about, some talking to themselves, others gesturing to the air. Jubiabá took him to the place where old Luísa sat singing in a weak voice, "I'm not going again, never again, never again."

Antônio Balduíno hardly recognized her. She was thin and bony, her eyes popping out of her dried-up face. He kissed the old woman's hand, and she looked at him indifferently.

"Auntie, it's Baldo."

"You know something? Those bad boys want to steal my *mingau.* You came to steal it, too, didn't you?" She started to get furious. But at once she smiled and continued her song. "I'm not going again, never again, never again."

Jubiabá took him back again. Balduíno watched the somber house that looked like a prison. In the streetcar, Jubiabá asked if he still had the *figa* he had given him. Antônio Balduíno pulled it out from inside his shirt and showed it to him.

"That's good, my son. Keep it always. It brings good luck."

Before they got out, he gave Antônio Balduíno ten cents.

He only went back to the asylum once. It was with Jubiabá again, to attend the funeral of old Luísa. In front of the poor black casket, he saw almost all those he knew from the hill. Again they were all very kind to him and hugged him. A few people cried. They went to the cemetery where they gave Antônio Balduíno a shovel to throw dirt over the coffin. And afterward, the old woman's body remained there, and only Antônio Balduíno kept her memory with love in his small heart already so full of hate.

It was on the day of old Luísa's funeral that Jubiabá, to entertain him, told the story of Zumbi dos Palmares on the way home from the cemetery.

"The name of that street is Zumbi dos Palmares, isn't it?"

"Yes, sir."

"Do you know who Zumbi was?"

"No." Balduíno was sad, thinking of running away once again, and at first he didn't pay much attention to the story, in spite of the fact that it was Jubiabá who was telling it.

"It happened a long, long time ago, in the days when Negroes were slaves. Zumbi dos Palmares was a black slave. Black slaves were beaten a lot, so Zumbi was beaten, too. But back in the land where he was born, he wasn't beaten. Because there Negroes weren't slaves, they were free. They lived in the woods working and dancing.''

''And why did they come here?'' Balduíno was beginning to be interested.

''The white men went there to get Negroes. They tricked the Negroes because the Negroes were foolish, they had never seen white people and didn't know how bad they were. The white people had no more eye of mercy. They would bring black men and beat them with whips. That's how it was with Zumbi dos Palmares. But he was a brave Negro and knew more than the others. One day he ran away. He got together a band of black men and was free, just like in his own land. Then more black men ran away and joined Zumbi. There got to be a big city of Negroes. And the Negroes started to take revenge on the white men. So the white men sent soldiers to kill the black men who ran away. But the soldiers were too weak to kill the Negroes. More soldiers went. And the Negroes beat the soldiers.''

Antônio Balduíno's eyes were wide, and he trembled with enthusiasm.

''So then they sent a whole lot of soldiers, a thousand times more than the number of Negroes. But the Negroes didn't want to be slaves anymore, and when Zumbi saw they were losing, he threw himself off a cliff so as not to be whipped by a white man ever again. All the other Negroes did the same. Zumbi dos Palmares was a brave man and a good one. If there had been twenty of his kind back then, black men wouldn't have been slaves.''

On the day his aunt died, Antônio Balduíno had found a friend to take the place of old Luísa in his heart: Zumbi dos Palmares. And from then on, he was his favorite hero.

There were some consolations in that life complicated by Amelia's bullying. First, there was Lindinalva to play with. He was capable of spending hours and hours without moving, looking at her face, which was like that of a saint. Then he discovered the movies, and they were a revelation for him. Instead of cheering for the cowboys as all the other kids did, he always cheered for the bad Indians who were against the white hero. He had come to understand the meaning of race, and of an oppressed race, from the stories on the hill; they still throbbed within him. There was also Zé Camarão, who came to teach guitar to some fellows that lived in the old house at the end of the street and gave Balduíno lessons, too.

The work at the Comendador's house wasn't heavy: He waited on table, washed the dishes, went to do the shopping, and took messages. Senhor Pereira was even thinking of taking him to work in his commercial establishment.

"I'd like to do something for this boy," he would say. "He's smart, the little black devil."

Antônio had learned to dissimulate in order to avoid beatings. Now he smoked in hiding, swore under his breath, and lied unabashedly.

It was the Comendador's idea of bettering Antônio Balduíno's life, giving him a job in his store with a salary and the possibility of making something of himself, that obliged the boy to run away. By this time, Antônio Balduíno was already fifteen and had put up with Amelia's hatred for three years.

The thing that precipitated his flight was this: When the Comendador announced one Sunday that Antônio Balduíno would start to work in the warehouse the following month, Amelia had an attack of fury. She was overcome with jealousy, not understanding why her employers protected the Negro boy and wanted to make him into someone.

"Niggers are a worthless race," she would always repeat. "Niggers ain't people."

And she started to think up a way of demoralizing the boy completely. Then one day she saw Antônio Balduíno sitting on the kitchen steps gazing at Lindinalva with religious adoration. The girl was now eighteen. She was seated on the veranda, sewing. Amelia clapped Balduíno on the shoulder.

"Aha! You shameless nigger! Looking at Miss Lindinalva's legs, are you?"

Balduíno hadn't been looking at anything; he had been remembering the good times when they were smaller and he and

Lindinalva had played in the orchard. But he was as alarmed as if he really had been looking at the girl's legs.

The story reached the Comendador's ears. Everybody believed it, even Lindinalva, who could never again look at Antônio Balduíno without fear and disgust.

The Comendador, though he was a good man, knew how to be cruel when he was angry.

"So, you no-good tramp, I bring you up like a son, I try to help you, and this is how you act!"

Amelia added, "That nigger is downright shameless. When Dona Lindinalva was taking a bath, he was spying through the keyhole."

Lindinalva ran off, almost sobbing. Balduíno wanted to say it was a lie, but since they all believed Amelia, he didn't say anything. He was given a terrible thrashing that left him lying down, his entire body aching. But it wasn't just his body that hurt. His heart ached because they hadn't believed in him. And, as they were the only white people he respected, he began to hate them, and all other whites along with them.

That night he dreamed of Lindinalva. He saw her naked and woke up. Then he remembered the vices that the boys practiced on the hill. He was alone, but he wasn't alone. He slept with Lindinalva, who smiled at him with her calendar face, opening her white thighs and offering him her hard, girl's breasts. And from then on, whatever woman he slept with, Antônio Balduíno was sleeping with Lindinalva.

In the wee hours of the morning he ran away from Zumbi dos Palmares Street.

CHAPTER 4
Beggar

Antônio Balduíno is now free in the religious city overlooking the Bay of All Saints, the city of pai-de-santo Jubiabá. He is experiencing the great adventure of liberty. His home is the whole city; his job, to roam through it. The child of the poor hillside slum has become the owner of the city.

Religious city, colonial city, black city of Bahia. Sumptuous churches embroidered in gold, houses with blue-tiled fronts, ancient two-story buildings inhabited by misery, streets and hills paved with cobblestones, strong old men, historical places, the harbor—principally the harbor—everything belongs to Antônio Balduíno. He alone is the owner of the city, because he alone knows it all. He wanders through all its streets, taking part in whatever uproar or disaster might be happening. He knows all its secrets. His job is inspecting the life of the city that belongs to him. He watches all its movements, is acquainted with all its brave men, goes to its colorful fiestas, sees the travelers on and off all the ships. He knows the names of all the commercial sailboats and is friends with all the canoe men who stop in Porto da Lenha. He eats at the most expensive restaurants, uses the most luxurious automobiles, sleeps in the newest skyscrapers. He can move anytime he likes. And since he is the owner of the city, he doesn't pay for food, transportation, or housing.

Free in the old city with its huge houses, he has dominated it and become its owner. The men who pass don't realize this, of course. They don't even look at the ragged black boy who smokes a cheap cigarette and wears a beret over his eyes. The elegant women who give him coins shrink away from him so as not to get dirty from his touch.

But in truth, Antônio Balduíno is the emperor of the black city of Bahia. A fifteen-year-old emperor, a smiling rover. Perhaps even Antônio Balduíno himself doesn't know it.

He wears a cap, a pair of cashmere trousers, torn and spotted, and an enormous suit jacket inherited from someone much taller than he, a jacket that in winter is pillow and overcoat; such are the clothes of the city's emperor. And the black boys who surround him are his most beloved subjects, his honor guard. An entourage without a special uniform, they wear rags and sandals abandoned in trash cans, but they know how to fight like no other honor guard in the world.

The emperor has a large *figa* tied around his neck. He and his circle of urchins carry razors, knives, and switchblades concealed in the waistbands of their trousers.

Antônio Balduíno came forward.

"A handout, for the love of God."

The fat man measured the black boy from head to toe with the avid eyes of a man of affairs. He buttoned his coat, shaking his head ironically.

"A big kid like you asking for money! Go find a job, you tramp. No shame, some of 'em . . . go to work!"

Antônio Balduíno glanced quickly over the street, which was full of people. Then he said, "I came from the country, sir. I had an awful time crossing through the backlands. God knows they're dry, not a drop of rain. I'm out of work, but I'm looking for a job. I just want a nickel for a cup of coffee. Anyone can see you're a good man."

He looked to see what effect this speech was having, but the man started to walk away.

"I've heard that kind of lie before. You should go to work."

"I swear by the sun that's shining on us it isn't a lie. I traveled here under a sun so hot it was fearful. If you have a job I'll take it, sir. I'm not scared of work. But I haven't eaten since yesterday, I'm falling down from hunger. You're a good man, sir."

The man made an impatient gesture, put his hand into his pocket, and tossed him a coin.

"Don't bother me anymore. Get lost."

But the black boy kept following the man. It was because the cigar the man was smoking was more than half gone, and Antônio Balduíno adored cigar butts. The man thought about everything the boy had said. Could it be true what these beggars said all over the city? The man looked at their angry faces and grew suddenly afraid. He buttoned his suit coat again and went into a bar to drink something and build up his courage. Antônio Balduíno swooped down on the cigar butt and opened his hand that clutched the coin thrown by the man. It was a silver coin worth two mil-reis. He tossed it up in the air, caught it in his quick hand, and ran over to the others, who were discussing soccer.

"Guess how much, fellows?"

"Five hundred reis."

Antônio Balduíno laughed aloud.

"Two mil-reis."

"He fell for it like a sitting duck," said Antônio Balduíno with a scornful gesture. "I know how to sing."

Now they all laughed with clear, ringing laughter.

The passersby see only a group of boys—black, white, and mixed—who are begging. But in reality it is the emperor of the city and his honor guard.

When groups of elegant women dressed in expensive silk appeared, their painted faces scattering smiles, Antônio Balduíno would whistle a special signal, and the group would come together. They would form a line with Gordo in the front because he had a sad, hungry-sounding voice and a stupid-looking baby face. Gordo would put his hands on his chest, make a penitent expression, and address himself to the group of women. He would stop in front of them, blocking the sidewalk, and the boys would encircle them. Then Gordo would sing.

"Give alms to seven blind boys.
I'm oldest, he's next,
At home are the rest.
Papa's a cripple
And Mama's so ill,
Give alms to seven orphans
All blind, if you will."

By the time the song was finished, Gordo would be nearly crying, his expression contrite, his eyes tragic. He looked like he really was blind, with six blind younger brothers, a sick mother, a crippled father, and nothing to eat in their poor house. He would keep it up:

"Give alms to seven blind boys,
I'm oldest, he's next,"

and point to whoever was nearest. At the end he would stretch his fat arms to include the whole group and sing loudly.

"Give alms to seven orphans,
All blind, if you will."

The others provided the chorus. "All blind . . ."

Gordo would shake his rolls of flesh and stretch out his dirty palm, waiting for the handout, which was almost always generous. Women always gave them alms, often out of pity for those ragged children of the street, thinking of their own children safe in the comfort of their houses. Others gave alms to get rid of the barrier of filthy urchins who were like an accusation. The more daring ones would make little jokes.

"Well, now, how can that be? You said seven, but I see more than ten. They're orphans, but they have a mother and father who are sick, blind but they can see everything. How can that be?"

They wouldn't answer. They would close the circle tighter and Gordo would go back to his monotonous chanting.

"Give alms to seven blind boys . . ."

Not a one resisted. The urchins would come nearer and nearer, their dirty, ugly faces drawing closer to the elegantly made-up faces of the women. It was horrible when they all opened their mouths for the chorus. Gordo was like a professor, never letting them stop the song. The handbags would open and the coins would fall into Gordo's hand, which he removed from his chest. The children would fall back, and Gordo would thank the ladies.

"Ma'am, you will meet a handsome bridegroom who will arrive on a ship."

Many would smile, others would grow sad. And in the streets and narrow alleys, the laughter of the urchins would resound, happy and free. Afterward they would buy packs of cigarettes and drink glasses of rum.

There was a blond boy. He was the youngest. Perhaps he wasn't even ten yet. A round face like a processional saint, curly hair, delicate hands, blue eyes. He was called Phillip, and they nicknamed him Phillip the Beautiful. He had no story at all except that his mother, an old Frenchwoman who earned her living in the brothels of the Rua de Baixo, had once fallen in love with a student. After he graduated, he left for Amazonia. Their child was lost in the streets, and the woman in alcohol.

The day he joined the group there was a big fuss. It was because while they were sleeping, squeezed together in the doorway of an apartment building, lying on old newspapers, Toothless tried to pull down Phillip the Beautiful's trousers. Toothless was a strong mulatto boy of sixteen. He would spit between his stumps of teeth, making a special noise, and could spit anywhere he aimed, an ability that constituted his great distinction. So Toothless, a mean character, grabbed Phillip and started pulling down his pants. Phillip wriggled away and started yelling. They all woke up. Antônio Balduíno rubbed his eyes and asked, "What's all the fuss about?"

"He thinks I'm a queer but I'm not." Phillip was about to cry.

"Why don't you leave the kid alone?"

"It's none of your business. I'll do what I want . . . he's a little piece of candy."

"Look here, Toothless, whoever messes with the kid messes with me."

"You just want to screw him yourself. It ain't right."

Antônio Balduíno turned to the other boys, who were in doubt.

"You guys know I never wanted to screw anybody here. I

only like women. If the kid was a fairy, then fine. But in that case he wouldn't be here with us 'cause we don't want any fairies here. The kid's straight, nobody messes with him."

"And what if I do?"

Antônio Balduíno sensed that all the boys were on his side.

"Try it."

He got up. Toothless did the same, thinking that if he beat Antônio Balduíno he could take over the gang. They stared at one another.

"Hit me," said Toothless.

Antônio Balduíno punched him. Toothless wavered but didn't fall down. They grabbed hold of each other, the gang cheering. Toothless was down, but he twisted around and stood up. A blow from Antônio Balduíno knocked him over again. When Toothless got up, he had a switchblade open in his hand. It glimmered in the dark.

"Coward! You don't even fight like a man!"

Toothless came at him with the knife, but Antônio Balduíno had learned *capoeira* from Zé Camarão on Capa-Negro Hill. He turned a cartwheel and threw his legs into Toothless, who fell flat on the floor, the knife bouncing far out of reach.

Antônio Balduíno finished by saying, "If you mess with that kid, you mess with me. Next time I'll take your knife."

Toothless slept by himself in another doorway. Phillip the Beautiful became an established member of the gang.

Phillip's specialty was old ladies. The minute an old lady would appear on the street, he would straighten the bow tie he always wore, throw away his cigarette, thrust his hands into his bottomless pockets, hide his razor, and walk sadly toward the lady.

"Good morning, ma'am. I'm an abandoned child. I don't have any father or mother. I don't have anybody to take care of me. I'm hungry . . . so hungry."

He would start to cry. He possessed a special talent for crying anytime he wanted. The tears would run down his cheeks and he would sob loudly, "I'm hungry . . . my mama . . . you have children. Have pity . . . mama."

He was gorgeous when he cried, his fair, round face bathed in tears, his lips trembling. There wasn't a woman who didn't say, "Poor little thing, so small and already motherless."

They would give him fat handouts. Three times he was invited to live in rich houses belonging to rich ladies. But he loved the liberty of the streets and remained faithful to the group where he was already very much respected, since he was one of the most efficient members. Even Toothless treated him with respect when he came back from an encounter with an old lady.

"Got us a big fiver!"

The urchins' laughter would ring through the streets, hills, and alleys of the city on the Bay of All Saints, the city of pai-de-santo Jubiabá.

The strangest member of the group was Viriato the Dwarf. He was given this nickname because he was very short, even shorter than Phillip, although he was three years older. Truncated and stocky, he had immense strength for his age. Even when he took a bath, he still gave the impression of filth and misery. When the group was formed, he had already begun his career of begging in the city streets. His flat head frightened people. And to make an even stronger impression, he walked bent over, which made him look hunchbacked and even shorter. It was hard to get a word out of Viriato. And when the others' laughter rang out freely, he would only smile.

But he never bothered anybody, never complained when the gang didn't do very well, and was happy with whatever there was to eat and with the cigarette butts he got to smoke. Antônio Balduíno liked him, submitted many decisions to his opinion, and showed him great respect.

During the day, Viriato the Dwarf didn't move around much with the gang. He would stay seated in Rua Chile, his legs bent under, body curved, flat head bowed down on his neck. Without a word he would stretch out his hat to passersby. He looked as though he were a part of the door where he was sitting, a tragic sculpture, a church gargoyle. He always took in a good haul. At the end of the afternoon, he would meet with the gang and deposit in Antônio Balduíno's hands the results of his day's begging. After the numbers were tallied up, and he had received his part, he would go off into a corner, eat, smoke, and sleep. He went along with the others on their ramblings through the city when they chased after the housemaids in the sandhills, brawled, and partied, but he showed little enthusiasm. He would accompany them just to have something to do. He was the only one in the group of begging urchins who took his profession seriously.

At the end of the afternoon, Antônio Balduíno would sit down on the ground, call the band of boys around him, and gather up the money they had gotten during the day. They would turn out the pockets of their old trousers, pull out the coins and occasional bills, and deposit them in the hands of their chief.

"You, Gordo, how much?"

Gordo would count his money. "Five thousand eight hundred."

"And Beautiful?"

Phillip, with a superior gesture, would hand over his haul.

"Sixteen mil-reis."

It wasn't necessary to call Viriato.

"Twelve thousand one hundred."

The others would be coming up. Antônio Balduíno's cap would gradually fill with coins and bills. Last of all, he himself would go through his pockets and add up his day's haul.

"I didn't do so well. Seven mil-reis."

They would add it up, usually on their fingers. With the help of Viriato the Dwarf, they would divide the number among them.

"There are nine of us. That's six thousand six hundred for each one." And he would ask, "Is that right, fellows?"

It was. They would line up in front of Balduíno, who would give each boy his share. Sometimes there wasn't change.

"Toothless owes you five hundred reis."

"Well, let's don't forget it. Last time somebody forgot to pay me three cents' change."

They would get something to eat and then spread out over the city searching for mulatto girls to take to the sandhill near the docks, crashing poor parties in the hillside slums, or drinking rum in the bars of the lower city.

One day something unusual happened. When Zé Casquinha turned in his haul, he smiled an enigmatic smile. Antônio Balduíno said, "Three mil-reis."

"Plus this."

He threw a ring into the black boy's hat. Its stone sparkled in the light of the street lamp. There was one large stone surrounded by a dozen smaller ones. Antônio Balduíno raised his eyes and affirmed, "You stole this, Zé Casquinha."

"I swear I didn't. A girl gave me a handout and went away. When I looked around, this ring was lying next to me. I even ran after her, but I couldn't find her."

"Lying to me?"

The boys looked at the ring, which was passing from hand to hand. They paid no attention to the conversation between Balduíno and Zé Casquinha.

"Now tell me how it was, Zé."

"I'm not lying, Baldo. That's really what happened."

"And you went after her?"

"All right, that was a lie. But the rest is true, I swear."

"Okay, and now what are we going to do with this?"

Phillip laughed. "Give it to me! I was born to wear rings."

They all chuckled. But Antônio Balduíno asked again, "What are we going to do with it?"

Viriato the Dwarf murmured, "I'll pawn it. We'll get a lot of money—"

Phillip interrupted again, "I'll buy me some new clothes—"

"You can get them in a trash can."

"But we can't pawn it, Viriato. Don't you see, that gringo pawnbroker won't believe the thing is ours. He'll call the police and we'll all end up in jail."

"Yeah, you're right."

"Give it to me to wear," teased Phillip.

"Quit bugging me."

"I think the best thing is for us to keep it a while. When the woman has forgotten all about it, then we'll decide."

So Antônio Balduíno tied the ring around his neck next to the *figa*.

Antônio Balduíno went up to the man who was wearing an overcoat in spite of the summer weather. The gang watched from the corner.

"A handout for the love of God."

"Go find a job, you tramp!"

This time the street was deserted. Nobody passed through that particular alley. And the man with the overcoat was in a hurry. There was a red flower in his buttonhole. Antônio Balduíno came closer, the gang following.

"Give me a coin . . ."

"I'll give you a punch in the face, you no-good!"

The boys drew closer.

"You're a rich man. You can give us a lot of money."

The man didn't say anything more, for he was now surrounded by the gang.

Antônio Balduíno's face was very close to the man's. The Negro boy's hand was hidden in his pocket. A razor appeared.

"A big handout."

"Thieves, eh?" the man had courage to say. "When they start out as kids, they really go bad—"

Antônio Balduíno laughed, opening the razor. The others closed in on the man in the overcoat.

"Here, thieves."

"You'd better watch out, we might meet you again someday."

"I'm going straight to the police."

But they were accustomed to this threat and paid no attention. Antônio Balduíno took the ten mil-reis, put away his razor, and the whole gang ran off, scattering through the nearby streets. They would commit these offenses when the carnival celebration was near, or when it was time for the fiestas of Bonfim or Rio Vermelho.

One day Rozendo got sick. He ran a high fever and grew delirious at night. He didn't eat anything. The first night he laughed and said, "It's nothing, it'll go away."

The others looked and laughed, too. But on the second night, Rozendo started to be afraid. When he wasn't delirious, he would groan in a low voice. And he told the others, "Go call Ma. I'm going to die. Ma . . ."

Troubled, the others looked at him without knowing what to do. Their happy eyes grew sad. Balduíno asked, "Where does your mother live?"

"I don't know. When I ran away she lived in Porto da Lenha.

But she moved. Look for her, Baldo. Look for her, I want my ma . . ."

"I will, Rozendo."

It was Viriato who took care of the sick boy. He gave him strange medicines, the contents of which only he knew. Somewhere, nobody knew where, he found a blanket to spread in the doorway where Rozendo slept. And he would tell the patient funny tales and anecdotes that seemed even funnier because they were told by Viriato the Dwarf, who rarely spoke and almost never laughed.

Viriato asked, "What's your mother's name?"

"Ricardina. She's living with a truck driver. She's a heavyset woman, still young, well preserved . . ."

The sick boy would get agitated when he spoke of his mother.

"I want my ma, I want her. I'm gonna die."

"Don't worry, tomorrow Baldo and me'll bring her here."

Phillip cried, and this time his tears were not fabricated. Gordo prayed, mixing up parts of different prayers, and Antônio Balduíno clutched his *figa*.

The next day Balduíno stayed with Rozendo in the darkest part of the stairway. They were thinking about calling Jubiabá that night. But around the middle of the afternoon, Viriato the Dwarf brought a fat black woman. Rozendo was delirious and didn't recognize her. She threw her arms around him and took him away. They went in a taxi. Antônio Balduíno asked, "Do you have money, ma'am?"

"Not much but enough with God's help."

Then Antônio Balduíno remembered the ring he was wearing around his neck.

"We'll give Rozendo this. For the doctor."

The others looked at it with a touch of envy. The black woman asked, "Did you all steal this? Are you thieves? Was my son hanging around with thieves?"

"We found it in the street."

The woman seized the ring. But Antônio Balduíno still detained her, asking, "Do you want me to bring Jubiabá to your house? He can cure Rozendo."

"Can you do that?"

"Yes, he's my friend."

"Oh, then bring him, honey. Bring him."

Rozendo was in the taxi, yelling, saying he wanted his mother because he was going to die.

Antônio Balduíno asked Viriato, "How did you find her?"

"It was hard, because she wasn't living with the truck driver anymore. Now it's a carpenter."

He stared at the street, which was filling with traffic. Suddenly he said to Balduíno, "What if I get sick? I don't have a mother or a father or anyone."

Antônio Balduíno put his hand on Viriato's shoulder, and Gordo trembled.

Jubiabá went to Rozendo's house and cured him. One sunny morning the gang went to visit their friend. Rozendo was already sitting in a chair his stepfather had built, and they laughed a lot, remembering their adventures together. Rozendo said he wasn't going to be a beggar anymore, that now he was going to be a man and work as a carpenter with his stepfather. Antônio Balduíno laughed. Viriato the Dwarf grew serious.

The emperor of the city eats in the best restaurants, has the most luxurious cars at his disposal, lives in the newest skyscrapers. He pays nothing. In the afternoon he goes with his gang to a restaurant and says a word to a waiter. The waiter knows it isn't smart to argue with these boys. He gives them the leftover food, rolled up in newspapers. Sometimes there is even food left over from the gang's meals, and they throw it into the garbage cans. And old beggars eat the leftover leftovers.

He waits for an automobile that suits his taste to go by, because the emperor of the city doesn't want just any car. When he sees one that is very luxurious, he jumps up on the rear end of it and travels through entire neighborhoods. And if a prettier one comes along, Antônio Balduíno says good-bye to the first, mounts the second, and continues his tour of the city he has conquered.

He and his honor guard sleep in the doorways of the newest skyscrapers where all the employees know that those urchins have razors, switchblades, and knives.

This is when they don't want to sleep in the sandhills above the docks, looking at the enormous ships, the stars in the sky, and the mysterious green sea.

CHAPTER 5
Street Kid

The sea is his oldest passion. From the top of Capa-Negro Hill he has already gazed at it fondly, studying the variations of its surface: blue, light green, and then dark green, tempted by the vastness and mystery he senses in the great ships at rest in the port, in the small sailboats that the tide rocks to and fro. The sea brings to his heart a peace that the city cannot give. However, he owns the city, and no one owns the sea.

He comes to see it at night. Almost always he comes alone and lies down on the white sand of the small sailboat landing. There he sleeps his soundest tramp's sleep, and there he dreams. At times he brings the whole group of boys. Then they go to the big harbor where the transatlantic ships dock. They go to see the men who mysteriously embark at night, carrying overcoats and packages under their arms; they go to see the men whose work is to unload the ships. They are black and look like ants carrying enormous burdens. They walk bent over as if, instead of sacks of cocoa, they were carrying their own unlucky destiny upon their backs. And the cranes, like gigantic monsters making fun of the men, lift incredible burdens and swing them through the air. They screech and squeal on their tracks, driven by men in overalls who are mounted inside the brains of the monsters.

Other times Antônio Balduíno goes accompanied but not by the gang of street kids. He takes a black girl his own age or a little older to sleep without dreaming on the sand of the harbor. These times he does not see the peacefulness of the sailboats, the mystery of the oceangoing ships, or the giant cranes. He goes to certain places that only he and a few other boys know about, places where there is nothing to be seen except the green vastness of the ocean. Antônio Balduíno likes the ocean to see his lovers, to know that in spite of being only fifteen years old he is already a man who can take a mulatto girl on the soft, mattresslike sand.

But alone or accompanied, he always looks at the sea as a road leading homeward.

He is certain that someday the sea will bring him something, and though he doesn't know what it will be, he waits and hopes for it.

What does Antônio Balduíno, who is only fifteen years old and is already the emperor of the black city of Bahia, lack? He doesn't know, nor does anyone else. But something is missing, and to find it he will have to cross the ocean or wait for the ocean to bring it to him in the hold of an ocean liner, the bottom of a sailboat, or even fastened to the body of a shipwrecked sailor.

One night at the docks, the men stopped their work suddenly and ran to the water's edge. There was a bright moon, and the stars were so brilliant that one didn't even notice the light of a small bar that was called Drowned Man's Lantern. The men found an old coat and a battered hat. A few Negroes dived into the water. They came back with a body. It was an old black man, one of those rare black men with white hair, who had thrown himself into the sea. Antônio Balduíno thought that he had gone down the homeward road, that he, too, might have come to the docks every night. But a stevedore explained, "It's old Salusitano, poor devil. He'd been looking for work ever since he left the docks."

The man glanced behind him and spat in anger.

"They said he couldn't keep up with the work anymore 'cause he wasn't strong enough. He'd been living from hand to mouth, hungry all the time. Poor devil."

Another added, "That's how it always is. They work us to death, and then, when we're not fit for anything else except to throw ourselves in the ocean, they send us away." It was a thin mulatto man who spoke.

A muscular Negro said, "They eat our meat and then throw

away the bones. During slave days, at least they would save the bones to chew on."

A whistle blew, and they went back to their cargo and the cranes. But first, someone covered the old man's face with the old coat.

Then women came and wept.

The black men of the docks stopped their work on another occasion. This time the night was without stars or moon. From the guitar of a blind man in Drowned Man's Lantern there came old songs of slave days. A man got up on a packing crate and began to speak. Others arrived and moved closer, surrounding him. When Antônio Balduíno and his gang got there, the man was already leading the crowd in yelling, "Viva!"

Antônio Balduíno and his gang joined in loudly, "Viva!"

He didn't know what he was cheering for, but he liked to cheer. And he laughed because he enjoyed laughing.

The man on top of the packing crate, who looked Spanish, threw the crowd a fistful of pamphlets, which were quickly distributed. Antônio Balduíno took one and gave it to the stevedore Antônio Caroço, a friend of his. Then somebody yelled, "Here come the police!"

The police grabbed the man who had been speaking. His speech was about the misery in which the masses lived, and he had promised a new nation where everyone would have bread to eat and a job. That was the reason for his arrest, and since the others didn't understand why he was arrested for that, they protested: "You can't! You can't!"

Antônio Balduíno shouted "You can't!" too. This was the kind of thing he liked best. In the end, they took the little man away, but the workers kept the pamphlets he had passed out, and those who hadn't gotten one borrowed one from their friends. It was a group of hands stretched out against the soldiers who had arrested the speechmaker. A group of strong black faces. Their extended hands recalled the gesture of breaking shackles. From the Drowned Man's Lantern came slave songs.

The whistle blew uselessly. A fat man with an umbrella and a rosy face said, "Rabble!"

Who knows how the sea will show Antônio Balduíno his way home. By means of a drowned body, a suicide? Or by the arrest of a man who speaks about bread and the gestures of the others who protest?

They were good, free years, those years when he and his gang dominated the city, begging in its streets, fighting in its alleys, sleeping in its harbor. The group was united, and the boys had a certain esteem for one another. They only knew how to show that esteem by slapping each other on the back and swearing. To profane a companion's mother in a soft voice was the greatest sign of affection any of those laughing black boys knew how to express.

Yes, they were united. When one got in a fight, they all fought with him. Everything they earned was fraternally divided among them. They had self-respect, and loved the fame of the gang. One day they beat up another gang of street kids that begged in the city.

When this group appeared, led by a black boy of about twelve, Antônio Balduíno made an effort at diplomacy. He sent an emissary to Terreio Square, where they were hanging out. It was Phillip the Beautiful, who was a good talker. But he couldn't even get close to them. He was driven away, hooted at, and he came back miserable, his eyes full of tears of rage. He told Antônio Balduíno the whole story.

"Was it because you went there putting on airs, Beautiful?"

"I never even got close. They started in calling my mother names. But I'll get one of those guys and bash his head."

Antônio Balduíno thought a while.

"I'll send Gordo."

Toothless was affronted. "Send somebody else? What for? We should go over there and bust their faces. Give 'em a lesson. They come taking our bread away, and you want to make peace. You shouldn't even have sent Beautiful. We've been disgraced. Let's go over there right now."

The others supported him. "Yeah, Toothless is right. Let's go."

But Antônio Balduíno interrupted. "No. I'm sending Gordo.

Maybe they're all hungry. If they want to keep part of Baixa dos Sapateiros for their territory, I'll leave them alone."

Toothless laughed.

"Looks like you're scared, Baldo."

Antônio Balduíno's hand closed on his razor, but he contained himself.

"Toothless, have you forgotten the day we found you and Cici starving down in Cidade de Palha? If we'd wanted, we could have finished you off then. But we didn't."

Toothless bowed his head and whistled under his breath. He no longer thought about the black boys in Terreio Square, and now it hardly mattered to him whether Antônio Balduíno finished them off or left them in peace. He was thinking about those hungry days, his father unemployed, spending in bars the money his mother scraped together by washing clothes. He remembered the beating he had gotten the day he had tried to get between the old lady and his father when the latter tried to take the money away from her by force. And his mother's screams. His father saying, "Shit, shit, shit" over and over.

Afterward, he ran away. He remembered the hungry days he spent in the city, his meeting with Antônio Balduíno and the gang, and his life from then on. Where might his mother be? Had his father found a job? When he was working, he didn't drink or beat the old lady. He was affectionate and brought presents. But there wasn't much work, and when the old man was out of a job, he would drown his sorrows in rum. Thinking about all this, Toothless felt a knot in his throat and a terrible hatred for the world of men.

Gordo left on his mission, in spite of the smiles of Phillip the Beautiful.

"If I couldn't do anything, how can you?"

Viriato the Dwarf murmured, "Talk good, Gordo. We don't want to fight. We just want everyone to stay in their own territory."

They waited in Rua do Tesouro. Gordo crossed himself and walked toward Terreio Square.

He took a long time to come back. Viriato the Dwarf said, "I don't like this."

Beautiful smiled. "He's probably in some church praying."

Cici thought Gordo was getting things straightened out, but they were all anxious that something had happened to their ambassador. And something had, indeed. Gordo finally returned, crying.

"They grabbed me and beat me up, and they threw away my holy medal, the one I wear around my neck."

"And didn't you do anything?"

"How? There's about fifty of them and I was alone."

And Gordo continued, "I got there and they were all laughing, making fun of Beautiful. They started swearing at me right away, calling me a pig. 'Here comes the pig,' that's what they yelled."

"Well, so what? They swore at my mother," said Phillip.

"But I didn't pay any attention. I went up to them and tried to talk. They didn't give me time. They grabbed me. I kept saying I'd come in peace. And look what they did to me. There's more than twenty of 'em."

"Okay, if they want to fight, let's fight right now."

They got up and went happily off, clutching their knives, talking about all manner of different things.

The Terreio Square gang disappeared after the fight, undoubtedly disbanding. The members may have bummed around separately, but in truth they never again appeared as a group. Antônio Balduíno's gang came back radiant, except for Gordo, who hadn't managed to find his holy medal, given to him by Padre Silvino.

Gordo was very religious.

For this reason, Gordo crossed himself and trembled on the day that Antônio Balduíno saw Lindinalva. He understood everything on that day, and although he didn't say a word to Antônio Balduíno, he felt even closer to his leader.

They were in Rua Chile when they saw a young couple who seemed to be sweethearts. The boys got into line, Gordo in the front, and went toward them. Sweethearts always gave good handouts. Gordo clutched his hands together on his fleshy chest and began singing, "Alms for seven blind boys . . ."

They surrounded the couple. But when Antônio Balduíno looked closer, he saw that it was Lindinalva and a young man with a red ring on his finger. Blues music was playing in a snack bar nearby. Lindinalva saw Antônio Balduíno and clutched at her boyfriend's chest in a gesture of fear and disgust. Gordo sang, and nobody noticed the little scene. Antônio Balduíno shouted, "Stop! Let's get out of here!"

He ran off. The gang was speechless with surprise. Lindinalva's eyes were closed. The young man asked her, "What's the matter, dear?"

"Oh, it's those awful beggars," she lied.

The young man gave a superior laugh.

"You're very fearful, darling."

He threw a coin toward the boys. But they were far away by this time, coming up to Antônio Balduíno, whose face was hidden in his hands. Viriato the Dwarf asked, "What's the matter, Baldo?"

"Nothing. I know those people."

Toothless had gone back and gotten the coin. Gordo, who had understood everything, crossed himself and then went over to Antônio Balduíno and told him a funny story about Pedro Malazarte, the comedy hero. Gordo told a lot of stories and was very good at it. But no matter how happy the tale was, it always turned sad when told by Gordo; inevitably, he put in angels and demons. But he narrated very well, embroidering all the details, telling many lies and then believing them himself.

They lived this free life for two years. Two years running through the city, attending soccer games and boxing matches, sneaking into the Olympia movie theater, and listening to the stories Gordo would tell. They didn't notice that they were growing up, becoming men, and that the song about the seven little blind boys wouldn't work for them anymore. They were big strong Negroes, laying mulatto girls beside the docks, bumming around the religious city of Bahia. They began to get smaller handouts, and one day they were arrested for vagrancy and disorderly conduct.

A mulatto man with a straw hat and papers under his arm, who was a police detective, got some soldiers together and took them away.

First they went to the police headquarters where they were told nothing. Then they were taken to a gloomy corridor where only a tiny ray of sunlight penetrated through a crack in the wall. They could hear the voices of the prisoners singing. Some soldiers came with rubber thongs, and the boys were beaten without knowing why, for they had been told nothing. Thus they got their first tattoos. Phillip the Beautiful got a scar on his face. The mulatto man who had spotted them laughed, dragging on a cigarette. The prisoners were singing down below, or up above, nobody knew where. Their song spoke of the world outside, of liberty and light. And the rubber thongs whistled over the backs of the street kids. Toothless yelled and cursed everybody. Antônio Balduíno tried to kick the soldiers, and Viriato the Dwarf bit his lips with rage. Gordo's prayers were no help, but he prayed in a loud voice, "Our Father, who art in Heaven . . ."

And the thongs whistled. They didn't stop beating them until blood ran down their bodies. The prisoners sang sadly.

They spent eight days in jail, got their names in the police files, and finally were let go on a bright sunny morning. They went back to bumming through the city.

They went back, but they didn't stay. Slowly the group dissolved. The first to go was Toothless, who joined a gang of pickpockets. Sometimes they would see him go by wearing a suit, old shoes, and a scarf tied around his neck, whistling softly as was his custom. Cici went away, too; they never knew where. Jesuíno went to work in a factory, got married, and had a batch of children. Zé Casquinha signed up as a sailor.

And Phillip the Beautiful was killed under the wheels of a car. It was another sunny morning, and Phillip was growing handsomer all the time. Even the whip scar that had marked his face gave him an adventurous air. He had found himself a new tie and was commemorating his thirteenth birthday. The others laughed and joked with him. Then they saw something sparkling in the asphalt of the street, as bright as a diamond. Balduíno saw it first and said, "It looks like a diamond."

Phillip the Beautiful got excited.

"Oh, I'm going to get it to wear on my finger. It's my birthday present!" He ran into the middle of the street. Viriato even cried out to warn him that there was a car coming. Phillip looked up, laughing, and it was his last smile. The car left him a bloody heap, a pile of flesh and entrails that still moaned. He died smiling, to thank Viriato for his warning. His face was untouched, and it was beautiful, radiant, the face of a prince. The body was taken to the city morgue. An old, painted woman came, sobbing, *"Mon chéri, mon chéri."*

And she kissed the face of Phillip the Beautiful. But he no longer saw anything, nor knew it was his mother who was there. Nor did he know that the group got back together again for his funeral. Toothless came, Jesuíno, even Cici came from wherever he had been. Only Zé Casquinha couldn't come because he was a sailor and traveling far away. Phillip's mother and the other women from the Rua de Baixo brought flowers. The gang dressed him in a cashmere suit, bought from a Turk who sold clothes on the installment plan.

Only Viriato the Dwarf, who grew more and more shrunken and distorted, kept on as a beggar. The others were scattered through the city in diverse jobs, as factory workers, tradesmen, stevedores. Gordo took to selling newspapers because he had a good voice. Antônio Balduíno went back to Capa-Negro Hill where he hung around with Zé Camarão, practicing *capoeira*, playing the guitar at parties, and going to Jubiabá's *candomblé* ceremonies.

Every night he would go to the docks to watch the sea, looking for the road toward home.

CHAPTER 6
Drowned Man's Lantern

When Mr. Antônio bought the Drowned Man's Lantern from the widow of a sailor who had set it up years ago, the bar already bore that name. Above the door hung a crudely painted board depicting a mermaid rescuing a drowning man. The sailor who had established the bar had gotten off a cargo ship one day and put down anchor in the dark old salon, which had once been a colonial mansion. He had fallen in love with a mulatto girl who made rice pudding for his customers and furnished lunches for the dockworkers.

Why he called the bar Drowned Man's Lantern, no one knew. But they knew that he had been shipwrecked three times and had traveled over the whole world. Before he died, he married the mulatto girl so she could inherit the bar, which had built up a faithful clientele. She sold it to Mr. Antônio, who had had his eye on it for a long time due to its convenient location. Mr. Antônio didn't like the name of the bar. He could see no reason for calling it such a strange name, and a few days after the business transaction, the board was changed. The new placard displayed the poorly drawn figure of a Portuguese caravel and beneath, a name: CAFÉ VASCO DA GAMA.

But it happened that the customers viewed the new name with suspicion and didn't go in. What with the new sign and the thorough cleaning that had been done inside the barroom, they didn't recognize their grimy port of rest, where they could drink their rum of a night and converse beside the harbor.

Mr. Antônio was superstitious. The next day he fetched the old sign from the rear of the premises and put it back in its place. He stored the board that had the Portuguese caravel for such time as he might possess a café in the center of the city. With the sign of Drowned Man's Lantern, the mulatto woman who had been the sailor's lover came back, and once again made rice pudding for the customers, furnished lunches for the stevedores, and slept in the same bed she had occupied before. Except that now she was sleeping with a talkative Portuguese man instead of a taciturn sailor. If someday Mr. Antônio should move to the center of town to set up a café called Vasco da Gama, adorned with Portuguese sailing vessels, she would still be in Drowned Man's Lantern, cooking rice pudding for the customers, furnishing lunch for the stevedores, and sleeping in the same bed with the new proprietor.

The clientele came back to Drowned Man's Lantern. There, blond and black sailors discussed long ocean cruises. Sailboat captains conversed about the markets along the coast where they took their boatloads of fruit. They played guitars, sang sambas, told tall tales in the immense starlit nights. Women from the Ladeira do Taboão would come down to the Drowned Man's Lantern.

Antônio Balduíno, Zé Camarão, and Gordo were among the most frequent customers. Even Jubiabá appeared from time to time.

Though Antônio Balduíno was Zé Camarão's most dedicated *capoeira* pupil, he was even better at the guitar. Very soon he superceded his teacher and got to be equally renowned. Often, as he bummed through the streets of the city, he would start to drum his fingers on his straw hat, singing a verse of a song he had made up out of his own head.

"A black man's life is really fine,
Parties every night,
Lots of rhythm, lots of rhyme
Black girls to hold you tight."

He was always a great success at parties.

* * *

"The Lord of Bonfim protects me,
He's powerful and strong.
I was a carefree playboy
Until you came along."

There wasn't a *cabrocha* who didn't fall in love.

One afternoon a very well-dressed man appeared on the hill and asked for Antônio Balduíno. They pointed out the Negro, who was talking with a group of people. The man came up, dragging a cane across the ground.

"Are you Antônio Balduíno?"

Balduíno thought he might be someone from the police.

"Why do you ask?"

"Aren't you the one who makes up sambas?" asked the man, pointing to him with the cane.

"Yeah, I make up some little things."

"Want to sing one for me to hear?"

"Well, if you don't mind my asking, why should I?"

"Might be I'd buy one."

Antônio Balduíno was needing money to buy a pair of new shoes he had seen at the Agua de Meninos market. He went to get his guitar and sang a few sambas. The man liked two of them.

"Want to sell me these?"

"What do you want 'em for?"

"I like them."

"Okay, I'll sell."

"I'll give you twenty mil-reis for the two."

"Fair enough. Whenever you want more . . ."

The man made Antônio Balduíno whistle the music and took notes on a paper full of little lines. Then he wrote down the words.

"I'll be back for more one day soon."

He went down the hill, dragging his cane. The people of the hill stared at him. Antônio Balduíno stretched out in the door of the little store and put the two ten-mil-reis notes on top of his naked belly. He was thinking about the new shoes he would buy and the length of chintz he would give Joana.

That night in a downtown café, the cane-carrying man who

had bought the sambas said, "I composed two fantastic samba pieces."

He sang, drumming his fingers on the table. The sambas later came out on records and were sung over the radio. People played them on the piano. The papers said, "The greatest hits this carnival season are the sambas by the poet Anísio Pereira. They'll drive you wild!"

Antônio Balduíno didn't read the papers or listen to the radio or play the piano. He continued to sell his sambas to the poet Anísio Pereira.

Joana wore her hair loose. She kept it carefully straightened, and perfumed it with a scent that made Antônio Balduíno dizzy. He would press his flat nose against the nape of her neck, lifting up her hair to breathe in her perfume. She would laugh.

"Get your snout off my neck."

He would laugh, too.

"You smell good enough to eat."

He would throw the girl backward onto the bed. Her voice sounded far away.

"You dog!"

On the day he turned up wearing his new shoes, carrying the chintz for Joana's new dress under his arm, she was also singing one of the sambas that he had sold to the man with the cane. Antônio Balduíno said, "You know what, Joana?"

"What?"

"I sold that samba."

"Sold it, how?" She didn't know how anyone could sell a samba.

"Some little man turned up on the hill and bought two sambas from me for twenty mil-reis. Pretty good, huh?"

"But why did he want them?"

"How should I know? I think he must be crazy."

Joana thought for a minute. But Antônio Balduíno gave her the length of material.

"I bought this for you with the money."

"Ooooh, how beautiful!"

"And look how swanky my new shoes are."

She looked and threw herself around Antônio Balduíno's

neck. He laughed aloud, satisfied with life, happy with the business he had conducted. And as he smelled the back of Joana's neck, she sang his samba. She was the only person who sang it knowing that it was really Antônio Balduíno who had composed it.

Balduíno told her, "Today we're going to the macumba at Jubiabá's house. It's your saint's day, honey."

They went to the macumba session and afterward lay down on the sand where they made love furiously, Antônio Balduíno seeing in Joana's body the body of Lindinalva.

They often went to the Drowned Man's Lantern, although Joana wasn't fond of the place.

"So many whores go there. They might think I was one, too."

Joana worked as a maid in a house in the Vitoria neighborhood and rented a little room in Quintas. She liked to go and make love near the docks, but she only went to the Drowned Man's Lantern to satisfy Antônio Balduíno's whim. When the two of them went together, he would sit alone with her at a table, drinking beer and smiling at the others who greeted him. He would show off his girl friend and then leave, laughing and winking as though to say that they were now on their way to the harbor.

Much more often, however, Antônio Balduíno would go with Gordo, Joaquim, or Zé Grandão. They would drink rotgut rum, recount their adventures, laugh as only black men know how. On the night of Gordo's birthday, Viriato the Dwarf appeared. He had changed a lot in the past few years. Not that he was any taller or stronger. Rather, he was all in rags and tatters, leaning on a rough cane.

"I came to drink to your health, Gordo."

Gordo called for rum. Antônio Balduíno asked, "How are things going, Viriato?"

"So-so."

"You sick?"

"No. This getup is to take in more handouts." He laughed his tight-lipped laugh.

"How come you haven't been to see us for so long?"

"I dunno . . . didn't really feel like it."

"I heard you'd been sick."

"Yeah, I was. Bad case of malaria. The public health people grabbed me . . . I went through hell. If I get sick again I'd rather die in the street."

He accepted the cigarette that Joaquim offered.

"They threw me in there without anybody to care what happened to me. You know what it's like?"

Gordo didn't know, but he was frightened.

"At night, the fever would come. I thought I was gonna die. I remembered I didn't have anyone to mourn me—" He stopped.

"But you got well," said Baldaíno.

"Not really. Malaria comes back. One of these days I'll die in the street like a dog."

Gordo clapped his black hand on the table in Viriato's direction.

"What do you mean! You're not gonna die, brother!"

Joaquim tried to laugh.

"Ugly dishes don't break."

But Viriato went on: "Baldaíno, you remember Rozendo? He got sick but he had his mother, who came to get him. It was even me who found her. And Phillip the Beautiful, when he died, there was his mother, who came to the funeral. She brought those flowers and there were a lot of women."

"One of 'em had gorgeous legs," interrupted Joaquim.

"Everybody has a father, a mother, somebody. I don't have anyone."

He threw his cigarette away and ordered another glass of rum.

"What's our life worth? Do you remember that time that we got beaten like dogs by the police? Why did they do that to us? Our life is good for nothing. We don't have anybody."

Gordo trembled. Antônio Baldaíno was looking into his glass of rum. Viriato the Dwarf got up.

"I'm bothering you guys. But I live alone, and I get to brooding."

"You leaving?" asked Joaquim.

"I'll catch the crowd coming out of the movies."

He shuffled out, bent over his staff, covered with rags.

"He's gotten used to walking like that," said Joaquim.

"Why does he only talk about sad stuff?" Gordo didn't know, but he felt sorry because he was very good-hearted.

"He knows more than we do," affirmed Antônio Balduíno.

At the next table, a mulatto man with a briefcase was explaining to a Negro, "Moses commanded the sea to divide, and he crossed over with all the Christians."

"I talk to amuse myself," said Joaquim.

Gordo complained, "He shouldn't have done that today, today is my birthday."

"Done what?"

"Talk about sad stuff . . . he took all the fun out of it."

"Aw, come on. Let's go have a bash at Zé Camarão's house," invited Antônio Balduíno. "We'll get us some girls."

Gordo paid the bill. At the next table, the mulatto man was telling the story of King Solomon, who had six hundred wives.

"Wow, some man," said Antônio Balduíno, chortling.

They had their bash, flooded themselves with rum, and made love to some good-looking mulatto girls, but they didn't manage to forget Viriato the Dwarf, who had no one to treat his malaria.

Joana would throw fits on account of other girls that were equally loved by Antônio Balduíno. Any *cabrocha* that crossed his path was automatically his. A strong, rowdy young man of eighteen, he had gained considerable prestige among the dark girls of the city: maids, washerwomen, cooks who sold traditional Bahian foods like *acarajé* and *abará.* He knew how to talk to them. When he found one he liked, he would always take her to the sandhills where they would curl up together, unmindful of the sand that got in their hair.

He would make love to them and never see them again. They passed through his life like the clouds that floated across the sky and served for the comparisons he made.

"Your eyes are as black as that cloud up there."

"Ooooh! It's going to rain!"

"Then let's go. I know a place where we'll be nice and cozy."

But Joana had that perfume on the back of her neck. She

stuck to him, fought when she learned he had gone off with some other girl. It was even said she had a magic spell cast so he wouldn't leave her. She had gotten a pair of Antônio Balduíno's undershorts and tied some black chicken feathers up in them, along with five copper coins and a mixture of palm oil and manioc flour. She put the whole thing beside Antônio Balduíno's door on a night when the moon was full.

At the party at Arlindo's house in Brotas, she had made an awful fuss just because Antônio Balduíno had danced a few times with Delfina, a redheaded mulatto girl. She had wanted to fight the other girl and even snatched one of the shoes off her feet. Antônio Balduíno laughed aloud, enjoying the dispute.

Back home, Joana asked him, "What did you think was pretty about that pest?"

"Are you jealous of her?"

"Me! Jealous of that piece of hide? An old hag already falling apart? I don't know what you saw in her!"

"Ah, that's what you don't know. She has her secrets."

Antônio Balduíno laughed and rolled over the bed with her, smelling her perfumed neck.

He remembered when he had met her. It was at a party in the Rio Vermelho neighborhood. He went after her at once, playing things on his guitar. She fell for him right away. The next day, a Sunday, they met and went to the matinee at the Olympia. She told him a very long story to prove that she was a virgin, and he ended up believing her. He began to lose interest, but he kept the date they had made for Thursday because he had nothing else to do that night. They strolled through the Campo Grande park, he without talking much because she was a virgin, and virgins didn't really interest him. When it was almost time to go back, she told him, "Look, I can see you're very nice and respectful, so I'll tell you the truth. I'm not really a virgin."

"Oh. You're not?"

"It was my uncle, an uncle who lived in my house. It was three years ago. I was all alone, my mama had gone out to work."

"And your father?"

"I never knew him. My uncle took advantage of me, he grabbed me and forced me."

"What a disgrace!" At heart, Antônio Balduíno sympathized with the uncle.

"I never had anything to do with men for three whole years. But I like you."

This time Antônio Balduíno could see that it was all her invention, but he didn't say anything. He didn't let her go back to the house where she worked that night, and since he had nowhere to take her, they went to the docks, to look down at the ships and the sea.

Then they rented the room in Quintas where every night Joana would throw jealous fits and tell lies.

Balduíno didn't believe the lies, and he was starting to get bored with her.

One stormy night they were at the Drowned Man's Lantern when Gordo came in very upset. Joaquim, who was talking to Antônio Balduíno, said, "Here comes Gordo."

"Do you guys know what happened?"

"The stevedores found a body down in the harbor."

That was common, and they weren't impressed. But Gordo added, "It was Viriato."

"Who?"

"Viriato the Dwarf."

They ran out. There he was beside the docks. A group of men surrounded the body. It must have been in the water for about three days, for it was swollen large. The eyes, wide open, seemed to pin themselves on the group. The nose had already been chewed a little by the fish, and you could hear crabs making a strange noise inside the belly.

They took the corpse to the Drowned Man's Lantern, pushed two tables together, and put the body on top of them. The crabs made noises under Viriato's skin like rattles being shook. Mr. Antônio brought a candle from the counter to place in the hand which would no longer open.

Joaquim said, "He only grew taller after he died."

Gordo was praying.

"Poor thing! He didn't have anyone."

Some of the men who were drinking rum came to see. The

women looked and drew away in fear. Mr. Antônio was still holding the candle, for nobody had the courage to put it in the dead man's hand. Antônio Balduíno took the candle and went up to the body. He pried open the thick hand of the drowned man and placed the candle in it. Then he spoke.

"He was all alone, friends. He was trying to find the road home, and he went by way of the sea."

Nobody understood. Someone asked where he had lived. Jubiabá, who was just arriving, wanted to know what had happened.

"Good evening to you all. What's this?"

"He was looking, pai Jubiabá, he was looking for the eye of mercy. But he didn't find it, and he killed himself. He had no father or mother, nobody to take care of him. He died because he didn't find the eye of mercy."

Nobody understood, but they trembled when Jubiabá said, *"Ôjú, ànun fó ti ikà, ôkú."*

In his saddest style, Gordo told the story of Viriato the Dwarf to one of the men who was drinking rum, omitting no detail. According to Gordo, Viriato had once seen three angels and a woman dressed in purple, who was his mother, calling him up to heaven. So then he threw himself into the water.

Suddenly, in the midst of all those people, Antônio Balduíno felt as though he were alone with the cadaver, and he was afraid. Terribly afraid. He trembled, his teeth chattering. He remembered everyone: his aunt Luísa, who had gone crazy; Leopoldo, who had been murdered; Rozendo, sick and calling for his mother; Phillip the Beautiful, crushed by the car; old Salusitano drowning himself in the harbor; and now the body of Viriato the Dwarf, full of rattling crabs.

And he thought that they were all very unlucky, alive or dead. Those who would be born afterward, too. But he didn't know why they were so unlucky.

The storm put out the lights in Drowned Man's Lantern.

CHAPTER 7
Macumba

Exú, the devil, had been driven away so he wouldn't upset the ritual proceedings. He went to some distant place, such as Pernambuco or Africa.

The night was falling behind the houses, and it was one of those calm, religious nights in the city on the Bay of All Saints. From Jubiabá's house came the sound of instruments: drums, gourd rattles, the metallic *agogô,* the mysterious sounds of the macumba ceremony. They lost themselves in the stars, in the silence of the city night. At the door, black women were selling *acarajé* and *abará.*

And since they had sent Exú away, he went to bother other ceremonies farther off, in the cotton plantations of Virginia or the shanties of Favela Hill.

In a corner at the back of the clay-floored room, the orchestra was playing. The instruments' monotonous rhythms resounded inside the heads of those who listened. It was enervating music touched with longing, music as old as the race, this music made with drums, gourd rattles, *agogôs.*

The audience, squeezed around the room against the walls, had its eyes fixed on the *ogãs,* who were seated in a square in the middle of the room. The priestesses, called *feitas,* whirled about them. As full members of the *candomblé* body, the *ogãs* were important, but only the *feitas* could receive the spirit of a deity, or *orixá.* Antônio Balduíno was a member, and Joaquim also, but Gordo, who wasn't yet, sat in the audience, very close to a thin, bald white man who was watching the scene with rapt attention and trying to accompany the monotonous music by slapping his knees. Opposite him, a young Negro dressed in blue lost himself in the music and chanting, forgetting that he had come only to observe. The rest of the audience, made up of black or mulatto men, pressed itself beside fat Negro women dressed in petticoats and low-cut blouses, their necks laden with beads. The priestesses danced slowly, shaking their bodies.

Suddenly an old Negress, who was leaning against the wall in front near the bald man, and who for a long while had been trembling nervously with the music and chants, received the spirit of a deity. She was taken to the dressing room. But since she was not a priestess of that *candomblé* assembly, she remained there until the spirit abandoned her and entered a young black girl, who then also went into the priestess's room.

The deity was Xangô, the god of lightning and thunder, and he had chosen a *feita* this time. The girl came out of the dressing room wearing the costume of that deity: a white dress and white beads streaked with red. In her hand she carried a small rod.

The high priestess of the *candomblé* assembly began the song to welcome the deity: *"Edurô dêmin lonan ô yê!"*

The audience joined in the chorus. *"A umbó k'ó wá jô!"*

The high priestess was saying in the Nagô song, "Make way for us who have come to dance."

The *feitas* whirled around; the *ogãs* and the audience paid reverence to the deity by stretching their hands toward him, arms at sharp angles, palms turned toward the deity: *"Okê!"*

They all shouted, *"Okê, Okê!"*

Black men and women, mulattoes, the bald man, Gordo, the student, the whole audience encouraged the deity: *"Okê, Okê!"*

Then the deity went into the midst of the *feitas* and danced among them. He was Xangô, god of thunder and lightning, and wore white beads streaked with red upon his white clothes. He came and bowed to Jubiabá, who was in the middle of the *ogãs* and was the greatest of all the priests. The god circled the room again and bowed to the bald white man who had come at Jubiabá's invitation. Xangô paid his respects by bowing three times in front of the person, squeezing the shoulders in a hug, and kissing him lightly on both cheeks. Now the high priestess was singing.

"Iya ri dé glê ô
Afi dé si ómón lôwô
Afi ilé ké si ómón lerun."

She was saying,

"The mother decks herself with jewels,
She adorns her children's necks,
She puts new beads about her children's necks."

The *ogãs* and the audience chimed in at the chorus, reciting an onomatopoeic chant that was supposed to suggest the noise of the beads "all rattling and clattering." *"Omiró wónrón wónrón wónrón omiró."*

At this point Joana, who was already dancing as if she were in a trance, was possessed by Omolu, the goddess of the bladder.

She came out of the dressing room in a multicolored costume, predominantly bright red, with pants resembling old-fashioned bloomers, their embroidered edges appearing under the skirt. The trunk of her body was almost nude with only a white cloth tied around her breasts. Joana's trunk was perfect, her hard, pointed breasts thrusting through the cloth. But nobody saw the *cabrocha* Joana. Not even Antônio Balduíno saw his lover Joana, who slept without dreaming in the sand of the sailboat landing. It was Omolu who danced before them with thinly covered breasts, Omolu the terrible goddess of the bladder. From the high priestess came the monotonous chant of welcome: *"Edurô dêmin lonan ê yê!"*

The music of the drums, gourd rattles, and metallic *agogôs* never changed; it repeated itself over and over. Yet it excited those present to a crazed pitch. Again the audience sang in chorus. *"A umbó k'o wá jô!"*

They were paying homage to the goddess. *"Okê! Okê!"*

And Omolu, who was dancing among the priestesses, came and greeted Antônio Balduíno. Then she greeted the persons in the audience who had been invited to attend: Gordo; the black student, who was generally liked; the bald man; Roque; and various others.

Now they were all excited, and they all wanted to dance. Omolu was choosing women from the audience to dance. Antônio Balduíno moved the trunk of his body as if he were rowing a boat. He stretched out his arms to greet the deity. An air of mystery spread over the room; it seemed to come from everything: the spirits; the music; the chants; and principally from Jubiabá, small and ancient.

They sang another of the macumba songs in chorus. *"Êolô biri ô b'ajá gbá kó a péhindá."*

They were singing that "the dog shows his tail when he walks." Oxossi, the god of hunting, also visited Jubiabá's macumba ceremony. He wore white, gold, and a little red, a bow strung with an arrow hanging from one side of his belt. On the other side he carried a quiver. He wore a metal helmet trimmed in green cloth, and this time he carried a staff tipped with many thick cords. It wasn't always that Oxossi, the great hunter god, brought his corded staff.

The bare feet of the women stamped on the clay floor as they danced. They swayed their bodies as part of the ritual, but this swaying was as sensual as their warm black bodies, as seductive as the African music. Sweat ran freely; all were intoxicated by the ritual and the dance. Gordo trembled, unable to see anything except the confused figures of women and spirits, capricious spirits of the distant forest. The white man stamped his well-shod feet on the floor and said to the student, "I might dance myself any minute."

The deity paid reverence to Jubiabá. Arms at sharp angles greeted Oxossi, the god of hunting. Lips were pursed, hands trembled, bodies shook in the hysteria of the sacred dance. Then suddenly, Oxalá, the greatest of all the gods, appeared, knocking down Maria dos Reis, a black girl of fifteen with a rounded, virgin's body. Oxalá divides himself in two: Oxidian, who is young, and Oxolufã, who is old. This time he appeared as Oxolufã, old and bent, supported by a decorated staff. He came out of the dressing room attired in white to receive the reverence of the audience, who all bowed lower than ever.

"Okê, Okê, Okê!"

Only then did the high priestess sing, *"Ê inun ójá l'a ô lô, inun li a ô lô."* She was advising, "Prepare yourselves, O people of the market place, for we are going to invade."

And the audience chanted, *"Erô ójá é pará món, ê inun ójá li a ô lô."*

"Be careful, O crowds of people, we will enter the market place." Yes, they would enter the market place because they were with Oxalá, the greatest of all the spirits.

Oxolufã, the old Oxalá, paid homage only to Jubiabá. He danced among the priestesses until Maria dos Reis fell to the floor, awakening suddenly, still shaking her body as though dancing, foaming at the mouth and genitals.

Everyone in the room was crazed with excitement as they danced to the sound of the instruments. All four spirits danced among the priestesses, circling the *candomblé* members. Oxossi, the god of the hunt, Xangô, god of lightning and thunder, Omolu, goddess of the bladder, and Oxalá, the greatest of all deities, rolled and wallowed on the floor.

On the Roman Catholic altar in one corner of the room, Oxossi was St. George; Xangô, St. Jerome; Omolu, St. Roque; and Oxalá, Our Lord of Bonfim, most miraculous of all the deities of the black city on the Bay of All Saints, the city of the pai-de-santo Jubiabá. His ceremony is the most beautiful, since it is pure macumba.

In the main room they had offered popcorn to the audience, and back in the kitchen, goat meat and mutton cooked in palm oil was served with pepper-seasoned rice. On macumba nights, the Negroes of the city met at Jubiabá's house and exchanged their news. They talked late into the night, discussing what had happened during the last few days. But that evening they were constrained because of the white man who had come from very far away just to attend Jubiabá's ceremony. The white man had eaten lots of goat meat and had licked his chops after the peppered rice. Antônio Balduíno learned that this man wrote ABC's and traveled all over the world. At first he thought the man must be a sailor, and Gordo confirmed that he was a traveling man. He had been brought there by the poet who bought Antônio Balduíno's sambas. The man wanted to see a macumba session, and the poet said that only Antônio Balduíno had the prestige to get him invited to Jubiabá's house. In spite of this compliment, Antônio Balduíno hadn't felt much disposed to speak to Jubiabá. This business of letting white people—especially unknown ones—come to the macumba sessions was no good. The man could be a police detective wanting to arrest everyone. Once they had locked Jubiabá up overnight and had taken away his image of Exú. Zé Camarão, who was as artful as they come, had to go down to the police headquarters and steal the image back, right out from under the guards' noses. When Zé returned with Exú under his coat, there was rejoicing. And they had had an all-night session in order to appease Exú, who was furious and might later disturb other ceremonies.

That was why Antônio Balduíno didn't want to take the white man. He only spoke to Jubiabá when the black student, with whom he was acquainted, told him, "I'll guarantee the man. It's as if he were me."

Then Balduíno wanted to know all about the white man's life. When he learned that he wandered all over the world seeing everything, he grew enthusiastic. Who knew that someday that man might write *his* ABC?

The white man said good-bye after telling Jubiabá that the session was the most beautiful thing he had ever seen. The student went along with him, and the blacks breathed easier. Now they could talk freely, discuss their affairs, talk about what they liked, lie as they wished.

Rosado said to Antônio Balduíno, "Did you see my new tattoo?"

"No."

Rosado was a sailor who passed through Bahia once in a while and who had once brought them news of Zé Casquinha, who was sailing far-off seas and even talking gringo language. Rosado's back was entirely filled with tattoos, including girls' names, a vase of flowers, a knife, and a whip.

He laughed. Antônio Balduíno admired his back with a certain envy.

"Looks nice."

"There's an American guy on the ship who has a map on his back. It's a real beauty, man."

Antônio Balduíno thought of the white man. He would like to see that. But he had left as though he were running away, because the Negroes were uncomfortable in his presence. Antônio Balduíno thought he would have a tattoo done on his back, but he hadn't decided what kind it would be. He would like to put the sea and a picture of Zumbi dos Palmares. There was a Negro at the docks who had Zumbi's name tattooed all over his back.

Damião, an old Negro, smiled. "Y'all want to see a back with marks?"

Jubiabá made a gesture to stop him, but he had already ripped off his shirt. They all saw that his hair was white. On his back were scars from a whip. He had been beaten on the plantations and put in stocks during the days of slavery. Just below these scars, Antônio Balduíno saw the mark of a brand.

"What's that, uncle?"

When Damião realized he was talking about the brand, he suddenly grew ashamed and covered his back. He wouldn't talk anymore but only stared at the city lights below them. Maria dos Reis smiled at Antônio Balduíno. Old men who had been slaves had their secrets.

Since Joana had left alone in a fit of jealousy, and Maria dos Reis had gone home with her mother, Antônio Balduíno went down the hill with Gordo and Joaquim. He was taking his guitar along to have a wild party.

But Gordo went home early, since he lived a fair way off with his grandmother, an octogenarian with a goatee on her chin, who long ago had lost all notion of reality. She lived in a different world, telling stories that got mixed up with each other, their characters turned around, and never reached any conclusion. In truth, she wasn't Gordo's grandmother at all. Gordo had invented that story out of shame at having sheltered and supported the old woman, who before had wandered homeless about the city. But he treated her as if she were his grandmother, bringing her food, talking with her for hours on end, going home early so the old woman wouldn't be alone. At times they would see Gordo with a length of dress material and would think he was going to give it to some flirtatious *cabrocha.*

"No, it's for my grandmother, poor thing. Her clothes wear out fast because she's always lying down on the dirty floor. She's getting a little soft in the head."

"Is she your father's mother or your mother's, Gordo?"

Gordo would get embarrassed. The others knew perfectly well that Gordo had never known father nor mother. But Gordo had a grandmother, and many of them envied him.

After Gordo said good-bye, Antônio Balduíno and Joaquim went down Ladeira da Montanha street, whistling a samba. The hill was deserted and silent. There was only one poor window lit by a lantern where a woman was hanging out the diapers of a newborn baby. They could hear the voice of a man talking inside the bedroom.

"There now, son, there now."

Joaquim said, "That one will be asleep on his feet at work tomorrow. He's playing nursemaid."

Antônio Balduíno didn't answer. Joaquim continued, "It's no use. What's the use?"

"What?"

"Nothing . . . nothing."

Antônio Balduíno asked him, "Have you ever noticed how good Gordo is?"

"Good?" Joaquim hadn't noticed.

"Yes, good. He's a good fellow. He has the eye of mercy wide open."

It was Joaquim's turn to be quiet. Soon he laughed aloud. "You're right. Gordo is a good fellow."

"So what're you laughing about?"

"Nothing. It's because I only just now realized that Gordo is a good fellow."

They went downhill without further comment. Antônio Balduíno was still thinking about the macumba and the bald man who had traveled all over the world. The man had gone away; in truth, he had run off. Antônio Balduíno thought that that man could be Pedro Malazarte. But he had fled when he saw that the Negroes were embarrassed. Antônio Balduíno remembered Zumbi dos Palmares. If there had been another Zumbi, that old

Negro wouldn't have been whipped. He would have been a fighter. Then he wouldn't have to be ashamed before a white man. The man had left in gesture of solidarity, and he wouldn't come back. However, one day that man would write Antônio Balduíno's ABC, a heroic ABC recounting the adventures of a free, happy black man, a fighter with the courage of seven.

Thinking about this, Antônio Balduíno grew happy again and laughed.

"You know something, Joaquim? I'm gonna end up taking that girl's cherry."

"Whose?" Joaquim's interest was lively.

"Maria dos Reis's. She's starting to fall for me."

"Which one's she?"

"The one Oxalá chose. That real young one."

"Hey, that one's refined stuff, Baldo. She's engaged to a guy in the army. You're going to get yourself into hot water."

"Who says? She's falling for me for sure. I got nothing to do with soldiers. I'm going to take her to bed, that's what. The soldier can go to hell." Joaquim knew that Antônio Balduíno would make love to the girl without caring a fig for the soldier. But he didn't like fights with army men, and he advised his friend, "You better leave her alone, Baldo."

He had forgotten that when Antônio Balduíno died he would be sung in an ABC ballad, and that all heroes in ABC ballads fought with soldiers and made love to damsels they met and conquered in a single night.

They went through the sleeping Lower City. There was nobody to party with; the Drowned Man's Lantern was closed. No one in the streets, not even a *cabrocha* to take to the sandhills. Not a single bar where they might drink a last nightcap. They walked on aimlessly, Joaquim yawning. Finally they turned down an alley and saw a mulatto man and woman who were talking like recent sweethearts. Joaquim said, "A mulatto girl, brother."

"That one's ours, Joaquim."

"But she's with a man, Baldo."

"You're going to see how this is done."

And with a jump, Antônio Balduíno accosted the woman. He shoved her hard, and she fell down in the street.

"So, you bitch, I'm working my ass off and you're after another man! You shameless whore, I'll teach you!"

He whirled to face the mulatto man, but before he could say anything the man asked, "She's your girl friend? I didn't know."

"Girl friend? She's my wife, married by the priest, y'hear? By the priest!" He advanced toward the man.

"I—I didn't know! Excuse me, sir. She didn't mention . . ."

He backed away and disappeared around the first corner. Antônio Balduíno laughed deliriously. Joaquim, who had drawn away from them since a fight should be one-to-one, came up.

"It worked, huh?"

Both of them let out peals of laughter that awakened the sleeping city. A chuckle came from the ground: It was the little woman getting up. A mulatto girl with rotten teeth and yellowish skin, hardly worth all the effort. But since there wasn't another woman available, the only thing to do was to take this toothless creature to the boat landing. Antônio Balduíno went first, then Joaquim.

"She may not have any teeth, but she's not bad," said Joaquim.

"She wasn't worth it," said Baldo.

He lay down on the sand, took up his guitar, and began to play. Joaquim put his feet into the water. The woman, who was fixing her dress, came up to them and began singing the song Antônio Balduíno was playing on the guitar. At first she sang softly, then in a full voice, and her voice was lovely and strange, almost masculine. She filled the whole harbor with her voice; even the sailboat crews woke up, and mariners appeared on the gunwales of the ships as the day broke over the bay.

When the sun came in through the poor window on Ladeira da Montanha, the woman woke the man. He had to go to a distant factory and needed to get up early. He said to the woman, pointing to the baby, "This little so-and-so didn't let me get a wink of sleep. I'm dead tired."

He threw some water on his face, looked at the bright morning, and swallowed some weak coffee. His wife warned, "There's no bread, on account of the milk for the child."

The man made a resigned gesture, kissed his son, patted his wife on the shoulder, and dragged on a cheap cigarette.

"Send my lunch at noon."

When he went out into the morning, which was becoming a bright blue day, and down Ladeira da Montanha toward the factory, he met Antônio Balduíno and Joaquim, who were coming along with the toothless woman trailing behind them. Balduíno yelled, "Jesuíno, is that you?"

It was Jesuíno, who had been a beggar in their street gang. He was almost unrecognizable, he was so thin. Joaquim laughed.

"You don't look so good, brother."

"My wife just had a baby, Baldo. I want you to be the godfather. One day I'll take you to meet the old lady."

He went off down the hill, toward the factory, which was on the other side of the bay in Itapegipe. And he had to go on foot, since bus fare was out of the question because of the child's milk. His wife was hanging diapers in the window, and she, too, was thin and pallid. There had been neither coffee nor bread left for her.

CHAPTER 8
Fighter

Jubiabá's house was small but pretty. It was situated in the middle of a lot on Capa-Negro Hill, a large yard in front, an orchard stretching out behind.

The spacious front room took up most of the house. Jubiabá and his guests ate at a table with a bench on either side, and there was an easy chair facing the door of the room where the pai-de-santo slept. On the benches beside the table, black men and women talked. Two Spaniards and an Arab were there as well. On the walls were numerous photographs of the priest's friends and relatives, framed in pink or white shells. Inside a glass-doored case, an African deity fraternized with a picture of Our Lord of Bonfim. The picture showed him saving a vessel from shipwreck. However, the idol was much prettier, since it was a black woman with a lovely body, holding one of her generous and well-made breasts in a gesture of offering. She was Iansã, the goddess of the waters, whom the white people called Saint Barbara.

Jubiabá came out of the bedroom, dressed in a beautiful smock that was embroidered across the chest. It reached down to his feet, and he was wearing nothing else. A black man got up from the table and helped the old medicine man to sit down.

The Negroes came and kissed Jubiabá's hand. The Spaniards and the Arab did the same. One of the Spaniards had a swollen jaw with a cloth tied around it. He drew closer to the priest and said, "Pai Jubiabá, I have a tooth that aches something awful. *Caramba!* I can't work, can't do anything on account of it. *Caramba!* I've spent a fortune on dentists, but they don't help. There's nothing left for me to do!"

He untied the cloth that covered his chin. His jaw was enormously swollen. Jubiabá doctored it.

"Put wood-mallow tea on it and recite this prayer:

St. Nicodemus, heal this tooth!
Nicodemus, heal this tooth!
Heal this tooth!
This tooth!
Tooth!"

He concluded, "You should say this prayer on the beach. Write it out on the sand and erase one word at a time, you know? Then go home and apply the tea. But without the prayer it won't work."

The Spaniard left five mil-reis and went home to apply the cure.

Then there came a Negro who wanted sorcery done. He whispered into Jubiabá's ear, and the pai-de-santo, aided by the Negro, got up and went into the bedroom. They came back a few minutes later. The next day there appeared a strong charm (manioc flour mixed with palm oil, four mil-reis in ten-cent coins, two copper pennies, and a young vulture, still alive) at the door of Henrique the Baker, who caught a mysterious disease and died a short time later. A Negro woman also wanted a spell cast, but she didn't lower her voice nor enter the bedroom. She said, "That shameless Marta took away my man. I want him to come back home." She was revolted. "I've got kids, she hasn't."

"Bring me some strands of her hair and leave the rest to me," answered Jubiabá.

The medicine man received many people who wanted sorceries performed. He recited prayers over some, holding a bunch of magic herbs. And in the wee hours of the morning, things were found cluttering the streets of the city, objects that passersby drew away from in fear. Often rich people would come to see Jubiabá, white bosses wearing rings, moneyed people with cars.

When Antônio Balduíno went into the room, there was a soldier speaking with the old priest. He was trying to talk softly, but his voice, charged with emotion, was audible to everyone.

". . . seems like she doesn't like me anymore. She's stopped listening to me. I think she's falling for somebody else. But I don't want that to happen, pai, I want her for me . . . I love her. I'm crazy about her."

The soldier's voice was on the point of breaking. Jubiabá asked him something and he answered, "Maria dos Reis."

Antônio Balduíno started, then smiled. He began to pay attention to their conversation. But the pai-de-santo was finishing the soldier's consultation.

"You'll have to bring me some hairs from under her arm and a pair of her underpants. I'll fix things so she'll never leave you. She'll be tied to you like a dog."

The soldier went out with his head bowed, trying not to let anyone see him.

Antônio Balduíno drew close to Jubiabá and sat on the floor.

"He really seems to like her."

"Do you know her, Baldo?"

"Isn't she the one Oxalá possessed during the ceremony?"

"The soldier loves her; he's going to have a spell cast. Be careful, Baldo."

"I don't give a shit for soldiers."

"But he loves her."

"Sure seems to."

Idly, Balduíno scraped the ground with a stick. He was only eighteen, but he looked twenty-five. He was strong and tall as a tree, free as a wild animal. He had the brightest, happiest laughter in the city.

He left Joana, never again saw the toothless girl with the masculine voice who sang his sambas, and wanted nothing more to do with the *cabrochas* who went to the sandhills. With Gordo for company he hung around Maria dos Reis's house. He composed a samba for her which went like this:

"Maria, you're the girl for me,
You stole my heart away.
Once I was footloose and fancy free,
Don't torment me this way . . ."

He didn't want to sell this samba. He sang it once at a party she came to, looking at her the whole time. The soldier was already suspicious, and he hadn't yet managed to get the hairs from his fiancée's armpit to take to Jubiabá. Maria dos Reis contented herself with only smiling at Balduíno. She looked sadly at the soldier because she knew he loved her and would kill a man for her sake. She remembered the letter he had sent her godmother, Dona Branca Costa, asking for her hand in marriage. She had put it carefully away in the bottom of a trunk at home. It said:

Most Esteemed Senhora Dona Branca,

Today more than ever before I am transported to a pleasureable Paradice by my most Intimat and heartfelt feelings, on account of which I am obliged to declare sincerely to yourself, exelent Lady, that I love with a pure and saintely afecction youre esteemed Maria.

It is a sentiment that will never be extinguished rather the passing of Time together, with your most atenttive kindness will cause to increase Eternally between us a Love that must surely lead to the Heavenly state of true bliss. With these Solemn intentions I take this most radiant oportunity to ask, excellent Lady, for the hand of your genteele and enchanting Maria, in marriage.

It would be the greatest adventure to posses this most brilliant jewl of youre noble heart. For which I shal forthwith exert myself to give you and the members of your grashious family this most brilliant sastifaction. Sertain that you will not refuse my request, I awayt a favorable response. I close offering you my expressions of Elevated esteme and consideration.

Osório, Private

The godmother didn't want Maria dos Reis to marry a soldier, but she held her ground and got engaged, although she had to leave her godmother's house. They had set the marriage for August, as soon as he got his corporal's stripes the captain had promised, when Maria dos Reis met Antônio Balduíno at Jubiabá's house. He didn't send her letters, nor speak about marriage; he was jobless and wrote sambas.

At Riberinho's party, Antônio Balduíno had given her a card that looked like this:

folding this side means yes	folding this side means no
MY SOUL SUFFERS FOR YOU	
And will be happy if the young lady would accept my declaration of love. Returning this card intact, you will give me hope.	

She hid the card between her breasts. She ran into the bedroom of Mrs. Riberinho, where the men's hats were laid, and also Antônio Balduíno's guitar. Cândida went with her and saw the card.

"Who's it from, girl?"

"Guess."

"I dunno. Wait a minute, I'll tell you." She thought. "Oh, I give up. Who?"

"From Antônio Balduíno."

"Eeeeh, that one there's no good. He's the devil himself in the form of a man. He ruins every girl he touches. You be careful, dos Reis—"

"Well, I don't know why."

"What about Osório?"

Osório was the soldier. Maria dos Reis grew a bit sad, and instead of folding over the corner that meant yes, she gave Balduíno back the card intact. For Antônio Balduíno it was just the same as if she had folded the corner that meant yes.

Now he went to talk with her in the doorway of her house in the Brotas neighborhood on the days when the soldier didn't appear. Since the soldier only came on Thursdays, Saturdays, and Sundays, the rest of the week belonged to Antônio Balduíno, whose hands had already felt the heat and firmness of that virgin body. One Tuesday there was a party in Cabula, and Maria dos Reis went with some girl friends. They met Antônio

Balduíno in Cabula Square. He was very elegant with red shoes and a red shirt and was smoking a cheap cigar. They talked for a while. In a newsstand Antônio Balduíno bought a number to learn Maria dos Reis's fortune. They opened the rolled-up scrap of paper and it was number 41. The owner of the newsstand, a fat Spaniard, went to see what corresponded to that number. He yelled, "Forty-one . . . a box of face powder."

On top came a little paper telling her fortune. She read it.

"Many tears lie ahead. There will be disgrace and violence. Your present romance is ill-fated."

Antônio Balduíno laughed, but Maria dos Reis grew sad.

"What if Osório comes along?"

It seemed she had spoken on purpose. Osório, in uniform, was approaching the group. He said immediately, "I was already suspecting it, but I didn't want to face the truth. I never thought you'd do this."

His voice had that tearful tone of church masses. Osório spoke while Maria dos Reis hid her face in her hands. Her girl friends giggled uneasily, saying, "Now, Mr. Osório, don't do that."

"Do whatever you want," said Antônio Balduíno, shrugging his shoulders.

The soldier slapped Antônio Balduíno in the face, but the Negro ducked and threw his legs into the soldier's. Osório fell down and got up with his saber drawn. Antônio Balduíno opened his razor.

"Come on, then, if you're a man."

"I'm not scared of anyone."

Maria dos Reis screamed, "Baldo, for the love of God!"

Her friends were crying, "Mr. Osório! Mr. Osório!"

"I don't respect uniforms," said Antônio Balduíno, knocking away the soldier's saber. Osório already had a razor slash across his face.

After disarming the soldier, he threw away the razor and waited for Osório in the dark. People were coming—bystanders, police, and more soldiers. Osório threw himself on top of Baldo and received one of the Negro's heavy punches. He fell down flat on the ground. A gringo who was watching the fight pulled Antônio Balduíno to one side, saying, "Get lost fast, because there's a lot of soldiers coming. Good punch! Later I want to talk to you."

The Negro picked up his razor and went running toward Maria dos Reis's house. He was just in time, because there were soldiers coming from all directions, and when they saw their companion wounded, fights broke out. The confusion became general.

Maria dos Reis hid Antônio Balduíno in her own room; her mother was asleep and saw nothing. When he left in the wee hours of the morning, the body of Maria dos Reis was still warm and soft but no longer virgin. It had been better than Oxalá, the greatest of all deities.

In the Drowned Man's Lantern some days later, Antônio Balduíno met the gringo who had helped him to get away from the soldiers. He was just coming in with Gordo when he heard someone call his attention. "Pssst!" It was the gringo.

"I've been looking for you for ages. Ever since that day. I walked all over the place and didn't find you. Where've you been?"

He pulled up chairs, offered cigarettes. They sat down. Baldo thanked him.

"If it weren't for you that day, I'd have gotten beat up by those soldiers."

"That was a good punch you gave him. A beautiful punch."

Gordo, who hadn't been there, asked, "What punch?"

"The one he gave the soldier. *Per la Madonna,* what a beautiful punch!"

He ordered a beer.

"You ever been a boxer?"

"No. I know *capoeira,* though."

"Well, if you wanted to, you could be a champion."

"Champion?"

"Per la Madonna, I swear it. That punch . . . magnificent!"

He looked at the Negro's enormous hands and patted his shoulders, feeling the muscles in Baldo's arms.

"A champion, a champion." He spoke like someone reminiscing. "All you have to do is want to."

Antônio Balduíno wanted to. "How?"

"You could even fight in Rio, maybe in North America."

He took a swallow of beer.

"I used to be a trainer a long time ago. I trained boxers that are champions all over the world today. But none of 'em could have stood up to that punch of yours. Beautiful."

By the time they left the bar, Antônio Balduíno had been contracted by Luigi, the trainer, with Gordo to go along as their assistant. They were all rather drunk by then. The next day Antônio Balduíno said to Maria dos Reis, "I'm not a bum anymore. I'm a boxer. I'm gonna be a champion. Someday I'm going to Rio, maybe to North America."

"You're going away?"

"I'll take you along, honey."

It was better than Oxalá, the greatest of the deities.

The newspapers announced the first fight a few months afterward. Now he was Baldo the Negro. Luigi gave interviews, and a newspaper even published a picture of Antônio Balduíno with one arm forward to deliver a punch, the other in an attitude of defense. Maria dos Reis glued this picture up on the wall of her room.

The adversary was called Gentil, and advertised himself as the Navy heavyweight champion. Actually, he was a stevedore from the docks.

In Sé Square, the boxing fans were gathered. The clientele from Drowned Man's Lantern were there, including Mr. Antônio, as well as the inhabitants of Capa-Negro Hill and all Antônio Balduíno's friends. The referee, an army sergeant in civilian clothes, stepped up into the ring first. He said, "We're going to see a fierce fight, folks. I ask the public to show lots of respect and applaud plenty."

Gordo arrived, bringing a bucket and a bottle. A yellowish man came up on the other side, carrying the same things. Then up stepped Antônio Balduíno, accompanied by Luigi. All the people from the hill, the Drowned Man's Lantern, the sailboats, and the canoes shouted, "Antônio Balduíno! Antônio Balduíno!"

The referee introduced him. "Baldo the Negro."

The other boxer then entered and was applauded by the audience.

"Gentil, champion of all weights, from the glorious Navy!" yelled the referee.

Clapping and cheers from the audience. The people from the hill, the sailboats, and the bar looked at the mulatto with irony.

"He's gonna get a beating."

Antônio looked at his adversary and smiled. Luigi advised him, "Punch him hard. Go for the mouth and eyes. Real hard."

Nervous, Gordo was praying for his friend to win. Then he remembered that boxing was a sin and stopped praying, terrified.

A signal sounded, and the fighters advanced toward each other. Behind them the crowd roared.

Antônio Balduíno was declassified for using a *capoeira* blow in the midst of the fight, which was a very fierce one, showing all Baldo's fine qualities as a boxer. The audience wasn't satisfied with the outcome and booed the referee, who had to leave quickly with the protection of the police.

The papers published Antônio Balduíno's picture, and one of them sold out because it carried his biography. Thus it was discovered that he had composed the sambas of the poet Anísio Pereira, a fact that scandalized the social and literary circles of the city.

They conceded him a rematch. There was a great crowd, and this time he wasn't applauded only by the people from the hill, the sailboats, and the Drowned Man's Lantern. Mr. Antônio had bet twenty mil-reis that the Negro would win. The referee announced, "Baldo the Negro."

The entire crowd cheered lengthily.

In the fifth round, the mulatto Gentil was no longer the Navy heavyweight champion. He was knocked out cold on the floor of the ring. Gordo wiped the sweat off Antônio Balduíno. Then they all went to the Drowned Man's Lantern to drink up the twenty mil-reis Mr. Antônio had won.

It was Maria dos Reis who went away. Her godmother had had another child, and the godmother's husband, who was a public functionary, had been transferred to Maranhão. Maria dos Reis went with them. Antônio Balduíno missed her because she didn't remind him of Lindinalva, pale and freckled.

He got very drunk that night, looking at the ship that had taken her away, and thought about signing on as a sailor. She took along his picture, the one where he had one hand stretched out to attack, a smile on his lips and in his eyes.

He beat all the adversaries standing between him and the

champion of Bahia, a boxer called Vicente, who had stopped fighting because nobody was good enough to beat him. After Antônio Balduíno's appearance and successive triumphs, however, Vicente began to train rigorously again, seeing in the Negro a danger to his title.

A week before the fight, the city was already filled with placards and signs. There was a sketch of two men punching each other.

VICENTE
BAHIAN CHAMPION OF ALL WEIGHTS

VS

BALDO THE NEGRO

Disputing the Bahian Championship

SÉ SQUARE, SUNDAY

Vicente gave an interview to the papers, declaring that he would win in the sixth round. Antônio Balduíno replied the next day that in the sixth round the Bahian champion would already be out cold on the floor. They exchanged insults, and public enthusiasm grew. Many bets were laid, and Antônio Balduíno was indisputably the favorite.

Before the sixth round, Vicente really was knocked out on the floor of the ring, and Baldo the Negro was the Bahian champion of all weights.

He agreed with a rematch with Vicente and beat him again. Luigi was walking around in a daze and could only talk about going to Rio. He began setting up deals with impresarios in the nation's capital. Antônio Balduíno made love to the mulatto girls in the sand, drank in the Drowned Man's Lantern, went to Jubiabá's macumba sessions. His happy laughter rang in the streets of the city.

One day a boxing champion from Rio appeared, making a big fanfare and challenging everyone. A fight was set up between him and Antônio Balduíno. There was much interest in the city in the match between the two champions.

The night before the fight, Antônio Balduíno was chatting in the Drowned Man's Lantern when he was singled out by the Rio champion's manager.

"Good evening."

"Good evening."

Antônio Balduíno offered the man a beer.

"I wanted to talk to you in private."

Gordo and Joaquim went off to another table.

"It's this. You see, Claudio can't afford to lose."

"Can't afford to lose?"

"Because he's costing me a lot of money. If he loses to you, he won't be able to fight here anymore . . . right?"

"Right."

"But if he wins, he'll get other matches around here with other guys, and pay his expenses."

"So?"

"So I'm offering you a hundred mil-reis to lose. Afterward you have a rematch."

Antônio Balduíno raised his hand but dropped it on the table.

"You talk to Luigi?"

"Luigi's an asshole. He doesn't even need to know about this." The man smiled. "And you'll get your rematch before we leave, okay?"

"You got the money with you?"

"I'll give it to you after the fight."

"Nope. No good. But if you want to give it to me tonight—"

"And what if you don't lose?"

"And what if after I lose you screw up and don't pay?" Antônio Balduíno had already gotten up. Gordo and Joaquim were watching from the other table.

"Don't get upset," said the manager. "Sit down."

He looked at the Negro, who was belting down a glass of rum. "I'll take you at your word. Here, under the table."

Antônio Balduíno took the money. There were only fifty mil-reis.

"You said a hundred."

"I'll give you the other fifty afterward."

"No."

"I don't have it now, really."

"If you want a deal, give it to me now."

He took the other fifty and went over to Gordo's table. When the manager left, Antônio Balduíno laughed until his sides ached.

The next day, after the fight and the sensational defeat of the Rio champion, the manager came to look for Antônio Balduíno in the Drowned Man's Lantern. His face wore a terrible expression.

"You're a cheat."

Antônio Balduíno only laughed.

"I want my money back!"

" 'Whoever robs a thief gets a hundred years' relief.' "

"I'll go to the papers, I'll go to the police!"

"Go ahead."

"You're a thief! A thief!"

Antônio Balduíno knocked the manager over, too. The people in the bar, who hadn't expected to see another fight, applauded.

"He wanted to buy me, folks! He gave me a hundred mil-reis so I'd lose to that cancerous bag of bones. I said I would. This is so he won't buy men anymore. I only sell myself for friendship, folks! Now let's drink up his money!"

The entire Drowned Man's Lantern laughed. Antônio Balduíno left and went to see Zefa, a *cabrocha* who had come from Maranhão, bringing him messages and a kiss from Maria dos Reis—except that instead of one, she had delivered several. He gave her a necklace of red beads he had bought earlier that day with some of the money from the Rio champion's manager.

Luigi was talking seriously about going to the capital.

His career as a boxer ended the day Lindinalva got engaged. In the same newspaper that announced his fight with Miguez the Peruvian, Antônio Balduíno read the notice of the engagement of "Lindinalva Pereira, daughter of the industrialist, Comendador Pereira, of this city, to the lawyer Gustavo Barreiros, glorious offspring of one of the most illustrious Bahian families, author of brilliant poetic verse and an orator of the first order."

He went on an all-day drinking binge, was knocked out in the third round because he was simply unable to fight anymore or even defend himself from the Peruvian's blows. A rumor went around that he had been bought. He didn't explain his fiasco to anyone, not even to Luigi, who cried that night, cursing and tearing out his hair. He didn't even confide in Gordo, who looked at him with the eyes of someone who always expects the worst. He never went back into the boxing ring again.

On that cold night of his defeat, he went to the Bahia Bar since he didn't want to go to the Drowned Man's Lantern. He sat down at a table in the rear with Gordo and was drinking silently when a man came up to them and asked that they buy him a drink. Balduíno looked at him.

"I know that guy. I can't remember from where, but I know him."

The man's eyes were glazed. He licked his lips.

"One for the road. Buy it for me, friend . . ."

Then Antônio Balduíno saw the scar on the man's face.

"That was my work."

He thought for a minute and then slapped his forehead.

"Aren't you Osório?"

Gordo added, "A guy who was in the army."

"Yeah, I used to be a sergeant."

He pulled up a chair and sat down.

"I used to be a sergeant." He licked his lips. "How about a nightcap, huh?"

Balduíno laughed. Gordo felt sorry.

"Then this woman came along, a woman—pretty! Whoo-ee! Pretty. You'd have to see her to believe it. She was my fiancée, see. I was waiting to be promoted to corporal—"

"But weren't you a sergeant?"

"Yeah, that's right. I forget. I guess I was waiting to be promoted to captain. The captain had promised me, see . . . the captain. Gimme another drink? Boy, bring another drink here 'cause my friend's payin' . . . we set the date for the wedding. There was going to be a big party. She was gorgeous, gorgeous . . . but she left me for another guy."

"And that scar?"

"Oh! He was the one who did it. But I spilled his guts out. She was a beauty. A real beauty."

"She sure was."

"You know her?"

"Don't you remember?"

They drank all through the night and left arm in arm, the best of friends, chuckling together. Maria dos Reis and their careers as boxer and soldier were completely forgotten. But suddenly Osório said, "Hey, you were the guy!" He drew away from Antônio Balduíno.

"But I lost everything, too."

They embraced each other again and staggered off down the street.

"She was a beauty."

Antônio Balduíno was confusing the black Maria dos Reis with the white Lindinalva.

CHAPTER 9
Boat Landing

Great canoes lie motionless upon the still water.

The sailboats, their sails furled, sleep in the darkness. Even so, they give one the impression of departure, of travels to the small ports up and down the coast with their large marketplaces. But now the sailboats are asleep, their picturesque names lettered close to their prows: *Flying Packet, Homeless Traveler, Morning Star, Solitary One.* Tomorrow morning they will shove off quickly, sails unfurled to the wind, and cut through the water of the bay.

They will go to load up with vegetables, fruit, bricks, or roofing tiles, and pass through all the markets. Later they will return laden with fragrant pineapples. The *Homeless Traveler* is painted red and is faster than the others. Mestre Manuel is asleep in the prow. An old mulatto, he was born in a sailboat and has always lived in them.

Antônio Balduíno knows the history of all these sailboats and canoes. Ever since his childhood he has liked to come here and lie on the landing beach, his hair cradled in the pillow of sand, his feet in the water, which is warm and pleasant at this time of night. Sometimes Balduíno fishes in silence, his face breaking into a smile when he catches a fish. However, generally he just watches the sea, the ships, and the dead city behind.

Antônio Balduíno wants to go off somewhere, to travel through unknown lands, make love to unknown women on unknown sands. Miguez came from Peru and beat him.

A ship whistles at the breakwater and departs, illuminating the night. It is a Swedish vessel. Only a little while ago the sailors were walking through the city, drinking beer in the bars, reveling in the arms of the mulatto girls of the Barroquinha section. Now they are upon the dark sea, and tomorrow they will be in some distant port in the arms of white or yellow women. One day Antônio Balduíno must sign on and travel through the world. He has always dreamed of this. As he falls asleep, lying in the sand, he looks at the sailboats and the stars.

The ship is disappearing.

The city stretched the arms of its churches toward the sky. From the harbor he could see the slanting streets and enormous old houses. Lights were shining on the hilltops, and white clouds scampered across the sky like flocks of sheep. They looked a little like Joana's teeth. Every time Antônio Balduíno found a good-looking girl he would tell her, "Your teeth look like clouds."

But now that he'd lost the fight, what girl would look at him? They were even saying he'd been bought.

He lost himself looking at the dark city skyline. There was a star right above his head. He didn't know which star it was, but it was pretty, large, twinkling as it shone. He imagined himself a sailor arriving at a distant foreign port like the one he saw in his dreams every night. Because Antônio Balduíno dreamed of disembarking in other lands. The clouds drifted through the sky. They were enormous white sheep. There was no one in the Lower City. Besides, it was the first time he had ever dreamed this way, awake. Bahia wasn't Bahia anymore, and he was no longer Antônio Balduíno, who used to go to the macumba sessions at Jubiabá's house, no longer Baldo the Negro, who had been beaten by Miguez the Peruvian. What city might that be in front of him, and who was he? He looked toward the port and saw the ship. Naturally it was time to be getting back; they must be waiting for him on board.

He looked at his sailor's uniform, somersaulted to his feet, and said aloud, "I'm going aboard."

A voice answered him, "Huh?"

But he didn't hear, staring again at the city bathed in the pale light of the moon. He remembered the boxing match.

Suddenly, from high up on a hill, there came the sound of drums.

A dark cloud covered the moon. He touched himself, and the

sailor's uniform had disappeared; he was wearing white trousers and a red striped shirt.

The noise from the hill grew louder. It came like a supplication, like a cry of anguish. Then he saw that the city was Bahia again, very much the Bahia whose streets, hills, and alleys he knew so well, and not a lost port on some island in the vast ocean. It was Bahia, where he had been beaten.

Now he didn't look at the stars anymore, nor the clouds. He didn't watch the flocks of sheep in the sky. What had become of the sailboats that had fled from before his eyes?

He only listened.

From all the hills came the sound of drumbeats, a sound that on the other side of the ocean had been a call to war, an announcement of combat or hunting. Today it was a supplicating sound; enslaved voices were screaming for help, legions of Negroes extending their hands toward the sky. A few of those Negroes whose hair was white bore whip scars on their backs. Today, the macumba sessions sent forth those lost sounds. They were like a message to all black people, those who were still fighting and hunting in Africa, or those who groaned under the white man's whip. Drumbeats on hills. Antônio Balduíno, lying in the sand of the sailboat landing, heard religious sounds, anguished and confused, warrior sounds, slave sounds. They came in through his ears and stirred up the deaf hatred that lived within him.

Antônio Balduíno rolled over in the sand, desperate. He had never felt such anguish, such loathing as that which writhed inside him. He saw long lines of Negroes; he saw the old man with the brand on his back whom he had met at Jubiabá's house; he saw callused hands beating the ground. He saw black women having mulatto children, the sons of the white masters. He saw Zumbi dos Palmares transform the music of slaves into the drumbeats of warriors. Jubiabá, noble and serene, telling the slave people proverbs. But he had lost the fight, had taken a beating from Miguez like a man who had sold himself.

But he saw nothing more because the disturbing light of the moon returned, and the sounds died out on the hills, in the darkened alleys, in the cobbled streets.

With the dying of the drumbeats and the dizzying light of the moon, he found himself before the freckled white face of Lindinalva.

She was beautiful, smiling. She made the drums and the hate disappear. Antônio Balduíno gently touched her face to take away the intimidating vision, and then stared fixedly in the other direction. Once again his eyes focused on the lights of the sailboats and on Mestre Manuel, who was walking along the landing. But in the midst of the lights was Lindinalva, dancing. All because he had lost the fight and was demoralized.

He closed his eyes, and when he opened them, he saw only the sad, small light cast by the single bulb in the Drowned Man's Lantern.

CHAPTER 10

A Sad Song Comes from the Sea

The light from the Drowned Man's Lantern shines like an invitation. Antônio Balduíno gets up from the caressing sand and leaves the sailboat landing. With long strides he walks toward the bar.

The weak light bulb barely illuminates the sign showing the pretty woman with the fish's body and the jutting breasts. Above her, a star painted in red pours a bright light over her virgin mermaid's body, making her look mysterious. She is rescuing a suicide from the water. Underneath the picture is the name: DROWNED MAN'S LANTERN.

From inside comes a cry. "That you, Baldo?"

"Yeah, it's me, Joaquim."

Gordo and Joaquim are sitting at one of the greasy tables. Joaquim calls to him again, his hands placed above his eyes to see better in the vacillating light of the signpost.

"Come on in. Jubiabá's here."

In the small room, almost enveloped in darkness, are five or six tables where canoemen, sailboat hands, and sailors are drinking. Rum is served in thick glass tumblers. A blind man plays the guitar but nobody listens. At one table, pink-faced blond sailors, Germans from a cargo ship loading in the port, swill beer and sing drunkenly. Two or three women who have come down tonight from the Ladeira do Taboão to the Drowned Man's Lantern are with them. They laugh a lot, but they have a worried air because they don't understand the sailors' song. The Germans have their arms around the women and are kissing them. Under the table are innumerable empty beer bottles. Antônio Balduíno passes nearby them and spits. A sailor picks up a glass, and Balduíno prepares for a fight. The blind man whines his song over the guitar; nobody hears him. Antônio Balduíno remembers that Jubiabá is in the bar, lowers his arm, and goes to sit down next to Gordo and Joaquim.

"Where's Jubiabá?"

"He's in the back with Mr. Antônio, doctoring his wife."

Mr. Antônio is an old Portuguese who lives with a mulatto woman whose pocked face resembles a bladder. A pallid youth waits on tables at a run. He greets Antônio Balduíno, "Good evening, Mr. Baldo."

"Bring me some rum."

Gordo listens to the sailors' song.

"It's pretty."

"But do you understand it?"

"No, but it gets me in here."

"Gets you?" Joaquim doesn't understand.

But Antônio Balduíno understands and no longer wants to fight with the Germans. Now what he would like is to join in their song and laugh along with the women. He drums his fingers on the table and whistles. The sailors are drunker than ever; one of them is no longer singing, his head resting on the table. The blind man plays his guitar, whines his song in the dark. Nobody hears him except the pallid waiter serving the tables. In between hurried trips to fetch glasses of rum, he watches the blind man with admiration, smiling.

Then from far away, from the darkness of the sea, comes the sound of a singing voice. In spite of the starlight, no one could see who it was, nor where it was coming from, whether from the canoes, the sailboats, or the old fort out in the bay. They only knew it was coming from the sea. A strong voice, far-off.

Antônio Balduíno looks out: everything black. There is only the light of the stars and the glow of Mestre Manuel's pipe. The Germans are no longer singing, the women have quit laughing, and to the disappointment of the pallid waiter, the blind man has stopped moaning over his guitar.

Jubiabá is back at his table, and Mr. Antônio is again behind the bar. The wind, invading the room like a caress, brings the sweet melancholy of the voice. Where does it come from? The sea is so large and mysterious that it is impossible to know who is singing this sad old waltz tune. But it is a black man who sings, because only black men can sing like that. Mestre Manuel is silent. Is he thinking about the cargo of pineapples that will be loaded onto his sailboat at dawn over on Itaparica island? No. He is listening to the singer. He turns toward the place where the voice seems to come from, the voice that fills up the mystery of the sea. Gordo's eyes are dreaming. Naturally, the song gets him. He and all the others turn in the direction of the ocean: Where was the Negro voice coming from?

"Lord, give me respite from my woes . . ."

Is the singer an old soldier in the crumbling fort? Is he a young country fellow arriving in a boat to sell oranges in the Água de Meninos market? Or a canoeman in Porto da Lenha? Could he be a black crewman from some fast-traveling schooner, remembering his sweetheart in a distant port?

"Lord, give me respite from my woes,
Take away this pain
So I see it no more, no more."

From where comes this sad tune that floats over sailboats and canoes, breakwater and docks, the Drowned Man's Lantern, the entire harbor, and loses itself in the hills of the city of Bahia?

Gordo sees at once that Antônio Balduíno is nervous. He thinks about Lindinalva and judges that the Negro's song is only for Balduíno, who is so lonely. But the song is for everyone, not just for Antônio Balduíno. It is for Gordo, Mestre Manuel, the German sailors; it is for all the Negroes of the canoes and sailboats, for all the blond sailors of the Swedish ships, for the sea itself.

The lights of the city twinkle on the hillsides. A little while ago, the beating of *candomblé* drums filled the streets. But now the city is far away and the brilliance of the stars is much closer to the men than the electric lights. Antônio Balduíno sees the coals glowing in Mestre Manuel's pipe. The voice of the singer penetrates him, then suddenly withdraws, fleeing to the sea outside. But it returns, vibrating inside the barroom. A sadness falls.

"I'm so lonely that all I can do
Is cry, is cry . . ."

Nobody speaks. Jubiabá stretches his hands out on the table. Gordo is trembling. Antônio Balduíno sees Lindinalva's pale, freckled face in the waters, in the sky, in the clouds, in his glass of rum, in the eyes of the consumptive boy who waits on tables.

The yellow moon once again pours over the Drowned Man's Lantern. The voice, borne away on the wind, is softer now. Gordo trembles; Mestre Manuel smokes slowly. Inside the bar, the voice comes and goes with the breeze.

"Have mercy on me,
Turn your eyes,
Your sacred love
Toward me . . ."

The sad tune dies away. The blind man searches for it with his darkened eyes.

Jubiabá mutters some words that no one hears. Joaquim asks, "Got a cigarette, man?"

He smokes, inhaling deeply. The sailors drink beer. The women's eyes are drawn toward the sea. Jubiabá stretches his skinny legs and looks out into the night. The moon has made everything yellow on land and turned the sea and sky to silver. The old waltz drifts back. The Negro voice is much closer now.

"Take away this pain
So I see it no more, no more."

The voice comes closer and closer. Mestre Manuel goes back to his pipe, which shines like a star. A sailboat is crossing the bay far out. It moves silently, also listening to the sad tune brought on the wind. Antônio Balduíno feels like saying, "Have a good trip, friends!"

But he stays quiet, listening. The voice fades away with the breeze, then comes back very softly.

"So I see it no more, no more."

The moonlight enters the bar. The sailors listen as though they understood the Negro's tune. The women, who do understand this time, no longer laugh. Joaquim says, "What's the point of coming back?"

Gordo gives a start. "What did you say?"

Antônio Balduíno says to Jubiabá, "Pai Jubiabá, I had a strange dream tonight, lying down by the landing."

"What did you dream?"

Jubiabá is withered and tiny in his chair. Gordo wonders how old Jubiabá might be. How many years past one hundred? Antônio Balduíno is enormous, strong. Instead of describing his dream he says, "I saw that black man with his back branded, pai Jubiabá."

The voice might have been inside the bar.

"I'm so lonely that all I can do
Is cry, is cry."

Antônio Balduíno says, "Crying, just crying . . . that man who was branded on his back. I saw him in the dream. It was horrible. I feel like punching those sailors."

Gordo says in alarm, "Why?"

"Black men always beaten down . . . beaten down."

Jubiabá stands up, his wrinkled face open with hate. Everyone pays attention.

"It happened a long time ago, Baldo."

"What?"

"The story I'm telling you. Your father's father was a boy. It was on a plantation of a rich white master, over in Corta-Mão."

A sad tune, an old waltz sung by a Negro in an unknown place, dominates everything.

"Lord, give me respite from my woes."

* * *

Jubiabá was saying, "We were a whole lot of Negroes. We had just got off the ship and didn't know the talk of the white masters. This was a long, long time ago, there in Corta-Mão."

"What happened?"

"Mr. Leal didn't have an overseer. But he had a couple of gorillas, black monkeys, chained with a heavy chain. The master called the male Catito and the female Catita. The male went around with a cup tied to the chain and a whip in his hand. He was the overseer."

What has happened to the old waltz that no longer fills the hearts of these men? Why has it left them alone with Jubiabá's story? Where is the voice of the Negro who was singing? Now only the blind man moans over his guitar and everyone listens. The sickly youth collects coins in a china dish for the blind man, who is his father. One customer says, "I won't give him anything. The old guy can't even sing."

But everyone looks at him in such a way that he puts a coin into the dish.

"Just joking, kid."

Jubiabá's voice: "The female gorilla, Catita, would kill chickens. She would run loose among the slave houses. The male would take us to the plantation and sit down under a tree. When Negro didn't work he would beat Negro. Sometimes he beat them for nothing. He killed Negro with his whip."

The lights tremble in the Drowned Man's Lantern. The blind man plays a rhythmic song on his guitar.

"Mr. Leal liked to turn Catito loose after the black women. Catito would kill them so he could rape them. One day, this master let Catito loose after a young black girl who was married to a young Negro. Mr. Leal had visitors."

Gordo's entire body is trembling. The sad old tune is drifting back again, far away now. The blind man's guitar has stopped; he is counting the change he has collected.

"Catito threw himself on top of the black girl, and the man went for Catito."

Jubiabá looks far away into the night. The moon is yellow.

"Mr. Leal shot the Negro, who had already stabbed the gorilla twice. The Negro woman died, too. There was blood all over the place. The visitors all laughed, very much amused. Except a little white girl who went crazy that night when she saw the gorilla and the black man."

The sad tune, close by.

"But that night the Negro's brother killed Mr. Leal. I knew him; he told me the story."

Gordo is beside Jubiabá. Mestre Manuel's pipe shines like a star. In the darkness of the sea, a voice sings a sad song.

"Take away this pain
So I see it no more, no more . . ."

The voice is loud, sonorous, full of longing.

Jubiabá repeats, "I knew the brother."

Antônio Balduíno clutches his knife in front of his chest.

CHAPTER 11
Ojú ánun fô iká li ôkú

Jubiabá said, "Ôjú ánun fô iká li ôkú."

Yes, Antônio Balduíno knew very well that the eye of mercy had run dry, and that only the eye of badness was left. In the mysterious night of the harbor, full of strange music, he longed to laugh again, for laughter was his cry of freedom. But he had forgotten how to laugh. He was demoralized. He was no longer the emperor of the city; he was no longer Baldo the Boxer. Now the city was strangling him like a rope around the neck of a suicide. They were saying he had been bought. And the ocean beating against the rocks, the lighted ships that put to sea, the sailors who left with a lantern and a guitar were irresistible calls. That was the homeward road. Viriato the Dwarf had gone down it; so had old Salusitano, and others as well. On Antônio Balduíno's chest were tattooed a heart, an enormous *L,* and a sailboat.

He took Gordo and fled. They would travel the coast in a sailboat. In the small towns, in the open country, in the sea, he would search for his laughter, for his way home.

PART II
Diary of a Runaway Negro

CHAPTER 12
Sailboat

The *Homeless Traveler* cuts through the water, which reflects the stars. It is painted red all over, and its lantern spreads a yellow light around it like the light of the moon that has just appeared, coming out from behind a cloud. From another sailboat that is crossing the bay someone shouts, ''Who's coming there?''

''Have a safe trip! Good-bye!''

The road of the sea is wide. The murmuring waters glide past. A fish jumps into the light of the lantern. Mestre Manuel is at the helm. Gordo is going without understanding why. Antônio Balduíno is stretched out in the sailboat, looking at the spectacle of the sea. From the hold comes a smell of ripe pineapples.

A soft breeze passes, and a bright star shines in the sky. A samba comes into Antônio Balduíno's head, and he taps out its rhythm against his knee. Now he is whistling, and soon he will find his lost laughter. The samba comes out, speaking of women, mischief, and free black men, about the stars in the sky and the wide road of the sea. It asks:

''Where will this road lead, Maria?''

And later it says,

''The stars of the sky are in your eyes,
The sound of your laughter is in the sea,
You're a sailboat lantern shining for me.''

It says this kind of thing. It also says that the Negro Antônio Balduíno only likes two things: mischief and Maria. In the language he speaks, mischief means liberty; Maria means a mulatto girl.

Where would this road lead? For Mestre Manuel, who is an old sailor, it has no mysteries.

"Here"—he shows them—"is where the sea makes love to the river."

They have crossed the bay and are entering the Paraguaçu River. On its banks are old feudal castles, the ruins of sugar mills and of past fortunes. There are colossal, ghostlike shadows. No wonder Gordo says, "Feels like it's haunted by a headless mule."

The sound coming now from the water is the lovemaking of the sea and the river. And the noise that comes from the forest behind must be some priest's lover who died and turned into a headless mule and still haunts these dark woods that have covered the graves of Negro slaves.

The sailboat glides smoothly in the calm water of the river. At the rudder, Mestre Manuel smokes his pipe. He points to some black crowns of rock. The way holds no mysteries for him. Antônio Balduíno has just sung his samba, and Gordo already knows it by heart. He thinks it is the best samba that Antônio Balduíno has made yet, because it speaks of women, mischief, and stars. He asks, "Don't sell any more sambas, Baldo."

The black man laughs. The sailboat goes up the river, gaining speed.

"Nobody can catch her," says Mestre Manuel, stroking the boat as if he were caressing a woman.

A wind comes to fill the sails and refresh the men. From the hold comes the ripe pineapple smell.

Mestre Manuel has owned a sailboat for many years. Antônio Balduíno was a child when he met him and came to know the *Homeless Traveler*. But long before that, Mestre Manuel was already sailing from port to port along the Bahian coastline, taking fruit to the markets, bringing bricks and tiles for the construction work in the suburbs of the city.

He looks about thirty years old. Nobody would attribute to him the fifty years he actually carries on his back. He is all one color, a dark bronze, and it is hard to say if Mestre Manuel is white, black, or mulatto. He is just a sailor the color of bronze, a sailor who rarely speaks and is respected throughout the harbor zone in the port of Bahia, from the Água dos Meninos market to the harbor bars, as well as the bars of all the tiny ports where he docks his boat. Gordo breaks the silence with a question.

"Did you ever see anyone drown, Mestre Manuel?"

Manuel abandons his pipe and stretches his legs.

"One day there was a storm at the mouth of the river. A sailboat turned over and the wind put out all her lanterns. It was a terrible day, it looked like Judgment Day."

Gordo assures himself that the night, at present, is clear and friendly.

"I was sailing that night, too, hanging on through the storm. My lantern had also been blown out, and nobody could see his hand in front of his face."

Antônio Balduíno, who likes the life of the sailboat captains, smiles. But Mestre Manuel is serious. He takes a pull on his pipe.

"We could see the lights of Bahia. They looked real close, but they were getting farther and farther away. We couldn't seem to come in toward them. That night the sea was wild, it was angry with the river."

He became even more serious.

"It's bad when the sea is angry with the river. . . . It always means a storm."

"What about the sailboat?"

Mestre Manuel seemed to have forgotten about the sailboat.

"It was carrying a family that was coming home from the festivals in Cachoeira. They were in a hurry to get there, and they didn't wait for the ship, which would only leave the next day. The papers mentioned that"—he takes another pull on the pipe—"they were in a hurry and they all ended up in the sea. We only saved the bodies. Even so, two of them were never found."

The *Homeless Traveler* goes fast, leaning to one side, following the river that is full of curves and changes, opening suddenly into basins and closing afterward into narrow channels.

"I remember the water going *glug-glug-glug* inside the overturned sailboat." Mestre Manuel imitates the water. "*Glug-glug-glug* . . . it sounded like it was eating something."

"Wasn't there a woman crying for her fiancé? Or the guardian angel of the drowned?" asks Gordo, trembling.

"Drowned people don't have any guardian angel. The Mother of Waters lures them after her in order to take them."

The business about the guardian angel and the fiancé is Gordo's invention, but he affirms he saw it in the papers.

"But you weren't born yet."

"Well, then it was another time. Didn't you see it?"

Gordo thinks it is a bright new star that is shining just behind them. He cries out in the happiness of the discovery.

"Look what a beautiful new star! It's mine, it's mine! It's afraid someone will steal it, will take it away from the one who found it."

The others look. Mestre Manuel is scornful.

"That's no star. That's the *Flying Packet* coming. She was in Itaparica when we passed; she's catching up with us. She wants to race you." Mestre Manuel is talking now to the *Homeless Traveler,* caressing her. He turns to his companions.

"That boat's fast; Guma is a good helmsman, but nobody can catch this one here, you'll see."

Gordo is sad because he lost his star. Antônio Balduíno asks, "How do you know it's the *Flying Packet,* Manuel?"

"By her lantern."

But the lantern is just like the light of any other sailboat. The only reason Antônio Balduíno doesn't agree with Gordo about it's being a new star is that it keeps moving all the time. However, he doubts that it is the *Flying Packet.* It might be any of the fast sailboats of the port. He waits. Gordo looks at the sky to see if he can discover another star to replace the one he lost. But those that are shining are already well known, and they all have owners. The sailboat draws closer. Mestre Manuel goes slowly, waiting. Sure enough, it is the *Flying Packet.* Guma yells, "Want to race, Mestre Manuel?"

"Where are you going?"

"Maragogipe."

"I'm going to Cachoeira, but we'll race as far as Maragogipe. I'll bet you a big fiver."

"It's a bet."

Antônio Balduíno bets, too. Guma accepts from the helm.

"Okay. Let's go."

The sailboats are exactly side by side, and the *Flying Packet* gains distance. Balduíno warns, "Watch out for my ten mil-reis that are in the fire, Manuel."

The captain smiles. "Let 'im run."

He yelled down below, "Maria Clara!"

The woman who was asleep and dreaming awakens and appears. Mestre Manuel introduces her.

"My boss lady."

Their surprise is so great they are speechless. She, too, is silent, and even if she had been ugly, she would have looked beautiful standing there in the leaning sailboat, her dress billowing in the wind, her hair flying. A smell of the sea mingles with the smell of pineapples. The back of her neck, her lips—Antônio Balduíno thinks—must smell like the sea, taste like saltwater. And he feels a sudden wave of desire. Gordo thinks she is a guardian angel and wants to say a prayer. But she's nothing of the kind; she is the wife of Mestre Manuel. He tells her, "I'm racing with Guma. Sing a song."

The song helps the wind and the sea. These are secrets that only an old sailor knows, secrets that are learned in a life lived with the sea.

"I'll sing the samba that young man was singing."

They are all fascinated by her. No one knows if she is beautiful or ugly, but they are all in love with her at this moment. She is the music that buys the sea. Standing with her flying hair abandoned to the wind, she sings.

"Where will this road lead, Maria?"

The *Homeless Traveler* races over the water, making a noise. Again the *Flying Packet* can be seen, a luminous point in the night.

* * *

"The stars of the sky are in your eyes . . ."

That white object is the sail of the *Flying Packet*, which is gaining on them.

"The sound of your laughter is in the sea . . ."

Where would this crazy race end? Wouldn't they crash against a snag of black rocks and go to sleep in the bottom of the river? Mestre Manuel steers with his eyes closed. Antônio Balduíno trembles with pleasure at the woman's singing. For Gordo she is an angel, and he prays.

"You're a sailboat lantern shining for me."

They pass close by the lantern of the *Flying Packet*. Guma tosses a package of money into the *Homeless Traveler:* fifteen mil-reis. Mestre Manuel puts five into his pocket and calls, "Have a good trip, Guma! Have a good trip!"

"You, too!" His voice comes from behind them.

Antônio Balduíno takes the ten mil-reis he won.

"Buy a dress for her, Manuel. She's the one who won the race."

"The way of the sea is wide, Maria . . ."

Antônio Balduíno wonders where the bald white man might be who came to the macumba session that time in Jubiabá's house. Where was he, that man whom Antônio Balduíno thought was Pedro Malazarte, the adventurer? He mustn't forget this sailboat trip when he writes the ABC of the brave fighter Antônio Balduíno, who loves freedom and the sea.

Now that the river is wide, Mestre Manuel turns the helm over to Antônio Balduíno. He goes with the woman to the stern of the boat. They are hidden behind the cabin, but the others can hear the sounds of bodies making love; low cries, supplications for kisses. A high wave comes, washing over the lovers. They laugh between kisses. Now they must be soaking wet, and their love even better.

Antônio Balduíno imagines throwing the sailboat against the rocks of the river. They would all die, and the cries and kisses would be extinguished in the water. Gordo, who has lost a star and an angel tonight, says, "He shouldn't have done that."

CHAPTER 13
Sweet Smell of Tobacco

Sweet smell of tobacco, sweet smell of tobacco! It invaded Gordo's wide nostrils, making him dizzy. The sailboat only stayed in port for the market days of Cachoeira and São Felix, the neighboring cities. Then it made off for other small ports: Maragogipe, Santo Amaro, Nazaré das Farinhas, and Itaparica, taking Manuel and his wife, who sang during the night and smelled of the sea. It set sail in the nostalgic morning, its canvas opening in a farewell.

Antônio Balduíno stayed on in the old town of Cachoeira, measuring the length of its streets as they roved pointlessly up and down them. They smelled the city's odor, a sweetish scent of tobacco that came from São Felix across the river, from the white factories that took up whole blocks and were as fat as their owners. The smell made one dizzy, caused one to think about distant things. It obliged Gordo to invent or repeat long stories. In the cigar factories there was no work for men. Only women, pallid, emaciated, and sad-eyed, manufactured expensive cigars destined for ministerial banquets. Men were no good at this work, for their hands were too large for this type of job, which, nevertheless, was heavy and hard.

On the rainy afternoon they arrived, they crossed the Paraguaçu River, which separated the two cities. The enormous bridge was behind them. Gordo was telling a story. Gordo was really a born poet and had he known how to read and write, he could have made a living writing ABC and stories in verse. But Gordo had never been to school and contented himself with narrating in his low, sonorous voice the cases he heard about, the old legends he learned in the city, and the stories he made up when he drank. He would be even better at it if he didn't always put in so many angels. But Gordo was also very religious.

The canoe avoided the rocks. The river was low, and men with rolled-up trouser legs and bare backs were fishing for their dinners. Gordo was saying, "So Pedro Malazarte, who was a very clever fellow, said to the man, 'It's an enormous herd of pigs, there are more than five hundred . . . no, more than a thousand, two thousand, three thousand, I've lost track there are so many.' The man with the pot could only see the tails buried in the sand. There were a whole bunch of black tails rustling in the wind. They were all moving as if they really were live pigs buried in the sand.

"And Pedro Malazarte said, 'What's more, these are magic pigs. When they make dung, money comes out instead. All five-mil-reis notes. When they get bigger, notes of ten mil-reis, and even a whole conto-de-reis when they're old. I'll trade all this for your pot.' "

"And didn't the man get suspicious?" asked the canoeman.

"No, the man was a fool and was only thinking about the pigs. He made the deal and traded his pot full of beans and meat for the herd of pigs. Pedro Malazarte advised him: 'Just leave them buried until tomorrow morning. In the morning they'll come out and produce some money.' So the man waited for the pigs to appear. He spent the afternoon, the night, the next day, and the next. He's still there waiting to this very day. If you want you can go and see him."

The canoeman laughed, and Antônio Balduíno wanted to hear the part about the pot. He loved the stories of Pedro Malazarte, an adventurer who knew how to trick people and led a funny life. He imagined him really existing, going all over the world, knowing things from all the countries, because Pedro Malazarte had even gone to heaven once, to take some money to a rich widow's departed husband, who was living in misery in a trashy hotel in Paradise. And he was almost certain that the bald man who had come to the macumba ceremony at Jubiabá's was Pedro Malazarte himself, in disguise. Hadn't that man been all over the world and seen everything?

"I bet that bald man who went to pai Jubiabá's macumba session was Pedro Malazarte."

"Who?" Gordo couldn't remember.

"That day Oxalá possessed Maria dos Reis."

"Oh, I know! But he wasn't. That white man is a traveler, he writes ABCs. I know all about him. He ran away from his father's ranch one day on a bay horse. His father was a rancher and raised horses. Then he went all over the world on his bay horse, writing the ABCs of the bravest men he met, and of the wickedest women."

"He's going to write my ABC."

"Yours?"

"The bravest man he ever saw was Antônio Balduíno. I'm man enough for anyone. He told me so himself."

Gordo looked admiringly at his friend. Antônio Balduíno was carrying two knives under his jacket, one on each side. The canoe beached on the mud of the landing.

This dizzying smell comes from the factories. The men who were fishing are going back home, carrying fish for their meager supper. At the same time, a long, shrill whistle comes from the factories. It is the end of the day's work. Antônio Balduíno goes to find himself a mulatto girl to make love with from among the factory workers. He stands on the corner, laughing at Gordo's stories, waiting for the women to pass by.

But they leave their job sad and tired. They come out dizzy from the sweet tobacco smell with which they are saturated: It is in their hands, their dresses, their bodies, their genitals. There are many of them, a legion of women who all look sick and unhappy. Some smoke cheap cigars after having manufactured very expensive ones. Almost all of them chew tobacco. A blond man converses with a little mulatto girl who hasn't yet lost her complexion in the factories. She laughs and he murmurs, "You could get a raise."

Antônio Balduíno says to Gordo, "That's the only one worth screwing. But she's with the foreman."

The women pass silently as if they were drunk from the smell of tobacco, enter the darkening, narrow streets, and walk toward the unlighted alleys at the bottom of town. They walk sadly, conversing in low voices, still afraid of the fines imposed for talking inside the factories. A pregnant woman with a thrusting belly goes by them and stops just ahead to kiss a man who has some fish in his hand. They continue arm in arm, and she tells him about the fine she is forced to pay when she stopped working during a momentary stab of pain in her heavy belly. Suddenly she says, "And the wages I'll lose when I have the kid! So many days."

Her voice is tragic and anguished. The man lowers his head, clenching his fists. Antônio Balduíno overhears and spits in disgust.

Gordo is trembling. The cigar-factory women pass. Huge billboards parade their products. And in a bar window, the advertisement: BEST CIGARS IN THE WORLD: FOR BANQUETS, DINNERS, AND LUNCHEONS. The women who manufacture the cigars go by. They look so sad that no one would guess they are going home to their husbands and children. Gordo says, "It's like a funeral procession."

The pretty mulatto girl goes off with the German. The pregnant woman cries against her husband's arm.

In the hotel in Cachoeira, which is comfortable, even sumptuous, young German men drink whiskey and eat dinners specially prepared for them. Girls come from Bahia to sleep with these pleasant blond youths, the sons of the owners of those factories where the women work. They chat over their drinks about the salvation of Germany by Hitler and Nazism, and about the next war, which they expect to win. Later when the drink goes to their heads, they will sing fighting songs. A child interrupts their dinner to say, "Give alms to my mother, she's dying . . ."

The full moon, which comes out from behind the hills and shines upon the river, is not seen by the blond Germans. On the riverbank, the husbands of the factory workers sing to guitar music and the women present their children to the moon.

"Your blessing, friendly moon,
Take this baby for yourself
And help me to raise it."

* * *

At the end of the drizzly afternoon, the canoeman came up to Antônio Balduíno and Gordo.

"So, friends, aren't you going to eat supper?"

"We are, yeah. . . ."

"You want to eat at my place? It's poor folks' food, there's nothing but fish, but you'd eat with our good wishes."

He turned to Gordo.

"You can tell my old lady some of those stories. She'll be comin' home from the factory. I got five girls and two boys."

He smiles, waiting for their answer. They enter an alley that gives onto a muddy street, which reminds Antônio Balduíno of the Capa-Negro Hill.

Inside the houses, the red lights of the lanterns shine. Children play in the doorways, making dolls and animals out of the black clay soil.

"Here," says the canoeman.

The walls are dirty with smoke. Hanging on them, a picture of Our Lord of Bonfim and a guitar. An infant sleeps on a bed made of boards. He might be three months old, if that. He wakes when the man kisses him and stretches out his little hands, his small black mouth laughing. Another child, barely big enough to walk, grabs its mother's skirts. Its belly is swollen, like those of the others who are making clay dolls outside.

The canoeman makes introductions.

"Couple of friends. This one here"—he points to Gordo—"can tell a beauty of a story. You'll see."

The woman chews tobacco. She has turned-up lips and the yellow face of those who suffer from malaria. She takes the fish from the man and goes into the kitchen. They hear her voice calling the children.

Antônio Balduíno takes up the guitar.

Gordo asks, "Is life hard here?"

"Jobs are hard to find, yeah. Here there's only work for women, the men just fish or pick up a little change running canoes."

"And do the women earn a lot?"

"Huh! Almost nothing. And they make 'em pay fines, plus

they lose wages when they have kids or get sick. They age fast, get used up. We slice things thin here, friend."

"It's sad."

"Sad?" The man laughed. "There's people who starve, all right. When a woman leaves one factory, she can't get a job in the other one. They have a scheme, and we don't eat fish every day, either."

A black youth stands in the doorway, silent. He nods in agreement. Gordo feels guilty for having started such an unpleasant conversation.

"Well, God will provide—"

"By sending sickness maybe. My old lady has that picture, but I don't even believe in God anymore. I've been starving before. One night we didn't even have food for the youngest one, who at that time was her." He pointed to a little mulatto girl of about five. "God has forgotten about poor folks."

The woman appeared in the door behind them and spat a dark stream of saliva.

"Don't blaspheme, man! God will punish you."

The black boy in the doorway says, "In my heart, I don't believe, either. Only from the mouth outward. Know what? That German dog is after Mariinha, telling her he'll raise her wages. Where's God?"

Gordo prays in a low voice. He asks God not to let the German take Mariinha away, and prays that on the canoeman's table there will be enough food. Antônio Balduíno knows that Gordo is praying and that it is useless. He says, "It may be heresy, folks, but what this black man here wants is to kill all the white people. Kill 'em without pity."

The fish is served. The black youth disappeared and a few months later was condemned to thirty years in prison for killing the German who left Mariinha with a child and without a job. The food is little for so many mouths, and the children complain, asking for more. The red light of the lantern casts enormous shadows.

Gordo has told the story about Pedro Malazarte and the pot of food, and the children fall asleep. One of them still clutches in her small black hand a clay doll with a crippled arm. In her dream the black clay doll is a blond china doll that says

"Mama" and closes its eyes to sleep. They go out to the riverbank where men are singing to the full moon. Women in patched dresses walk along the breakwater. The river passes and disappears below the bridge.

Gordo sings the *Ballad of Vilela,* which Antônio Balduíno accompanies on the guitar. The men all listen attentively to the story of the famous fight between the bandit Vilela and the "second-lieutenant slave trader." The lieutenant was heroic; Vilela even more so. It is a song of heroes.

"The lieutenant, he was valiant
And never did he faint,
But braver was Vilela,
Who died a fighting saint!"

"Nice," says a man.

"I never heard tell of a bandit turning into a saint," interrupts a thin little woman.

"There's a lot of bandits who deserve to be saints," a man explains, tapping his fingers against the rampart wall. "You all ever see a bandit rob poor people? Bandits are poor, just like us. They have hearts like us. I like bandits."

"God save you, man! Maybe you didn't see what they did to Colonel Anastácio. They left the man with his ears cut off. Nose, too. They even cut off his parts. He looked like an animal, God forgive me."

They laugh, remembering how the man had looked. But the fellow who is tapping the wall says, "Maybe you don't remember what Colonel Anastácio did to one-armed Simon's daughters. There were four of 'em, and the colonel didn't leave one in peace. Ruined every single one. The old man nearly went crazy. If he'd had any more, the colonel would have had more to take to bed. Bandits are the ones who get revenge for us." He turned to Gordo. "Sing us another song, friend."

But it is Antônio Balduíno who begins to sing sambas and songs that make all the women sad.

From the church bell comes the nine o'clock chimes.

"Let's go dance the samba at Fabrício's house, folks," a strong Negro man invites.

A group goes. The rest go toward the houses or linger at the landing to look at the moon, the river, the bridge, the only movie house they have.

Fabrício received his guests with a glass of rum in his hand.

"Want to wet your whistle?"

They all wanted to, and the glass passed from mouth to mouth, a thick tumbler that Fabrício filled conscientiously up to the brim. The canoeman introduced Antônio Balduíno and Gordo.

"A couple of friends."

"Come in, come in! This is a house for friends," he said, distributing great hugs.

They went in. A mulatto man with a little mustache was playing the harmonica. Couples circled about the room. Antônio Balduíno didn't smell the characteristic smell of black people; even there, in the distant neighborhood, the sweet smell of tobacco dominated. The couples circled; the man with the harmonica bent over and straightened up as he played. At the end of his tune, he was so excited that he played and danced at the same time, brushing against the couples who passed within reach of his hand.

When the music stopped, the canoeman shouted, "Folks, this black man here plays the guitar like an angel, and this fat guy can tell a beautiful story."

Antônio Balduíno said to Gordo, "I'm thinking I'll find me a woman here."

He went into the kitchen to drink some rum with the owner of the house, and when he came back, he played his best sambas on the guitar at the insistence of the girls. Gordo sang. The man with the harmonica was resentful but said nothing. When Antônio Balduíno finished, he said to him, "Let's have a drink, brother. You really play good."

"Oh, I just scratch at the guitar. Now you're an expert."

The man indicated some girls to Antônio Balduíno.

"That one there's willing. Look here, my girl has a friend. Why don't you try her out?"

The man went back to playing the harmonica. Now the whole room was dancing. Their feet beat on the floor, their navels rubbed against each other, their heads touched. They were all drunk, some on rum, others on music. The men clapped to the rhythm. Bodies joined together at the waist and then separated, twisted alone and joined together again, belly to belly; crotch to crotch.

"Oh, my love . . ."

The stomping and clapping went on, the men with instruments among the dancers. The room was upside down, sideways, then suddenly right side up again, then it wheeled crazily and they were dancing on the ceiling. The lanterns made it even more confused. Shadows danced on the walls, gigantic and frightening. The floor disappeared, their feet couldn't feel it anymore; only the bodies had feeling and where they touched they sparked desire. The women seemed made of springs, their entire bodies undulating in the dance. Their hips grew wider, their buttocks swayed by themselves, as if they had a life of their own. The men and women danced, the shadows cast by the lantern light. The room had disappeared, the light had gone out, you couldn't see anything at all. There was only the drum rhythm, the sweet smell of tobacco, and the navels finding each other. Even the desire disappeared—everything disappeared—and now it was pure dance.

Antônio Balduíno writes a name in the sand of the river: Regina. The woman beside him, languid with the tiredness of love, smiles with satisfaction and kisses the black man. But a little wave comes and erases the name written with the point of his knife. Antônio Balduíno lets out a peal of laughter that makes everything tremble. The woman grows angry and begins to cry.

CHAPTER 14
Hands

Stretching over the hill, the tobacco field seemed to have no end. First there was a high, level plain that rose to meet the hill and sloped away on the other side in an endless field of low, broad-leafed plants.

The wind rustled the leaves, and if it weren't for the cloth sacks protecting them, the seeds of the tobacco plants would be wasted.

The women, who were bent over picking the leaves, straightened up with tired gestures and began to move. They were the last ones to stop work. One of them was old and wrinkled while the other, who was smoking a fifty-cent cigar, was a robust young woman. The men walked ahead of them, and they all seemed like hunchbacks. They were carrying bundles of tobacco leaves, which they would hang in front of the houses where they would be protected from the strong sun and the rain. The leaves that were already dry would give way to the newly picked ones, forming a curtain in front of the workers' houses.

There were four houses built at the four corners of a square. In the quadrangular central area, the men met to talk and play the guitar. The old woman went into one of the houses where her husband kept an eye on the pot of beans that was cooking. The girl passed the time of day with the men who were in the "square," which was what they called the area between the houses.

Gordo, who was missing his grandmother, said, "She was left all alone with only God to help her . . . who'll give her food?"

"Never mind, she won't die of hunger."

"That's not what I mean." Gordo was confused. "I'm only saying . . ."

The woman put her hands on her hips to hear more comfortably.

"So what is it?"

"It's just that she's old and worn-out. She can only eat if somebody feeds her with a spoon."

The woman laughed; the men joked.

"That sounds more like a girl friend of yours. This business of keeping her fed . . . she pretty?"

"I swear it's my grandmother, I swear. She doesn't have any teeth, and she's kind of soft in the head."

Other men were arriving. Antônio Balduíno lay down in the middle of the central square, his naked belly turned upward.

"I'm dog-tired."

Gordo asked him, "Isn't it true I have a grandmother? Don't I have to feed her with a spoon?"

The men laughed. The woman interrupted, "Is your wife so old, Gordo, that you call her Grandmother?"

More laughter to increase Gordo's confusion.

"I swear it! I swear." He made a cross with his fingers and kissed it.

"Bring her out here, Gordo. I'll feed her with a spoon. I'll even marry her!"

"She's my grandmother, I swear."

"It doesn't matter. An old one's just as good."

Antônio Balduíno propped himself up on one arm.

"I'm thinking inside here"—he tapped his head—"that you're all a bunch of idiots. Gordo has a grandmother, he really does. And Gordo has a guardian angel, too. Gordo has things nobody else does. Gordo is good, you don't know how good."

Gordo was embarrassed and confused. The men were quiet, and the girl looked at him with alarm.

"Gordo is good, the rest of us are bad. Gordo, he . . ." He stared off at the fields of tobacco that stretched as far as the eye could see.

Ricardo murmured, "I'd take her, even if she was old."

But before going into her house, the younger woman came up to Gordo and asked him, "Will you pray for me? Pray to your angel, to make Antônio get a little money together for us to go to the cocoa plantations." She gazed at the tobacco leaves. "There's money there, lots of it."

Ricardo said, "This year the work is heavy. The harvest is a big one, and Mr. Zequinha don't hire any more men. It's a miracle he hired you two."

"We were starving over in Cachoeira. That's why we came."

"To earn ten cents a day."

A donkey brayed out in the field. Antônio Balduíno said to the old man who was coming out of the house, eating, "Say hello to your father, old man, he's complaining."

"Any why don't you ask your grandfather for his blessing? I knew your mother pretty well."

They laughed. Antônio Balduíno lowered his voice.

"That Totonha woman is sure a good piece."

"You mess with her and see what happens! Antônio has four dead men on his back already. He doesn't fool around, and he's a crack shot."

"All I know is, I'm horny. Two months without a woman . . ."

The old man laughed. Ricardo looked at him angrily.

"You're only laughing because you're married. You have a woman! She might be an old piece of hide, but at least she's a woman. Me, it's been almost a year since I've even seen a filly in bed."

"I'm not laughing about that. When I came to these parts to harvest tobacco, it was that way already. I went through hard times until I got Celeste. She was born here; she was still almost a child. Today she's an old hide, but back then she was a real temptation . . . men were after her worse than buzzards after a carcass. But they were all scared of old João; he was fierce. He had said that any man who took his daughter away from him was a dead man. But I hadn't even got near the scent of a woman in two years. I said to myself that that business of dying was nonsense; we only die when our time comes. One night it was drizzling rain. I called Celeste over to talk. The old man was inside his house, cleaning his repeating rifle. He even spoke to me, laughing. I wasn't scared before, but I was scared then. But Celeste was already coming, and I couldn't stand it any longer. Right there, in some bushes close by, I knocked her down."

The men's eyes were lowered. Antônio Balduíno scratched the dirt with his knife. Ricardo was slapping his hands together impatiently.

The old man continued, "It had been two years since I had been near a woman. Her dress got all torn. I ran off into the jungle and waited for the old man to shoot me."

"And then?"

"The next day I got up my courage and went back to talk to old João. He was cleaning his rifle, and when he saw me, he put down the gun. I knew he was going to kill me, but I was already wanting Celeste again. I went up and told him everything. I told him I wanted to marry her, that I was a good man and a hard worker. Then he got a mean look on his face, and I thought for sure my hour had come. But he didn't do anything, he just said, 'This was bound to happen. There are no women here, and a man needs a woman. Take her home with you but marry her.' I could hardly believe it, but João added, 'I am pleased you came to tell me everything. You acted like a man.' Then he called Celeste and told her to go with me. And he went back to cleaning his rifle. But when we left, I swear he was crying."

The men were silent. The wind stirred the tobacco plants, the wide leaves reminding them of the strange genitals of women.

Ricardo swallowed dryly and said, "I don't know how anybody can work without a woman. Here there's only these two married ones."

"What about Miss Laura's daughter?"

"I'd marry her if she wanted," said Ricardo.

Antônio Balduíno stuck his knife into the ground. A tall black man affirmed, "One of these days I'll take her to bed, whether she wants to or not."

"But she's only a girl of twelve!" said Gordo in alarm.

The mountains behind covered in mist. The far-off railroad track. Occasional trains whistled, with women waving goodbye from the windows. The men followed the road to the markets, driving donkeys laden with fruit or cattle to sell in Feira de Santana. Sometimes they carried enormous sacks in their callused hands, sometimes they prodded their donkeys along or drove cattle ahead of them. Huge herds went by, the cowboys chanting sadly, "Ooouuuuuu booiiiiiiiii . . ."

And the hands that reached toward the earth; large, callused hands that picked the fragrant tobacco leaves. The hands went up and down with a certain rhythm, always the same. They seemed like people crying. The work made the back ache, a sharp, prolonged ache that continued on into the night. Zequinha would go by, looking at the work, giving orders, arguing. Piles of tobacco leaves would accumulate, and when the afternoon ended, the men would have earned ten cents that they never saw because they already owed the boss unknown amounts.

With their ugly, callused hands, they waved farewell to the trains that went whistling by.

Four people lived in the mud-wattle house: Ricardo; black Filomeno; Antônio Balduíno; and Gordo. Filomeno only talked about shootings and deaths; that is, when he talked at all, because generally he stayed quiet and listened. On the wall above the rude boards where he slept, Ricardo had glued up the picture of a movie actress, completely nude except for a fan she held over her crotch. He had put the picture up on the wall very carefully, a picture the boss's son had given him when he came to the ranch about three years ago. He had placed the lantern in such a way that its red light clearly illuminated the actress, whose nakedness seemed an invitation. Gordo had a saint above his bed, a saint he had "traded" for five hundred reis at the Bonfim fiesta. At the foot of Antônio Balduíno's hard-board bed, he placed the *figa* that Jubiabá had given him and the daggers he wore in his belt. Filomeno had nothing.

They went out to the "square" after supper, and as they had no cinema, theater, or cabaret, they played the guitar and challenged each other at singing. The rough hands of the black men drew from the strings melodies that filled the country folk from all the tobacco plantations with emotion, both joy and sadness. They sang melancholy songs, happy sambas, and Ricardo was always ready to meet a challenge. His hands ran expertly over the guitar strings, no longer the callused hands that knew earth and the hoe. They were artist's hands, quick and sure, that brought to the men's hearts the stories of loves and battles. The hands that before had earned bread now gave joy in the land without women. The guitars strummed far into the night, providing the cinema, theater, and cabaret. The quick hands ran over the strings, spreading music through the tobacco fields, which looked eerie in the moonlight.

When silence falls over everything, when the sound of the guitars dies away and the men stretch out on their rough makeshift beds, the lantern out, Ricardo looks at the picture of the nude actress with the fan covering her crotch. As he fixes his eyes on her, she begins to move. But now she is dressed and they are no longer on the tobacco plantation. They are in a great city, a city that Ricardo has never seen, a city full of lights, with many cars and avenues, bigger than Cachoeira and São Felix put together. It might be Bahia, or maybe even Rio de Janeiro. Women pass, blond ones, dark-haired ones, all smiling at Ricardo, who is elegantly dressed in cashmere and wearing red shoes like the ones he saw once in a store in Feira de Santana. The women laugh. They all want him, but he is with the actress, whom he met in a theater and who is hanging onto his arm in such a way that her breast rubs against his chest. Now they are going to eat supper in a chic restaurant where all the women wear low-cut gowns and everyone drinks expensive wine. He has already kissed the actress many times, and undoubtedly she loves him, because she lets him squeeze her breasts and lift up her silk dress beneath the table. But suddenly she's back in the picture again, with the fan over her crotch, because the boards are shaking a lot, and Antônio Balduíno stirs in his bed across the room. Ricardo waits angrily for everything to become quiet again, pulling the ragged blanket up to his chin. He goes back to the restaurant with the woman. From there, they will soon be getting into a car that takes them to a perfumed bedroom. He undresses her little by little, enjoying each of her enchantments in turn. Now he cares little that the bed is creaking and that Antônio Balduíno stirs. No, no, it isn't his own callused hand on his penis. It is the blond crotch of the blond actress, who wears neither dress nor fan, and who loves Ricardo, tobacco-plantation worker. Let who will wake up, because he's not doing anything extraordinary, he's making love to a pretty woman with firm breasts and a round womb. His hand is a woman.

The actress has gone back to the picture, her fan in place. On the road a lantern light shines, illuminating the tobacco fields. Ricardo rests his head against the hard boards of his bed and falls asleep.

One Sunday Ricardo said he was going fishing on the river. He had bought a bomb with which he hoped to kill a lot of fish. He invited the others, but Gordo was the only one who wanted to go. They talked the entire way. When they reached the riverbank, Ricardo removed his shirt, and Gordo lay down on the grass. The fields of tobacco stretched out behind them. A train passed. Ricardo prepared the bomb and lit the fuse. He was smiling. He stretched his hands out in front of him, but before he could throw the bomb, it exploded, taking with it his hands and his arms and drenching the river with blood. Ricardo looked at the stumps of his arms, and it was as if he had killed himself.

CHAPTER 15
Wake

Miss Laura's daughter, Arminda, who used to run through the tobacco fields after work with the childish abandon of her twelve years, no longer runs. Her face is worried as she works. One day she even asks Zequinha permission to go home. It is because Miss Laura has been lying on her bed for a week, swelling up with an unknown disease. Before, Arminda was happy, swimming in the river like a fish and exciting the men with the sight of her girl's body. Now she only works, for if she doesn't, she will starve.

On Tuesday she didn't even go to work. Totonha, coming from the sick woman's house, announced, "Well, the old lady kicked the bucket."

The men stopped working for a moment.

"At least she was old enough."

"She's swollen up like an ox . . . it's scary."

"What a strange disease."

"Nobody can tell me that wasn't a bad spirit."

Zequinha was coming up. The men bent over the tobacco leaves again. Totonha spoke to him and then told them, "I'm going back to stay with the girl. The wake will be tonight."

Filomeno whispered to Antônio Balduíno, "Wish it was me. If I were alone with her, God help her!"

Gordo took a gulp of rum, because he was very much afraid of dead people. At lunchtime, they exchanged stories of dead people they had seen, telling anecdotes of illness and death. The black Filomeno didn't talk. He had a plan in his head. He was thinking about Arminda, about the freshness of her girlish body.

* * *

The lanterns seemed to walk. The wavering lights approached the mud-wattle house. The people couldn't be seen, only that red light that flickered and grew dim like a suffering soul. In the doorway, Totonha was receiving the visitors who had come to the old woman's wake. She distributed embraces and received condolences as if Miss Laura had been her relative. Damp-eyed, she narrated the sufferings of the dead woman.

"Poor thing, she screamed so much. But with that awful disease . . ."

"It was an evil spirit."

"She swelled up, her belly was all bloated."

"Now she's gone to her rest."

A woman crossed herself. Black Filomeno asked, "What about Arminda?"

"She's inside, crying. Poor thing, she's left without anyone in the world."

She offered rum, which they all drank.

In the only bedroom of the house, two benches were pushed against the wall. Some barefoot men and women, their heads uncovered, sat beside the dead woman. On the other side of the room was an old chair where Arminda sat weeping tearlessly, sobbing aloud from time to time. Her eyes were covered with a red handkerchief. The new arrivals went up to her and squeezed her hand, though she didn't move. No one said a word.

In the middle of the room, stretched out on top of a platform, which, on normal days, served as bed and dining table, was the bloated cadaver, looking as if it might explode. A chintz cover with great green-and-yellow flowers covered the body, leaving exposed only the wrinkled face with its twisted mouth and the enormous flat feet with their splayed toes. When the men turned around, they stared at the dead woman's face; the women crossed themselves. A candle placed near the cadaver's head spread its wan light over the immobile face, still twisted in an expression of suffering. Those paralyzed eyes seemed to pin themselves on the company, who were now all seated on the benches, whispering. A bottle of rum passed from hand to hand. They drank from it in large gulps. Two men went outside to smoke. Zequinha arrived and patted Arminda on the head. Then the prayers began, led by Gordo.

"Lord take this soul." Those present responded in chorus, "Pray for her."

Antônio Balduíno lifted his eyes and peeked at Arminda. She was across the room, crying. But the swollen face of the dead woman impeded his seeing her properly.

Filomeno is also looking at the orphan. Antônio Balduíno can see very well that the eyes of the black man are resting on Arminda's bosom, which rises and falls with the sobs that shake her. And Antônio Balduíno is angry. He murmurs to his neighbors, "That miserable nigger doesn't even respect the dead."

But he, too, is staring at the breasts trembling under her dress. Suddenly, Filomeno's gaze turns, and he looks at the people who are in the room. Everyone can see he is afraid. What can Filomeno be afraid of? thinks Antônio Balduíno. And he looks, almost laughing, at the neckline of Arminda's dress. The lantern light falls upon the place where her breasts begin. And it wants to go farther . . . yes, the lantern light wants to spread over Arminda's breasts like a hand. She is tempting it. Antônio Balduíno follows the scene with shining eyes. Finally, the light manages to get inside the neckline. Naturally, it is now squeezing the breasts that rise and fall. Antônio Balduíno smiles and almost mutters, "It got there, the pest!"

But now he, too, removes his gaze and trembles. For didn't the dead woman fix her paralyzed eyes on him in an expression of hatred? Antônio Balduíno looks at the floor, at his rough hands, but he senses that the angry gaze of the cadaver accompanies him. He thinks, Why in hell doesn't the old woman pay attention to that pest Filomeno, who wants to screw her daughter?

Then he remembers that his own intentions are just as bad and flees from the old woman's gaze. He looks at Gordo, whose mouth opens and closes as he recites the prayers for the dead. He wants to see if he can concentrate on a fly entering Gordo's mouth. But the dead woman looks at him, and Filomeno ogles Arminda's breasts.

"That devil of an old hag is still taking care of her daughter, she hasn't died yet."

"Huh?" said his neighbor.

"I didn't say anything."

Gordo is chanting. Antônio Balduíno repeats with everyone, "Pray for her."

That fly just might go into Gordo's mouth. It was almost inside, but then Gordo shut his lips. There it goes again. It lights on his nose. It's waiting for Gordo to open his mouth again. Now. But the fly buzzes off and lights on Arminda, on the other side of the room. Filomeno shifts in his chair. Antônio Balduíno imagines what Arminda's breasts would be like outside her dress. What big nipples they have. They actually make little dents in her dress. The fly is sitting on top of one of them, right smack on the left one. She obviously isn't wearing a brassiere. Her breasts would be firm and fleshy. Why is she crying? thinks Antônio Balduíno. She has large eyes with long lashes. With the sobs that agitate her breathing, her breasts almost spill out of her neckline. The fly took off again, lighting on the dead woman's face. How swollen she is! She hardly fits on the table. And her face is enormous, the skin greenish and the eyes popping out. But why is she staring at Antônio Balduíno? What is he doing wrong? He's not even looking at Arminda. But Filomeno is; he hasn't taken his eyes off her. So why doesn't the old stiff leave Balduíno alone and look somewhere else? But how deformed she is, how ghastly! The fly has settled on her nose. Are those beads of sweat shining on her dead face? Naturally, she wants prayers. Antônio Balduíno, instead of praying with the others, is staring at her daughter. He joins in the chorus.

"Pray for her."

He is amused, because he speaks up so loudly that he startles Filomeno, who repeats tardily, "Pray for her!"

It's the wrong time. Gordo is already saying something else. The bottle of rum goes around. Antônio Balduíno takes a large swallow and tries to look at Arminda again. But the dead woman is persecuting him. By now her eyes have swollen so much that when Balduíno looks past her he can see only half of Arminda's face. What he sees very clearly are the dead woman's eyes following him with hatred. Could she somehow have guessed that he is going to ask Arminda for a drink of water, just so he can get her into the other room with him, where he plans to grab her? Dead people know everything. Certainly she has already discovered this and will not let him go. He sees her frightful face. No one has a face like that. Arminda's face is cheerful. Even when she cries, as she is doing now, she has a happy face. Why is it that people like that exist? The dead woman's face is green and covered with sticky droplets of sweat. Antônio Balduíno rubs his hands together, wanting to free himself of the vision. He looks at the ceiling. But he senses that the ghastly eyes are fixed on him. He spends a long time studying the rafters and the blackened roof tiles. Suddenly he lowers his eyes and looks at Arminda's breasts. He smiles in satisfaction: This time he fooled the old dead hag. But this time it's worse, much worse: She twists her mouth in rage, her eyes popping out farther than ever. A fly perches on her mouth. It looks like a cigar butt, black with saliva. Antônio Balduíno tries to accompany the prayers. And when he thinks the dead woman is no longer watching him, he opens his mouth to ask Arminda for a drink of water. But there are those dead eyes looking right into his with an air of challenge. He prays some more, takes another drink of rum. How many times has the bottle been past him? This one is down to the end. How many more would there be to open? At a wake you use up a lot of rum . . . and now that the dead woman isn't watching, Antônio Balduíno gets slowly up, edges around the table, and touches Arminda's shoulder.

"Come give me a sip of water."

She gets up. They go out into the backyard, where there is a vat of water and a mug. Arminda bends over to fill the mug, and Antônio Balduíno can see down the front of her dress. Then he clutches the girl's arms and whirls her around to face him. She stares at him in alarm. But he sees nothing except her mouth and breasts. He is going to hug her tightly, and his mouth starts toward Arminda's, though she doesn't yet understand. But the cadaver's eyes come and place themselves between the two. Old Laura has left her place on top of the table and come to interfere. She is protecting her daughter. The dead know everything, and she knows what Antônio Balduíno intended to do. She is there between the two, looking at the black man. He lets Arminda loose, puts his hands over his eyes, dumps the water out of the mug, and staggers blindly back into the room. The cadaver on the table is bloated bigger than ever.

The Negro Filomeno laughs as if he understands Antônio Balduíno's idea in asking for a drink of water. Undoubtedly, he's going to do the very same thing. What a fool, thinks Antônio Balduíno, to imagine he has some advantage. When he gets there, he'll find the dead woman watching him. She knows everything, sees everything. But the cadaver's eyes don't follow Filomeno. Can it be possible that she's going to let that filthy Negro touch Arminda? For he has gotten up to ask Arminda for a drink of water, and the dead woman hasn't done a thing. Antônio Balduíno murmurs to the impassive face, ''Go on! Go on! Don't you see that? Don't you see? That nigger is up to no good.''

But the dead woman pays no attention to his warning. She actually seems to be laughing. A sound is heard in the back. Arminda returns to the room, and now her tears are of a different kind. Her dress is wrinkled across the bosom. The Negro Filomeno comes in smiling. Antônio Balduíno wrings his hands in rage, gets up and says aloud to Gordo, ''Didn't you say she was a girl of twelve? Where's her dead mother, why didn't she do something?''

Zequinha observes, ''He's drunk.''

Someone closes the cadaver's eyes.

CHAPTER 16
Flight

In his belt, under his coat, Antônio Balduíno carries two knives.

Zequinha goes for him with a sickle in his hand. They grapple together and roll over in the hard clay of the road. Zequinha falls down, and the sickle flies far away. When he gets up and runs at Antônio Balduíno again, he sees the knife in the Negro's hand. He stops, irresolute, tries to calculate the blow. Then he jumps. Antônio Balduíno steps back, his hand opening, and the dagger falls to the ground. Zequinha laughs with his eyes, and quick as a cat, bends to take his enemy's weapon. As he bends, Antônio Balduíno takes the other knife from his belt and stabs Zequinha from behind. Antônio Balduíno always carries two knives in his belt . . . and his laughter frightens his opponents more than the fight, the stabbing, or the blood.

It is night, and the black man makes for the jungle.

He has to make a path through the woods. He runs between the trees; their branches close behind him. It is easily three hours that he has been running this way, like a dog pursued by ill-intentioned boys. In the silence of the jungle one can hear crickets. He runs without a set direction; he is lost, penetrating the brush, avoiding the roads, his aching feet tearing themselves on thorns. His denim pants are torn from top to bottom. He didn't even see when that happened. The endless jungle is before him. In the darkness he can see nothing. Now he stops and hears the sound of brush cracking. Who's coming? Is it his pursuers? He tenses to listen, his hand on his razor, the only weapon he has left. He makes himself almost invisible behind a tree and smiles, thinking that the first pursuer who passes him will sleep forever. The razor is open in his hand. Fleeting as a vision, a jungle inhabitant goes by him. What kind of animal is it? Antônio Balduíno doesn't recognize it; he smiles at his own fear. Fighting open a path, he goes on. Blood drips from his face. The jungle is implacable toward those who violate it. A thorn has cut Antônio Balduíno's face, but he sees nothing, feels nothing. He only knows that he has left a dead man behind on the tobacco plantation. The dagger in his back is Balduíno's, driven in by his own hand. But he has no remorse for what he did. It was all Zequinha's fault. He was the one who did everything to start the fight. He had been picking on the Negro a lot. What happened was bound to come about. What's more, if he hadn't grabbed the sickle, Antônio Balduíno wouldn't have pulled out his knife.

Up ahead the woods thins. Between the leaves, the black man sees the stars shining. The sky is bright. White wisps of cloud drift through the sky. If there were a mulatto girl with him, Antônio Balduíno would tell her that her teeth looked like those white clouds. He stops and admires the starry night sky. He sits down in a clearing, no longer remembering the fight. If Maria dos Reis were there . . . But she went with her family to São Luiz do Maranhão. She went by sea, in a black ship all full of lights. If she were there, they would make love in the silence of the jungle. The black man looks at the stars. Who knows, maybe Maria dos Reis is looking at the same stars. The stars are everywhere. Are they the same ones? wonders Antônio Balduíno. Maria dos Reis is seeing that star, and Lindinalva, too. When he thinks about Lindinalva, he grows irritated. Why is he thinking about her? She's white, she has freckles on her face, and has nothing to do with a black man like him. It's better to think about Zequinha, lying in the clay with a dagger in his back, than to think about Lindinalva, who hates black people. If she knew he was running away, she would undoubtedly tell the police. Maria dos Reis would hide him, but not Lindinalva.

Antônio Balduíno's thick lips spread in a smile, because he remembers that Lindinalva knows nothing about this and could not denounce him. He grows impatient with the stars, which make him think of Lindinalva. Viriato the Dwarf hated the stars; he had said so once. When? Antônio Balduíno doesn't remember. Viriato hardly talked about anything except his sadness over being all alone. And one day he went down the road to the sea, like that other old man who was fished out of the water one night when the dockworkers were loading a Swedish ship. Had Viriato found his way home? Gordo said that those who commit suicide go to hell. But Gordo is crazy, he doesn't know what he's talking about. Balduíno misses Gordo. Gordo doesn't know anything about this, either; he doesn't know that Antônio Balduíno has knifed Zequinha in the back and killed him. Gordo had left for Bahia two weeks ago because he missed his grandmother, who had no one to spoon-feed her. Gordo is very good; he would be incapable of knifing anybody. He was never a fighting man. Antônio Balduíno remembers perfectly the days of his childhood when he begged in Bahia. Gordo knew how to ask for alms better than anyone. But he was no good at fighting. Phillip the Beautiful used to laugh at him. He was handsome, Phillip the Beautiful. When he got run over by a car and died on his birthday, everyone cried. His funeral was like a rich person's. The women from the Rua de Baixo had brought flowers. An old Frenchwoman cried. She was Phillip's mother. And they had dressed him in a beautiful suit of cashmere and put a new tie around his neck. Phillip must have been pleased. He was elegant, and appreciated a tie.

Antônio Balduíno got in a fight on account of him once. He smiled to remember the fact. Toothless had taken a good thrashing. He had come at Balduíno with a switchblade, and Balduíno hadn't pulled out any weapon at all. With Zequinha, he had pulled out a dagger. He is certain now that he never liked Zequinha, that he had taken a dislike to the fellow ever since his first day in the tobacco fields. And if Antônio Balduíno hadn't stabbed him, someone else would have. Filomeno, the black man, detested Zequinha, too. It was all because of Arminda. Why did Zequinha have to start living with her? They had gotten there first.

On the night of the wake, Antônio Balduíno didn't take her home only because the dead woman wouldn't take those swollen eyes off him. And hadn't Filomeno felt her breasts? So why did Zequinha interfere? She was a girl of twelve, Gordo was always saying so. A girl of twelve. Gordo meant that she wasn't grown-up yet and that to sleep with her would be wicked. But Zequinha did, so he deserved to be stabbed. It was true that if Zequinha hadn't slept with her, Filomeno or even Antônio Balduíno himself would have. Yes, he knows that wasn't why he buried his knife in Zequinha's back. She was a twelve-year-old girl. But he killed the foreman because he had taken her, and the black man wanted her for himself. She was only twelve years old, but she was already a woman . . . or was she? What if Gordo was right? What if she were still a girl and sleeping with her wicked? Well, then Zequinha wouldn't do it again, because he was lying on the clay road with a knife in his back. However, what good was that? By now, black Filomeno had no doubt taken her home with him. That is the law of the tobacco plantations. Women are rare creatures, and when one is left without a man, another man takes her home at once. Unless she perfers to walk the streets in Cachoeira, São Felix, or Feira de Santana. That would be the real evil. Because she was a girl of twelve, all the men would want her. She would age fast and take to drinking rum. Her breasts would fall. She would quit washing her hair, catch terrible diseases, and be forty years old by the time she was fifteen. Maybe she would drink poison. Others threw themselves into the river on dark nights. It was better for her to stay with Zequinha, picking tobacco in the country. But Zequinha was stabbed to death. Antônio Balduíno hears voices through the woods. He moves in their direction to listen. The noise is still indistinct. Is it men passing on the road? But the road is a long way off, in the opposite direction. Where the noise is, there's nothing but a little trail. Antônio Balduíno moves closer. Now he hears them. The men are close, separated from him only by a thin strip of woods. They are men from the plantation. They are all carrying rifles and smoking, sitting down in the trail. They are after Antônio Balduíno, the Negro who stabbed the foreman. And they don't know that he is very close by, almost laughing. However, he trembles when he hears the men say he is surrounded, that he will either be captured or die of hunger. Antônio Balduíno moves away from them slowly, soundlessly, and hides himself again in the jungle. On the opposite side of the woods is the road. But there would be men on it, too, and all around the thick patch of jungle. He is surrounded, held at bay like a damned dog, and will either die of hunger or be taken prisoner for murder. The noise of the crickets irritates him. At Zequinha's house they would be holding a wake. Filomeno would be there, thought Antônio Balduíno, ogling Arminda and planning to take her home with him—unless he was out there armed with a rifle. If he could just stab Filomeno, too. But he is fenced in on all sides, cowering like a hunted dog in the underbrush. He is beginning to feel hungry and thirsty.

His feet hurt from walking. He could have just beaten Zequinha up. Wasn't he Baldo the Boxer? Hadn't he knocked out hundreds of men in the Sé Square in Bahia? Yes, he could have easily thrashed Zequinha, if only he hadn't come at him with that sickle. Men don't fight with sickles, and treachery must be repaid with treachery. That was why he had pulled out one knife and let it drop, in order to stick the other one into Zequinha's back. The only person who had gained something out of it all was Filomeno, who must be at the wake right now, staring at Arminda. He would kill Filomeno if he could get to Zequinha's house. The cadaver, wound in its back, must be stretched out on the bed. No doubt Filomeno had put Balduíno's dagger in his belt and would later put Arminda in his house. Filomeno was the one he should have killed. Now here he was, surrounded, trapped in the woods. If it weren't for his thirst, everything would be all right . . . but his throat is dry. He doesn't mind his feet hurting, nor his torn clothes, nor his face that bleeds from the thorn scratches. The only thing that matters is his throat burning with thirst. He would like to eat, too. In these woods there were no fruit trees. It wasn't the season for guavas, there wasn't a single guava on the trees. A snake passes by, hissing. The crickets make an unbearable noise. Now he can no longer see the stars, for the jungle is thick. His thirst increases. He smokes. Fortunately his cigarettes and matches were in his pocket. What time was it? Midnight maybe, or later. The cigarette makes him forget his hunger and thirst. How long has he been smoking? He doesn't even remember anymore. Even back on Capa-Negro Hill he was already smoking. He used to get punished for it. If his Aunt Luísa could see him now, what would she say? She used to thrash him, but she liked him. She went crazy, poor thing, from carrying so much *mingau* and *munguzá* to Terreio Square to sell. In front of her house on the hill, people used to meet and talk. One day that man from Ilhéus came, who told stories about courageous bandits. Now Antônio Balduíno was trapped as if he, too, were a famous bandit. If the man from Ilhéus could see him now he would certainly admire him and add his story to those he told long into the night. Balduíno wanted to have his ABC written, too. He thought that the bald man who had come to Jubiabá's macumba session would someday write his ABC. Gordo said that the bald man's whole life was spent writing ABCs of the most courageous men he met, and that was why he went all over the world riding a bay horse. Did Antônio Balduíno already deserve an ABC? He doesn't know. Maybe the man from Ilhéus would one day tell his story, and the men and boys from some other hills would admire him and want to become like him. Ah, if he can just get out of these woods where he is surrounded by armed men, he will deserve to be sung in an ABC. How many men were after him? If they had all come from the plantation, there would be more than thirty. But probably not all of them had come. Filomeno hadn't, he had stayed behind with Arminda, telling her lies, promising her things. He knew that nigger . . . a man who never talks is a bad man. He squeezed his razor. Though it is the only weapon he has, he would attack Filomeno right now if he saw him. It would be another verse in his ABC. With only a razor, he attacked and killed a bad man who carried a rifle. He throws away the useless cigarette. Hell, his throat is dry. His stomach burns, and his face throbs with pain. He touches the thorn scratch with his hand. Now that it has stopped bleeding, it hurts badly. It is a large cut; it tore open his whole face. His hands and feet are bleeding, too. And this thirst that tortures him, the men who surround him, the crickets that make so much noise! The underbrush grows thinner and he sees the stars again. If there were just some water. If only it would rain. But there are no dark clouds in the sky, only wispy white ones that the wind carries away. The moon comes out, a great bright moon more beautiful than ever. Oh, the desire he had to be on the boat landing in Bahia with his guitar, with that woman who had the masculine voice, singing a waltz, some old song that spoke of love. Then they would roll over in the sand, their bodies twined together. Ah, how good it used to be! That star reminds him of the sign at the Drowned Man's Lantern. He would have a drink, listen to the old blind man singing to the guitar, talk with Gordo and Joaquim. Maybe Jubiabá would come in and he would ask for his blessing.

Pai Jubiabá doesn't know that he is trapped in the woods; he doesn't know that he killed Zequinha. But Jubiabá would understand; he would place his hand on Antônio Balduíno's head and speak in Nagô. No, he wouldn't say that the eye of mercy had run dry, that only the eye of badness was left. Why should he say that? Antônio Balduíno still has the eye of mercy wide open. He killed Zequinha, yes . . . but it was because he was going to bed with a twelve-year-old girl. A little girl, she wasn't even a grown woman! Let them ask Gordo if they wanted. A girl, a girl whose mother was still taking care of her when she died. Let them ask Gordo if they wanted. But it's useless to lie to pai Jubiabá. He knows everything because he is a pai-de-santo and draws strength from Oxalá. He knows everything just like that old dead woman. No, Balduíno killed the foreman because he wanted Arminda for himself. She was twelve years old, but she was already a woman. Gordo doesn't understand these things. How could anyone believe Gordo? Gordo doesn't know the first thing about women, he only knows about prayers. And besides, Gordo is very good, he doesn't have an eye of wickedness. Pai Jubiabá ought to cast a spell to kill that nigger Filomeno. Filomeno is bad, his eye of mercy was dry. A charm to kill him, a strong charm that used hairs from a woman's armpit and vulture feathers! Why is pai Jubiabá shaking his head? Ah, he is saying in Nagô that Antônio Balduíno's eye of mercy has also run dry. Yes, that's it. Antônio Balduíno pulls out his razor, his throat cracking with thirst. If Jubiabá repeats that, he'll kill him, too. And then he will slash his own throat with the razor. In the dark blue sky he sees the old Negro. It isn't the moon, it's Jubiabá. He's repeating, repeating what he said. Antônio Balduíno lunges at him with the razor in his fist and almost runs into his pursuers, who are talking as they go along the road. Jubiabá disappears. Balduíno is thirsty. He runs back into the thick forest where he cannot see the moon, nor the stars, nor the landing dock in Bahai, nor the Drowned Man's Lantern. He throws himself on the ground, stretching his hands in the direction of the road.

"Tomorrow they'll see if I don't get away. I'm a man . . ."

His face hurts and he is thirsty. But when he closes his eyes, he falls asleep at once, and no dreams disturb him.

He wakes with the twittering of the birds. He looks all around him and doesn't understand why he is there and not on his hard-board bed at the tobacco plantation. But the thirst that clutches his throat and the pain of his scratched face remind him of the happenings of the night before. He is hiding in a patch of woods; he killed a man yesterday. And he is thirsty, crazed with thirst. His face has swollen during the night. He runs his hand over it.

"A poisonous thorn. Just what I need . . ."

He squats on the ground, thinking what to do. Maybe they had left only a few people to surround him during the day. His face hurts. He is thirsty. He walks slowly forward, avoiding other thorns and moving quietly. Now, in the daylight, he can get his bearings. The road is to his right. But he goes toward the trail where there is less chance of people. If it weren't for his thirst, he wouldn't mind. He isn't hungry now, although his stomach aches. But he can tolerate that. The thirst is the awful thing; it seems to strangle his throat like a cord. No, he must get out, even if he goes to prison. He cannot stand the thirst any longer. He would fight until they shot him, but he had to get to water. The funny thing was that nobody liked Zequinha, and everyone liked him. But the boss gave orders, no doubt, and whoever didn't go to surround the criminal would be fired. If there were people on the trail, there would be a fight. He might die, but he would take someone with him.

"One goes with me."

He laughs so loud, he seems happy. And he is, yes, because he has decided to fight for his life and have done with it. The thing he loves most is to fight. Only now does he realize it. He was born to fight, to kill and one day to die of a shot in the back, a stab in the chest, maybe even a razor slash. Those who came back would tell that he had died like a real man, a true *macho*, with a razor in his hand. And who knows, perhaps they would tell their friends and children the story of Antônio Balduíno, who was a beggar, a composer of sambas, a boxer, a trouble-maker who killed a man because of a girl and died defending himself against twenty. Who knows?

He stumbles onto the pool of water, drinks in great gulps, and washes the cut on his face.

Water! Water! Why had he never noticed before how delicious water was? Better than beer, better than wine, even better than rum. Let them surround them now, let them corner him like a dog. What did it matter! He had water to drink and to wash the swollen, stinging cut. He lies down beside the pool and rests, confident, smiling, happy. During the dark night, he didn't see the pools of water. There are many of them; muddy, dirty water, but delicious. He spends a long time lying there, thinking. When he runs away, where will he go? He might go into the backlands, take shelter at some ranch, become a cow-hand. There were so many murderers hiding out in the backlands. If they pressed him too hard, he could join a band of outlaws and live the life he had always admired. The worst is that now he is hungry. Maybe he could find some fruit to eat, the way he had found the water. He goes through the woods, examining the trees. He doesn't find a thing. But as the day wears on, maybe he can kill and eat an animal. He has matches, he can make a fire. No, he can't do that, because it would call the attention of the men who are waiting in ambush on the road. Then he remembers to look and see if there are still many after him. He touches his face, which hurts more all the time. It's an ugly cut. The thorn must have been poisonous. Pai Jubiabá knows marvelous remedies for that kind of wound. They are made with leaves, leaves from the jungle. There must be some of those leaves around here. He looks at the ground. But which ones would work? Only pai Jubiabá knows; he knows every-thing. Balduíno approaches the strip of woods that separates him from the trail. He looks: There are the men, all of them. None of them went to work today. If the boss let the workers off, he really is out to liquidate Antônio Balduíno. The men are eating dried beef and talking. Balduíno turns around slowly. He puts the razor back into his belt, pensive, then suddenly he laughs.

"They won't get anywhere with me."

The worst things are not having anything to eat and to be alone at night. He was never afraid to stay alone before, but today he doesn't want to. He starts thinking nonsense, seeing Jubiabá, remembering places he has been and people he used to know who are dead. He even sees Lindinalva. If he could keep from seeing Lindinalva, there would be no problem. He thinks about Arminda, who by now must be shacked up with the black Filomeno. But it wasn't Filomeno's fault. If he didn't take Arminda, someone else would have. There aren't any women on the tobacco plantations. That was why Ricardo agitated in his bed so much at night. How did he manage now that he had no hands? He was living in Cachoeira, begging for alms. Did he have a woman? Who knows, perhaps he had found one to take care of him. He deserved as much; he was a good fellow with a friendly way about him. If he had been on the tobacco plantation, would he have gone after Antônio Balduíno? There is a mist in front of his eyes. It's hunger; he's heard about this. And desperately, he goes in search of food. When night falls, he smokes his last cigarette and can barely see what is before him. His swollen face drives him mad with pain.

Staggering like a drunken man, he walks toward the place where the pools of water are. He hasn't eaten anything since lunch yesterday, because when he fought with Zequinha, they hadn't yet had supper. As he lurches along, there are many companions with him. Where has he seen that thin man who shouts, "Where's Baldo, who knocks down the white guys?"

The man is shouting and laughing. Where has Antônio Balduíno seen him? Now he remembers: It was during that boxing match with a German he had beaten. He smiles. The man had jeered, but Baldo had beaten the white man, leaving him out cold on the floor of the ring. He will get away from his pursuers, too, and reach freedom. But why is Gordo praying the prayers for the dead? He hasn't died yet. Why do they all answer, "Pray for him"?

Why are they all responding in chorus? Don't they see that they're hurting Antônio Balduíno, who is hungry, his face cut with an ugly scratch where the mosquitoes light? They go on chanting. Antônio Balduíno lies down near a pool of water and drinks. Then he stares at the entourage accompanying him. Stretching out his hands, he begs them to go away and leave him in peace.

"Go away! Go away!"

But they don't. Old Laura, Arminda's mother, has just arrived, her eyes swollen, body bloated, tongue out. She is laughing at him.

"Go to hell! Go to hell!"

He rises. They are all after him. Even Gordo, who was such a good friend. Jubiabá says that the eye of mercy has run dry in him. It's true, yes, it's true. But let them leave him alone because he'll soon die, and he wants to die like a man, and with them around he can't, he can't. . . .

They pray the prayers for the dead. He trips on a tree root and falls down.

He allows himself to lie there on the ground. When he gets up, there is resolution in his eyes.

The road is off to his right. He goes in that direction with firm steps, walking erect as though he weren't hungry, as though he hadn't been cut off from human beings for two days and haunted by ghosts. The razor is in his hand.

"One of them will go with me."

But his sudden appearance on the road leaves the men dumbfounded. He still has the strength to knock down one of them, who was in front of him. He breaks through the group with the razor shining in his hand and disappears into the darkness.

A few random shots ring out.

CHAPTER 17
Boxcar

"It was already full of maggots."

The old man was treating the cut on Antônio Balduíno's face, which was swollen and deformed-looking, as red as an apple. He had put herbs mixed with earth on the cut; Jubiabá would have done exactly the same.

"Thank you, old man . . . you're good."

"It'll heal up real fast. This leaf is holy, it works miracles."

The Negro had arrived there, exhausted from his flight away from the tobacco plantations through the forest that bordered the road. The old man lived deep in the jungle in a filthy hovel with some mandioca plants out front. He had given him food and bed and treated his face. Then he had explained that Zequinha had escaped by a hair's breadth but that the boss wanted to catch Balduíno and give him a beating which would serve as an example.

Antônio Balduíno laughed. "I'm tough, uncle. It's hard for trouble to get hold of me." He drank a mug of water. "Now I'm going to take off. If I can repay you one day I will, old man."

"Take off? What for? If you do that, the cut won't heal, son. Just lie down there. Stay hid out here for a while. Nobody will suspect nothin'. I'm a peaceful man."

Antônio Balduíno spent three days waiting for the cut to heal. He ate the old man's food, drank his water, slept on his bed.

He tells the old man good-bye.

"You've been good to me."

He follows the railroad track. When he reaches Feira de Santana, he'll look for a truck to take him back to Bahia. And he is happy on account of his adventure, his fight, his escape from capture. He is invincible, the most courageous man in these parts. Up there in the sky are the stars that witnessed the way he fought. And if the men who had surrounded him hadn't been so overwhelmed by his courage, he would have taken one with him to the stars, to the great blue sky. He would have shone there with the razor in his hand. Maria dos Reis would have seen him, the woman with the masculine voice, even Lindinalva. Gordo, who always wanted to have a star, might have discovered him. He would have played a trick on Mestre Manuel, making him think he was the light from a sailboat that wanted to race with the *Homeless Traveler*. He would hear Maria Clara sing his sambas. All this would have happened if the men hadn't been so stupid when he appeared on the road with his razor in his hand and a cut on his face. They would have fallen on him, and he would have taken one with him. Maybe they would have riddled his body with bullets. But men who die fighting and take someone with them turn into stars and have an ABC on earth telling of their deeds. He would be a red star with a razor in his hand. Jubiabá always said that courageous men turned into stars. Antônio Balduíno lets out a peal of laughter that silences the crickets and frightens the animals in their dens. A smell of leaves spreads itself in the silent darkness as a breeze sighs, announcing rain. The leaves bend, exuding perfume. Ahead of him on the track, a lantern shines against something black. Men's voices argue. It is a train that has stopped. It would be heading for Feira de Santana with the passengers who came from Bahia to Cachoeira by ship today. The men are examining a wheel. Antônio Balduíno goes around to the other side and finds a freight car. If the door is unlocked, he'll go by train. He pushes the wide door with all his strength, and it gives. He jumps in as quickly and subtly as an animal, closing the door after him. Only then does he see that he has startled some figures who hide themselves in the depths of the boxcar between the bundles of tobacco.

"Hi, folks. I come in peace. I don't like to pay for a ticket, either."

He laughs.

* * *

The woman is pregnant. Her belly still hasn't grown too big, but one can easily see she is expecting. One of the two men is old and holds a staff. He smokes, almost asleep. In the darkness of the boxcar, the burning point of his cigarette makes the staff look like a snake ready to strike. The other man wears the trousers of an army uniform and an old cashmere suit coat. He has no beard, but he is trying to show off a sparse mustache that is sprouting on his upper lip. He constantly passes his hand over this imaginary mustache as he talks. A kid, thinks Antônio Balduíno.

The train was stopped, which was why they kept quiet. There had been a problem of some sort, a common occurrence on those trains. For half an hour they had remained quiet, waiting for the train to start up again. They could hear voices outside, and the man in charge of the train would certainly cause problems for the clandestine travelers if he discovered them. When Antônio Balduíno spoke, the old man opened his eyes and said, "Keep your trap shut, man, if you want to travel. Otherwise they'll throw us off."

And he gave a glance at the pregnant woman. Antônio Balduíno wondered if he were her husband or father. He was old enough to be her father, but he could also be her husband. He imagined that woman with her big belly walking to Feira de Santana. She would give birth before she got there. The black man laughed softly. The youth in army trousers looked at him, twisting his mustache. He didn't seem very happy about Antônio Balduíno's arrival. Just then they heard voices approaching. It was the man in charge of the train, explaining the delay to the first-class passengers.

"Just a small difficulty. We'll soon be on our way."

"But we've lost almost an hour!"

"These things happen on any railroad."

"This is a disgrace!"

Soon afterward, a shrill whistle, prolonged and sad, announced their departure. Even hidden in a boxcar with the doors closed, Antônio Balduíno said good-bye.

"Missing someone?" asked the old man.

"Only if I missed the snakes." Antônio Balduíno laughed.

But he lowered his head and spoke without looking at anyone. ''I do miss a girl.''

''Pretty?'' asked the young man, twisting his mustache.

''Gorgeous, man. Looked like a city girl.''

''And you left her?''

''She belonged to someone else. And he didn't die.''

''I know of a man who stole a woman,'' said the old man.

''I know of a guy who knifed somebody on account of an old broad. Then he spent two days starving, hiding out in the jungle.'' Antônio Balduíno began telling his own story.

''Was he scared?''

''Shut up, kid. What do you know? He was scared all right, and surrounded on all sides. If you want to know what kind of man he was, just come after me.''

''You mean, it was you?'' The boy looked at him with more respect.

The pregnant woman remained silent. But when she let out a moan, the old man commented, ''That man was right when he said this train was a disgrace. If the first-class folks complain, too bad for us, who are bumming a free ride!''

''I gave the baggage boy two mil-reis to let me in here,'' groaned the woman.

''When I was in the army, I used to ride first class for free,'' bragged the boy.

''First class?'' Antônio Balduíno doubted it.

''Yes, siree, first class. I guess you do know that soldiers have privileges. You live out here in the sticks and don't know anything.''

''I'm not from around here, junior. I'm just traveling to amuse myself. I was born in Bahia. You ever hear of a fighter called Baldo? Well, now you're looking at him.''

''Ah, are you Baldo? I saw you fight Chico Moela.''

''I beat him good, didn't I?'' The black man smiled.

''Yeah, it was a tough fight. I got in free, soldiers have privileges.''

''So why'd you quit?''

''My time was up. And then—''

The old man opened one eye. ''What happened?''

"A corporal. Just because he had stripes . . . corporals and shit are all the same thing. But he didn't think so."

"He started picking on you?" The old man rested his arm on his staff.

"Yeah, this mulatto girl, she liked me. He kept making trouble for me, and I was locked up all the time. Just so I couldn't go out on my days off. You should see what I did to his face."

"I'm getting to like you, kid. How old are you?"

"Nineteen."

"You ain't seen nothing yet, kid. I'm tired of living," said the old man bitterly.

"Tired, why?" asked Antônio Balduíno.

"Son, I've done everything, I've been through so much. Around here everyone has heard of Augusto da Cerca on account of a fight I had once. What did I get out of it? Nothing but sickness . . . nothing else."

The ex-soldier offered cigarettes. Antônio Balduíno lighted one. By the light of the match he saw the face of the woman, who was gazing at the sky through a crack in the door. She had the tired air of one who had lived a hard life. The old man was still talking. "I used to have lots of cattle to bring to Feira de Santana. A whole lot of cattle, more than you could see at once. I used to have tobacco fields before the Germans came here. I used to have land . . . a whole lot of things."

He paused, apparently asleep, but he began to talk again in a hushed voice.

"I even had a family, would you believe it? Nobody would. But I had two daughters, and I even sent them to school. They were pretty as a picture. It's all gone though, you hear me? All. The cattle went. A white man cast a spell on one of my daughters and carried her off, where I don't know. The other one lives over in Cachoeira, looking like a crazy woman with her hair cut off, walking the streets. At least I know where that one is, but what about the other?"

The woman took her eyes off the door.

"Do you hate whores?"

"They're lost. They cut their hair off and paint their faces red."

"You don't know what their life is like. You don't know anything. What do you know?"

The old man became confused.

The ex-soldier said, "Once I had a lover who was a streetwalker. She would go and earn her living until midnight, then I'd go to her house and stay there until the next morning. It worked fine."

"And you, why are you mouthing off?"

"I wasn't saying anything."

"Oh, weren't you!" answered the woman angrily. "You talk without knowing anything. Just to hear yourselves talk. Me, if I'm here and haven't died of hunger, it's only because God didn't want it that way."

Antônio Balduíno wondered about her pregnancy, but he didn't ask anything.

The old man opened his eyes and said, "I shouldn't say anything, God forgive me. And even if she weren't my daughter, how else could she make a living? She supports me, and it's true she respects me. When I go to see her she always throws the men out. If only she hadn't cut off her hair."

The woman laughed.

Antônio Balduíno said, "Poor people's life is miserable. Poor people are just like slaves."

The ex-soldier told them, "I used to know a corporal who said the same thing."

"Was he the one who took your girl friend?"

"No, that was another one. And Romão didn't take her. I was the one she liked."

"But she ended up with the other man." Balduíno laughed.

"You didn't know her . . . she was really beautiful. There wasn't a woman could touch her for looks."

The train stopped at a station. Silence returned to the boxcar. Men were talking outside, very near. Someone called, "Good-bye! Good-bye!" And someone else, "Tell Josephina hello."

Very close there came a whisper, "You'll forget . . ."

It was the pained voice of a woman. A man protested that no, he wouldn't forget.

"Don't fail to write . . ."

A kiss, and the train whistle cutting the good-byes short.

Then the noise of the wheels on the tracks. The ex-soldier explained, "The train is saying, 'I go with God, I go with the devil.' Doesn't it sound the same?"

"So it does."

"My mother told me that when I was still small enough to sit in her lap. Another train, a big one that pulled a lot of cars, said something different. It was like this: 'Bread-and-butter, tea-and-coffee, bread-and-butter, tea-and-coffee.' Just alike, huh?"

He grew thoughtful, remembering.

"Is your mother still alive?" the woman asked.

"I'm going to visit her. She cried a lot when I signed up. You know how women are. The old lady thinks I'm still a little kid." And he smoothed down the nonexistent mustache.

"Things are the same everywhere," said the woman. She turned to Antônio Balduíno. "Did you see that woman at the station, asking the man to write to her?"

"I heard them talking."

"She'll never see him again. Me, too." And she fell silent.

"How's that?" asked the old man, opening his eyes.

"Nothing . . . just nonsense." She started to whistle.

"It's a rotten world," the old man spat with disgust. "We're born to suffer."

"Life's good, old man. You're only talking that way because you don't fit in." The ex-soldier laughed.

"Life's good for people with money," affirmed the woman.

"So you have a mother?" Antônio Balduíno asked, turning to the soldier. "I never knew mine. My aunt went nuts . . . and Gordo has a grandmother."

"Who's Gordo?"

"A guy you don't know. A good guy—"

"Good?" scoffed the old man. "Ain't nobody good. What's good in this world?"

"Gordo's good."

But the old man seemed to have fallen alseep again. The woman answered, "There are people who are good. But poor folks are born miserable. Poverty makes anybody bad."

The train was going swiftly now. The ex-soldier lay down on the floor of the freight car, watching the woman's face. She was very worn-looking, and her belly was ugly. But even so, Antônio Balduíno perceived a smile on her lips. She looks at the sky through the crack in the door.

"It's poverty, y'know? That's why I don't blame him. He left me with this belly."

"Your husband?" asked the genteel ex-soldier.

"I'm a streetwalker. I was never married."

"I thought so."

"What else could he do? He had no money at all. How could he support a kid? He ran away at night like a thief and left all his things behind. But I know he loved me."

"He ran off when he found out you were going to have a kid?"

"Yeah. I had quit the streets to live with him, see. I was taking in washing; it was just as if we were married. He was good to me, he really was. He could have been a saint on an altar."

"You sure like him a lot."

"It's true. He was a saint. One day I told him I was going to have a baby. I was very happy. He stood there stupidly, his mouth open. Then he laughed a lot, kissed me . . . everything was so good."

"I have a girl friend back home," said the ex-soldier. "She's really good-looking. One of these days we're getting married."

Anyone who looked at him now would say he was dead. With his eyes closed and a smile on his lips, his handsome face was as happy as a dead man's.

The woman shook her head. She had doubtless lived a hard life, for her still-young face wore a tired expression. She felt sorry for the ex-soldier. He was so handsome and so inexperienced. He was going to get married.

But Antônio Balduíno asked, "And then what happened?"

She continued, "It was because he was poor. We could hardly make ends meet, even in the hole where we lived. His money, along with what I earned washing clothes, wasn't enough. It was because of that."

She felt sorry for the ex-soldier, who listened anxiously, his head propped up on his arm.

"So one night he took off. I didn't see him go. He left all his things. I found out that he ran away so as not to see the child go hungry."

"And now?"

"They say he's working in Feira de Santana. I came to look for him."

The soldier was sad. He was thinking now about money to support his future wife and the children they would someday have.

"But she's so pretty. And then, I'll work. I'm not scared of work."

The woman encouraged him.

"That's right."

But she was doubtful, they could all tell.

Antônio Balduíno said to the woman, "I'll be your child's godfather."

"I made him a little cap. An old lady gave me some old diapers. That's all he's got. He'll come into the world suffering."

The ex-soldier said, "Better not to get married. She's so pretty."

The train pulled into São Gonçalo station.

Passengers got off. The sleeping city is full of parks. A child in a home nearby is wakened by the noise of the train. They hear its crying. The woman smiles happily.

"Before long, it'll be your turn," said Balduíno. "You'll have one crying at night."

"I hope it's a boy."

With the whistle of the departing train, the old man woke up.

"There's good people. I was lying. My daughter is good. I'm talking about Maria. Zefa, no, she's no good. Never sent any news. Who knows, maybe she's dead. But Maria's good, she gives me money. But she fights with me because I drink. I drink on account of Zefa because I don't know where she is. Maria's good."

The old man's head nodded again as he went back to sleep.

The ex-soldier said to the woman, "He's crazy, that's for sure. So you want a boy? I want a boy, too, when I get married. They say there's men who feel the labor pains when their wife has a kid."

He is happy again and looks at the woman without the

slightest desire. His heart is pure, and he thinks with great tenderness about Maria das Dores, who is in Lapa waiting for him. He smiles because he thinks how surprised she will be to see him. What a shame his mustache hasn't really grown yet . . . It's still so short. She probably wouldn't recognize him at first.

"Do you think she'll know me?"

"Who?" Antônio Balduíno roused himself.

"Nothing. Just thinking."

The old man woke up, trembling with cold. The wind blew, announcing a storm. It enveloped the train, making it sway on the tracks.

"This thing will end up turning over with us inside," said Antônio Balduíno.

"Poor people have to suffer. Some are born to have fun, they're the rich ones. Others are born to suffer: the poor. It's been like that since the world began."

Now the ex-soldier was happily asleep, snoring soundly. He didn't hear the wind whistling past.

"There's going to be a heavy rain," said the old man as he limped to the door and peered out.

"I came from a place, uncle, where the people were really miserable. They earned ten cents a day."

"The tobacco plantations?"

"That's right."

"You have no idea, son. I've lived here years and years. I've seen things to make your hair stand on end. You know something?" A strange light comes into his eyes, and he moves his staff away so as to stand up. "Poor folks are so unfortunate that when shit is worth money, their assholes tighten up."

Antônio Balduíno laughed. The old man lost his balance and rolled on top of the bundles of tobacco. The woman helped him up.

"Hurt yourself?"

The soldier snores. The woman comes closer to Antônio Balduíno and says in a low voice, "I didn't tell him so he wouldn't be sad." She points to the ex-soldier. "But to tell you the truth, I don't really know why Romualdo left me. Maybe it was on account of being so poor. That's what I think. A neighbor woman said that he left me for another girl, somebody called

Dulce . . . do you suppose he did?'' Her voice grew louder. ''But that wasn't it. He wouldn't leave me like this.''

The soldier slept happily as a dead man.

''This way, carrying a kid. But why did he leave?''

Antônio Balduíno lighted a match, and in its glow he saw that the woman was crying, her shoulders shaking. Confused, the black man tried to find something to say and murmured, ''Don't worry. It'll be a boy.''

CHAPTER 18
Circus

The encounter with Luigi was entirely by chance. Antônio Balduíno had spent the rest of the night bumming about Feira de Santana. The ex-soldier had taken the road to Lapa at once, the old man had found a place to stay, and the woman had gone to look up a girl friend. In the morning, Antônio Balduíno tried to hitch a ride to Bahia in a truck. He came up to one that was loading and said casually to the driver, "You going to Bahia, brother?"

"Sure am," answered the driver, a thin, smiling mulatto. "Want to send something?"

"Yeah, I want to send this black man here," he said, tapping his chest and grinning.

"Bahia is a damn good place to be now, with all the festivals."

Antônio Balduíno jumped up beside the driver, accepting a cigarette.

"I miss the place, brother . . . it's been almost a year since I left there."

The driver sang.

"Bahia is a lovely place,
As long as I'm somewhere else."

"Aw, don't say that. Bahia is good. I'm dying to get back."

"Want to go today in my truck? I'm leaving after lunch."

"But I haven't got a red cent, man."

"Spent it all on the women?" The driver laughed.

"Who knows?" Balduíno winked.

"No problem. I'm not taking anyone along. You can be my assistant."

"Fine."

"If we get stuck, you can help push."

"What time you leaving?"

"After lunch. One o'clock, one-thirty."

"Okay, I'll see you then."

"Where you going?"

"To see some friends."

"One o'clock, here."

"Good enough."

Antônio Balduíno wandered through Feira de Santana. He didn't have any friends to visit, but he didn't want the driver to know that he wasn't going to eat lunch. He would eat dinner in Bahia, though, either with Gordo or with Joaquim, or perhaps even with Jubiabá. He walked along thinking these things, and as he was bumming a cigarette he heard someone shout, *"Per la Madonna!* It's Baldo!"

He turned around. In front of him was Luigi, sparse-haired and dressed in worn-out clothes.

"Luigi!"

Luigi grabbed him by the shoulders, spun him around and said happily, "Magnificent!"

"What are you doing here, Luigi?"

"Ill winds, my friend . . . ill winds."

"What the hell does the wind have to do with it?"

"After you threw over your career, Baldo, things never went well for me again."

He looked at the Negro sadly.

"Such a fine career you had going . . . a shame. You threw it all away and never even said where you were going."

"I got mad that time when I got beat."

"Nonsense, nonsense! What boxer doesn't lose a fight once in a while? Besides, you were drunk as a pig."

"But what are you doing in these parts, Luigi? You got a new fighter?"

"Fighter? There will never be another one like you."

Antônio Balduíno laughed, satisfied, and punched Luigi playfully on the chest.

"Never again . . . I'm with a circus now."

"Circus?"

"A terrible business. I can't even tell you."

They went into a bar. Luigi ordered coffee, and Antônio Balduíno said, "Buy me some cigarettes. I'm down to nothing, Luigi."

He knew he could talk frankly to the Italian. He remembered something and said, "You were the only one who didn't appear to me when I was surrounded in the jungle, as good as dead."

"I didn't know about that! What happened?"

"Nothing. I was almost dying of hunger. I saw everyone, you know, Luigi? They came to pester me, singing songs about the dead. You're the only one who didn't."

Luigi still hadn't understood properly. Antônio Balduíno narrated his fight with Zequinha, the flight through the jungle, his visions. He spoke somberly, without details, because he was dying to find out about the circus.

"What kind of business is it, the circus?"

Luigi shook his head sadly.

"It's just awful, a real mess. When you left, I was out of a job."

"You lost everything?"

"That's about it. That was when this circus turned up, the Grand International Circus. It belonged to a countryman of mine named Guisepe. He made money in Bahia, but he had all kinds of problems, debts galore. I went in with him as a partner. What a rotten businessman! We've been in some real holes . . . *per la Madonna!* The circus doesn't pay anything, and the overhead is beastly. We hardly cover expenses. We're almost broke."

Luigi waved his hands, describing the details. Antônio Balduíno said, "It's the devil, all right."

Luigi looked at him again and said, "But I have an idea that might change things. I need you."

"Me? I was never a circus performer."

"You weren't a boxer, either, and I got you started."

They both smiled, remembering old times. By the time they finished their coffee, Antônio Balduíno was hired by the Grand

International Circus as a fighter. The Negro went back to see the truck driver.

"I'm not going to Bahia after all, brother."

"Women won't let you?" The driver laughed.

"Who knows?" The Negro winked.

Balduíno's verbal contract with Luigi affirmed that he would have room and board and money when there was any. The money made little difference to Antônio Balduíno.

The sign was still lying on the ground. The large blue letters read:

GRAND INTERNATIONAL CIRCUS

Beside the signboard was Guisepe, sleeping like a pig.

"Drunk again," said Luigi. "That's how he always is."

He pushed him with one foot. Guisepe incoherently murmured some words, "I ask you to be silent . . . it's time for the death-defying leap . . . one word and the great artist . . . can lose . . . his life."

Some men were digging holes in the ground. Others were setting up the grandstand. They all worked, artists, grooms, roustabouts. Luigi took Antônio Balduíno to his quarters. The first thing the black man saw was his picture in fighting gear as it had appeared in the Bahia newspapers.

Luigi sank down on his bed, which was nothing more than a divan that also went on stage for the Snake-Man's act, and continued to explain to Antônio Balduíno, "Five contos to whoever wins. Nobody will dare to fight, you'll see."

"But there has to be a fight, or else the crowd'll get mad."

"Who said there wouldn't be? We'll hire somebody for twenty mil-reis. There'd be plenty of takers. You'd give 'em a professional thrashing."

"And what if it's somebody who's really out to beat me?"

"It won't be."

"But what if it is?"

Luigi pointed to the picture on the wall.

"Aren't you a fighter anymore, man?"

Antônio Balduíno nodded, stroking the picture and whistling.

Luigi commented, "You think it's all behind you? Then you're getting old."

"In those days I didn't have this scar on my face."

"It'll be good to impress people."

Someone was knocking at the door. Luigi opened it. It was a little woman complaining about her salary, which she hadn't received for the last month and a half.

"I won't go on working this way! Don't expect to see me tomorrow."

"But tomorrow you'll get paid, my dear."

"Every day the same story, every single day! 'Tomorrow you'll get paid.' For two months now I've been hearing the very same thing. Well, I'm tired of it! Don't look for me tomorrow."

"But tomorrow you really will get paid. You don't know what's going to happen." He turned to Balduíno. "This is Fifi, our trapeze artist. She's a little upset."

The little woman looked at the Negro.

"And this is the celebrated Baldo. I'm sure you've heard of him."

The woman never had, but she nodded her head yes. Luigi spoke quickly to impress yer.

"That's right . . . the greatest fighter in Brazil. In Rio there was no one who could match him. He's just arrived from Bahia today; I sent for him, and he hired a car and hurried over."

The woman was suspicious.

"What did you use to hire this phenomenon, Luigi? Sounds like a lie to me. I bet anything I've seen that black man driving a truck around here. Look here, mister, if you left your job thinking you're going to earn money here, you're mistaken. Money's something nobody has in this circus."

She whirled around and started toward the door. But Antônio Balduíno was quicker, and he grabbed her angrily by the arm.

"Just a minute, lady. I really am a boxer. I was Bahian champion of all weights. Don't you see there on the wall? That's my picture."

The woman looked and was convinced.

"Oh, well, then . . . but why did you come here? You sure won't make any money."

"I came to help out a friend." He patted Luigi on the shoulder. "A true friend."

"Oh! Well, if that's how it is—"

"And tomorrow you'll see money by the bucketful."

The woman was all apologies.

"There's a truck driver who could be your twin. He really looks just like you."

She was still smiling from the door. Antônio Balduíno looked at Luigi.

"That talk about Rio didn't stick, brother."

Luigi was writing the announcement for the next day's circular. Balduíno read over his shoulder.

"I want my name in nice big letters . . . this size." And he opened his arms to show the size they should be.

When he recovered from his drinking bouts, Guisepe became active and resolute. It seemed he would take care of everything, resolve the difficult situation of the circus, pay the crews' and artists' salaries. But his activity was limited to liberal gestures and extravagant words.

"Let's get going here. You're not working. The gallery should be set up already! You're getting me into a panic. Without me, nothing goes forward!"

And when an artist complained, "All you know how to do is ask for money! Isn't art worth anything? In my time, we would work for the sake of art, for the applause, for the flowers. Flowers, do you hear? The young girls used to throw us flowers. Embroidered handkerchiefs, too. I could have a whole collection of them if I wanted. But I care nothing for these things. In those days one thought about art. A trapeze performer was an artist!" He turned to Fifi. "Do you hear me? An artist!"

Fifi would get angry.

He continued, "And today, what do I see? A girl like you, who is actually promising, talks only of money, as if the applause meant nothing."

"I can't eat applause."

"But it's for the glory of it. Man shall not live by bread alone. It was Christ Himself who said that."

"Christ was not a trapeze artist."

"These days . . . now, in my time . . . applause, flowers, handkerchiefs, you see, all those things had their value. So you want money, is that it? All right, tomorrow you'll have your money. I'll pay you everything, everything."

But he would always end up saying, "You know, Fifi, we're not doing too well. What can I do, poor wretch that I am? I'm just an old artist. I've been all over Europe. I have my photo albums over in my tent. Now here I am, and I have to get along as best I can. Do you think I have money? All I have are debts. Be patient, Fifi. You're a good girl."

"But Guisepe, I don't even have a decent costume. My green outfit is shameful. I can't appear in it anymore."

"I promise the first money we earn will go to you."

And he would go out to give useless orders, complain about the delayed work, inspect what Luigi had done, disagree with everything, and finally enter a bar where he would recount, to any stranger who would buy him a drink, his glories as a trapeze performer.

One night when he was staggering back to the circus wagons, having marked the foreheads of several boys with charcoal so they could get into the show for free, he met Antônio Balduíno. The black man appeared to be contemplating the stars, though he was actually spying on Rosenda Rosedá, the black ballerina who was one of the principal attractions of the Grand International Circus. By the light of the candle inside her tent, he had seen the black girl changing her clothes, and her back looked like velvet. The Negro was singing one of his best sambas:

"My girl is made of velvet,
So soft she makes me tremble."

When he saw Guisepe coming, he pretended to be looking at the stars. Which one was Lucas da Feira? Once they had shown him the star into which Zumbi dos Palmares was transformed, but it isn't shining here. It only shines in Bahia; on macumba nights, when the Negroes worship Oxóssi, god of the hunt.

Zumbi's star watches over Negroes, shines when they're happy, grows dim when they are sad. Was it Gordo who had told him that story? No, it was pai Jubiabá, one night on the docks. If it were Gordo, he would have put in an angel. Pai Jubiabá was the one who knew things about Zumbi dos Palmares and other great and valiant Negroes. He might just as well take another peek at Rosenda Rosedá, because Guisepe is weaving about so much he won't be here soon. But she has put out the light and disappeared. If it weren't for Guisepe—that drunk!—he would have seen her naked. She would be a real catch. The circus might not have money, but as long as she stayed Antônio Balduíno would stay, too. What a gorgeous girl! At the Drowned Man's Lantern she would be a howling success. They'd all sit there with their jaws dropping off.

Guisepe came up. When he went to shake hands with the Negro, he almost lost his balance.

"I'm so tired. The work kills me. I work like a dog around here."

"Anyone can see."

He went on by. It took him almost half an hour to get to his quarters.

He's liable to set fire to the tent when he lights his candle, thought Antônio Balduíno as he approached. But Guisepe had lighted the candle and was now sitting at a small rickety table. On it were some beautifully bound books, damaged by time. Curiosity absorbed the black man, who spied on him like a thief. What was there in those books that made Guisepe caress them with so much love? He touched them the same way Balduíno touched the flesh of a girl's thigh, stroking them gently, carefully, luxuriously. But when Guisepe turned around, Antônio Balduíno saw his eyes. There are men who grow sad when they drink; others grow happy, laugh and sing. But Guisepe is one of those who get sad and start crying. Antônio Balduíno couldn't resist; he went into the tent of the sad, drunken Italian.

It was in Italy, and it was springtime. The man there in the album, the one with the mustaches, was his father. His whole family were circus owners. In the oldest photo, the one yellowed with time, was his grandfather in uniform. He wasn't a general; he was the owner of the circus, the Grand International Circus. But back then it was a real circus. The lions alone numbered more than thirty. Twenty-two elephants, tigers . . . all sorts of animals.

"I had a few drinks, but I'm not lying."

Antônio Balduíno believes him. His father's mustache was admired. He was a boy, but he still remembered. When his father climbed up on the trapeze, it seemed that the circus would fall down from the roars of applause. The crowds would go wild. And his leaps from one trapeze to another, the death-defying leap through the air, three somersaults without anything to hang onto . . . it was enough to stop people's hearts. His mother was a tightrope walker. She dressed in blue and looked like a fairy godmother. She would balance herself with a Japanese parasol. He was from a family of circus people and inherited everything when his father died. Countless lions, trained horses. He used to pay a fortune in salaries to the performers, the most famous ones in Europe.

"And they were all paid on Saturday. There was never a delay."

One day the king, the king himself, had come to his circus. What a day that was! He knew Antônio Balduíno didn't believe him, because here he was, drunk and poorly dressed. But he had been applauded by the king and not the king alone. The whole royal family, who had sat in the most luxurious box seat. It was springtime in Rome. When the king appeared, Holy Mary, what a sight. He had never seen anything like it.

"I thought the applause would never end."

His picture from those times was there in the album. Yes, dressed in a swallowtail coat. That was how he went into the ring. Then he would remove his clothes piece by piece. The coat, the trousers, the starched shirtfront. He was soon dressed only in his leotard, as he appeared there in his other photo. And he was handsome, nothing like now. These days he was a skeleton. But back then, the women would go wild. There was a blond countess, covered with jewels, who had set up a rendezvous with him.

"And did you go to bed with her?" The black man was interested.

"A gentleman doesn't tell such things."

The king, with the entire royal family, was seated in the best box. Guisepe gave the double death-defying leap and—maybe Balduíno didn't believe it—the king couldn't contain himself, he stood up to clap. What a night that was! And Risoleta had looked prettier than ever. Their performance together was a great success. She had sold photos of the two of them to the spectators, that picture right in the center page of the album. In it Antônio Balduíno could see a woman bowing to acknowledge the public's applause, her hand held by a man dressed in a sort of bathing suit. If one looked closely, the man was recognizable as Guisepe.

"What a woman!" said Antônio Balduíno.

"She was my wife."

She sold that photo to the spectators, and there wasn't one left over. For wasn't it springtime, and she as beautiful as the blossoming flowers? She herself was a spring flower, and all the Romans wanted a souvenir of the season, which was ending. They bought her photograph. In another snapshot, she was standing, one leg raised, on a horse named Jupiter which was worth a lot of money. He had been left with a creditor in Denmark when the circus was there. That picture of Risoleta on the horse was taken just a few days before she fell. She was so beautiful that spring, so young, and nobody would have imagined that such an absurd accident could come about. Guisepe had never dreamed it could happen. "She fell down. That night there were so many people at the circus that it looked like a sea." The two of them were the big attraction that spring. Everyone talked about *I Diavoli*, the name by which they were known. When Risoleta appeared in the street, the ladies would stop to look at her. They imitated her dresses, because she knew how to be elegant; she was pretty outside the circus, too. The men were wild for her. The two of them were the success of the season, and spring was flowering in Rome. On that night the circus was packed.

"This picture shows her dressed to go out."

Guisepe looked at the picture, then walked to the bed and brought back a bottle of rum.

"Rum from Santo Amaro, eh?" Balduíno laughed.

Guisepe really was drinking too much. He didn't take his eyes off the woman's picture. But Antônio Balduíno saw that she had the sad face of a prisoner. Guisepe knew very well she didn't like circus life, that she had ambitions to enter society, go about well dressed and elegant, cause a furor among the men. But who could have guessed she would fall that night? They hadn't broken a mirror or anything. They entered the ring to thunderous applause. She bowed to the audience, and they climbed up. At first, everything went fine. But when they were executing the death-defying leap . . . Nothing like that had ever happened before. The trapeze didn't swing far enough. She couldn't catch Guisepe's legs . . . she was dashed to pieces on the ground. Even the time Rex the lion mauled John, the English lion tamer, it hadn't been so ugly. Risoleta had become a pile of flesh without face, without arms, without anything. Guisepe couldn't understand how he had the strength to come back down, why he didn't fall, too. Outside, it was springtime, and couples were going by. Afterward, the clown said that Guisepe had done it on purpose because he knew she had a lover. They went so far as to conduct an inquiry, but nothing was discovered. The decline of the Grand International Circus began on that day.

"It's like a novel," affirmed Balduíno. "All you need to do is write it. I'll tell Gordo."

"But do you think she had a lover? They said she did—they found the letters he wrote to her with her other things—but it was a lie, wasn't it? Circus people are rotten. You can't trust circus people. They're envious. She couldn't have had a lover! They were just jealous of her success. What makes me angry, what makes me drink, is to think that she could really have had a lover. There were the letters. But she was so good. Mind you, she didn't like that life. But she wasn't the type of woman to have an affair. Still, there were those letters. They talked about rendezvous. I just wish she was alive to tell me it was all a lie, all people's envy. Don't you think it was?"

Was he going to cry? He held his head in his hands and closed his eyes. Now it was Antônio Balduíno's turn to take the bottle of rum and drink an enormous gulp. Outside, it was another spring night.

* * *

"And the clown, what does he do?"

"He steals other men's wives!"

"Even that fat woman standing in the doorway?"

"She's not standing there, she's stuck!"

Bozo the clown is riding backward on a donkey. The circus dominates the lower end of town. Its numerous flags are flying, and there are two advertisements at the entrance. The band will play there in the evening, and black women will sell coconut candy. The city talks of nothing but the circus, the artists, the black woman who dances almost naked, and especially the boxer, Baldo, who challenges the men of Feira de Santana. The men comment about it in the big market. Luigi waited until Monday to launch his surprise, because on Mondays there was a cattle sale, and men came from all over the surrounding area to bring their cattle. The clown is crossing Market Square.

"Is there a show today?"

"Yes, sir!"

Boys in from distant ranches to sell molasses-sugar and cheese look enviously at the city urchins, who are following the clown and who will get into the circus for free. One fellow says to his friend, "Oh, I sure do love a circus!"

"I saw one once, one called the European. It was fun!"

"They say this one is good."

"At least it's big. If that clown is for real . . ."

"I'm going to stay overnight here so I can go."

"They say there's no more seats; they're all sold out."

Urchins plan to sneak in underneath the tent flaps. The clown continues his glorious parade among the country people. Employees of the commercial establishments peer out. In the middle of the marketplace, the clown stops and asks for silence.

"Ladies and gentlemen! Baldo, world champion of free-style fighting, boxing and *capoeira,* who has come from Rio de Janeiro ex-press-ly"—(he accentuated the expressly)—"to work in the Grand International Circus, earning three contos a month, board and room, and laundry privileges—"

"Wow," murmured a country boy.

". . . has the pleasure to challenge any man of this heroic city to a boxing match in the circus arena tonight, or during the time the circus is here. If there's a man among you who can beat Baldo, the circus will give him the amount of five contos-de-reis. Five contos-de-reis,'' he repeated at the top of his lungs. ''And Baldo is betting another conto that he can't be beaten. Is there someone who will take advantage of this opportunity? I announce in advance that two men have already come to the circus office to challenge the great champion, and he has accepted. Whoever wants to fight has only to appear at the Grand International Circus tonight. It will be a fight to the death, ladies and gentlemen! A fight to the death!''

And, as if he weren't tired of his speech, he continued riding through the city, mounted facing the animal's rear. The donkey would balk from time to time, and the clown would pretend to fall, holding onto its tail. He made the entire city laugh and gave the same discourse wherever people were gathered.

The whole town was talking about the perilous fight that was to take place. Everyone soon knew that a chauffeur, a store clerk, and a huge farmhand were disposed to accept the challenge of Baldo, the black giant, in the dispute for the five contos. Night fell on a nervous town.

When the farm laborer entered the ring, a wisecracking boy up in the gallery pointed at him and yelled, ''Hey, Joe, you know that pair of monkeys you ordered? The male one is here!''

Everyone laughed. The gigantic man started to get angry, but he ended up laughing, too. He was wearing sandals and carrying a staff, and laughed to think about the five contos-de-reis he would win fighting that fellow Baldo. In the country, he cut down trees with very few ax strokes and carried their vast trunks across enormous distances. And when he sat down, his smile was victorious, although modest and suspicious.

Black men entered, carrying chairs for the families who had box-seat tickets. The circus had no chairs; the spectators brought their own.

''That's why I always sit in the stands. It's cheaper, and you don't have to bring anything, just your body.''

''There comes the judge's houseboy.''

A black boy came in, placed the chairs in the box, went out for another load, and then accommodated himself in the stands.

Catcalls went up for a fellow who sat in a box: "Ooooooh! Chico the fish peddler! In a box, eh? Coming up in the world, eh, Chico?"

Outside, the lights and colors were beautiful. The signboard—GRAND INTERNATIONAL CIRCUS—shone in red, blue, and yellow, its light bulbs blinking. Black women in petticoats and necklaces were selling *popcoran, acarajé, mingau,* and *munguzá.* The whole square was illuminated by the circus lights. Urchins hung about the places where they might get in for free. There was sugar-cane syrup for sale, and a black ice-cream man was dying to sell his whole supply of ice cream, so he could hurry into the stands. He laughed heartily, enjoying in advance the jokes of the clown, who was so funny. People were crammed into line to buy cheaper tickets, and Luigi was rubbing his hands with joy. The old ladies were alarmed with all the excitement in their peaceful town, which normally went to sleep by nine o'clock. The circus revolutionized things, for a circus means news, travels, wild animals from other countries, adventure. Black men invented stories about the performers.

The music starts. The band is turning down the Rua Direita, and the sound of a carnival march can be heard. In the circus everyone stands up. Those who are on the top benches of the grandstand spy over the top of the sides of the canvas tent. The urchins at the entrance of the circus run after the Seventh of September Marching Band, who are coming, spruce and military, dressed in green and blue. Mr. Rodrigo from the drugstore is a fine man on the flute. The cornet's notes vibrate in the air and strike the ears of Antônio Balduíno, who runs out of his tent to see the musicians. A smart-looking bunch! They're so well dressed! That man marching backward is the director. Antônio Balduíno would happily have traded places with the thin man who walks backward, directing the Seventh of September Marching Band. It really is wonderful, thinks the Negro. Look how all the girls are watching that fellow! Everyone. He really is a hero of the city, a glory to Feira de Santana. The flutist is, too. Everybody knows them and greets them. The judge takes off his hat to them, and when the boys from the bank go on a partying spree, they invite the flutist to go with them, pay for his drinks, and treat him like an equal, as long as he brings his flute. But Guisepe jolts Antônio Balduíno out of his contemplation of the band. The Negro goes to his tent, carrying in his heart the desire to be a band director. The Seventh of September Marching Band enters the square where the circus is. Surrounded by people, they feel important, conscious of their prestige. At the entrance of the Grand International Circus, the director gives an order, and all the musicians stop. Everyone hears the military march the band executes at the circus entrance: the people in the grandstand, in the gallery, in the boxes, in the performers' tents. They all think it's divine, that Feira de Santana has, without doubt, the best musical group in the State of Bahia. The march completed, the musicians go into the circus and install themselves near the entrance on some board seats placed there especially for them. Now that the band has arrived, the spectators shout for the show to begin, for they've been waiting for a long time.

"Clowns! We want the clowns!"

The children scream, the men scream, and even the judge consults his watch and says to his wife, "They are five minutes late. Punctuality is a great virtue."

But Mrs. Judge isn't impressed; she is already tired of her husband's maxims. In the neighboring box, a group of store clerks, who pooled their resources to come, comment on the fight.

"D'you think it'll really be to the death?"

"Naw, the police won't let them."

"But they say this Baldo is a real animal. Agripino saw him fight in Bahia against a German. He said he's a bull of a man."

The people in the grandstand are stamping their feet. Grandstand people are ill-mannered, think the store employees. Whoever heard of a show starting on time? Grandstand people are vulgar. But the store clerks don't know anything. It's not for lack of manners that they are stamping their feet; they stamp, shout, and complain because they enjoy themselves all the more that way. A circus without wisecracks from the gallery, shouting, and complaints is no fun. All that is the best part of the circus: to get hoarse from shouting, to have sore feet from stamping on the boards of the grandstand.

A black woman yells, "Go pinch your grandmother's behind and leave mine alone!"

There is the beginning of a fight off to the left. That's what always happens when somebody bothers a married woman. A man falls off the gallery boards. But he gets up right away and goes back to his place, to violent catcalls and booing. Luigi came into the arena dressed in Guisepe's uniform, Guisepe being stewed to the gills. Silence fell over the circus.

"Honorable Public! Ladies and Gentlemen! The Grand International Circus thanks you for your presence at its opening show and hopes that its great artists will receive your genteel and benevolent applause."

Luigi played up his Italian accent to make a better impression. The roustabouts unrolled an old moth-eaten rug that covered the ring from one side to the other, and then the company was introduced, to hysterical applause. First Luigi came in, leading the horse Hurricane with his shiny saddle and bridle. Then came Fifi, the trapeze artist; the applause doubled. She was wearing a short green skirt that showed off her legs to the avid eyes of the Negroes, bank clerks, and judge. When she curtsied, the skirt went up another palm's breadth. The grandstand nearly collapsed under the noise. Bozo the clown came in doing pirouettes.

"Good evening to you all, folks."

Chuckles. He was dressed in wide blue breeches covered with yellow stars and sporting a red moon on the seat.

"I'm dressed like the sky with all the stars. This costume was given to me by my fairy godmother!"

He's so funny, that clown! The Snake-Man really looks like a snake in his skin-tight costume, covered with shiny, scalelike sequins. The costume outlines his body perfectly, and he seems sexless, like a little girl or a boy. All the men crack jokes until shouts for silence stop them. The fire-eater has red hair. The great juggler Robert enchants the women with his worn-out suit. To judge by the way they pronounce his name, he is French, and he has very straight hair, parted in the middle and plastered down on his head. Enchanting! He throws kisses, which are caught by the romantic damsels and clutched to their bosoms. An old maid sighs. "Pretty fellow," murmurs somebody in the general audience. Juju is hardly noticed because everyone is looking at the monkeys and the bear. The lion, in a cage at the back, howls lugubriously. Fiercely, too. A woman explains to her friend that she doesn't like to go to circuses because she is afraid of the lion getting loose. Lions make her nervous. Juju is getting old; she has wrinkles that the makeup can't hide, but still she has a well-built body. Rosenda Rosedá comes out dressed in a folkloric Afro-Bahian costume.

"Good evening, ladies and gentlemen!"

She runs leaping around the ring, her skirt lifting about her until it stands out straight like the circus tent itself. The men forget Juju, Fifi, the great juggler Robert, the bear, the lion, and even the clown; they see only the black Rosenda Rosedá, who wears a Bahian costume and sways her hips in a dance rhythm. Their eyes are full of lust. The store clerks lean forward in their box. The judge puts on his glasses. His wife says it's immoral. The black men in the general audience are already hoarse from shouting. Rosenda has conquered the public. Only Baldo, the Negro giant, hasn't appeared because he is behind the curtain holding back Guisepe, who wants to greet the public no matter what. The crowd screams for the Negro to appear.

"We want the fighter! We want the fighter!"

"Is he hiding?"

Luigi explains that Baldo, the Negro giant, the great world champion of boxing, free-style fighting, and *capoeira,* is doing his last-minute training and will appear at the time of the fight when he will take on the champions of this fair city. The company retires, and the show begins with Juju and her horse. Hurricane gallops around the ring. Juju has a whip in her hand and wears a vest. Her enormous bosom is squeezed into a tight blouse. She jumps up on the horse and rides standing on the animal's rump. For her, it is as simple as riding in a car. She turns a cartwheel on top of Hurricane. Clapping. She does more pirouettes and goes out of the ring as the people applaud.

"I've seen better things," says a man who is studied with admiration because he has traveled. He assures them he has been to Bahia and Rio.

"This stuff is worthless."

The men who want to applaud hesitate. But soon they lose

their shyness and clap loudly. After the band plays a samba, the clown somersaults into the ring. He argues with Luigi, grabs an open suitcase from which a pair of drawers hang visibly out, takes his cane, and starts to walk away. Then he does a few magic tricks.

Luigi asks him, "Did you go to school, Bozo?"

"Did I go to school! Why, I spent ten years studying Donkeology, and today I'm a renowned Doctor of Asininity!"

The crowd laughs uproariously.

"So tell me: In how many days did God make the earth?"

"I know—"

"So tell me."

"I know, but I'm not telling, so there, I don't want to."

"You don't know."

"Who said I don't know? I do so. Who said? I'll punch him in the face!"

And so, saying things like this, the clown made the people happy on the opening night of the circus. The store clerks laughed, the judge tittered, the black men in the grandstand let out peals of mirth. Only the man who had traveled thought it was worthless and that he had thrown away his ten cents. But he had long since lost his purity in the large cities where he was a student before his father died, and he had to get his hands dirty working for Mr. Abdula.

The monkey danced. The bear drank a bottle of beer. The asexual Snake-Man twisted himself all up in knots. It made one nervous. He put his head through his feet, turned his body to one side, and put his feet into his mouth. He lay down on top of a small box, touching it only with his feminine stomach, and brought his legs and head up to touch his back. He had a good act, but he irritated the men because he didn't have a defined sex, and they were uncomfortable not knowing if they should love him, think of him as a woman, or applaud him as one does a masculine hero. But in the eyes of the well-traveled man, a strange, criminal light was shining. The Snake-Man thanked them with his angelic face, threw kisses like Robert, the great juggler and bowed like Fifi the celebrated trapeze artist. The women caught the kisses, the men received the thanks. The well-traveled man left his place because, for him, the show was over. He carried his misery away with him in his heart and eyes and didn't sleep that night.

The great juggler Robert doesn't do his act this first night, to the disappointment of the women. In compensation, out comes the incomparable Rosenda Rosedá.

"The incomparable Rosenda Rosedá proudly appears before us at the golden peak of her career in the circus ring, to dance in a breathtaking torrent of ecstasy."

The breathtaking torrent is a wild *maxixe* dance. Could it be that under her wide, folkloric skirt she doesn't have anything on at all? It looks that way, because she shows her thighs halfway up, and nobody sees any bloomers at all. Around her neck she wears many strands of multicolored beads. Her legs do big *X*s. The judge's wife thinks that it's decidedly immoral and that the police shouldn't permit such things. The judge doesn't agree; he cites the Constitution and the Code, says that his wife isn't civilized, and doesn't want to talk. He wants to take a better look at the incomparable Rosenda Rosedá's legs. But now they all have something even better to look at, for she is shaking and rolling her hips. She has disappeared entirely; she is all hips. Her buttocks fill the circus, from the top of the tent to the dusty ring. Rosenda Rosedá dances. It is a mystic macumba dance, a sensually religious dance, fierce like the dances of the virgin forest. She is showing off her body, but it is hidden from the men; it hardly appears. Her skirt covers and camouflages her body. The men are irritated and concentrate on looking, but it's useless. The dance is too fast, too religious, and they are dominated by it. Not the white men, who are still fascinated with the thighs, buttocks, the sexiness of Rosenda Rosedá. But the Negroes are hypnotized. They lose themselves in the movements, the rhythm and cadence of the religious dance, a wild *maxixe,* and they think that she is possessed by some spirit. She reaches the golden peak of her career when she rests her buttocks on her legs and hears the deafening applause of the audience, which is on its feet, oblivious to the march the band begins to play. And once again she dances her "torrent of ecstasy," the breathtaking *maxixe,* religious dance offered by black people in macumba sessions to the gods of war and the bladder. Her skirts fly, her breasts bounce beneath the necklaces under the judge's gaze. The legs and buttocks of the black people dance in the grandstand, which is threatening to collapse. She is at the golden peak of her career in the circus ring. The judge stands up to applaud, just like the king with Guisepe. From beneath her skirt, Rosenda takes some rose petals, which she throws at the judge's bald head. Luigi's idea. The moment is a moving one. She is at the golden peak of her career in the circus ring. And when the show is over, a Negro wearing sandals will come and pick up a few of those rose petals, which holds the smell of Rosenda Rosedá's body, and put them next to his heart before he goes back to the tobacco plantations.

The clown comes in again, and the men calm themselves once more and laugh. Then Luigi appears, announcing, "Ladeees and gentlemen! Baldo, the Negro giant, whom you know by name, challenges any man of this city to a fight, which will be to the death. The circus will give a prize of five contos-de-reis to the winner, and Baldo bets one conto-de-reis on his own victory."

A buzzing spreads through the crowd. Luigi goes out of the ring and comes back with Antônio Balduíno, who wears over his muscular body a tiger skin that is much too small for him and hampers his movements. He crosses his arms upon his chest and looks at the spectators with a challenging expression. He knows that Rosenda is watching, so he wants to look like a real champion. She sold pictures and counted up the money in the tent. Then she said to him that she would watch the fight. However, up to now no one has accepted the challenge; Luigi explains to the honorable public that the two men who had come to the circus office hadn't shown up. If nobody came, Baldo would fight with the bear. But he had hardly finished speaking when the apelike farmhand got up and lumbered shyly into the ring.

"Is it true, this business about the five contos?"

"Absolutely true," said Luigi, shocked.

The man took off his sandals and shirt, leaving only his trousers. Luigi looked at Antônio Balduíno. The black man smiled to say that all was well. They brought a mattress into the middle of the ring, and Antônio Balduíno removed his tiger skin, wearing only a strip of bathing suit over his genitals. The scar on his face shone in the artificial light. The men applauded for the farmhand. Luigi again addressed the public, asking for a man who understood something of fighting to be the second referee.

One of the store clerks came down. He talked to Luigi, and they laid down the conditions. The Italian explained to the crowd, "The fight will end with the death or the surrender of one of the contestants."

He made the introductions.

"Baldo, the Negro giant, world champion of boxing, free-style fighting, and *capoeira,* the challenger."

He asked the peasant man something.

"Totonha de Rosinha, who accepts the challenge!"

Antônio Balduíno came to shake hands with the adversary. But the latter thought it was already the beginning of the fight and wanted to grapple with Antônio Balduíno. Luigi explained things to him and all was well. They stood on top of the mattress looking at each other.

Rosenda Rosedá watched Antônio Balduíno from behind. There weren't any five contos-de-reis for him, there wasn't even a salary, but there was the incomparable Rosenda Rosedá's warm body, and Balduíno felt happy. If he could have been the director of the marching band he would have been completely happy. The store clerk was counting.

"One, two, three . . ."

The peasant went after Balduíno, who ran around the mattress. The crowd booed the Negro, and Rosenda made a face at them. But suddenly Baldo turned around and punched Totonha smack in the face. The farmhand didn't even seem to feel it. He came after the Negro again, and Baldo barely managed to shove him back. This is a case for *capoeira,* thought Balduíno. He threw himself on top of the fallen peasant and socked his face. But Totonha grabbed Antônio Balduíno around the back with his legs and rolled over on top of him. This was when Antônio Balduíno saw that his adversary was an easy match. He didn't even know how to throw a punch; he had only brute force. When they got up, the black man drove home various punches, from which the farmhand failed to defend himself. They circled the mattress in this fashion until Totonho grabbed Antônio Balduíno by the waist, lifted him high in the air, and threw him on the ground as hard as he could. The black man was flattened out. He got up angry. Before he had been having fun, but now he was mad. He knocked the man over with a *capoeira* blow, got him by the arm, and twisted it cruelly. The peasant was pinned by the Negro's legs, and Baldo twisted his arm. The crowd applauded. The peasant yelled in pain and gave up the fight and the five contos. The audience booed as he left holding his arm, which looked broken. Antônio Balduíno bowed to the public and retired to much applause.

"The Negro's really good."

Behind the curtain he asked Rosenda, "How'd you like that?"

Her eyes were damp with enthusiasm.

An assistant came into the ring, carrying a board on which was written:

INTERMISSION

The people went out to drink sugar-cane syrup. The band played military marches.

Robert was one of the sergeants; Antônio Balduíno the other. The great juggler was extremely elegant in his French sergeant's uniform. However, Antônio Balduíno's was too small, having been made for the sword swallower who used to work in the circus years ago. It was far too tight for the black man, and the saber was ridiculously short. But if that were the only problem, all would have been well. The worst was that Fifi demanded to be paid her back salaries before she started the second half of the circus, in which the celebrated pantomime, "The Three Sergeants," would be acted. Luigi still hadn't figured up the circus's debts and didn't want to pay her until the next day. But Fifi wouldn't hear of it.

"Either you pay me now or I won't go out in the ring."

She had the part of the third sergeant and looked beautiful dressed in men's clothes. Red with rage, she threatened and shook her finger at Luigi. She ended up making him laugh uncontrollably.

"That uniform has taken you over. You're thinking you really are a sergeant."

"Don't you make fun of me, you hear?"

Guisepe came staggering in from the rear, talking about art and glory, and began to cry. Luigi begged Fifi to wait; he was going to figure up the accounts and pay her yet tonight. But the show had to go on! Just listen: The crowd was already impatient, stamping their feet and complaining. Luigi pulled at his sparse hair, almost desperate. Rosenda Rosedá was moved.

"Stop being such a wet blanket, girl! The show is going so well tonight. . . ."

Fifi knew that, she knew that. And she didn't like to be a wet blanket, either. Yes, the show had gone well; the applause was good. There was a big crowd. They were all happy and so was she. But folded against her breast was the letter from the headmistress of the school. And she had to be strong, she had to resist, she had to fight. It was two months since she had paid her daughter's tuition. If she didn't pay within ten days, the headmistress would send the girl back to stay with her. And she didn't want her daughter in the circus . . . anything but that! She must be strong, she had to be strong. But she couldn't look into the eyes of Luigi, who was pleading with her. Luigi had always been good to her, had really helped her. But if she didn't demand her money, he would soon postpone it until the next day, and the next day the circus expenses would come up, and the girl would be sent here, and good-bye to all her plans, all her dreams, kept alive during these four long years in which she had been making such a sacrifice to pay for Elvira's schooling.

When her daughter was born, she had just read *The Death of the Virgin Elvira.* Now she didn't even have money to buy novels; she sent everything to the headmistress of the school, and even so, it hardly covered expenses. If she weren't strong, if she didn't resist, all the castles she had built at such a price would crumble to pieces.

The town would be small, even smaller than Feira de Santana. A position as a first-class teacher would be hard to get. But housing is cheap in such places. It would have a little garden in the front where she would cultivate flowers; carnations were her passion. There would be a bench where she could sit and read her old novels with their yellow covers. The school would operate in the house itself. Elvira would teach the children, and she would help her daughter with the domestic work, do the cooking and straighten the house, would put red carnations on the teacher's desk. She would be a grandmother to the children who would learn their ABCs from Elvira. She would know all the people in the city. No one would know she had been a circus performer, a singer in second-class variety theaters, a whore in her worst days. Her white hair would give her the maternal air of genteel poverty. Her old age would be a happy one. She would make lace—would she still remember how?—for the dresses of the smaller girls. Everyone would love her, especially Elvira. When she grew completely senile, Elvira would hold her head in her lap and stroke her hair, as she did with the children. The house would have a garden in the front with red carnations. But for all this to happen, she needed to be strong, not a wet blanket.

And, red with shame, she took out the headmistress's letter, unveiling her secret. Luigi was moved; he put his hands on her shoulders and promised, "Fifi, after the act, I'll pay you, I promise. Even if we don't have money to feed the lion."

The crowd was whistling, booing the assistants and looking at their watches. The pantomime began. For an hour, Antônio Balduíno had been kissing Rosenda Rosedá. The black man didn't know his part very well; he was never good at memorizing things, but during the kisses he remembered perfectly. He smiled and winked at Rosenda, who seemed to be no good, either. But when it was time to go out, the Negro gave the dancer a smacking kiss on the cheek and whispered in her ear, "On the mouth it's better."

The pantomime was a great hit.

Guisepe was probably in his tent looking over his photograph album again. Robert had gone to the local cabaret to pick up a woman for free with his straight hair. Fifi was writing a letter to the headmistress of the school apologizing for the delay in payment and sending the money for the past two months. By the light of the candle in the distant tent, Antônio Balduíno could see Luigi figuring up the accounts. Poor fellow, he wasn't doing well with the circus. No matter how successful it was, things were already in such a mess that nothing short of a miracle could straighten them out.

Why is Rosenda taking so long to change her clothes? He is waiting for her, leaning against the circus entrance, the board with the darkened lights just above his head. The lion roars. Hungry, probably. The lion is very thin, he's skin and bones. The bear is still happy because he gets to drink a bottle of beer on the nights he performs. Luigi once thought of substituting water for the beer. So he filled the bottle up, and though he managed to fool the spectators, he couldn't fool the bear, who refused to drink. The number was a fiasco. Antônio Balduíno was amused when Rosenda told him that story. She is taking forever to get dressed. Rosenda Rosedá, what an odd name. She really was called Rosenda. The Rosedá was Luigi's invention.

A determined girl, that one, capable of getting what she wanted out of anybody. She used hard words when she talked and told stories about the hillside slums in Rio: Favela Hill, Salgueiro Hill. She described parties at the clubs there, the Ameno Jasmineiro, the Caprichosas da Estopa, the Lírio do Amor. She had an elegant way of moving her hips when she walked; you could tell she was from Rio. The truth was, Antônio Balduíno liked the girl. She was vain and silly, and every time the Negro thought he had her in his hands, she would slip away, but he was getting very fond of her. Isn't she ready yet? Why has she put out the light and opened the curtained doorway? She appears in the bright light.

"I was waiting for you."

"For me? Goodness, who'd have thought it."

They went for a walk, he telling of his adventures in the great world, she listening attentively. Enthusiastically, he recounts his flight through the jungle, the circle closed about him, the men dumbfounded when they saw him holding the razor. She moves close against the black man; her breasts touch his arm.

"It's a pretty night," he says.

"So many stars . . ."

"Brave black men turn into stars in the sky when they die."

"I still want to dance in a big theater, a real one. Like the ones in Rio."

"What for?"

"I love to dance. When I was a little girl, I used to keep the pictures of all the theater artists. Papa was a Portuguese, and he had a little store."

Rosenda Rosedá's hair is straightened with an iron. It is very straight, like a white woman's. Even straighter.

"What a silly girl," thinks Antônio Balduíno. But since he can feel her breasts against his arm, he says that she is really a sensation when she dances.

"Did you see? The people went crazy. They were all clapping."

She snuggles closer. He convinces her.

"I really like to see the *maxixe* danced right."

"I'd like to go on the stage. A man who used to live near us knew one of the doormen at the Recreio Theater. But Papa wouldn't let me go. He wanted to marry me off to a clerk he had, a smelly rat—"

"And you didn't want to tie the knot?"

"I'm not that stupid! I couldn't stand him. A Portuguese . . ." She seemed to have something else to tell.

Antônio Balduíno asked, "What is it?"

"After that I met Emanuel. Papa said he was a tramp without a cent to his name. And he was. He had nothing to live on. Just about like you, honey! Anyway, he took a liking to me. We danced in the Ameno Club and caused a real scandal. The old man got pissed off on account of the Portuguese guy, who really liked me a lot. He cursed me and put me out into the street."

"So what did you do?"

"First I went to live on the hill with Emanuel. But when he got drunk, he liked to beat up women. The very first time I packed my stuff up and got out. After that, I had to take whatever bones were tossed. I worked as a cook, a chambermaid, a nursemaid. It was a clown in a circus in Rio who got me started in this life. We were sweethearts and finally started to live together. There was this Spanish girl who was supposed to dance to the castanets, and one day she didn't show up. So I danced in her place. You should have seen the hit I made! But I had a fight with the clown and went to work for another circus. I ended up in this one, and here I am."

"Uh huh." Antônio Balduíno can't think of anything else to say.

"But one day I'm going on the stage for real. Even black as I am. Why not? In Europe there's a black actress, and all the white men just follow her around. A lady I used to work for told me—"

"I've heard of her."

"So, I'll get there. You're going to hear a lot about me someday."

Antônio Balduíno smiles. "You're like the moon."

"Good heavens, why?"

"Because you seem close to the rest of us, but you're really far away."

"I'm awfully close to you."

The black man squeezes Rosenda Rosedá's waist. But she runs to her tent.

Now he is at the city's sad nightclub. Today there are more people because of the circus; usually everyone goes home to bed at nine o'clock when the church bells ring. The elegant Robert is sitting at a table watching a woman who is dancing. Antônio Balduíno sits down.

Robert asks him, "You come to find a woman, too?"

"No. I came to have a drink."

The women are few in number and almost all old. Even the one Robert is watching is getting up in years; her makeup is heavy. Scattered among the tables, they smile at the men.

"Why don't you invite that one to sit down with you?"

"I'm ready to."

But there is a virgin in the corner. Why has that idea lodged itself in Antônio Balduíno's head? He has been drinking tonight, but he doesn't remember ever getting drunk on two glasses of rum. So why does he think that the girl with the straight hair and pallid face is a virgin? She sits in the corner, not looking at anyone or anything. She seems distant from the cabaret, the customers, the drink in front of her. If Gordo were there, Antônio Balduíno would ask him to invent a story about the abandoned girl who has no guardian angel, nobody in the world. And if Jubiabá were there, he would ask the pai-de-santo to cast a spell on the man who is exploiting the virgin, who makes her come to the nightclub and drink those drinks. Antônio Balduíno looks at Robert, who is winking at the old broad. Maybe the girl isn't a virgin, but who could possibly not see that she is a virgin and that a man is exploiting her? She is in the cabaret, at the table in the corner, but her eyes are not looking at anything; they are lost in something beyond the window. She must be thinking about her little brothers she left alone, about her sick mother. Her father is already dead. Is that why she is here?

She has come to sell her virginity tonight so she can buy medicine. For isn't her mother sick, almost dead, and without a doctor, without a single drop of medicine? Antônio Balduíno thinks about going up to her and offering her some money. The truth is, he hasn't a cent, but he would steal it from Luigi. A store clerk has asked her to dance. It's a tango. She is going to sell her virginity to whoever gives her the most money. But what does she understand about money? She might not even get anything, and her mother might die just the same.

Everything is useless. Her mother will die and the little brothers, too, from malaria, for their bellies are bloated and their faces pale. Some man or other—why not Robert the juggler?—will exploit her, will sell her young virgin body in the market. He will offer it to the peasants, the truck drivers, to all the men. She'll fall in love with the flute player, and Robert will beat her up; one day she'll die of tuberculosis like her mother, but she won't have a daughter who will sell herself for the money to buy her medicine. Balduíno will steal Luigi's money, the money for the lion's food, but he won't let her lose her virginity. He pushes himself forward and claps a hand on her companion's shoulder.

"Leave her alone."

"Mind your own business!"

The woman's eyes are distant.

"She's a virgin, don't you see? She's trying to save her mother's life. But it's no good."

The man shoves the Negro away with one hand. Antônio Balduíno is so drunk that he falls on top of a table. He cries like a baby. The young man goes out with the girl who, once outside, says, "He's so drunk he thinks I'm a virgin."

But why is the man laughing? She wants to laugh, she wants to laugh a lot at the drunken Negro, but she can't; there's a lump in her throat. A sudden anguish takes hold of her. Without explanation, she abandons the uncomprehending man, who is still chuckling, and goes alone to her room where she sleeps the sleep of a virgin and does not wake because she drinks cyanide.

In the cabaret, Antônio Balduíno, drunker and drunker, sings amid applause and takes the old broad away from Robert the juggler. A fight almost breaks out with the owner of the nightclub because they have nothing to pay for the drinks with. When Antônio Balduíno gets back to the circus, he goes into Rosenda's tent; he has drunk so much in order to do just that.

Luigi spends all his time with a pencil in his hand, doing arithmetic. The lion's constant howling isn't from ferocity, for he is as tame as the horse Hurricane. He is howling from hunger, because the circus has no money to feed him.

All Luigi's calculations are pointless. For two days now, Guisepe hasn't drunk a drop, because he can't get money even for a shot of rum, and nobody will lend it to him anymore. And for Guisepe, life without rum is sad. Rum transports him into the past, brings back from the dead those he loved. Without alcohol he has to face up to the difficulties of the circus, the lack of money that turns the performers brutish and lazy. After the opening night, the circus hasn't had another full house. These two weeks in Feira de Santana have been bad. In two shows, the circus presented all its repertoire, and in two shows the whole population attended the circus. They only drew a decent crowd the following Monday—a batch of country people who stayed on after their marketing. Even so, there weren't many because there was no fight, and what they really liked was the fight. No other adversaries had shown up to challenge Antônio Balduíno. It was no good for the circus to increase the winner's prize to ten contos-de-reis, nor for Baldo, the boxer, to bet two contos on his victory. The Negro's fame had spread through the area, and nobody wanted to risk the shame of losing. Now Antônio Balduíno himself lifted poles for the sparse crowds, fought with the bear, who let himself get beaten very easily, and ended up accompanying Rosenda Rosedá on the guitar. For him, it mattered little whether money did or didn't exist.

There was Rosenda. He thought of nothing else. The nights with her were well worth putting up with Guisepe's drinking bouts, Robert's silence, and the complaints of Bozo, who was forever lamenting his life.

He had abandoned his studies in the second year, although he had gotten good marks in all the subjects, except Civil Law, which he barely passed because of the professor's persecution of him arising because of a catcall he gave once in class. Bozo's father appeared to be rich; everyone said he was rolling in money. Certainly, he spent it freely; he lived in an expensive rented house, bought a piano for his daughter, hired French and English teachers, made plans to travel to Europe. No one spoke of his heart trouble; he didn't know of it himself. He died suddenly when he was crossing the street. When they examined his affairs, they found he had left debts upon debts. That was how Bozo (using his old school nickname) had come to be in a circus ring, wearing a blue costume with yellow stars and a red moon on the seat of his pants.

He repeated this story daily and always finished by saying, "I could have graduated. I would have joined the police, I had talent for police work. By this time I could have been an officer."

Fifi would mutter that God gives to each his destiny. Antônio Balduíno would escape to Rosenda's tent where he would forget Bozo; forget Fifi, who wanted to have a happy old age; Guisepe, who wanted to die; Luigi, who did arithmetic; and Robert, who didn't say anything, not even complain about his salary.

In order for the circus to be able to travel to Santo Amaro, they sold the horse, Hurricane, and part of the boards from the grandstand. Luigi did more figuring. Nobody wanted to buy the lion, and the lion ate a great deal. One night Robert disappeared, no one knew to where. Luigi thought that he must have stolen some money from the small amount the Italian had put away in the tent for the next day's expenses. But Robert hadn't taken anything. He must have boarded the ship that left that night for Bahia. A man appeared to fight with Balduíno and was beaten in the first round; with the profits from this fight, the circus moved on to Cachoeira, passing once again through Feira de Santa in two trucks. When it had come the first time, it had occupied seven, and that was only because of Luigi's stinginess in crushing everything together to economize vehicles. Now they could fit into two trucks, and there was even space left over.

Guisepe remembered that when they traveled to France, they had possessed a real fleet, for they had two ships, and thirty-four enormous cars carried the performers across the land. Guisepe spent the whole trip boozing and remembering the great days of the Grand International Circus. Luigi pins his hopes on Cachoeira and São Felix. They are two neighboring cities, and São Felix has two cigar factories. Maybe he can even equip the circus in São Felix. But he is interrupted by Fifi, who asks how she is going to send money to her daughter's school this month. Luigi shrugs his shoulders.

"I don't even know how we're going to eat."

Bozo tells his life story once more to the Snake-Man, who listens indifferently. In the other truck, Antônio Balduíno and Rosenda Rosedá laugh loudly. Antônio Balduíno takes his guitar and sings a samba that starts like this: "Life is good, honey . . ."

Fifi doesn't agree, nor does Bozo. Guisepe cries; Luigi is impatient. Only the Snake-Man remains indifferent.

They set up the circus in São Felix. Circuses are a poor people's recreation, and São Felix is a city of factory workers. A Negro who used to be a sailor accepted the challenge to fight with Antônio Balduíno. The fight was vastly publicized. Luigi rubbed his hands together, satisfied with life, and could already listen to Antônio Balduíno's sambas without getting irritated. The clown went through the city, the men commented, the women laughed. On opening night, the front of the circus was all lit up, the band came with urchins trailing behind them, black women sold *munguzá* at the entrance. The important people brought chairs, and lots of people from Cachoeira came, too. Since the company was reduced without Robert and the horse Hurricane, Luigi didn't make introductions. Fifi came out first and walked on the tightrope. Then the clown entertained the spectators. Rosenda Rosedá danced. This time Antônio Balduíno didn't accompany her on the guitar because tonight he was Baldo, the Negro giant. Juju did an act with the monkey and the bear. Up above were some trapezes. Fifi was going to do another number to fill in the show. When the time came, the roustabouts prepared the trapezes, which swung back and forth in the air. Everyone looked up. Fifi came out in her green skirt, took a bow, and climbed up. She was testing the trapeze when a figure invaded the ring wearing a worn-out cashmere suit and weaving about as if drunk. It was Guisepe. Luigi started to go after him, but as the crowd was applauding, thinking it was another clown, he let him run through the arena and yell at the spectators, "She's going to fall! She's going to fall!"

The public laughed. And they laughed even harder when he affirmed, "I'm going to save the poor thing!"

Nobody could hold him back; it was too late. He climbed up the rope with an agility that nobody would have thought possible and loosened the other trapeze. Fifi, on the opposite side, stared at him in fright, not knowing what to do. The crowd didn't notice anything. Luigi and two of the assistants climbed up the trapeze. Guisepe let them get close, and when he saw they were almost next to him, he swung away on the trapeze, let go in midair, gave the most beautiful death-defying leap of his entire career, and searched with his anguished hands for the other trapeze. He fell into the ring, and his anguished hands, looking for the trapeze, seemed to wave farewell. Ladies fainted, people ran for the door, others went up to the body. His hands seemed to say good-bye.

PART III
The A.B.C. of Antônio Balduíno

CHAPTER 19
Winter

The winter washed everything away. It even washed away the spot of blood that remained in the place where the ring of the Grand International Circus had been. Luigi sold the grandstand boards and the big tent; the monkey went to one of the German factory owners. He distributed the money among the employees and declared the circus dissolved. Juju went off to the city of Bonfim where another circus was performing, to see if she could find a job. Before leaving, she said to the others, "I've never seen a circus as broke as this one. But even so, I liked it."

Luigi took the lion and Fifi and traveled through the cities of the interior, making shacks into theaters, charging five hundred mil-reis for an entry fee. The Snake-Man held a show for his own benefit in the local theater and then disappeared. Antônio Balduíno thought that if the Snake-Man went to the tobacco plantations, they would take him for a woman. At times he looked like a woman, and at other times like an adolescent boy. In Cachoeira the Negro had seen a man who had attended the circus's opening night in Feira de Santana. He was a well-traveled man who had been to Rio and Bahia, and he had left the circus right after the Snake-Man's number. He had fled in an automobile. Only later did they discover that the police were after him for robbing the money from a store where he was employed.

When Luigi divided up the things that he couldn't manage to sell, the bear went to Antônio Balduíno and Rosenda. Rosenda didn't realize that this had been shared between Antônio Balduíno and Luigi. The Negro said, "We can't cut the animal in two. I'm thinking we might be able to earn some money with him in the Água dos Meninos market."

"Or in the theater," ventured Rosenda.

"That, too," agreed the black man, who didn't want to fight.

At the docks, they learned that Mestre Manuel's sailboat would arrive in two days. So they waited for the *Homeless Traveler*.

But the winter churned up the river. Heavy rains darkened the face of the water. The river ran high, bringing trees it had uprooted on the plantations, bodies of animals, and once even a door that the water had ripped off a house. The crowns of rock had disappeared, and the men didn't go into the water to fish for their lunch anymore. The river was treacherous, growling like a wild animal from the jungle. Groups of people would watch it from the bridge as it curled by underneath, like a serpent. From above came the sweet smell of tobacco. The river had swallowed two sailboats this winter. One of the factory women wore mourning to work.

Great sheets of rain fall every night. In such weather there is no reason for Rosenda Rosedá to leave Dona Raimunda's boardinghouse, to invent this business of taking a walk. She has undoubtedly gone to Cachoeira. What she wanted was to leave Balduíno there like a fool, taking care of the bear, which is restless because of the rain that pours down on the roof with a sound like the river. The place smells of tobacco. They can't leave the bear alone, it is true. Buy why did she go out at this hour? Antônio Balduíno pounds his fist on the table. If she thought he was stupid, that he didn't see through her, she was wrong. Did she think he hadn't seen that German following them the night Guisepe died? He had been hanging around them ever since, trying to talk to them, saying things. Twice, Antônio Balduíno had wanted to collar him and ask him what he wanted. Now he remembers that one afternoon he said to Rosenda, "I'm going to ask that gringo if he ever saw me before."

Rosenda thought it wasn't worth it, that it was silly to fight, and that probably the gringo wasn't even looking at them. She had steered him away. When they want to, women can blind men's eyes, but now his eyes were wide open, and he understood. She had gone out to meet the white man. They would go somewhere, and she would open her thighs for him. What a shameless hussy! It was true she was exciting in bed, but he wasn't about to be made a fool of. He had always prided himself on leaving his lovers first, and Rosenda wanted to deceive him. Where was she? Had they gone to some hotel? They probably had, for the German had lots of money. But he would catch them and teach them a lesson. The rain falls on the roof. Is it really worth it to go out and look for them? Maybe it would be better to stay here, lock the door of the room, and make Rosenda sleep in the street. However, he has hardly formulated this thought when he begins to crave her slender, warm body. When she sleeps with a man, it is as if she were dancing. She knows things, that girl! Antônio Balduíno smiles. The night is cold, the rain pours down in sheets. A cat rubs against his legs, looking for warmth. The old bed is soft. A good mattress, the one in this room. There were lots of expensive hotels that didn't have a mattress as comfortable.

And Rosenda, in what sort of bed was she now, with her German? Maybe the mattress was hard. She deserved a beating. It wasn't worth it for a man to kill somebody because of a tramp like Rosenda. He had stabbed Zequinha, but Arminda was a girl of twelve who knew nothing about life. That Negro who killed a white man the other day went to prison for eighteen years, but Mariinha was a virgin and engaged to the Negro. What he should do was beat the German up and leave Rosenda. But it's so cold! He puts the cat on his lap. The contented animal rubs its head on his legs. This way he won't go out to look for them. The bear is restless. Maybe he is afraid of the rain, or maybe he misses someone. Can bears miss people? Poor bear . . . how many years has it been since he saw a female? Antônio Balduíno can't go a week without a woman; he smiles with satisfaction. Maybe the bear was castrated. He goes and examines it. It isn't castrated, nor is it a male. It's a female, that's what it is. What would he do with that bear in Bahia? It would be fun to turn it loose on Capa-Negro Hill. They would think it was a werewolf. The rain lessens. He gets up, shooing the cat off his lap. He would go look for Rosenda. But she has just come in, smiling to show off her white teeth.

At once she sees that Antônio Balduíno is angry. She smiles and comes up to him.

"You mad, honey? Was it the bear?"

"You're making a fool of me. You think I don't know you went to meet that gringo?"

"Good Lord, what gringo?"

Can it be genuine, the surprise stamped on her face? But Balduíno remembers that women are false, treacherous creatures. Every time he thinks about bad women, he remembers Amelia, the cook at the Comendador's house. Amelia would lie cynically, though from her face you would think she was telling the absolute truth. Rosenda could very well be lying to him with that innocent face of hers.

"So where were you?"

"Can't I even go out and talk to the neighbor woman?"

"Neighbor woman?"

"Just go ask Mr. Zuca's wife. I was over there. She used to know some relatives of mine who lived around here."

The bear grows more and more restless. Antônio Balduíno has little desire to argue now. He is disposed to accept all her excuses. What he wants is to lie down on the soft mattress with Rosenda's warm body next to his. The rain, heavier again, runs off the roof. There is a small hole in the middle of the room where the dripping water makes a hole in the beaten clay floor. The bear paces back and forth as far as its chain allows. Rosenda grabs it, pats its fur. But the bear is still impatient. Rosenda's caresses are no good. Antônio Balduíno, stretched out on the bed, thinks of a way to make up. He wants Rosenda next to him, her body close to his, her belly dancing against his own. Maybe tomorrow he'll beat her up and abandon her, but tonight he needs her—her body, her warmth. The worst is that now he has started a fight and he can't give in too fast. Still angry, she pats the bear. He doesn't know how to start. He closes his eyes, but she doesn't come to bed. Outside it's still raining; the wind whistles down the street and enters through a crack in the door. Doesn't she feel the invitation? She is very angry. Maybe she's telling the truth. She could have been talking to the neighbor, that woman of Mr. Zuca's who knows everything about everyone. She takes off her dress. It isn't wet. If she had walked a long way, if she had gone somewhere with the German, she would come back soaked to the skin, that was certain. He had been thinking nonsense here all by himself. The cat curls up against his feet and warms them comfortably, but the rest of his body is abandoned to the cold. The rain beats on the roof. He remembers some verses Gordo knows about the music of the rain on the roof and a woman who arrives in the middle of the night. He isn't sure if she came on horseback or on foot. Rosenda Rosedá slips out of her underwear, and now her breasts fill the room. Antônio Balduíno can see nothing else. Very few girls had breasts as pretty as hers, erect and firm. Antônio Balduíno throws his cigarette away.

Making an enormous effort he says, "Did you know that bear is a girl?"

"What?"

"That's right, the bear is female."

Her breasts rub against his chest. And amid the rain and the cold, as the wind howls in the street, Rosenda dances just for him. He pushes the cat away with one foot; it meows.

The *Homeless Traveler* docked in the heavy rain. Maria Clara makes them some coffee. They will leave early tonight, as soon as the sailboat is loaded. The bear is tied in the hold. Mestre Manuel brings news of Gordo, who buried his grandmother and went back to selling papers. Jubiabá was still alive and continued casting spells and holding macumba sessions. Joaquim is seen daily in the Drowned Man's Lantern with Zé Camarão. Antônio Balduíno wants news about everyone he knows and about the city, too, the docks, the ships that come and go. Again he is going over the mysterious sea. When he fled (he had taken a tremendous beating from the Peruvian, Miguez), he had forgotten how to laugh. His head had been troubled with Jubiabá's stories, the shame of getting beaten, the end of his career as a boxer, Lindinalva's engagement. Now he knew how to laugh again and would doubtless enjoy Jubiabá's tragic tales. He had seen a lot of misery during his two years of travel; his laughter had acquired a cruel tone. And on his face is the scar left by the thorns the night he was surrounded. Mestre Manuel asks him the history of that scar. Maria Clara watches them from the stern. Telling his story, Antônio Balduíno thinks about the sea, the cranes, the black ships that sail in the night.

It was on a stormy night like this that Viriato the Dwarf had entered the sea. The crabs crept into his body and rattled. Old Salusitano searched in the sea for the way home, too. And a woman had thrown herself into the water with a rock around her neck. The sailboat sways in the waters above the crown of rock. Today no one can see them; the waters have covered everything. Mestre Manuel does not let anyone take the helm.

It would be swift. The sailboat would run up against a rock; the conversation between Maria Clara and Rosenda Rosedá would end. (Maria Clara's hair is wild, blown by the wind, and from her comes the smell of the sea. Perhaps she has never lived in a house; perhaps she is a daughter of the sea.) Mestre Manuel's pipe would go out. And the waters of the river would cover everything, for the river is very high and even has waves like the sea. Mestre Manuel won't let anyone else take the helm. The wind shakes the trees on the riverbank. Far, far away shines the light of another sailboat. In the darkness of the forests, the fireflies wink. The wind carries the sailboat, which flies over the water faster than a motor launch. At this moment, in the midst of the storm, they are very near to death. One false turn of the rudder, and they will be thrown against the invisible rocks. Antônio Balduíno lies down with his belly to the sky, thinking these things. He cannot see a single star in the sky; only the heavy black clouds race along, whipped by the wind. From Maria Clara comes the scent of the tide. They are close to the sea. The sailboat has almost reached the river mouth. On the receding banks of the river, the small villages sleep without lights. Antônio Balduíno thinks that when all is said and done, life is absurd, not worth the trouble to live. Viriato the Dwarf knew this. The way of the sea is wide; today it is wide and revolted, its green surface agitated. The sea is an invitation. Ever since he was a child, he had thought about having an ABC recounting his courageous deeds, so that others might hear of them. He had become a brave and resolute man. But if he were swallowed by the waters now, no one would tell his story. A brave man doesn't commit suicide, except to escape the police. And a man of twenty-six still has lots of life to live; he still has to fight a great deal to deserve an ABC. But the sea is an invitation. There is the road home. Maria Clara smells of the tide. She speaks of the sea, tells things that happened to sailboat captains, stories of shipwrecks and drownings. She talks of her father, who was a fisherman and disappeared along with his tiny log raft during a storm. She smells like the ocean; it is always present in her, at once friend and enemy. It has incorporated itself in her, become a part of her. But nothing is a part of Antônio Balduíno. He has already been everything, and he is nothing. He knows he is fighting and that he needs to fight more. However, within him all this is still hazy and unclear. He feels in his weakened nerves that he is fighting a losing battle, as if he were punching the air. And the sea calls him now, as Maria Clara's lips called him on the trip out. In the distance, the lights of Bahia appear. The wind blows about their heads, bringing all the perfume of the sea that is in the body of Maria Clara. The twinkling lights of Bahia seem to offer salvation.

Rosenda Rosedá stayed at Gordo's house. Jubiabá came that night, and they kissed the old Negro's hand as he sat hunched in a corner. The lantern light (in Gordo's house there is no electricity) falls full on his wrinkled face. Gordo smiles in the joy of seeing his friend again. Everyone listens to Antônio Balduíno's stories. The bear sleeps in a corner. The next day, they decide, they will all go to the Água dos Meninos market, to see if they can earn some money from the bear's act. Then they go down the hill to the Drowned Man's Lantern and get drunk. Antônio Balduíno takes Rosenda Rosedá down to the sandhills and makes love to her in front of the sea. But she complains about the sand that hurts her body and gets into her iron-straightened hair. The black man laughs with pleasure. In the harbor are the figures of cranes.

The Água dos Meninos fair starts on Saturday night and goes on through Sunday noon. But it's best on Saturday night. Canoemen tie up their craft in Porto da Lenha, sailboat captains dock their boats in the small landing, men bring loaded animals, black women sell *mingau* and rice pudding. The passing streetcars are full of people. Everyone comes to the fair at Água dos Meninos. Some come to buy their supply of food for the week, others for the pleasure of the outing: to eat *sarapatel,* play the guitar, find a woman. The Água dos Meninos fair is a party. A black peoples' party, with music, laughter, and fighting. The booths are set up in rows. But the bulk of the merchandise is not in the booths. It is in great baskets and crates, or heaped on spread-out cloths. Peasants in wide straw hats, seated beside their wares, talk animatedly with the customers. Thick manioc roots, yams, mountains of pineapples, oranges, and watermelons. There are all the varieties of bananas in the Água dos Meninos market. They have everything for sale. A man with a parakeet sold "fortunes" on rolled-up bits of paper for two hundred reis apiece. Rosenda Rosedá bought hers. It said:

YOUR FORTUNE

"Do not trust those who flatter you, because it is all false. You are still ingenuous because you think everyone is like you. Be good-hearted and don't think badly of anyone. This will not take much effort, because you were born beneath a benevolent star. Your youth will be a flowing current of loves, and you will have many romantic misadventures. You will finally marry a boy to whom you will not give much importance at first, but in the end he will take possession of your heart. He will be the only one you love with true affection in your whole life. You will give birth to three lovely babies, and raise them with tender care; they will bring true peace to your heart.

"You will live eighty years. Your lucky lottery number is 04554."

Rosenda Rosedá laughed. Antônio Balduíno said, "You're going to have three kids."

"Once a gypsy told me I would have eight, and that I was going on a long trip. The trip came true; I came from Rio to Bahia. She was right."

But Antônio Balduíno thinks about the part of the fortune that says, "Your youth will be a flowing current of loves, and you will have many romantic misadventures." He is definitely getting very fond of Rosenda. It seems as though she is using Jubiabá's sorceries. Jubiabá hasn't come to the fair yet; it's too early for him. Today is Saturday, and many people go to consult the pai-de-santo. Suffering people. Some are sick and need medicine for their bodies: cuts, tuberculosis, leprosy, venereal disease. Jubiabá distributes herbs and prayers. Others come because they suffer from a woman's betrayal, or because they desire a woman who cares nothing for them. All come looking for strong spells, special charms, magic potions. On Sunday morning, the streets are full of objects that figure in voodoo spells. Pai Jubiabá protects love affairs and finishes them. He takes a woman out of a man's thoughts, puts a man into a woman's thoughts. He knows the secrets of important people, he knows the life of the poor; what doesn't he know in his little house on Capa-Negro Hill? Later he will be here, leaning on his staff, having cured people and straightened out everyone's business. He will come to the place they now stop. Gordo has arrived with the bear. Antônio Balduíno always upsets Gordo's life; Gordo quits selling papers and follows his friend. Then suddenly everything is over, and Gordo goes back to hawking papers with his sad, sonorous voice. Now he's got his hands full with the bear. At first he had been afraid of it, but later he grew accustomed to the animal and, as his grandmother had died, he was very affectionate toward the bear, which was eating very well indeed, even if Gordo had to go hungry. The bear is muzzled and ready to work for its living. Country people gather around Gordo, who invents a story for the bear. But he encounters a difficulty: Do bears have guardian angels or not? He has never heard. But stories without angels are no fun, and Gordo decides to give the bear one, when Balduíno comes and repeats what he heard Luigi say about the lion.

"This monster here, ladies and gentlemen, was captured in the African jungles. It is a three-time assassin, having killed a trio of intrepid animal tamers." (He remembers word for word the speech Luigi recited every night.) "He is an assassin, but he is going to perform, and you may all observe him; with care, however. Do not forget that he has killed three men. . . ."

Gordo examines the bear's muzzle and discovers that it has the soft eyes of a child and is incapable of killing anybody at all. It isn't right for Baldo to call it an assassin. But the bear is walking with his head lowered and the group around them increases. Rosenda reads the men's palms. They like it because she tickles their hands, and it makes their whole bodies shiver. Rosenda knows how to earn money. Laughing, she says to a loitering mulatto, "There's a *cabrocha* who is just crazy about you. . . ."

The man smiles at Rosenda. It could almost be her. She puts the coins away. Gordo collects money for the bear's performance in his straw hat. Antônio Balduíno, very elegant in red shoes and a red shirt, tells the animal's history. The marketplace swarms around them.

A car has broken down in the street. The driver crawls underneath it to search for the cause of the problem. A man addresses the nearby group, "Didn't I tell you? Machines are worthless . . . now, Lightning never broke down. Have you ever seen a horse break down?"

He has been telling the story of Lightning, a horse which belonged to his brother-in-law. He is against horseless carriages. He is an apologist for horses and oxcarts, and quotes the Bible. Jubiabá listens, shrunken up. Other men interrupt the conversation with words of approval.

When Jubiabá arrived, Balduíno and his companions had counted their earnings (fifty-nine mil-reis, a fortune!) and had wandered about enjoying the lively marketplace. The bear lumbered along behind them. In front of the booth where Joaquim drinks, they all stopped to listen to the man who told the story of the horse Lightning.

"Now, in those times, when they didn't have those things"—he pointed to the broken-down car—"men lived a long time. Methuselah lived nine hundred years. It's in the Bible."

"It is," agrees a light-colored old mulatto.

"Everybody lived for two hundred years, three hundred . . . a hundred was nothing. Look in the Bible."

"They say parrots live for over a hundred years."

The man looks angrily for the person who is interrupting. But when he sees it is Rosenda, he smiles.

"They used to. Noah lived for ages and ages. Back then they used oxcarts."

He sipped his rum.

The light-colored mulatto agreed, "That's right."

He wanted to prove that he knew about things, too. A black man agrees, nodding in admiration of the man quoting the Bible.

"A man could leave home in an oxcart, and he knew he would get where he wanted to go. Nowadays a fellow goes out in one of these contraptions"—he points to the demoralized auto—"and he has to stop before he's halfway there. Out of gas. With oxcarts, you're never out of gas. That's why today men die so early. Machines are not God's invention; they're the work of the devil."

The light-colored mulatto agreed.

The man continued, "In the times when they used oxcarts, women had babies when they were a hundred years old—"

"Come on, I don't believe that. I'm sorry, but for a woman to have a kid when she's a hundred years old, that I can't swallow," declared Antônio Balduíno.

They all laughed, except for the light-colored mulatto.

"Well, it's in the Bible," said the man.

But there was no way Antônio Balduíno was going to believe him. A woman have a baby at a hundred? No, he wouldn't swallow that. That man was making fools out of them, taking everyone in with those stories. And he prepares to say so when Jubiabá speaks up.

"In the days when they had oxcarts, there were black people dying of hunger. Today there still are. For black people it's the same thing."

The old mulatto agrees. "Ah! Now that's the truth." He warms to the topic. "For the poor folks . . ."

But behind them the fair is alive, and as Jubiabá listens to the man who hates cars (who is now recounting the history of a disease that has plagued him for many years), they go meandering off through the marketplace, stopping at the booths, talking to the peasants, eating things. A drunk looks at Rosenda and whistles.

"Wow! What a piece!"

Antônio Balduíno gets offended, but Rosenda doesn't let him fight.

"Don't you see he's drunk?"

"And doesn't he see you're with a man?"

No, the drunk doesn't see a thing, for he has stopped at all the booths that sell rum. But he could see Rosenda well enough, and recognized a gorgeous woman. As they walk away, Antônio Balduíno still wants to go back and demand satisfaction from him.

A little farther on, there is a disturbance. Jubiabá comes to tell them he is leaving. Coming along behind him is the man who hates cars, confident now that he will be cured through Jubiabá's prayers. The disturbance on the opposite side of the marketplace grows louder. Antônio Balduíno notes that Gordo is not with them.

"Where's Gordo?" he asks.

"He must be around somewhere with the bear."

Joaquim only has eyes for Rosenda. If she weren't Balduíno's, he might very well try his luck with her. How should he know where Gordo was?

"Gordo's in that fight," says Antônio Balduíno, moving away a little.

"Gordo?" Rosenda is alarmed.

Antônio and Joaquim run. Rosenda walks faster. Gordo is defending himself from the blows of a fellow who is yanking at the bear's chain. The men around are shouting, "Come on! Go, man!"

Antônio Balduíno shoves through the group and puts his hand on Gordo's shoulder.

"What does he want?"

"He wants to stick his cigar in the bear's nose."

"Just to see what he does," the man says, laughing, showing him his lighted cigar. The man has a scar on his chin and a sparse mustache on his upper lip. "He has such a funny face. I'm going to put the cigar up his nose."

Around them everyone laughs. Antônio Balduíno bites his

hand. Two mulatto men mutter something to the man with the cigar. Joaquim overhears from behind. The man with the cigar retorts, "Naw . . . hell, no, I'm going to do it."

"Go ahead," said Antônio Balduíno.

The man comes close to the bear. He raises the cigar. The bear draws back. Gordo nearly screams as the cigar approaches the animal's muzzle. But the man is knocked flat on the ground with a punch from Baldo the Boxer. The two mulattoes who were behind the man advance toward the Negro. But one of them is caught by Joaquim, and the other receives Antônio Balduíno's foot in the pit of his stomach. Gordo wants to hit the man with the cigar, who is getting up. But instead, he hits a Negro who has nothing to do with the affair. The Negro strikes him back, and his brother gets into the fight, too. Mestre Manuel, who was selling pineapples, rushes over with three more men. If Antônio Balduíno is fighting, then he's fighting, too. His three companions join in the fray. Various men try to stop the fight and get involved instead. A soldier pulls out a saber. But what's the good of a saber against so many sparkling razors? A guard blows his whistle uselessly in the street. Antônio Balduíno socks an unknown man with all his might, a man who had nothing to do with the fight but was trying to stop it. The man with the cigar hits somebody on his own side. Gordo takes the bear and moves out of the way, watching the scene. Rosenda Rosedá bites the men who attack Balduíno. Her dress is torn, and she brandishes a razor she pulled out of her garter. The entire Água dos Meninos market is fighting. They fight for the sake of fighting, without knowing the cause, for the sheer physical pleasure of grappling with one another, rolling in the sand, exchanging blows. The black men have forgotten everything: the yams, the mountains of tangerines, the pineapples, the manioc biscuits. What they want to do now is fight, because fighting is good, like singing, like listening to a story, like lying, like contemplating the sea at night in the harbor.

Gordo steals a bottle of beer for the bear.

Someone yells, "The cavalry's coming!"

As fast as it started, the disturbance stops. The men go back to their booths, to their mountains of fruit and vegetables. The cavalry finds nothing, just a little blood on the ground. A man covers the cut on his face with a handkerchief. The razors have disappeared. And the Negroes laugh, satisfied, because tonight they have enjoyed themselves.

The man with the cigar says to Antônio Balduíno, "That was a damn good fight."

He offers beer, pats the bear on the head. Rain falls, soaking the Negroes.

CHAPTER 20
Creole Dance

The Liberty Club was located in a building in the Rua do Cabeça. It was on the third floor, accessible by a narrow staircase. It consisted of a large room with chairs arranged around the walls for the ladies, a platform for the orchestra, and an open balcony of cement where drinks were served at small tables. Drinking was rigorously prohibited in the ballroom. Off the ballroom was the men's toilet. The little powder room where the ladies arranged their hair was very small, but it had a big mirror and a little bench for them to sit down, as well as a comb and a can of Brilliantine. On the days of the big dances—when carnival or the Bonfim fiesta draws near—the ballroom is decorated with flowers and multicolored strips of paper. But the only holiday that is close now is St. John's Day, June twenty-fourth, and from the ceiling hang numerous paper lanterns and balloons. The St. John's Day party will be crowded. The Liberty Club has traditions to uphold, and its June dance will doubtless bring together servants of the richest houses, mulatto girls who sell candy in the streets, soldiers from the 19th Division, Negroes from all over the city. It is the most famous creole club of the town. There aren't many such places in Bahia. The black people prefer to attend the macumba sessions where the religious dances of the spirits are performed and only come to the creole club on the days when there are big dances. But the Liberty Club prospered because it managed to win Jubiabá's support; he became honorary president. Besides this, there was a noisy jazz orchestra that had started out there and was now earning good money in parties all over the city. A rich people's party without the Seven Canaries' jazz was no good. The musicians even wore tuxedos. But they were at their best at the Liberty Club parties. There wasn't money in the world that could tempt them to play at another party on days when the creole club held a big dance. There they danced, too, wore whatever they pleased; they were among friends, and people made speeches. The Liberty Club was at its peak and had traditions to uphold. It prepared itself for the St. John's Day party.

Every time Antônio Balduíno saw the Seven Canaries, he thought about being a band director or a jazz musician. A band director would be better because he could wear a uniform and lead the marching, walking backward with a baton in his hand. Antônio Balduíno loved the bright colors of band uniforms. The jazz men wore ordinary clothes or, for rich parties, tuxedos that held no charm for Balduíno. But since he couldn't direct a marching band, he would have settled for being in a jazz group, the kind that features singing and tap-dancing.

It had been a long time since he composed a samba. He hadn't had time for anything in the tobacco fields. But now, although he had just returned to Bahia, he had already made up two sambas that were sung over the radio. What was more, he had written the ABC of Zumbi dos Palmares, telling his hero's life as he imagined it. According to his ABC, Zumbi had been born in Africa, fought with lions, killed tigers. One day, deceived by white men, he went aboard a ship, which brought him to slavery in the tobacco fields. But he didn't like to be whipped, so he ran away, banded together with other black men, killed many soldiers, and so as not to be taken captive again, threw himself off a cliff.

"Africa, I remember you,
Where first I came to be.
I hunted game, ate jungle fruit
And lived entirely free."

"Palmares was the place I fought;
I would not be a slave.
They sent a thousand soldiers
But not a one was brave."

"And so, Zumbi dos Palmares
Jumped off a cliff so high,
He said, 'A slave I will not be
And so, my people, good-bye.' "

Gordo memorized the ABC at once and recited it at parties, accompanied on the guitar.

Antônio Balduíno looked up the poet who had bought his sambas to see if he wanted to buy the ABC. But the poet only wanted the two sambas and said the ABC was worthless, that the verses were broken and other things Balduíno didn't understand. The black man grew very angry because he thought the ABC was very beautiful, and after receiving thirty mil-reis for the two sambas, he showered the poet with insults. The man didn't react. Balduíno, feeling lighthearted, went off and sang the ABC to Rosenda and Jubiabá, who thought it was very good. Through Mr. Jerônio of the market, Jubiabá arranged for the ABC to come out in the *People's Library* (a collection of the best popular poetry, wise sayings, stories, songs, speeches, prayers, useful recipes, etc., sold for the price of two hundred reis). It came out in the same issue as the "Tale of the Mysterious Ox" and "The Indian and the Newborn Babe," and was quickly memorized by the stevedores of the port; by the sailboat captains, who took it to the blind men in the cities of the coast; by the troublemakers of the city; by all the black people. All Antônio Balduíno thought about was getting into the Seven Canaries.

Balduíno was a member of the Liberty Club, but he didn't go there much. He always had other places to go, and in the Liberty Club they charged for drinks, and there was nothing to eat. It was only because of a girl friend that he had ever gone to the club at all. When he made one of his rare appearances, fat Mr. Juvêncio, the secretary and ballroom master, invariably said, "At last, Mr. Balduíno, you give us the honor of coming to the club. You seem to scorn us, you come so little."

Balduíno didn't scorn anybody. But in the Liberty Club he couldn't dance holding the girls close because it was forbidden, nor converse with his partner in the middle of the ballroom. Moreover, they frowned on getting drunk. All this displeased the Negro, who didn't know how to contain himself, who squeezed the girls while dancing, who very frequently got drunk.

He remembered the first time he had gone to the club. It was a long time ago. Almost as soon as he got there he had had a fight with Mr. Juvêncio. The orchestra was playing with delirious enthusiasm. The music was one of his sambas, among the first he had sold the poet. He asked a mulatto girl to dance—it was Isolina, his girl friend at that time. They started dancing around the room, and he held her very close, cheek to cheek. That was all it took for Mr. Juvêncio to interfere.

"Here, you can't do that!" Mr. Juvêncio was a very strict ballroom master.

"Can't do what?"

"This is no place for mischief."

"Who's doing any mischief?"

"You, with this young lady."

Balduíno slapped the secretary in the face. A disturbance started, but Jubiabá came over and straightened it out. Mr. Juvêncio explained that he had to maintain the club's standards. If he were to permit anything unseemly here, the families wouldn't come anymore, and what could he say to the parents of the young girls who had placed their confidence in the club? He didn't care who liked who. That wasn't the point. He had nothing to do with other people's romances. But inside the club, he wanted respect and strict observation of the rules. This wasn't a place for loose women. It was a recreational dancing society, period. Antônio Balduíno decided Mr. Juvêncio was right, and they made peace. The black man continued dancing and drinking. By chance Gordo had come, too, and they got very merry. But at about one in the morning, an army sergeant began to dance very scandalously with a white woman. Mr. Juvêncio complained, but he paid no attention. Mr. Juvêncio complained again. The third time he told the sergeant he must leave. The sergeant gave Mr. Juvêncio a push. Antônio Balduíno interfered, supporting Mr. Juvêncio, and knocked the sergeant down. Demoralized, he left fuming threats. Then Antônio Balduíno went to have a beer with the secretary. But wouldn't you know, the sergeant came back with a group of soldiers, and an ugly fight ensued. Everyone started hitting each other; lots of heads were broken. People locked themselves in the bathroom, and the soldiers even fired shots. The party ended with bashed heads and people in jail. Antônio Balduíno managed to escape. He became famous in the Liberty Club, and when he turned up, Mr. Juvêncio always ordered beer and made a great fuss over him. But in truth, he preferred the parties of Capa-Negro Hill, of the Itapagipe or Rio Vermelho neighborhoods, to the dances in the Liberty Club. At carnival time it was all right, because he could wear an Indian costume with red and green feathers and sing macumba songs. But for St. John's Day, he preferred to go to the party João Fransisco always gave in his house in Rio Vermelho with an enormous bonfire out front, lots of firecrackers, and hot-air balloons, and *canjica* to eat with homemade genipap wine. But this year he would have to go to the Liberty Club, for Rosenda Rosedá had made a special ball dress and wanted to make a splash at the club's party. Oh, was she vain! He certainly would prefer to go to João Fransisco's house.

Antônio Balduíno had been thinking for some time that Rosenda Rosedá was getting insupportable. She wanted to boss him around. One of these days he was going to send her packing. She was always wanting things; she made him sell the bear in order to buy a ball gown when she could have bought it on the installment plan from the Turk. That very day she had asked him for a necklace she had seen for twelve mil-reis in a store in Rua Chile. But when he went out to buy it, he met Vicente and learned that Clarimundo had been killed by a crane in the harbor, so he had given Vicente ten mil-reis for the funeral. The trade union was going to pay for the burial, but the stevedores wanted to get some money together for the widow and were taking up a collection. They were going to bring a wreath for the grave also. The poor man had been hit on the head by the crane's great ball of iron (he was carrying a heavy load and couldn't look up) and had left a wife and four small children. Antônio Balduíno gave Vicente the ten mil-reis and stopped in to talk with Jubiabá to see if the pai-de-santo could do anything else to help the woman. Balduíno had known Clarimundo very well. He was always cheerful and singing, and he had married a light-colored mulatto girl. "Solid as a brick," Joaquim always said. A good companion who would help out a friend in need if he had the money. Now he had died, and his wife would have to live on other people's charity. What good was it to work, to load ships, to live under heavy burdens? Afterward one died and left one's children with nothing to live on. Old Salusitano had thrown himself in the water. And from thinking so much about these things, Viriato the Dwarf had committed suicide one stormy night. Antônio Balduíno didn't like to think about these things. He liked to laugh and play the guitar, to listen to Gordo's beautiful stories or the heroic yarns of Zé Camarão. Today he is impatient because he is going to miss João Fransisco's party. He has to take Rosenda to the dance at the Liberty Club. On the way he would stop by Clarimundo's house to pay his respects to the dead man, who had been his friend. The best thing would be not to go to any party at all but to stay at Clarimundo's wake. He would go ask Jubiabá to perform the sending-off of the body. Jubiabá was very likely at home, talking with Gordo. Gordo's place was near Capa-Negro Hill, and once in a while Jubiabá would go down to chat with him. Jubiabá never changed. How old was he? He must be well over a hundred. He knows so many things, too. Yet Jubiabá adds to the anguish that from time to time takes hold of Antônio Balduíno. The medicine man says things that stick in Balduíno's mind and make him think about the sea into which Viriato threw himself, where the old Salusitano forgot his children's hunger. Antônio Balduíno feels a change in himself, senses that he isn't as happy as he used to be. Nowadays he thinks sad things. And right there in the street, the Negro laughs aloud happily. Passersby turn around in surprise. The black man continues to laugh. But he realizes that he is laughing more in order to irritate others than from happiness. He keeps walking, his easygoing pace hurried now, almost running. When he gets home, he is calmer; he thinks about the white suit he will wear to the dance that night.

"Get my necklace, honey?"

Antônio Balduíno looks at the black girl with a disconsolate face. Only now does he remember Rosenda's necklace. Of the twelve mil-reis, he had given ten to Vicente for Clarimundo's wife. The two mil-reis coins are in his pocket. Rosenda looks at him suspiciously.

"Didn't you bring my necklace?"

"Do you know what happened? Clarimundo got killed."

But it's no good telling Rosenda; she never knew Clarimundo.

"I wanted it so much, and you didn't get it! Just to be mean. Then you say you love me. But never mind."

It is the eve of St. John's Day, and everyone in the street is happy. Antônio Balduíno would like to be happy, too. People go by smiling, and the firecracker booths are full of customers. Everyone is getting ready to have a good time tonight. They would set off Roman candles and "fizzlers." The black people talked only of João Fransisco's party and the dance at the Liberty Club. Still, Antônio Balduíno can't be happy tonight. Clarimundo is dead, and he thinks only of the stevedore. Rosenda is complaining, acting like a spoiled brat. He doesn't answer her questions, and she starts to cry. At Osvaldo's house they are sending up a hot-air balloon; it's going to be a big one. In the two-story house across the street, girls are hunting for their fiancé's picture in a basin of water. Everybody is happy today. Only Balduíno is grieved and angry. Clarimundo's widow must be crying. But she has a reason: She has lost her husband. He has no reason except Rosenda's pouting. Even so, that is a silly reason. He could give her a good kick and go to João Fransisco's party. She is getting to be a pain in the ass. Antônio Balduíno goes out the door. Rosenda is crying in the bedroom, saying she won't go anywhere. The Negro takes his hat and heads for Jubiabá's house, to tell the pai-de-santo about Clarimundo's death.

When he got back, after talking with Jubiabá and Gordo (Gordo went off at once to the wake), he found Rosenda with a hostile face, getting dressed for the dance.

"Rosenda, you know we have to stop at Clarimundo's house for a while."

"Who's Clarimundo?" she asked sulkily.

"A stevedore who died today. I gave the money for the necklace to help pay for his funeral."

"And what are we going to do there?"

"Pay his wife a visit, poor thing."

"Like this, dressed for a party?"

"So what?"

But Rosenda is furious about the necklace and keeps muttering that it isn't right to go to make a condolence visit dressed for a party. All the while she goes on getting ready. Antônio Balduíno has some coffee. Rosenda's words reach him from the bedroom.

"Visit a dead man . . . whoever heard of such a thing?"

She really deserved to get beaten up, the conceited bitch! She wanted to wear the necklace to the party, decorate herself with blue costume jewelry. A necklace that cost twelve mil-reis . . . ten had gone to Clarimundo's widow. The other two were in his pocket. It would pay for some beer. A necklace around Rosenda's neck would be pretty. But red would be better than blue. Antônio Balduíno likes red. It was true Rosenda knew how to be a woman. In bed there was no one better. But outside that, she was spoiled, silly, full of little ways. A spoiled black broad. She liked people to make a big fuss over her. All she talked about was going on the stage; she wouldn't look for a job as a housemaid. She wasn't born for housework was what she said. The coffee was cold. It was too weak, too; coffee had to be strong to be good. Rosenda didn't even know how to make a decent cup of coffee. Clarimundo's wife could make a fine cup of coffee. If she didn't find another man, she would probably go hungry. Times were bad, and washing clothes wouldn't bring in enough to support anyone. What's more, she wasn't up to hard work. She was very thin.

Rosenda's voice comes from the bedroom. "You want to go or not?"

"Why?"

"You're taking forever to come change your clothes. What time do you want to get there? And we still have to go visit the dead man. Lord, what an inconvenience. I never heard of such a thing in my life. Paying a condolence call wearing a ball gown."

Antônio Balduíno puts on his white suit but, since he plans to stop at Clarimundo's house, he doesn't put on his red tie. He goes out hopping mad. So does Rosenda. They walk far apart as if they had never met each other. Hot-air balloons rise toward the sky. The bonfire is burning in front of Osvaldo's house. Firecrackers and Roman candles go off.

Clarimundo will not see the balloons go up for St. John's Day this year. On this date, a great bonfire had always burned at his door, and firecrackers had always popped. His friends had come to drink genipap wine and rum. Antônio Balduíno had come many times. They set off rockets to the dismay of careless passersby. Once they had sent up a colossal balloon, eighteen feet long, in the form of a zeppelin. It was a beauty. A newspaper had carried a picture of it the next day. The living room was always full of people. Today it would be full, too, but no bonfire would burn outside. Lying in his coffin, Clarimundo has closed his eyes. The balloons drift by overhead. Clarimundo doesn't see them. He doesn't see the bonfire in Osvaldo's house. Other years, they had laid bets to see who could make the bigger bonfire. This year Osvaldo won, because in Clarimundo's house there is only the candle that burns beside the cadaver. His face is unrecognizable. The iron ball of the crane had mashed in the head of the stevedore, broken his skull, flattened out his face. Today someone else sent up a balloon shaped like a zeppelin. Everyone runs to their windows to see it. It rises, lighted up, crossing the blue sky. Only Clarimundo doesn't see it because the crane killed him as he worked in the harbor. The other stevedores are there. The trade union is going to be in charge of the burial. Of those present, many will go to the dance at the Liberty Club. Jubiabá won't, for he is sending off the body. In his hand are trembling, sacred leaves. Very likely Gordo won't go, either. He will stay at Clarimundo's wake, helping Jubiabá with the prayers and sending-off. Balloons go by in the darkness. Clarimundo, black Clarimundo, has no bonfire in front of his house tonight. But the Negro Antônio Balduíno will get very drunk because of him. And from now on he will look at cranes as enemies.

The voice of Clarimundo's widow is resigned, and as she speaks, she releases them from an oppression.

"This was bound to happen. Every time he went out, I was afraid they would carry him home dead, killed by those cranes."

The oldest girl, ten, cries against the table. The smallest child, three, peeks out at the balloon drifting by. Jubiabá prays over the dead man. Antônio Balduíno will get very drunk tonight. The music of a samba comes from a house nearby, invading the dead man's home.

The Liberty Club ballroom is packed full. Laughter vibrates in the air. A smell of sweat fills the room, but no one notices it. The Seven Canaries jazz orchestra is in pandemonium. The couples can hardly move in the ballroom. Mr. Juvêncio leaves his function of chaperon and comes to greet Antônio Balduíno.

"At last you've given our club the honor . . ."

Mr. Juvêncio is wearing a blue suit. Balduíno introduces Rosenda, who has come in a green dress. They stay in the entrance until the music stops. The couples break apart in the ballroom, and they go in. The mulatto girls point to Rosenda Rosedá, whose green dress is a success. The men all stare at her. Rosenda says to Antônio Balduíno, "Haven't they ever seen a girl before?"

But in fact, she is pleased as punch. She smiles. Really, if she had worn the necklace, she would have been even prettier. Antônio Balduíno is proud of her. Everyone is staring at the two of them and whispering. Rosenda Rosedá sways her hips when she walks, as if she were dancing a samba. They stop in the middle of the ballroom under the chandelier. Rosenda goes to the powder room to fix her straightened hair. Black men come to talk with Antônio Balduíno. Joaquim is already half-drunk.

"It's a good party, brother. I've already had a few."

"I thought you were going to João Fransisco's party."

"Oh, I am. But first I thought I'd stop by here and take a look at things. It's nice here. Your girl friend's looking good, eh?"

"Rosenda? You want her?"

"I don't like other people's leftovers."

The men laugh. One asks Antônio Balduíno how he got the scar on his face. He lies, inventing a story of a fight with six men. Zefa is at the dance, and she gives Antônio Balduíno the eye. Then she comes up and complains that he "won't associate with poor people anymore." Rosenda comes out of the powder room smiling. Her teeth are white. Zefa looks at her enviously.

"Here comes your boss lady."

Rosenda sits down beside Zefa in the place Antônio Balduíno occupied. He has gone inside to have a drink with Joaquim and Mr. Juvêncio. There is an intermission in the dancing because the musicians need a glass of beer. But suddenly a carnival march explodes in the ballroom. Antônio Balduíno watches from his table. The dance floor is packed with couples; it's not worth dancing this number. He looks at his new red shoes. If he went to dance now, everyone would step on them. Joaquim compliments him on the shoes. Antônio Balduíno says he is going to get Rosenda and have a glass of beer. When he gets up, he sees her dancing with a white man. He turns to Joaquim.

"Who's that guy?"

"Who?"

"The one dancing with Rosenda."

"That's Carlos, a chauffeur. Thinks he's pretty tough."

Who had ever seen a girl come escorted to a ball and then dance with a stranger without first speaking to the gentleman who brought her? That's not right. Rosenda is making a fool of him. She was still angry about the necklace and wanted to make Balduíno jealous. Zefa wasn't dancing. She came over to their table and accepted a glass of beer.

"Your girl friend's good-looking, Baldo. See how she's smiling at that white man. Mr. Carlos is really something."

Joaquim asks Zefa to dance. Zefa goes off laughing; she is laughing at Antônio Balduíno. They all think that he is tied to Rosenda's apron strings, that she uses magic charms to keep the black man after her. Antônio Balduíno orders rum from the waiter, who has a wooden leg. A man at the next table wants to fight with everybody.

The black women sway in the ballroom. The orchestra throbs with enthusiasm. Rosenda is dancing. Carlos whispers in her ear. That's forbidden. Why doesn't Mr. Juvêncio complain? Balduíno thinks to himself, Am I really jealous?

What a pretty mulatto girl, the one seated next to that old fat lady. She has a first-class face. Small breasts. Laughing, Rosenda passes near the window. Why can't Antônio Balduíno think about the little mulatto girl? He orders more rum. It was all because of that necklace. But shouldn't he have given the money to Vicente for Clarimundo's wife? Clarimundo had been mashed to death by a crane. The necklace was blue. If it were at least red . . .

Rosenda goes by again, laughing. He'll end up telling that chauffeur off. Are they laughing at him? It seems they don't know Antônio Balduíno. He feels the contact of the razor tucked into the waistband of his trousers. It would leave a nice mark on someone's face. Besides, a blue necklace wouldn't look right with a green dress. Another glass of rum. If it were a red necklace . . . Tomorrow Clarimundo's wife would start to wash clothes. Hard, back-breaking work. She was so skinny, she would end up with tuberculosis. Rosenda deserved a beating. No woman had ever treated him like that before. The ballroom is full. The creole girls in their ball gowns dance like elegant ladies. Very few of them are as well dressed as Joana. But today Rosenda is prettier. The chauffeur is very pleased, exhibiting his success. Balduíno had given the money for the necklace to Clarimundo. The orchestra stops but is obliged to begin again by the clapping audience. At the next table a man wants to fight with somebody, anybody. Balduíno turns around.

"I'm with you, pal."

"Thanks, friend. Nobody can push me around."

The man complains to the waiter, complains to his table mate.

"Today I'll show 'em . . ."

Antônio Balduíno could easily ask Jubiabá for a charm to hold onto Rosenda, make her fall all over him. A black man sings with the orchestra, "Honey, you're scorning me."

But he doesn't want to cast spells to hold onto a woman. Actually, he cared very little if Rosenda left. What he wouldn't stand for was lack of respect. So! He had brought her to the party and she was dancing with someone else without the slightest concern. She wanted to make a fool of him. The women sway to the rhythm of the music. An old Negro is telling a story nearby him. The man who wants to fight interrupts with side remarks. A smell of sweat permeates the club. A fellow tries to convince a girl to go outside with him. Naturally, the chauffeur is asking Rosenda the same thing. She laughs.

Balduíno gets up. The money went to Clarimundo's wife. He comes over to the white man and pulls Rosenda's arm.

"Come and dance with me."

The chauffeur gets offended.

"The lady's with me."

"I brought her. I gave her this dress. She wanted a necklace, but I gave the money to Clarimundo's wife; he got killed by a crane."

He yanks Rosenda's arm, and she becomes indecisive, frightened. She knows very well that Antônio Balduíno likes to fight. But the chauffeur isn't about to give up the lady. The music stops, and they stand there arguing in the middle of the room. Mr. Juvêncio comes to say that it isn't permitted to stand talking in the ballroom. The chauffeur is offended and says, "Get lost."

Joaquim appears.

"What's going on?"

Rosenda grabs Joaquim by the arm.

"Baldo wants to fight just because I was dancing with this boy. Don't let him, Joaquim."

Now almost everyone is looking at them. The drunken man who wants to fight puts himself at Antônio Balduíno's disposal.

"Need me, pal?"

Mr. Juvêncio says it's all nonsense and asks the orchestra for music. A fox-trot begins. Antônio Balduíno takes Rosenda's arm. The chauffeur says, "We'll settle this later."

Rosenda becomes coy. Now that Balduíno has won her away from the other, she acts tender again, squeezing his arms. The Negro thinks she would be prettier if she were wearing a red necklace. The man who wants to fight has managed to start a commotion at the back. The chauffeur is at the door, watching them. The disturbance is quenched; the dance continues. Mr. Juvêncio claps his hands in the ballroom. This fox-trot sounds like a funeral march, it's so sad. Clarimundo is dead and won't see the St. John's Day balloons again. When they are through dancing, Antônio Balduíno goes up to the chauffeur.

"Look here, I just wanted to show you that you weren't going to take any woman away from me. But now you can have her, because I wouldn't touch that ugly piece of hide with a ten-foot pole.''

The creole band grows lively. Antônio Balduíno ends the night as bandleader of the Seven Canaries. Their director fell over drunk. The chauffeur disappeared with Rosenda. The dance hall smells of sweat, the Negroes laugh and join in the *maxixe*.

CHAPTER 21
Romance of the Ship *Catarineta*

Lindinalva sat on her balcony and read romantic poetry and novels. She especially liked the "Ship *Catarineta.*"

Here comes the Ship *Catarineta*
With many tales to tell.

Perhaps the ship *Catarineta* would bring her a fiancé. Once a little beggar boy had told her that her fiancé would arrive in a ship that skimmed over the waves. She waited for him. And while she waited, she read romantic novels and poems about love on her balcony.

After the marriage of the girl in the two-story house across from the Pereiras', Zumbi dos Palmares Street lost what little poetry it had. Never again did the young man cross the cobblestones and throw carnations onto the balcony. The newlyweds went to live in a busy street, and the windows of the old house were boarded up, hiding the portrait of the young military man whose death had killed all the joy of that family. Lindinalva grew sad when the girl and her suitor were married. She would watch her neighbor's courtship from the Comendador's garden, and take delight in the carnations the young man would toss his sweetheart. That courtship was the only romantic note of the entire street. But after their marriage, Lindinalva, who had never spoken to her neighbor, felt even more lonely and isolated. Amelia grew older in the kitchen. A year after Antônio Balduíno ran away, Lindinalva mourned her mother's death. The widowed Comendador divided himself between his business and the easy lovers he found. He started drinking (out of grief, the neighbors said), and Lindinalva was abandoned in the great old house where the geese had died and the flowers withered. She read the story of the Ship *Catarineta* and pulled the petals off roses. One day the fiancé would come in a ship. Lindinalva dreamed about this so much that she wasn't surprised when she learned that Gustavo (Dr. Gustavo Barreira, a lawyer from one of the best families in the city) had just come from Rio, bringing his degree and a firm determination to make a fortune. He was retained by the Comendador for advice about a business transaction and thus met Lindinalva. The freckles on her face, if they didn't allow her to be pretty, made her unusual. And her lean body with its high, pointed breasts tempted the lawyer's eyes. The engagement went blissfully, and Zumbi dos Palmares Street acquired a new life. They went walking arm in arm, and he said romantic things. The poppies in the yard across the street leaned over the wall to see the sweethearts. Red poppies, fleshy as lips. Once he said, "Poppies are an invitation to sin," and kissed her.

The wind blew the poppies, and Lindinalva was so happy she forgot the black boy Antônio Balduíno, whom she dreamed about when she had nightmares. Now she dreamed about her fiancé, about having a small house, a garden with poppies, lots of poppies red as sin.

The Comendador went bankrupt. (His house was squandered on women, the businessmen said.) The fiancé showed rare dedication, working very hard, but nothing could be done. The Comendador started living in the houses of the cheapest whores, and the fiancé came to see Lindinalva every afternoon. Finally, she moved out of the house, which had to be forfeited to the creditors. They went to live in a distant neighborhood, and the fiancé paid the household expenses. One stormy night, he slept there. The Comendador was at the brothels. The door to Lindinalva's room was only closed, not locked. Gustavo went in. She hid herself under the sheets, smiling.

But Lindinalva never thought it would all change so fast. They slept together many times, and at first everything was wonderful. Sweet nights of love, kisses that bruised the lips, hands that squeezed the breasts as though crushing the petals of poppies. But little by little he began staying away, complaining that his business wasn't prospering, pointing out the difficulties of the approaching marriage, which had been postponed three times. The Comendador died in a whorehouse, and the newspapers ran the story. Gustavo's sensibilities were offended; he declared that his career was irremediably damaged and did not appear at the funeral. A few days later he sent two hundred milreis. Lindinalva sent word that she wanted to see him; a week later he came. He was so somber and in such a hurry that she didn't cry, nor tell him she was pregnant.

CHAPTER 22
Song of a Friend

It was Amelia who told Antônio Balduíno that Lindinalva had become a prostitute. Amelia had grown maternal and tender when disgrace had fallen upon the Comendador's household. She had been mother and father to Lindinalva. But when they moved, Lindinalva insisted she look for another job and not accompany them. Amelia was perfectly willing to stay with Lindinalva, but Lindinalva angrily forbade it. Amelia had to go to work in the house of Manuel das Almas, a rich Portuguese who owned a bakery in the city. At that time, Antônio Balduíno was in the tobacco fields. When Lindinalva had the baby, it was Amelia who helped her. She had abandoned her job in order to come and stay with "the little girl," as she referred to Lindinalva. She used her own money for the baby's delivery and was a dedicated and able nurse afterward. So able that Lindinalva didn't feel any humiliation. Gustavo, who had married the daughter of a senator, sent one hundred mil-reis for the child and an anguished plea for silence. Lindinalva answered that he could put his mind at rest, for she would never reveal a thing. Once again she made Amelia look for a job and accepted the invitation of Lulu, a madame who owned the most expensive brothel in the city, to go earn her living in the Monte Carlo Boardinghouse. Antônio Balduíno heard all this with head bowed, stroking the scar on his face. The night outside was rainy.

The child, a boy, strong like his father, sad like his mother, went to live with Amelia. Lindinalva made her début at the Monte Carlo Boardinghouse in a low-cut ball gown. Lulu had given her instructions: order plenty of liquor, the most expensive kind. She should give preference to the fat colonels who came from the cocoa farms, tobacco fields, sugar plantations. Her slender, virginal appearance would please the old lechers. She should exploit them as much as possible. It was life. . . .

A slow waltz was playing when she went into the boardinghouse salon. In her brassiere was the key to her room, which she should give to the man who invited her to his table. With that key he would open the secrets of her body. Lindinalva doesn't feel like crying. But the music is sad. Couples waltz around the room, their feet dragging. It's still early and there aren't many people. Only two of the women are busy, at a table where some young men are drinking beer.

Lindinalva sits down at a table with some other women. A blond comments, "The beginner."

The women look at Lindinalva indifferently. Only a mulatto girl drinking rum from a wineglass asks, "What did you come here for?"

The music is slow and maudlin. Lindinalva's voice trembles. "I couldn't find a job."

A Frenchwoman offers cigarettes.

"I hope Colonel Pedro shows up today. I need money."

The mulatto girl looks at her glass and suddenly lets out a peal of laughter. The others, accustomed to Eunice's quirks, are unconcerned, but Lindinalva is alarmed. Why is the music so sad? They could just as easily play a happy samba. From the street comes a confused noise of voices and streetcars; the noise of life. The boardinghouse seems like a cemetery with music. It's because Eunice is saying, "We're dead and don't know it. Life is over for us. A fancy woman is as good as dead."

The Frenchwoman waits for Colonel Pedro. She needs money. Her relatives in provincial France wrote to say that her little brother is dying. They ask her to send some extra money since she is doing so well with her fashion shop in Brazil. She taps her fingers on the table.

"Fashion shop, fashion shop."

Eunice tosses off her glass of rum.

"All dead . . . all of us. This is a cemetery."

"I'm alive and kicking," retorted a young brunette. "That dumb Eunice has such ideas." She smiles.

Lindinalva looks at her. She is almost a child. A happy child with black hair. The blond is old; she has wrinkles and the distant air of someone who lives in another world. The music of the waltz fades away. Two men come into the house and order complicated mixed drinks. The brunette girl goes to talk to them. They pinch her thighs, order more drinks, whisper things in her ear. Lindinalva feels an immense sadness and a desire to stroke the brunette girl's head. Eunice asks for a cigarette. Did she feel sorry for the brunette girl, too?

"Fancy women are spit on by everyone," says Eunice, who thinks she is smiling.

Now the orchestra is playing a tango. The music speaks of love, of abandonment, of suicide. Some of the city's rich men come in. Lindinalva knows that businessman. When the Comendador's business was prospering, he once ate lunch at their house. The Comendador ended up in a brothel like this one; he died in a prostitute's room. How many of these women here had known him? How many had laughed at him? How many had hoped he would come so they could ask him for money? Now Lindinalva also hopes for some Comendador who will bring her money, who will buy drinks so Lulu will be satisfied and not put her out. The tango speaks of abandon. Here in the boardinghouse, Lindinalva doesn't want to remember her son. At this very moment he would be stretching out his arms to Amelia. When he learns to say "mama" he will say it to Amelia. When he smiles, Lindinalva will not be there. The two young men whisper with the brunette girl. What are they proposing to her? She shakes her head no. But it's a bad day, there aren't many customers. They insist, and she goes with both of them to the bedroom. Angry, Eunice spits forcefully. Lindinalva wants to cry. Lulu smiles and shows Lindinalva to the businessmen. She says something in a low voice. Eunice advises, "Your turn's come."

Lindinalva knows that man. He ate at the same table with her father and mother. She doesn't want to take him to bed. She'd prefer anyone else, even the Negro Antônio Balduíno. But the man beckons to her with his fat finger. Didn't the brunette girl go with two? Lindinalva gets up. Lulu motions for her to hurry up. Eunice lifts her glass of rum.

"Here's to your début."

The Frenchwoman shrugs. What does it matter? They are all dead, the tango is saying it. Eunice has already said so, too. She is no longer Lindinalva, the pallid girl who used to run in Nazaré Park. Lindinalva is dead; Amelia has her son. When she walks past Lulu, the madame tells her to order champagne. The brunette girl comes back from the bedroom with an air of alarm and tears in her eyes. The two young men laugh and trade impressions. Lindinalva orders champagne. Later, in the bedroom, the businessman (he had eaten at her house) asks her what her specialty is. But they are all dead, they have all died. Eunice drinks more rum, the tango sobs. Such was Lindinalva's reception.

She soon grew too worn and haggard for the expensive brothels. The rich men didn't find her attractive. Now her mouth always held the stale odor of rum. Eunice had already moved to the Rua de Baixo where the women charged five mil-reis. Today Lindinalva would go there, too; she had rented a room in the same house as Eunice. Earlier in the day, she had gone to visit her son in Amelia's little room. Gustavinho is beautiful, his large eyes lively, his mouth as fleshy as that red flower Gustavo talked about. Lindinalva doesn't even remember its name. Now she knows obscene words in French and all the slang of streetwalkers. But the little boy says, "Mama, mama," and she feels as pure as a virgin. She tells him stories, the same ones she heard from Amelia in the old days when she was Lindinalva. The madame of the house she had moved into said that her name would be Linda from now on. She tells the little boy the story of Cinderella and grows happy, so happy. (How wonderful, she thought, if the world would end at that very moment, if everyone would die.)

The women sit in the lounge behind the partly opened windows, calling to the men who pass by in the street. Some come in, others make jokes, some walk hurriedly away, carrying packages. Eunice is drunk, saying she has already died, that they are all in hell. The old Polish woman complains of her bad luck; last night she didn't find a man, nor today, either. Maybe she would have to go to the Ladeira do Taboão where the women charge a thousand five-hundred, do everything, and die early. Lindinalva is far away, with her son in Amelia's poor little room. He smiles and says "Mama." What a mad desire to kiss her son's fleshy lips, to keep telling him the story of Cinderella the rest of her life. The madame of the house turns on a Victrola in the dining room. Eunice's fallen breasts appear under her slip. She beckons the men from the window. Gustavinho, when he grew up, would perhaps pass through these streets. When this happened, Lindinalva would have died, and he will not find her behind the windows, calling to the men. He will remember her as someone sweet and pretty, who told him the story of Cinderella.

Eunice is saying they're all dead. The Polish woman asks to borrow two mil-reis. A long-haired youth answers Lindinalva's call. Eunice says, "Good luck, Linda!" and raises an imaginary glass.

In the bedroom, the boy asks her name, wants to know all about her life, says he is a poet, recites verses, tells her about his sick mother in the backlands, says she is beautiful as the acacias, compares her hair to the wheat fields, and promises to compose a sonnet about her. The Victrola in the dining room plays a hysterical samba. The boy likes a romantic tango. He asks Lindinalva's opinion about the political situation. "Disgusting, isn't it?"

Such was Linda's reception.

Lindinalva went down various hills. She went to live near the port district, on the hillside street called Ladeira do Taboão. From there the women only leave to go to the hospital or to the morgue. One way or another, they leave in an automobile: either an ambulance or in the red funeral car.

On the Ladeira do Taboão there are towels in the windows and black faces in the doorways.

Lindinalva had gone to see Gustavinho, who was getting over the mumps. He held out his arms and smiled with the joy of seeing his mother again.

"Mama, Mama!"

Then he made a serious little face and asked, "When are you coming to live with us, Mama?"

"Mama will come, son, one of these days."

"When you come it'll be so good, Mama."

Lindinalva passed near the old elevator that connected the lower part of the city to the upper. She smiled at the streetcar conductor and went to find number 32, where she had rented a room.

Gustavinho needed to gain weight. With the mumps, he had grown thinner. She pushed open the heavy colonial door with its great metal ring. The number 32 was daubed on with light blue paint, in very large figures. From above someone called, "Who's that?"

Lindinalva went up the dirty staircase, her eyes almost closed, her chest heaving. She had spent the night thinking. At first she had tried to sleep, but when she had managed to drop off, she had horrible nightmares in which she saw syphilitic women with enormous fingers banded together at the door of a tiny hospital. They were carrying an ambulance . . . No, it wasn't an ambulance; it was the body of the Comendador, who had died in a whorehouse. And then it was the body of Gustavinho, who had died of the mumps. Suddenly everything was gone, and there was only the Negro Antônio Balduíno, laughing loudly with pleasure, some coins in his hand.

She awoke sweating and got up to get a drink of water.

That was a horrible night in her life. Now Lindinalva didn't want to think. After all, it was destiny . . . that was how destiny was. Good for some, miserable for others. Each person was born with his fate; it didn't come in the ship *Catarineta.* If her fate was a bad one, what could she do?

Condemned, she went up the stairs. The night before, the mulatto woman who had rented the fifth-floor room to her had been frank.

"When you leave here, love, you'll go either to the hospital or to the grave." She looked through the window at the sky. "I've seen so many go."

Lindinalva climbs the stairway, her eyes distant. Where was the old Lindinalva who used to laugh and play in Nazaré Park?

Her back is bent; tears roll down her thin cheeks. Yes, Lindinalva is crying. Tears fall from her eyes, tears that melt the dirt off the staircase. Lindinalva walks bent over, her white, freckled face hidden in her arm. The tears slide off her sad face. Lindinalva has a son and would like to live for him. But from the Ladeira do Taboão the women only go to the cemetery.

On the fifth floor one woman says to another, ''It's Freckles coming. Don't try to talk, the poor thing is crying.'' The voice holds an ardent pity.

Such was Freckles's reception.

CHAPTER 23
Cranes

They will go to the Drowned Man's Lantern, to the harbor where the night is pretty. They leave Baixa dos Sapateiros and go down the Ladeira do Taboão. Finally, Gordo has discovered a star that no one has ever seen.

"Look! A new star! That one's mine."

Gordo has gotten a star, and he is very pleased. Jubiabá says that the stars are courageous men who died. Today a valiant man must have died, a man who deserved an ABC, for Gordo discovered a new star. Joaquim looks for one but can't find any. Antônio Balduíno wonders who died tonight. There are brave men everywhere. When he dies, he will shine in the sky, too, and Gordo will discover him. Or maybe he will be discovered by a child, a beggar urchin with a razor in his waistband. They like to wander through the deserted streets when the moon is full, illuminating the city with its yellow light. No one else is about; the windows of the houses are closed, the people are asleep. Once again they are owners of the city as in their days of begging. They are the only free men of the city. They are bums who live on what comes along, sing at parties, sleep in the sand of the boat landing, make love to the mulatto housemaids, have no set time to go to bed or get up. Zé Camarão, who is starting to age, never had a job. He had always been a hooligan, a known troublemaker, guitar player, *capoeira* fighter. Antônio Balduíno, his greatest disciple, has surpassed even the master. He has been everything: plantation laborer, boxer, and circus artist. However, he lives off writing an occasional samba and singing it at Negro parties around the city. Joaquim works three or four days a month when he feels like it. He carries suitcases for other porters who have too much to do. Gordo sells newspapers when Balduíno isn't in Bahia. When Balduíno arrives, he stops working and follows after the Negro in that pleasant vagabond life, doing nothing, running free about the sleeping city. Antônio Balduíno asks, "Shall we anchor in the Drowned Man's Lantern?"

"Sure."

The Ladeira do Taboão is silent at this hour of the night. The old elevator is no longer running, and its shaft towers over the buildings. A few lights shine down the street in the highest windows as the prostitutes coming back from the streets dispatch the last men.

Joaquim whistles a samba. They walk without speaking, and only Joaquim's whistle cuts the silence. Antônio Balduíno is thinking about what Amelia told him, the story of Lindinalva. Now she must have no pride left, and whenever he wants, he can possess her. She is no longer his boss lady, the rich daughter of the Comendador; she is a prostitute on the Ladeira do Taboão and sells herself to the men for two mil-reis. How things change! The day he wants, he can go up the steps of the building where she is and have her in his arms. He has only to pay a little change. He remembers when he ran away from Zumbi dos Palmares Street. If Amelia hadn't invented those lies he would have stayed on with the Comendador, seeing Lindinalva as a saint, working in the commercial establishment, maybe impeding his boss's bankruptcy. He would have been a slave. Amelia, wanting to do him harm, had actually done him a favor. He was free and could even possess Lindinalva whenever he wanted. She was freckled and had the face of a saint. He had never thought of desiring her, but ever since Amelia's lies about him spying on her as she bathed, he hadn't possessed another woman. No matter who he took to bed, he was making love to Lindinalva. Even when he slept with Rosenda Rosedá. He had given Rosenda to the chauffeur. Now she was dancing in a cheap cabaret and had become a prostitute as well. She had already sent to ask him for a loan. Rosenda was a vain woman, and now she was having to pay. Lindinalva wasn't vain, but she had hated him. She was getting paid back, too. She was living on the Ladeira do Taboão among the cheapest, most worn-out whores in the city. He could have her the day he wanted. So why isn't he happy, why does he grow sad and ignore the spectacle of the lovely full moon? Hasn't he waited all his life for the day to come when he might possess Lindinalva? Why doesn't he go up to the fifth floor of number 32, Ladeira do Taboão, and knock on Lindinalva's door? There is the house; they're passing right in front of it. The street slumbers, its silence broken only by Joaquim's whistling. Now, what cold wind blows off the sea, making Antônio Balduíno tremble? Suddenly a wild-haired woman darts out the door of number 32. The instant she appears in the doorway, Antônio Balduíno is certain she is Lindinalva. But the woman is a human rag, a figure who lost its name on the Ladeira do Taboão. It has a hollow, freckled face; thin, trembling hands; brilliant, feverish eyes. The wind lifts her hair. She stops in front of the men, agitates her arms, and wrings her hands in a gesture of supplication.

"Two mil-reis for a glass of beer . . . two mil-reis for the love of your mother."

The men are mute with surprise. She thinks they are refusing her.

"Then a cigarette . . . a cigarette. I haven't smoked in two days."

Joaquim gives her a cigarette. She clutches it in her thin fingers and laughs.

Yes, it is Lindinalva. Antônio Balduíno trembles uncontrollably. A cold wind blows off the sea. With her appearance, a profound terror invades him, causing him to shake, making him want to flee to the ends of the earth. But he is rooted to the ground, staring at Lindinalva's wasted, freckly face. She doesn't recognize him, nor even see him at all. She smokes her cigarette and asks in a sweet voice, a voice that reminds him of the other Lindinalva who used to run through Nazaré Park and play with the little black boy Baldo, "And the beer? You'll give it to me, won't you?"

Antônio Balduíno manages to get ten mil-reis out of his pocket and gives it to the woman who laughs and hiccups. Then, shaking with terror, he ran up the hill, stopping only when he reached Jubiabá's house, and sobbed against the pai-de-santo, who comforted him as on the day old Luísa went crazy.

When the terror passed (it lasted for days) he went back to Lindinalva's house. In the room where the double bed took up most of the space, Lindinalva was near the end. Amelia contained her tears. He went in softly, warned by the prostitute sobbing in the doorway. Amelia was not surprised to see him. She held a finger to her lips, signaling him to be quiet, and came over near him. He pointed to Lindinalva and asked, "Sick?"

"Dying."

With her approaching death, she had become again the Lindinalva of Zumbi dos Palmares Street. Her freckled face, the face of a saint, was serene and lovely. Her hands, which had played the piano and pulled apart roses, are the same. There is nothing left of the Lindinalva from the Monte Carlo Boardinghouse, of Linda from the Rua de Baixo, of Freckles from the Ladeira do Taboão. Once again she is the Comendador's daughter who lived in Zumbi dos Palmares Street and awaited a fiancé from the ship *Catarineta.* But she moves, and another Lindinalva appears. This one Antônio Balduíno never knew, but Amelia recognizes her. It is Gustavo's bride, Gustavo's lover, Gustavinho's mother, the smiling face of a young married woman. She murmurs something. Amelia draws near and holds her hand. She is saying that she wants her son, that they must bring him, as she is going to die. Amelia comes back crying. Antônio Balduíno asks her, "And the doctor?"

"He can't do anything more. He said there's nothing to do but wait for her to die."

But Antônio Balduíno won't accept that. He has an inspiration.

"I'll go get Jubiabá."

"Stop by my house and bring the child."

So Balduíno, who had come here to get revenge, to possess Lindinalva and afterward throw two mil-reis on her bed, insult her, tell her that white women were worthless, that a black man like him does what he wants, instead goes off to get pai Jubiabá and see if he can save her life. If she gets better, he will disappear. But if she dies, what will happen in his own life? There will be no other road left for him except the sea road Viriato the Dwarf had taken; Viriato, who also had nobody in the world. Only then does Antônio Balduíno understand that if Lindinalva dies, he will be alone, without a motive to live.

He comes back with the boy. Jubiabá wasn't home. Nobody knew where he had gone, and Antônio Balduíno's search was in vain. He cursed the old medicine man. The child holds the Negro's hand, and they get along very well. He has Lindinalva's nose, and freckles like hers on his face. He asks Balduíno lots of questions about everything. Antônio Balduíno answers them all, amazed at his own patience.

He carries the child up the steps. Choking back her sobs, Amelia advises, "She's almost gone . . . come in."

Antônio Balduíno deposits the child near the bed. Lindinalva opens her eyes.

"Son . . ."

She wants to smile, but it turns into a grimace. Frightened, the child begins to cry. Lindinalva kisses his cheeks, and Amelia takes him away. She wanted to kiss his fleshy lips, the lips that were Gustavo's, but she can't.

Now she is crying and doesn't want to die, she who prayed for death so often. She senses the presence of someone else in the room and asks Amelia, "Who is it?"

Amelia is confused, not knowing what she ought to say. But Antônio Balduíno draws near, his eyes lowered. If his friends could see him now, they probably wouldn't understand why he is crying. Lindinalva tries to smile when she recognizes him.

"Baldo . . . I was bad to you."

"Never mind."

"Forgive me."

"Don't say that. Don't make me cry."

She strokes his stiff hair and dies, saying, "Help Amelia raise my son, Baldo. Look out for him."

Antônio Balduíno throws himself down at the foot of the bed like a black slave.

He wants the casket to be white like a virgin's. But nobody understands him, not even Jubiabá, who knows so many things. Gordo only agrees because he is very good, but at heart he is uneasy because he never heard of a prostitute's casket being white. Only Amelia seems to understand.

"You cared a lot for her, didn't you? I made trouble between you. I was jealous because the boss liked you so much. I'd been with them for twenty years. I raised the little girl, and she deserved a better destiny . . . so sweet . . ."

Then Antônio Balduíno spread his hands out and explained in the heavy voice he had from time to time, "She was a virgin, folks. I swear she was. No one had her. She didn't belong to anyone. She made her living this way, but she didn't give herself. I was the only man who had her. Only me, folks. When I went to bed with a woman, I thought only of her. I want a white casket for her."

It was true, no one had possessed her because they had all bought her. Only the Negro Antônio Balduíno, who never slept with her, possessed her in all her forms, in the virgin body of Maria dos Reis, in the dancing hips of Rosenda Rosedá. He alone possessed her in the bodies of all the women he slept with. The love between the black Antônio Balduíno and the white Lindinalva had been amazing in its variety. She had been white, black, and mulatto, had even been a little Chinese girl in Maria Paz Street. She had been fat and thin; on a certain night beside the harbor she had had a masculine voice. She had lied like the *cabrocha* Joana. Amelia tries to explain to Balduíno that she can't have a virgin's burial, that she loved Gustavo, who possessed her without buying her. But Antônio Balduíno doesn't want to hear it; he believes that this story is another of Amelia's lies to keep him away from Lindinalva.

To help her son, Antônio Balduíno went to work as a stevedore in place of Clarimundo, who was killed by a crane. With a job, he would be a slave to the clock, to the foreman, to the cranes and the ships. But if he didn't work at a job, he would have no alternative but the road to the bottom of the sea.

The enormous shadows of the cranes fall over the water. The oily green depths call to Antônio Balduíno. The cranes brutalize men into slaves and kill them. They are the enemies of black men, the friends of the rich. The sea makes men free. He could take a deep dive and still have time to laugh freely. But Lindinalva had stroked his hair and asked him to take care of her son.

CHAPTER 24
First Day of the Strike

Antônio Balduíno had spent the night unloading a Swedish ship that had brought material for the railroad. On the following nights, it would be loaded with cocoa. Carrying a heavy bundle of rails, he went by a thin mulatto man called Severino, who said to him, "The streetcar guys are going to strike today."

This strike had been expected for a long time. Several times the workers of the company that controlled the city's power, telephone, and transit systems had tried to band together and demand a raise in salary. They had actually held a strike earlier but had been placated with promises that afterward were never kept. For eight days now, the city had been expecting to find itself without streetcar transportation or telephones. But the strike was always postponed; nothing happened. So Antônio Balduíno didn't attach much importance to Severino's announcement. But soon he heard a tall Negro say, "We should stick with them, help them out."

The cranes were depositing enormous rolls of iron on the docks. The Negroes carried the rolls toward the warehouses, looking like strange monsters, and as they worked, they conversed. The foreman's whistle gave orders. A white man wiped the sweat from his forehead, shaking it from his hand.

"Do you think they'll get anywhere?"

They came running back to the rolls of iron. Severino murmured as he lifted his burden, "Their union has money to back up the strike."

He hurried off with his load. Antônio Balduíno picked up pieces of railroad track.

"Every month, money goes to the union. So it has to back it up."

The foreman's whistle ordered the night shift to abandon its work. The day shift men were waiting and immediately substituted those who were leaving. The material for the railroad continued to go into the dock warehouses. The cranes screeched.

They leave in groups. At the entrance to the docks, Antônio Balduíno remembers a man who was arrested there once for making a speech. He was only a boy at the time, but he remembered the incident perfectly. He and his group had yelled, protesting against the man's arrest. They had yelled because they loved to yell, to boo the police, to throw rocks at soldiers. Today, he needed to yell again, as in those days when he ran free through the streets and didn't sense the cranes were enemies ready to bash in his head.

Antônio Balduíno comes through the streets alone. He stops to eat a dish of *mingau* in Terreio Square. Near the black woman's food stand men discuss the strike. Antônio Balduíno goes off, singing a song about the bandit Lampião.

"Mama, give me money
A cartridge belt to buy.
I'm joining up with Lampião
So Mama, don't you cry."

An acquaintance yells, "Hello, Baldo!"
The black man waves and continues to sing.

"Now Lampião he had a wife,
Whose heart was nearly broke.
She tried to make herself a dress
Of vapor clouds and smoke."

Now he sings under his breath, between his teeth, "Lamp, Lamp, Lamp, Lamp, Lampião."

With the paralysis of the streetcars, the city has grown festive. There is an unusual stirring of excitement. Groups of men go by, their conversation lively. Store clerks pass, laughing and joking because their bosses can't complain if they arrive late today. A young girl crosses the street hurriedly, afraid of something. Streetcar conductors and workers from the Public Utilities Company are everywhere. They discuss the heat. Antônio Balduíno envies them because they are doing something he would like to do, and he himself has nothing to do on this sunny morning. The groups pass. They are on their way to the union office, situated in a nearby street. Alone, Balduíno follows through the deserted alleys. A block away he hears the noise of conversation. It seems someone is making a speech in the syndicate office. He, too, belongs to the stevedores' union. Once they even asked him to be a candidate for the board. They must know he is brave. Suddenly, a drunken blond man with a cigarette hanging from his lip reeled over to block Balduíno's way.

"You going on strike, too, nigger? All because Princess Isabel decided to abolish slavery. Whoever saw a nigger that was worth anything? And look what's happenin' now! They're even going on strike, stopping the streetcars. They should all get whipped; Negroes are good for nothing but slaves. Go on to your strike, nigger! Didn't the idiots set all this rabble free? Get lost, you son of a bitch, before I spit on you!"

The drunken man spits on the ground. Antônio Balduíno knocks him flat on the cement with a hard push and brushes his hands clean. Afterward, he wonders why this man insults Negroes in such a way. The strike was begun by streetcar operators and public utility workers. Among them were many Spaniards, some even lighter-skinned than the drunk. But all poor people have become black; that was how Jubiabá explained it.

The sound of fighting comes from Terreiro Square. It's the bakery workers who have joined in the strike. The men who deliver bread have dumped their baskets in the street. The urchins fall on the loaves. Even maids from rich houses come to scavenge for free bread.

They find him in Amelia's room, crawling on all fours, playing with Gustavinho.

"I'm a werewolf!"

He jumps up. Severino puts a hand on his shoulder and tells him, "We need you, Balduíno."

"What is it?" asks the Negro, immediately thinking of a fight.

"The syndicate is going to have a meeting."

The Negro Henrique mops the sweat from his face.

"We had an awful time finding you."

They are staring at the white boy sitting on the floor. Confusedly, Antônio Balduíno explains to them, "He's my son."

"We want to join in the strike. We need your vote."

He leaves Gustavinho with Gordo and goes happily out, glad to be part of the strike. In the union office, there is a great uproar. Everyone is talking at the same time, and nobody can understand a thing. The board takes charge of the floor and asks for silence. A pale man says to Balduíno, "There are police here."

But Balduíno doesn't see any soldiers. "In disguise," the pale man explains.

Severino makes a speech. The public utility workers are not the only ones who are hungry. The dockworkers are also without food. Moreover, they have a duty to stick together with the public utilities workers; they are all brothers. They must adhere to the strike. Other speeches follow. One of the foremen, a little red-faced man who used to play dice with them at the Drowned Man's Lantern during his leisure hours, recites a speech saying that this is all nonsense, that he sees no reason for the strike, that they are all perfectly well off. But he is shouted down, booed. Black Henrique pounds his fist on the table and declares, "I'm just a dumb Negro, and I don't know any pretty words. But I know that there are men here with hungry children and hungry wives. Those Spaniards who drive the streetcars are hungry, too. We're black, they're white, but we're all poor and hungry."

The vote to join the strike passed, with the victory assured by Antônio Balduíno's vote. Only later was it discovered that many who had voted against them were people who didn't work at the docks, let alone belong to the stevedores' union.

A manifesto was drawn up. A commission was designated to convey the news of the dockworkers' support to the striking public utilities workers. Antônio Balduíno was part of this commission, and he was pleased because he planned to fight, get into trouble, yell—in short, do all the things he enjoyed.

TO OUR FELLOW WORKERS IN THE PUBLIC UTILITIES COMPANY:

The assembly of dockworkers, by a decision taken in their trade union, have resolved to adhere to the movement of their friends in the public utilities. They bring their unconditional support to the strike, in the battle for better wages and working conditions. Our friends at the Public Utilities Company can rely on the stevedores. Higher salaries! Eight-hour workdays! The abolishment of fines! These are things we all want.

Signed,
The Stevedores' Union Board

All the transport service was stopped; phones were dead. At night there would be no electric light. The utility workers had sent a memorandum outlining their demands to the highest officials of the company. They had replied that they would not agree and had appealed to the government to back them up. Newspapers weren't circulating due to the lack of electricity. There were many people in the streets, and groups of workers were talking on every corner. Cavalry patrols passed by. Rumors went around that the Public Utilities Company was contracting unemployed people at the price of gold in order to frustrate the strike. A lawyer—Dr. Gustavo Barreira, representing the workers' organization—approached the governor, and they discussed the situation at length. When he returned, he declared to the allied syndicates that the government found the workers' intentions just and that it would negotiate with the company directors. There was much clapping. Stretching out his arms, the young lawyer seemed already to be gathering the votes that would elect him a senator. Severino said aloud, "Double-talk."

Although Antônio Balduíno was tired of hearing so many

speeches, he liked them. This was something new for him, and he was enjoying it. It was good. He felt that at this moment they were the owners of the city. The owners of the truth. If the workers chose, there was no light, no streetcars, no phones for the sweethearts to chat over; the rails for the railroad wouldn't be unloaded from the Swedish ship. Nor would it take its bags of cocoa stored in Warehouse No. 3. The cranes were stopped, beaten by the enemies whom they used to kill. The owners of the cranes, the men who used to order the workers around, hid themselves in fear, afraid to be seen. Antônio Balduíno had always had great scorn for those who worked. He would have preferred to kill himself one night in the harbor than to work, if Lindinalva hadn't asked him to take care of her son. But now the Negro viewed workers with a new respect. They could quit being slaves. When they chose to act as one, nobody could control them. Those thin men who had come from Spain to work as streetcar collectors, those Herculean Negroes who carried burdens in the docks or maintained the machinery in the electric plants were strong and resolute, and they had the city's life in their hands. Nevertheless, they go by smiling, poorly dressed, often barefoot, and hear insults from those who are jeopardized by the strike. But they laugh because now they know that they are a unified force. Antônio Balduíno had discovered this, too, and it was as if he had become a new person.

The man with the overcoat got up from the table in the bar and asked a worker, "What's the strike all about?"

"To get a better salary."

"But what do you fellows need?"

"Money."

"You want to be rich, too?"

The worker grew confused. In truth, he had never thought about becoming rich. What he wanted was more money so his wife wouldn't complain so much, so he could pay for a doctor's visit (his little daughter was sick), to buy another suit of clothes since the one he had was threadbare.

"You want an awful lot. Whoever heard of workers needing so many things?"

The worker is confused. Antônio Balduíno came over to them. The man in the overcoat continued talking.

"Want some advice? Forget this nonsense about the strike. It's just agitators who want to disturb law and order, inventing these things. You'll end up losing the job you have and the money you're earning now. If you try to get too much, you'll end up with nothing."

The worker remembers his complaining wife and sick child. He lowers his head. Antônio Balduíno insults the man in the overcoat. "Who's paying you to tell that kind of story?"

"You're one of them, aren't you?"

"I'm man enough to push your face in."

"Do you know who you're talking to?"

"No, and I don't care, either."

Why should he care, if the city belonged to them? Today he could say what he liked, because they were giving orders in the city.

"I'm Doctor Malagueta, do you hear?"

"The doctor who works for the public utilities people, right?"

It was Severino speaking as he came up. Several workers came with him, including Henrique, the gigantic black stevedore. The man in the overcoat turned the corner. The worker who was talking with him joined the group.

Severino explained, "Boys, the strike is like those necklaces you see in the store windows. They have to be strung on a string. If you cut the string, all the beads fall apart. We need to hang together through this strike."

The worker, whose name was Mariano, nodded his head in agreement.

Antônio Balduíno went with them to the public utility workers' syndicate office to wait for the results of the conference between the government and the directors of the company.

At the board of directors' table in the union office, a black man was finishing a speech.

"My father was a slave. I was a slave, too, but I don't want my children to be slaves!"

All the chairs are occupied, and many men are standing up because there are no more seats.

A delegation of bakers comes to give its support to the strike and reads a manifesto encouraging the whole proletariat to join. "General strike!" they scream in the room. A police investigator smokes, leaning against the door. There are other plainclothesmen, but the workers pay no attention to them. Now a young man with glasses is talking, saying that the workers are an immense majority while the rich are a small minority. So why are the rich sucking the blood of the poor, living on their sweat? Why does this majority stupidly work for the comfort of the few?

Antônio Balduíno claps. All this is new to him, but what they are saying is right. He never knew it, but he always felt it. That was why he had never wanted to work. The ABCs said those things, but they didn't say them so clearly, they didn't explain. He was listening and learning as he used to in the nights on Capa-Negro Hill. The young man got down from the chair where he had been speaking. The black man who had spoken earlier moved nearer Antônio Balduíno, and the latter embraced him.

"I have a son, too, and I don't want him to be a slave, either."

The black speaker smiled. A student representative began to speak. The law students' organization was solidly allied with the strikers. In his discourse, the student called for all the workers, students, poor intellectuals, peasants, and soldiers to unite in the fight against capitalism. Antônio Balduíno didn't understand very well. But after the black speaker explained to him that "capitalism" and rich people meant the same thing, he cheered the orator. Suddenly, he felt like jumping up on a chair and speaking, too. He had something to say; he had seen many things. He pushed his way through the crowded room and got up on a chair. The workers asked each other, "Who's he?"

"A stevedore. He used to be a boxer."

Antônio Balduíno speaks. He doesn't make a speech, but rather tells what he has seen in the course of his vagabond life. He narrates the hardships of the peasants on the tobacco plantations where the men work and live without women. He tells them of the women in the cigar factories. They can ask Gordo if they think it's a lie. He tells what he has seen, explaining that he hadn't respected workers, people who held jobs. But he went to work because of his son. And now he saw that the workers, if they wanted, could free themselves from slavery. If the laborers on the tobacco plantations knew about this, they would join the strike, too.

They almost carry him out of the room in their enthusiasm. He still doesn't understand his triumph fully. Why do they applaud so? He didn't tell any pretty story, he didn't punch anybody, he didn't commit any courageous act. He only told what he had experienced. But the men applaud, and many embrace him as he goes past. An investigator stares at him so as not to forget his face. Antônio Balduíno is liking the strike more and more.

The young man with glasses goes out, and an investigator follows him. Dr. Gustavo Barreira telephones the union office from the governor's palace to say that the conference will be prolonged until the evening, at which time, possibly, they will have reached a solution.

''Favorable?'' asks the union secretary.

''Honorable,'' answers Dr. Gustavo from the other end.

The bells strike six o'clock.

CHAPTER 25
First Night of the Strike

The night is beautiful; there are no clouds in the deep blue, starry sky. It seems like a summer night. Even so, people stay at home. They will not go out walking tonight, for the city is dark; there isn't a single light bulb shining on the high black posts. Even the lamp in Drowned Man's Lantern is out.

The harbor has never been so silent. The cranes sleep; tonight the stevedores will not come to work. The crew of the Swedish ship goes off to the whorehouses. There is no movement in the commercial streets, either. People are fearful when there is no light. Inside the houses the red glow of kerosene lamps makes the shadows bigger. And the weak light of candles brings memories of wakes and dead loved ones. Antônio Balduíno remembers the tobacco plantations as he walks through the street. A man passes him, his back against the wall. He clutches his wallet through his suit coat. Whoever saw him would say he was clutching at his heart. The city is enveloped by the sounds of drums that come from the macumba session in Jubiabá's house. Today these drumbeats sound to Antônio Balduíno's ears like warrior music, the music of freedom. The star which is Zumbi dos Palmares shines in the bright sky. A student had once laughed at Antônio Balduíno and told him that that star wasn't a star, it was the planet Venus. But he laughed at the student because he knew that the star was Zumbi dos Palmares, valiant Negro who died so as not to be a slave. Shining in the sky, Zumbi sees Antônio Balduíno fighting so that Gustavinho will never be a slave. That day of the strike had been one of the most beautiful of Balduíno's life. As beautiful as when he fled through the jungle escaping from the surrounding gunmen.

As beautiful as the day he won the boxing championship after knocking out Vicente. Even more beautiful. Now he knows what his battle is about. And he is walking quickly so as to talk to all the Negroes who are at Jubiabá's macumba ceremony. He wants to tell them all: Gordo, Joaquim, Zé Camarão, Jubiabá himself. He doesn't understand why Jubiabá never taught him about the strike; Jubiabá, who knew everything. Zumbi dos Palmares, who is the planet Venus, winks at him from the sky.

Can it be that Exú, Exú the devil, is perturbing the ceremony? Can it be that they forgot to send him away, forgot to drive him far off to the other side of the sea, to the coast of Africa, to the cotton fields of Virginia? Exú is stubbornly trying to stay at the ceremony. Exú wants them to dance and sing in his honor. He wants greetings, wants Jubiabá to do him reverence and say, *"Ôkê! Ôkê!"*

Exú wants the high priestess of the assembly to ask them to let him through.

"Edurô dêmim lonan ô yê!"

He wants the audience to repeat in chorus, *"A Umbók'ô wá jo!"*

Exú will not go away. It is the first time that this has happened in a macumba ceremony in Jubiabá's house. The sounds of the drumbeats roll down the hill and die away far below in the alleys of the paralyzed city. The priestesses dance. The members look on in alarm. Antônio Balduíno goes quietly into the ceremony. He is an ogâ; he takes his place inside the circle of the dancing *feitas.* With Balduíno's presence, Exú goes away. Gordo says the ceremony is in honor of Oxossi. But before the god of the hunt can come to dance in the body of a priestess, Antônio Balduíno says, "Folks, you don't know anything. I'm thinking that you really don't know anything. You need to see the strike, to go to the strike. If the black people hold a strike, they aren't slaves anymore. What's the good of black people praying or singing to Oxossi? The rich people order Oxossi's festival closed. Once the police closed Oxalá's festival when he came as Oxolufã, the old man. And pai Jubiabá had to go with them; he went to jail. You remember, yes, you do! What can black people do? Black people can't do anything, can't even dance to their gods. Well, you don't know anything. When black people go on strike, everything stops, the cranes stop, the streetcars quit, and where's the lights? There are only the stars. Black people are the light, they're the streetcars. Black people and poor white people, they're all slaves, but they have everything in their hands. Folks, let's go on strike, because the strike is like a necklace. If we all hang together, it's something pretty. But if one bead falls down, the others have to fall, too. Folks, let's show them!"

And Antônio Balduíno goes out without seeing those who accompany him. Gordo goes with him, Joaquim and Zé Camarão also. Jubiabá holds out his hands and says, "Exú has possessed him."

At the union office they still await the results of the conference in the governor's palace. Severino repeats to whoever wants to hear, "They're trying to buy us off. Don't you see, that lawyer is yellow."

Others defend the lawyer. He is a learned man and knows many things. Right now he is giving his all for the rights of the exploited workers. A streetcar inspector makes a speech praising Dr. Gustavo. There are cheers mixed with booing.

The conference takes place in the palace salon. No conclusion is reached. Gustavo asks, in beautiful oratorical phrases, that the workers' demands be satisfied.

"Gentlemen, I do not ask, I insist!"

He speaks about humanity, about hungry men who work eighteen hours a day and often die of tuberculosis. He reminds them of the dangers of the social revolution if this state of things goes on.

However, the men who represent the company—a young American and an old gentleman who is a lawyer for the company and had once been a congressman—do not give in. The most they can do, declares the old lawyer, is to concede a fifty-percent salary increase. They only do this out of consideration for the people, so that the city doesn't have to do without transportation, lights, and telephones. For the workers, the solution will be excellent, he declares. But to give them all they ask is out of the question. They might as well turn the company over to them once and for all. Imagine the stockholders' reaction.

The workers are only thinking of themselves; they don't remember the foreigners who placed their trust in the Brazilian company when they invested their money. What would they say? They would say they had been robbed by the Brazilians, bringing certain dishonor to the name of the country. (The American nods his head in support.) He doesn't want to believe that Dr. Gustavo Barreira, who is a cultured and intelligent man (Gustavo bows) could think so unpatriotically, that he would wish to see the name of his country dragged through the mud in foreign places. Of course, the workers aren't thinking of this, which is understandable. They are ignorant men who already have more than they deserve and are taken in by the ideas of outside agitators. He does not refer—he underlines this emphatically—to Dr. Gustavo Barreira, whose honesty and talent he admires. (Gustavo bows again and murmurs, "I would never think of such a thing. My honor is above suspicion.") The company, so as not to allow these people to be wanting in anything essential to their comfort, would concede fifty percent of the raise demanded by the functionaries. Beyond that, they could do nothing.

The dinner hour arrives. The conference ends without results. The governor retires. The American offers Gustavo transportation in his automobile.

The company lawyer says, "Let's go have dinner together. With full stomachs we'll be able to discuss this far better."

How comfortable this Hudson is, thinks Gustavo, as he sits back in the automobile between the American and the lawyer. The American offers cigars. For a while they ride along in silence. The car is soft, the chauffeur uniformed. They pass near the streetcar tracks.

The lawyer asks the American, "And that idea of yours, Mr. Thomas?"

"Ah, yes."

The lawyer explains to Gustavo, "Imagine what a coincidence, sir. Only a few days ago we were mentioning you."

"Indeed we were," said the American, puffing on his cigar.

"I'm starting to feel a bit tired; I'm getting older," said the lawyer.

"You shouldn't say that."

"I won't say I'm not still able to practice law, of course. But the work in the company is very heavy for me. We, Mr. Thomas here and myself, were thinking about inviting someone to occupy the position of associate lawyer for the company. The firm has grown to the point of needing two lawyers, and you crossed our minds. No, don't think I'm saying this just to please you. Indeed no, sir."

Gustavo makes a gesture, protesting that his conscience didn't permit barter, and affirms that he would never imagine Dr. Guedes wanted to buy him, he was incapable of such a thing.

"The company thought about you, sir, or actually, I should say that Mr. Thomas and I"—Gustavo acknowledges him—"felt that you were the man because of your connections with the public services' trade union. You are a lawyer who knows the blue-collar man. Within the company you would represent the position of the humble working class. You would be a link between the workers and their company. There interests would be entrusted to you. You are a young man with a fine career ahead of you. The senate awaits. The nation is in need of your talents. Have no doubts that the company's intentions are the noblest possible. Many people think that the company has no interest in the well-being of its workers. They are mistaken. The proof that the company does indeed interest itself in their well-being could not be clearer: We invite their champion to be one of our own lawyers. That way, the workers will have a defender among the board members. And what a defender! I hope this will demonstrate, sir, the good faith with which the company acts."

The car is soft. Zuleika has been asking for a car. With the company in his hands, he could get to Congress during the next administration. The American is practical. "Your honorarium would be eight contos-de-reis per month, sir."

Gustavo protests that the question of money is the furthest thing from his mind; he is only interested in defending the workers who, he cannot deny, are at times excessive but who do have their reasons, after all. If he accepts, it would be as a guiding light for the rights of the workers. Of course, he doesn't support extreme measures, certainly not.

When dinner is over Dr. Guedes says, "Then you may take the good news to the workers, sir. We trust these children"—yes, they are hardly more than simple children, Dr. Gustavo affirms—"will go back to their jobs tomorrow. They will have a fifty-percent raise, and they owe this to the radiant talent and amiability of their lawyer, Dr. Gustavo."

After Gustavo leaves, the American spits.

"I've seen disgusting people before . . ."

Old Guedes laughs and orders champagne to commemorate the end of the strike.

"We'll put it on the company's bill, eh?"

A car for his wife, a reputation, a house in Copacabana, possibly a cocoa plantation. Fifty percent was quite a raise. The hundred percent the workers were demanding was too much. Besides, one always asks for more than one really expects to get. He had negotiated fifty percent for the workers. A victory, yes, indeed. And he had even kept his country's name from being tarnished.

At the syndicate headquarters Antônio Balduíno makes his third speech that day, just so that the son of Dr. Gustavo Barreira will not be a slave as he has been, as they all have been, black workers and white, in the docks, the bakeries, the public transport system, the light and telephone companies.

Head bowed, Mariano goes into his house. When he left that morning, his wife didn't know that the strike had been declared. Only at night does he have the courage to go home, to face her angry, fevered eyes and the listless gaze of his sick daughter. He is hardly inside when his wife screams, "Are you mixed up in this, Mariano?"

"In what?"

"Look at him, wanting to play the innocent little boy. I'm talking about this damned strike . . . you're mixed up in it, aren't you?"

"Why damned, Guilhermina? We want better wages, we want to get a little more money. It's for Lila's medicine. I don't see why you say 'damned . . .' "

"You want money? What you all want is to cause trouble, to hang around idle drinking in the streets until the wee hours. You think I don't know what you're up to? You think you're fooling me? You want medicine for Lila. If you were working the way you should, without getting mixed up in these things, you'd be an inspector already, and you'd be earning more. Strikes are the work of the devil; Padre Silvino says so every day. This is something the devil puts into the heads of crazy men like you. If you didn't get involved in such things you'd be an inspector."

Mariano listens without answering. When his wife finishes, and waits with her hands on her hips, Mariano only asks, "How's Lila?"

" 'How's Lila?' " she mimics. "She's just the same, how else should she be? You think a lot about her well-being, messing around with this strike. I'd prefer for God to strike me dead than to see my husband involved in the devil's doings."

She keeps away from Mariano as if he were the very devil himself. He goes to his daughter's bed and looks at her. She has an intestinal disease; the doctor said it was from eating dirt. These days, when he wasn't working, there was no food in the house. But probably Dr. Gustavo had settled everything with the company tonight, and tomorrow they would go back to work. He could pay for another visit to the doctor. He would bring medicine from the drugstore. But what if a settlement wasn't reached? What if the strike went on for eight, ten days? Then it would be awful, they would starve, the girl would die from lack of medicine. He doesn't want Lila to die. Even when Guilhermina was terrible, Lila smiled at him and kissed his bearded face. But the strike, Mariano, is a necklace of beads strung on a string. If one falls, they all fall. He hears Severino's voice and pushes the evil thought away, giving his daughter a kiss. From far away in the street, he still hears Guilhermina's angry voice.

The Negro Henrique picks his teeth with a fishbone. He puts his son on his lap and asks, "Do you know your lesson for tomorrow, fellow?"

The little black boy laughs, and putting his finger against his flat nose, guarantees that he knows it by heart. Ercídia comes out of the kitchen to say, "Tomorrow it'll be fish again."

"As long as we have fish, everything's fine, girl."

Henrique laughs with the boy. The little fellow is quick to learn, he can already do arithmetic.

"He's growing up strong, eh, Ercídia?"

The black woman smiles. The boy wants him to tell a story. Henrique says, "There was a black man who made a good speech at the union office today. He said our kids wouldn't be slaves anymore. You won't be a slave, will you, little fellow?"

"Will the strikers win?"

"Win? Why, of course! Who can stop us? It's in the bag, you'll see. It's a beautiful thing. There's this black man, Balduíno, who talks something wonderful."

He tells his wife about the day's happenings. His gigantic muscles ripple under his striped shirt. Then he picks up the boy and places him in front of his chair.

"Son, you're not going to be anybody's slave. You're going to be governor. There are many of us, and only a few of them. We'll end up ruling them."

He salutes the future governor and laughs aloud, secure in his strength, sure of the rightness of his cause. The black woman Ercídia smiles tenderly at her husband.

"Tomorrow we'll eat fish again."

The owner of the Two Worlds Bakery, a short Spaniard, recounts the day's events. His wife, sitting in her rocking chair, listens in silence. Their daughter taps out a samba with her fingers. The owner of the Two Worlds Bakery narrates the story of the strike and the day's principal happenings. The lantern light flickers. Miguel finishes his story and closes his eyes. His wife asks from the rocker, "But the bakery's still in business, isn't it, Miguel?"

"Oh, yes. With the men on strike, there will be some losses, but we'll make it up."

"Well, then I think those men are right. They live so miserably."

"Yes, they do. If it was up to me, I'd give them the raise. I said so at the meeting. The others, that Ruiz from the United

Bakeries, doesn't want to. Ruiz, anyway! He's never satisfied with anything, that man. If it was up to me, I'd give it."

The daughter interrupts.

"Why, Papa? Mr. Ruiz is right. We need so much money. I want that sports car and a radio. You promised me. Don't you remember? Now you want to give money to those shameless Negroes."

"Those who want everything at once end up with nothing," answered Miguel.

The wife reflects that her daughter was born in a comfortable home; she didn't escape the factories of Madrid in the third-class section of a ship like her parents. She had never gone hungry. She wants a car, a radio, and goodness knows what else. The black men want very little. She repeats to her husband, "Keep fighting for their raise, Miguel. Mr. Ruiz is a miser; he just wants to hoard his money."

The daughter dreams of a roadster that zooms down the street. Her boyfriend comes up to the window, saying, "I'm in favor of the strike. Because this way, with only the moonlight, you look even prettier."

When she has her car, she won't have to go out with the cashier from a dry-goods store. She'll go out with a student, somebody academic, and attend elegant parties.

Dr. Gustavo Barreira gets out of the taxi and goes up the union office steps two by two. Silence falls as he enters. The president moves aside, and he sits down at the officers' table, asking for their attention.

"Gentlemen, as your lawyer, I have worked all afternoon, together with the directors of the Public Utilities Company. But the best proof of my honest labors is the good news I bring you. Gentlemen, I will be concise. The problem is entirely solved"—the listeners lean forward to hear better—"thanks to the efforts put forth by your humble patron. After discussing the matter the entire afternoon, we came to the conclusion that the strike will be rightly settled, with honor on both sides, if we all compromise a little." Buzzing in the room. "On the one side, the company's intransigency softened. They had reached the point of refusing to negotiate with the workers while they were still striking, and not only did they agree to bargain, but actually reached a settlement, after hearing my arguments. The workers would concede fifty percent of their demands, and the company would give them a fifty-percent raise, with the new salary scale to be implemented immediately."

"Is this workers' politics or lawyers' politics?" interrupted Severino.

"The best politics." Dr. Gustavo smiles his most endearing smile. "And it is the right politics to gain, little by little, that which can't be gained all at once. If you give ears to the professional agitators, your battle will be lost, for extreme measures can work against you, like a double-edged knife. Then hunger will come knocking at your doors; misery will inhabit your homes."

"The union has money to back up the strike."

"Even if it goes on forever?"

"It'll have to end, because the city can't get along without lights and streetcars! They have to give us what we want. Brothers, let's not weaken!"

Dr. Gustavo is red with anger.

"You don't know what you're saying. I am a lawyer, I understand these things!"

"We know how much we need to keep from starving!"

"That's right, brother!" shouts Antônio Balduíno.

A young man asks for the floor. The men begin to clap as soon as he appears at the speakers' podium.

"Who's he?" Antônio Balduíno asks Henrique.

"He's a mechanic. His name is Pedro Corumba. Somebody wrote an ABC about his family; they went through hell in Sergipe. I've read it . . . he's an old hand at strikes. He's started 'em in Sergipe, Rio, São Paulo. I know him. Later I'll introduce you."

Pedro Corumba was saying, "When I go out, I tell my children, 'You are brothers of all the workers' children in Brazil.' I say that because I may die, and I want my children to continue in the fight for the redemption of the proletariat. Friends, we are being double-crossed. This isn't the first time I have participated in a strike. I know a betrayal when I see it. The workers cannot believe in anyone who is not a worker himself. Other people compromise, deceive. This fellow here''—he points to Dr. Gustavo—''is yellow. Who knows but what he already has a job in the company, or if they offered him a bribe?''

Dr. Gustavo bangs on the table, protests, says that the speaker is insulting him and that he is capable of losing his temper. But all the workers' eyes are on Pedro Corumba, who continues, ''Friends, we are being double-crossed. We cannot accept this proposal the company has made. If we do, they'll think we're weak, and tomorrow they'll take away the raise and leave us with nothing gained. We've started this, and we must see it through to the end. I prefer to die rather than abandon the strike that has begun. We shall win. We have to win. The proletariat is a force, and if it knows how to conduct itself, if it knows how to direct its power, it will have what it wants. Comrades, our proposals must be met. No compromises! Down with Dr. Gustavo Barreira and the Public Utilities Company! Hurrah for the workers! Hurrah for the strike!''

''Hurrah!'' The crowd's eyes are opened. Mariano smiles, black Henrique shows his teeth.

Antônio Balduíno says, ''The dockworkers agree with our friend Mr. Corumba. They are still waiting for their case to be resolved. They are for the utility workers' strike and hope that these people support them. They do not want a compromise. They want their proposals accepted as they are, and not halfway.''

He proposes that Gustavo Barreira, who was betraying them, be expelled from the floor. If Antônio Balduíno had known that he had been Lindinalva's lover, Gustavo wouldn't have left the room alive. The lawyer retires under protection of the police investigators. He is booed all the way down the stairs. But then there is a call for silence. Severino speaks and advises them that now the battle will be crueler, more difficult, for their enemies will say that they don't want to reach an agreement. He proposes that a manifesto be published for the public to read, and presents a manifesto he has already written. It is approved. The manifesto explains that they were betrayed, but that they will keep on fighting to the end and will only go back to work when the company accepts the conditions originally laid out.

A dark-haired man asks to be heard. He is against the continuation of the strike. He feels they should accept the fifty-percent raise; at least it's something. Those who demand too much at one time end up losing everything. Dr. Gustavo was right; what strength do workers have? Workers have no power at all . . . the police could stop the strike anytime they wanted.

"How? How could they?"

"But of course they could! We should be happy with the raise." He proposes that the assembly approve the termination of the strike and give Dr. Gustavo a vote of thanks.

Voices shout, "Sellout! Traitor!"

Others ask that they hear the speaker out. Various workers, among them Mariano, are half-agreeing with the dark-haired fellow. Fifty percent is something. If afterward they got nothing, it would be much worse. When the young man sits down, he is weakly applauded. But Antônio Balduíno yells from the place where he sits, "Folks, your eye of mercy has dried up. Is only the eye of badness left? You seem to have forgotten us dockworkers, and the bakery men, too. If you want to let them double-cross you, go ahead. Each one is his own man. But if you're dumb enough to risk losing everything in order to gain a tiny bit, I guarantee you I'll break the first head that goes out that door. I'm in the strike to win!"

Severino smiles. Many are impressed with Balduíno's speech. Gordo, who never saw anything like it, is trembling. The black man who spoke that afternoon speaks again. He shows that there was a betrayal, that they were sold out. Pedro Corumba gets up, too, citing examples from the strikes in São Paulo and Rio when they trusted in promises of lawyers pretending to be the workers' friends. But the audience is indecisive, the men converse among themselves, and those who accept the proposal gain a following.

The president wants to put it to a vote. Those who agree with the continuation of the strike should stand. Those who think they should accept the company's proposal should remain seated. But before the vote can be taken, a young worker dashes up to the platform and yells, "Comrade Ademar was arrested when he went out of here this afternoon. The company is paying people to break the strike!" He pauses for breath. "And they say the police are going to force the bakers to deliver bread tomorrow!''

Then the assembly rises as one man and votes, arms extended and fists clenched, for the continuation of the strike.

CHAPTER 26
Second Day of the Strike

Why sleep on such a beautiful night? Antônio Balduíno doesn't go to bed. He spends the rest of the night walking through the city with Gordo and Joaquim, putting up Severino's manifesto that explains the motives for the continuation of the strike. All the light posts have manifestos, as do the walls in the Ramos do Queiros and Baixa dos Sapateiros neighborhoods. A group led by Henrique has gone in the direction of Rio Vermelho. Some go to the Estrada da Liberdade area; others in the opposite direction to Calçada, and still others to the Lower City. Bahia is filled with manifestos, and everyone will know the reasons why the workers continue on strike. The Public Utilities Company is not generally liked, and the small businessmen, who view the workers with sympathy, come to work by bus. The company spreads the rumor that the price of streetcar tickets and phone and light bills will go up if the strikers win. But their strategy fails, for it only arouses greater animosity toward the company. The climate of good humor continues among the population; they are on the workers' side.

Antônio Balduíno (how much he had learned that day and that night!) explains the strike to Gordo and Joaquim. He is amazed that Jubiabá knows nothing about the strike. Jubiabá knows stories of slave days and things about spirits; he is free, yet he has never taught the enslaved people of the hill anything about the strike. Antônio Balduíno can't understand it.

From the direction of Pelourinho Hill comes the sound of a disturbance. Men go running by. From the syndicate office the noise of a shot is heard. Someone goes in saying, "The police want to force the bakers to deliver bread."

A group of men leaves the union office. But the commotion is over; on the ground remain the baskets that had held the day-old bread the bakery owners wanted to force their employees to deliver. A bakery worker with a black eye explains, "Cavalry soldiers came, but we didn't give it to them."

Another says that the Galega Bakery intends to deliver day-old bread, having hired unemployed people at double the normal salary. Moreover, the bakery guaranteed them a job for the rest of their lives.

An old oven operator yells, "We can't let them!"

Many people lean out the windows on Pelourinho Hill. New groups are constantly arriving from the union headquarters of the Public Utilities workers. Voices applaud the oven operator.

"Let's show them that they can't break the strike!"

Antônio Balduíno invites, "We'll bash in their heads!"

"No, we won't," says Severino. "We'll go there and explain to them that they shouldn't let themselves be used against other workers just like them. We don't need to make any trouble."

"But why so many speeches when we can just bash in their yellow faces?"

"They're not yellow. They just don't know anything. We've got to explain to them." Severino knows what he's saying.

Antônio Balduíno stops talking. Little by little, he is learning that in the strike, it's not one man alone who gives orders. In the strike they make up one body. The strike is like a necklace, but he doesn't feel sad at not being the leader of the strike. They are all leaders. They obey what is right. This struggle is different from any he has experienced in his whole life. What did he ever get from his other struggles? Their only outcome had been his being enslaved by the cranes, looking at the sea as a road home. But with the strike, the struggle was different. They were going to lose some of their slavery, gain more liberty. One day they would hold an even bigger strike, and they would not be slaves at all. Jubiabá knows nothing of this struggle. The men who are going to deliver the bread must not know, either. Severino is right. It's no good beating them up. The best thing is to convince them. And the black man follows the group toward the Galega Bakery, which is in Baixa dos Sapateiros.

The delivery men are about to go on their rounds. With the great baskets on their heads they look like masquerade figures. Severino climbs up on a light post and hangs on by one arm as he speaks. He explains to the men that they must be united with their brothers who are asking for a raise. That they shouldn't serve the bosses' interests by delivering the bread, that they shouldn't betray the class to which they belong.

"But we have no jobs," says one of them.

"And is that a reason to take someone else's away? Is it fair for you to take away the place of another man who is fighting for everyone's good? It's a betrayal."

A carrier puts down his basket of bread. Others follow suit. The crowd screams with enthusiasm. Even the more recalcitrant, like the man who interrupted, and others with families to support, set down their baskets before the enthusiasm of the crowd. Two who still want to deliver the bread are impeded by their very companions. Amid screams of "Hurrah for the strike!" they all go to the bakers' union office.

But later that afternoon things grew ugly for the bakers. Gordo, who had gone to eat and had taken a long time, brought them the news. The owner of the United Bakeries had sent to Feira de Santana to bring back oven men and kneaders. They had brought the men back by car, and on the next day there would be bread, for the men had already started to work this afternoon.

Panic began to spread among the bakers. Men were sent to the Public Workers' union office and to the stevedores' syndicate. If the United Bakeries managed to offer bread for sale, the bakers' strike could be considered finished, and the strikers would have lost not only the raise they asked for, but their jobs as well. Such a turn of events would seriously affect the strike of the Public Utilities workers and stevedores. If the bakers were beaten, the strike would lose an arm. It would be much easier to defeat the rest. Words fell thick as rain in the bakers' union office. Meanwhile, there was a rally in Castro Alves Square, calling for the liberation of the worker who had been arrested yesterday. In the midst of the rally, somebody announced the bakers' situation and told how the United Bakeries intended to break up the strike. Then the rally took on a more violent character, and they all went down to the bakers' union office. People were coming from the stevedores' union, too. Gordo went to the public utility workers' union to tell them the news.

At the bakers' union (the room was small for so many people) those representing the bakers, stevedores, Public Utilities workers, and students were speaking. A worker from a shoe factory spoke, too, saying his factory would hold a general strike if the situation called for it. More and more people were arriving at the union office. Severino was already hoarse and losing his voice. A manifesto was drawn up calling all the workers together for a general strike; it was resolved that they would impede the work of the bakers who had come from Feira de Santana.

The United Bakeries was made up of three large establishments. One was in Baixa dos Sapateiros, a second in the Vitoria neighborhood, and a third in a street downtown. The strikers joined together in three large groups and went to stand in front of the bakeries. Severino and a handful of men went to talk with workers from other factories and the bus and taxi drivers. All were preparing for a general strike. The Public Utilities Company and the company in charge of the docks refused to negotiate with the strikers. They would only acknowledge their proposals when the men came back to work. The bakery owners were trying to defeat the strike, too.

In the downtown area and in Vitoria, it was easy to stop the men hired by the bakery from working. They had been lured into coming by formidable promises, but in the very beginning Ruiz, the owner, refused to pay half of their money in advance as he had promised. He said he would only pay them the next day when the work was done. After an appeal to their feelings of solidarity, and after seeing the strikers' determination not to let them work, the new arrivals consented to go back to Feira de Santana by car. They left, cheering the strike.

But at the United Bakeries outlet in Baixa dos Sapateiros, things went differently. When the strikers came, the police were already festooning the bakery. Armed detectives had mingled with the workers. The group of workers stood in the street, waiting for the newly hired bakers to arrive. When the truck that was bringing them turned into the street, a worker placed himself in front of it, impeding its progress. Immediately, another man climbed up on a post and began a speech explaining to the bakers of Feira de Santana what the situation was and what the bosses were trying to do. The street was crowded. Men who had nothing to do with the strike stopped to see what was happening. One said to his friend, "I bet they go back."

"Five says they stay."

Boys and girls who had been playing in a nearby alley went to watch the spectacle. They enjoyed the excitement, as Antônio Balduíno had when the agitator had been arrested at the docks years ago. The children yelled when the workers did, enjoying themselves immensely. Mounted on his post, the worker continued his speech. The bakers of Feira de Santana listened, and some were convinced they should go back.

Suddenly, bullets rained. The detectives were shooting; the cavalry was attacking the workers. People were trampled underfoot in the running and pushing; hand-to-hand fights broke out. Antônio Balduíno had knocked over a man when he saw Gordo run in front of him, eyes popping out, the folds of fat on his face bouncing. The worker was still speaking, even amid the gunfire. Antônio Balduíno then saw that Gordo was gathering up the body of a small black girl who had been shot. He ran down the street, screaming, "Where is God? Where is He?"

The bakers from Feira de Santana went back in the same truck that had brought them. Two strikers remained flat on their backs in Baixa dos Sapateiros. One was dead, but the other could still smile.

Who is that Negro running through the calm or busy streets of the city, his arms stretched out? Why is he blaspheming, crying, asking for God? Why does he hold his arms out in front of him as if he were carrying something, and pass blindly without seeing the men and women who look at him, the life that moves about him, the sun shining? Where is he going, impervious to everyone? What is he holding in his arms, what is it he cradles with such affection? What is the invisible bundle that he cuddles gently to his chest? This fat, sad-eyed Negro traversing the streets at the rush hour, what does he want? To all who pass near him he repeats the same anguished question, "Where is God? Where is God?"

His voice is desolate, tragic. Who is this man, who leaves a deep impression on those who pass him in the city? Nobody knows.

The strikers know it's Gordo, who went crazy when he saw the bullet from a detective's revolver kill a small black girl in front of one of the United Bakeries outlets on the day of the rally. They know that he is carrying the cadaver of the girl to the house of the pai-de-santo Jubiabá, and that he always repeats the same question, "Where is God?"

He was very religious, and he went crazy. Now he walks with his arms extended as if he were still carrying the dead girl's body; He doesn't harm anyone; he is a tame madman.

However, not even they know everything. They don't know that ever since the day of the rally, Gordo has carried that little black girl in the certainty that at any moment God will remember her, will show that he is good, and will raise her up to play with other children in the streets of Baixa dos Sapateiros. On that day Gordo will stop repeating his question and will lower his arms. His eyes will lose their sad expression. But if he knew that she had died, that her poor coffin had been buried a long time ago, then he, too, would die. For even God's eye of mercy, which is as big as the world itself, would have dried up. Then he wouldn't believe anymore and would die, disgraced and damned. So, harmless madman, he walks about with arms outstretched, cuddling to his chest the thin body of the black child who died at the rally. It doesn't matter that people can't see the small bullet-ridden body. It weighs down Gordo's arms, and he feels its warmth as he presses it against his heart.

CHAPTER 27
Second Night of the Strike

The city had lost its festive tone. After the first gunfire, rumors invaded the city, and little by little the movement in the streets lessened. The buses were running, but the rare passengers went quickly home again, afraid of fights and stray bullets.

"Bullets can't read addresses."

Inside the houses, the atmosphere among the families was almost one of terror. The encounter between the striking bakers and the police in Baixa dos Sapateiros assumed tremendous proportions: eighteen dead, dozens wounded. It was rumored that the syndicates would be attacked and the strikers dispersed by force. The ladies trembled and locked their doors as they lighted candles and lanterns inside their houses. The city was tense.

There was no dinner at Clovis's house. He was supposed to bring some food from the city, and Helena waited all afternoon. He didn't come home. The most mixed-up rumors were circulating. When she learned of the shooting in Baixa dos Sapateiros, she ran out into the street. But they told her that Clovis wasn't there when the shots broke out; he had been in the group that went to close down the bakery in Vitoria. She returned home less worried and continued to wait for her husband. They had three children, who were running about the dooryard, playing tag. What would she give them to eat? The cold stove waited uselessly in the kitchen. There was nothing left; they had even finished off the manioc flour. Already she had borrowed food for lunch from her neighbors, promising to pay it back when her husband returned. They, too, were in need, poor things, since the people who lived in that alley were either bakers or stevedores and were all on strike. She thought they were right, that their small salary was insufficient. They were within their rights to ask for more, to stop working until their bosses raised their wages. But she was afraid of the days ahead. There was no more food in her house, and in the neighbors' houses it would soon be gone, too. Where would the unions find money to sustain so many? If the strike went on much longer, they would be starved out. She went to the window. In the house next door, Ercídia appeared.

"Did Clovis come home yet, Helena?"

"No, Ercídia."

"Well, he may not tonight. Henrique said that I shouldn't wait for him. The strike's in full swing, and the men have to be out in the streets."

The black woman smiled.

"I'm going to have supper without him."

She smiled again, but why isn't Helena smiling back? What's the matter with her? She is crying. Ercídia goes next door to her neighbor's house.

"What is it, Helena?"

The stove in the kitchen is cold and empty. The black woman pats her neighbor on the head.

"Never mind, girl, don't worry. Over at my house there's enough fish for us all. And they'll win the strike and we'll all have more money."

Helena smiles through her tears.

After making sure the children were settled and sleeping, Helena puts a shawl over her shoulders and heads for the Graça neighborhood where Dona Helena Ruiz, the wife of her husband's boss, lives. She had been a washerwoman for Dona Helena, a lady who always tried to help the poor, and who called her "Namesake" without the slightest pride.

"Now you do these sheets up right, Namesake. I want them good and white."

In spite of being very wealthy, Dona Helena continued to do much of her own housework. She said that a person with nothing to do will occupy his mind with evil thoughts. And even though she had many parties to attend, movies to see, outings, etc., she always found time to look after her home. Her husband begged her to let the maids do everything, to enjoy her youth, beauty, and leisure, but she never listened.

"If I let the maids do everything, you'll never again have decent-looking clothes. And besides, I enjoy it."

Her husband would kiss her cheek, and later they would go to the movies, feeling very close. He would tell her about his business, speak proudly of the prosperity of the United Bakeries (he was intending to open another branch in Itapegipe), and she would smile, delighted with the husband God had given her. He would say, "You give me courage. If it weren't for you, I don't know what would become of me."

It had been through Dona Helena that Clovis had gotten a job in the bakery. The washerwoman had spoken to her mistress, and the next day Clovis had found a place. She hadn't seen Dona Helena in two years, ever since Clovis had gotten the job. Thinking about all this, the laundress made her way to Ruiz's house. Would Dona Helena still remember her namesake?

Dona Helena is in the living room embroidering something. Her husband is taking a bath upstairs, having come home very hot and tired after a day spent in conferences and in finding men to work in the bakeries.

As soon as she learns that the laundress has come to speak to her, Dona Helena calls her into the living room. She puts down the embroidery she has been doing by lantern light (her husband always complains, "You'll ruin your eyesight, Helena!") and smiles at the woman whose eyes are glued to the floor.

"So, Namesake, you've never come back to see us!"

"I've been so busy, Dona Helena. The children don't leave me time for anything."

"You know I've never found anyone who could do up the laundry as well as you?"

Helena smiles, a bit shy. Dona Helena remembers that she has come to ask for something.

"What do you want?"

Helena doesn't know how to begin. She twists her hands, grows embarrassed. Dona Helena asks, "What's wrong? Did something happen to your husband? Or is it your children?"

"Well, not exactly, Dona Helena. It's the strike."

"Ah! The strike. Ruiz is all upset about this strike, too."

"But if he wanted to—"

Dona Helena doesn't know about anything. The washerwoman tells her about life in the alley where the men earn a pittance in the bakeries and support their families on this meager salary. She tells her about the sick children. Now, during the strike—a fair strike to get a few cents more—the families were going hungry. Her children had eaten that day only because a neighbor lady had taken pity on them. But there were others going hungry.

Dona Helena is astonished.

"Children going hungry? Good heavens, can it really be?"

Yes, going hungry. And a little black girl died in a gunfight this afternoon. She was fortunate. The others, at home, asked for food and cried, "If this goes on, we'll have to go out begging. And the men want so little!"

Dona Helena rises, upset. Certainly Ruiz doesn't know about this situation. If he knew, he would have already raised his employees' salaries.

He is such a good man. . . . Dona Helena takes the washerwoman to the kitchen. She makes up a package of the best food in the house for her and gives her twenty mil-reis in addition. When the laundress goes off, bent and crying like a slave, Dona Helena says to her, "Don't you worry, Namesake. I'm going to talk to Ruiz right this minute. He doesn't know about these things. But I'm going to tell him, and he'll raise the men's wages at once. You'll see. He's so good."

Antônio Ruiz, owner of the United Bakeries, puts on a silk shirt as his wife comes into the room. Seeing her face, he asks in alarm, "What's the matter, darling?"

He goes up to his wife and kisses her.

"Are you sad? How about going to the movies today?" He laughs. "Oh, but the strike won't let my love see movies."

"It's about the strike I want to talk to you, Ruiz."

"Are you getting into politics, dear?"

In the next room, the couple's daughter sleeps in a storybook cradle surrounded by dolls.

Dona Helena remembers the children who are going hungry in the alleys.

"You need to come to terms with those men, raise their wages."

The husband turns about with a jerk.

"What?" His voice holds a brutality she doesn't know. But then he is sorry and says in a smooth voice, "My love, you don't understand these things."

"Who said I don't? I know more than you!" Dona Helena sees before her eyes the picture of starving children. "I know things you don't."

And she narrates emotionally to her husband the things the laundress Helena told her. At the end she smiles victoriously. "Didn't I say I knew things you didn't? Your little wife is very well informed!"

"But who told you I don't know all that?"

"You know? . . . and . . . you know?"

It seemed as though someone were hammering Dona Helena over the head. The blows were so hard that she lost her voice. Her husband moved closer to her.

"What is it, Lena? I know about it, yes."

"And you don't do a thing? You don't give those men a raise? Do you agree with this crime?"

"What crime, Lena?" Ruiz's surprise is not feigned.

"What crime?" Dona Helena grows more and more upset. "You mean, you don't think it's a crime to let these men, their wives and children—children, Ruiz—go hungry?"

"But, my dear, I didn't say that. Ever since the beginning of the world, it has been like that. There have always been poor and rich—"

"But, Ruiz, there are small children starving. Did you ever imagine little Heleninha going hungry? My God, it's horrible."

Ruiz paces nervously up and down.

"But why are you involving yourself in this? You don't understand these things."

"And you, who are so good . . . or seemed so—"

"I'm just like everybody else. Neither better nor worse."

There is silence in the bedroom. From the neighboring room they hear the strong breathing of their daughter. Ruiz explains, "Do you know what it is they want?"

"What they want is very little."

"But we can't give them anything. If we give them this raise today, tomorrow they'll want another, and then another, and one day they'll want the bakeries themselves."

"Well, I know there are children going hungry. And they really do earn so little. You never told me you knew about these things. I had no idea. If I had known—"

Ruiz grows irritated.

"If you had known, what would you have done? You have no notion of such things. I'm defending your automobile, your house, Leninha's education. Do you think I ought to go to work for those bastards?"

"But they want so little, Ruiz. It's impossible you should enjoy other peoples' suffering."

"I'm not saying I enjoy it. But this isn't the time to get sentimental; the situation is very serious. I can't be myself alone; it can't have anything to do with my feelings. I'm the boss, and I have to defend my interests. If we give those men an inch, tomorrow they'll take a mile. Do you want to give up the car, the house, the maids to help you with Leninha? I'm defending all this, I'm defending what is ours, our money . . . defending your comfort!"

He walks across the room and stops in front of his wife.

"Do you really think, Lena, that I get pleasure from knowing that there are people going hungry? Of course I don't. But war is war."

The daughter's breathing comes from the next room. Children going hungry, children with nothing to eat, crying for their supper. And her husband thinking it's all so natural. Her husband; whom she knows to be a good man, incapable of hurting a fly. There must be some mystery in all this, mystery that she doesn't understand. But the children are starving, meaning that if Ruiz hadn't prospered, it would be Leninha who was going hungry. Weeping, she begs her husband to concede the workers their raise.

"It's impossible, dear. Impossible. It's the one thing I can't do for you."

And once again he tries to explain that this is a war, that if he gives them an inch they'll take a mile, that a month later they will want another raise.

"I have to subject them to hunger."

He comes close to his wife and strokes her hair.

"Don't cry, Lena. . . ."

He puts his arms around her. Children are starving in the alleys.

"Don't come near me. You're horrible! Don't touch me."

And she sits there, sobbing and miserable, pitying herself, pitying her husband and envying the strikers. As she cries she murmurs, "Hungry children . . ."

Clovis stayed at the union office to hear the speeches. After the shooting, the strike took on a new character. The men are spoiling for revenge. It is difficult to contain them. Manifestos are put out, demanding the immediate release of the imprisoned strikers. Contradictory reports circulate. At one point a worker ran into the room and warned that the police were coming to attack the union office. Everybody prepared to defend it. But it was a false alarm. Nevertheless, the attack is awaited momentarily. At nine o'clock that evening, the stevedores' case is resolved in favor of the strikers. However, they decide not to return to work until the demands of the bakers and public utilities workers are also met.

Everyone goes to the other union offices to take them the news of this decision. Amid the speeches, another piece of news explodes. The police grabbed several workers and intend to force them to work under the threat of beatings. The syndicate is as agitated as the sea. They all go out. Commissions go to hold conferences with the bus and taxi drivers. Others go to talk to diverse types of factory workers. A large group marches to the offices of the Public Utilities Company to show their protest. Their courage is raised to an exalted pitch. It is ten o'clock.

A car is parked in front of the Public Utilities Company. It is a Hudson belonging to the director, an American who earns twelve contos a month. He is coming down the steps, a cigar in his mouth. The driver starts the car. Antônio Balduíno yells from the group of strikers, "Let's grab him, folks! Then we'll have a prisoner, too!"

The director is surrounded. The guards who were watching

the building run. Antônio Balduíno seizes the man by an arm and tears his white suit. The crowd screams, "Lynch him! Lynch him!"

Antônio Balduíno raises his arm to deliver a blow, but he hears Severino's voice saying, "It's no good hitting the man. We're workers, not murderers. Let's take him to the syndicate office."

Angrily, Antônio Balduíno lowers his arm. But he understands that he must conform, that the strike is not carried out by one man alone but by all. Amid an uproar, the American is taken to the Public Utilities workers' union.

The news of the American's capture spreads swiftly through the city. The police want him to be released. The American consulate moves into action. The strikers demand that the political prisoners be let go and that no one be forced to work under police threats. At eleven, the prisoners appear at the syndicate, reporting that the American consul talked the police into releasing them for fear the workers would kill the company director. The latter is let go in peace after hearing a few insults. Great enthusiasm reigns in the union office. Antônio Balduíno says to Henrique, "I don't care about him. But if I ever get my hands on that Dr. Gustavo . . ."

And he rubs his hands together, happy with life. The strike is very good.

Half an hour later, a manifesto is read amid great cheering: The bus and taxi drivers, together with the workers from the two textile factories and one cigarette factory, declare themselves on strike the next day unless the bakers' and Public Utilities workers' demands are met tonight. Pedro Corumba begins a speech: "A united body of workers can dominate the world."

Antônio Balduíno embraces a fellow he never saw before.

At midnight a message comes from the governor's palace. The representatives of the Public Utilities Company and the owners of the bakeries communicate to the strikers' commission that they have decided to meet the workers' demands in full. The new salary scale will be in effect starting the next day. The strike is over with complete victory for the workers.

Antônio Balduíno goes to Jubiabá's house. Now he looks at the pai-de-santo man to man, equal to equal. And he tells him that he discovered what the ABCs taught, that he found the right road. The rich people had let their eye of mercy dry up. But when they want, they can cause the eye of badness to dry up, too. Then Jubiabá, the magic man, bows before Antônio Balduíno as if he were Oxolufã, the old Oxalá, greatest of spirits.

CHAPTER 28
Hans, the Sailor

In his pocket, Antônio Balduíno fingers the one hundred twenty mil-reis he won this afternoon in the lottery. Night falls gradually over the city. A few days ago there was no electricity. The strike paralyzed everything. No, not everything. Because, thinks Antônio Balduíno, it was his own life that had been paralyzed. The strike had shown him another road, and he had found the desire to fight again. A month had passed. Still, even today, he sings under his breath a samba entitled "The Victory of the Strike," which came out the day after the workers' triumph. Antônio Balduíno sings, remembering the incidents of those two days.

"A syndicate of workers
Rose up to go on strike
They wanted higher wages
And others thought alike.
So through the common effort
They reached a common goal
The Public Utilities Company
Had to pay the toll."

The words, written by Permínio Lírio, were sung to the music of "It Makes You Bitter." The samba was widely sold in the city. The day after the strike was over, nothing else was sung in the streets where the trolley cars once again circulated. For Antônio Balduíno, the strike had been a true revelation. At first, he had loved it because it meant fighting, disturbance, and trouble, things he had enjoyed ever since he was a child. However, little by little the strike began to take on new aspects for the ex-boxer. It was something more serious than fighting and commotion. It was a battle directed toward an end; a fine battle, for it meant knowing what one wanted. Taking part in the strike together, they all liked each other, defended each other, and fought against slavery. The strike deserved an ABC. The samba Antônio Balduíno sings in passing isn't enough.

"There wasn't light to see by,
Nor was there bread to eat.
The telephones were silent,
No trolleys crossed the street.
No newspapers were printed,
So no one read the news.
The strikers stuck together
And thus they could not lose."

What the samba says is very true. Those men whom Antônio Balduíno had always scorned as slaves incapable of reacting had paralyzed the whole life of a city. Antônio Balduíno had thought that he and his semicriminal friends, who took for granted the use of razors and switchblades, were the free ones, the strong ones, the owners of the religious city of Bahia. This certainty had made him morbid, almost suicidal, when he had to go to work in the docks. But now he knew it wasn't that way. The workers had been slaves, but they were fighting for freedom. The samba itself says,

"The factories were halted
For days, the owners feared,
Until the workers triumphed
And all Bahia cheered."

From what he had learned through the ABCs read at night on the hills, from overhearing the conversations in front of his Aunt Luísa's house, from Jubiabá's sayings, he had judged that the way to fight against enslavement was to be a troublemaker, to live as he pleased and refuse to work. But that wasn't what the struggle was about. Not even Jubiabá knew that the true stuggle was the workers strike, the revolt of those who were enslaved. Now Antônio Balduíno knows, and that is why he smiles so broadly. Through the strike he regained his free, happy laughter. He sings the last two verses of the samba in such a loud voice that he frightens the pallid, virginal prostitute watering a flowerpot in the window of an old house on the Ladeira da Montanha.

Night has fallen, and the moon rises over the sea to join the stars. Gordo must be walking down Rua Chile—his arms stretched out, lookking for God. Zumbi dos Palmares shines in the sky. For white men it is the planet Venus. For black men like Antônio Balduíno, it is Zumbi, the Negro who died so as not to be a slave. Zumbi new those things that Antônio Balduíno has only know learned. The sailboats sleep. Only the *Homeless Traveler,* carrying pineapples, sets sail with its lantern glowing. Maria Clara goes standing up, singing. From her comes a powerful smell of the sea. She was born on the sea; the sea is her enemy and her lover. Antônio Balduíno loves the sea, too. He always saw the road home in the sea. When Lindinalva died, he had wanted to go down the road of the sea to find happiness in death, for he thought his ABC was lost and he would never do anything again. But the men of the docks, the men of the sea, had taught him about the strike. The sea had shown him the right road home. He gazes at the green ocean made golden by the moon. From far away comes the voice of Maria Clara.

"The way of the sea is wide, Maria."

An old man down on the docks plays a mouth organ. The music spreads itself softly over the sailboats, the canoes, the transatlantic ships, the great, mysterious sea Antônio Balduíno loves. If it weren't for the strike, he would have given up being sung in an ABC, given up seeing Zumbi dos Palmares shining like Venus. A figure walks by in the distance. Could it be Robert the juggler, who disappeared mysteriously from the circus? But he doesn't realy care. The harmonica music is plaintive. Maria Clara's voice has disappeared in the sea. Mestre Manuel is no doubt at the helm. He knows all the secrets of the sea. He will make love with Maria Clara by the light of the moon. The waves of the sea will wash over their bodies, making their love even better. The pale sand of the boat landing is silvery in the moonlight—the same sand where Antônio Balduíno has made love to so many mulatto girls who were all the freckled Lindinalva. If it weren't for the strike, his drowned body would be deposited in the sand, and the crabs would rattle inside him as they had inside the body of Viriato the Dwarf. The light of a sailboat shines. Will the wind take it away to the melody that the old Italian is playing on his mouth organ? One day, thinks Antônio Balduíno, I have to travel, I have to go to other lands.

One day he will take a ship, a ship like that Dutch one all lit up in the harbor, and will depart along the wide way of the sea. The strike saved him. Now he knows how to fight. The strike was his ABC. The ship is preparing to leave. The sailors have heard about the strike; they will recount in other lands how the workers struggled. Those who stay behind wave good-bye. Those who are leaving wipe their tears. Why cry when leaving? To depart is a good adventure, even when one departs for the bottom of the sea like Viriato the Dwarf. But it is better to depart for the strike, for the struggle. One day Antônio Balduíno will depart in a ship and will lead strikes in all the ports. On that day he will wave good-bye, too. Good-bye, folks, I'm leaving. Zumbi dos Palmares shines in the sky. He knows that Antônio Balduíno will not dive to his death in the sea after all. The strike saved him. One day he will wave good-bye with a handkerchief from the deck of a ship. The music of the harmonica cries a farewell. But he won't wave good-bye like those men and women of the first class, who wave to their friends, parents, brothers, and sisters, to their crying wives or sad fiancées. He will wave good-bye like that blond sailor who is in the stern of the boat and waves his cap at the whole city, at the prostitutes from the Ladeira do Taboão, at the workers who had held the strike, at the idlers in the Drowned Man's Lantern, at the stars among which is Zumbi dos Palmares, at the sky and the yellow moon, at the old Italian playing the harmonica, at Antônio Balduíno, too. He will wave good-bye like a seafaring man. He will bid them a fond farewell, for the strike had taught him to love all those, whether black, white, or mulatto, whether on land or sea, who were shaking off the fetters of slavery. The Negro Antônio Balduíno raises his big callused hand in response to the farewell salute of Hans the sailor.

THE ABC OF ANTÔNIO BALDUÍNO

A man as brave as Baldo
Would be difficult to find.
He always got in trouble
But his heart was good and kind.

He fought with many foremen;
Girls melted at his smile.
For fighting or for loving
No one could match his style.

But one day he was murdered
By a traitor mean and vile.

The ABC of Antônio Balduíno, bearing on its red cover a picture of the Negro taken when he was a boxer, is sold for the price of two hundred reis on the docks, in the sailboats, in the open markets (especially the Mercado Modelo in Bahia), and in the bars. It is bought by young peasants, fair-skinned seamen, young stevedores, and the women who love the peasants and seamen and the smiling Negroes on whose chests are tattooed an anchor, a name, or a heart.

Pensão Laurentina
(Conceição da Feira), 1934
Rio de Janeiro, 1935

OBSERVATIONS

The reader's attention is drawn to the glossary included in this book. Many of the terms used by the author are regional to the State of Bahia, and particularly to the city of Salvador, its capital, where the story takes place. The city is often referred to as "Bahia" (meaning *bay* in English) because it is located on the Bay of All Saints. The Paraguaçu River empties into this bay.

Salvador's enduring African flavor sets it apart from other Brazilian cities.

—Translator

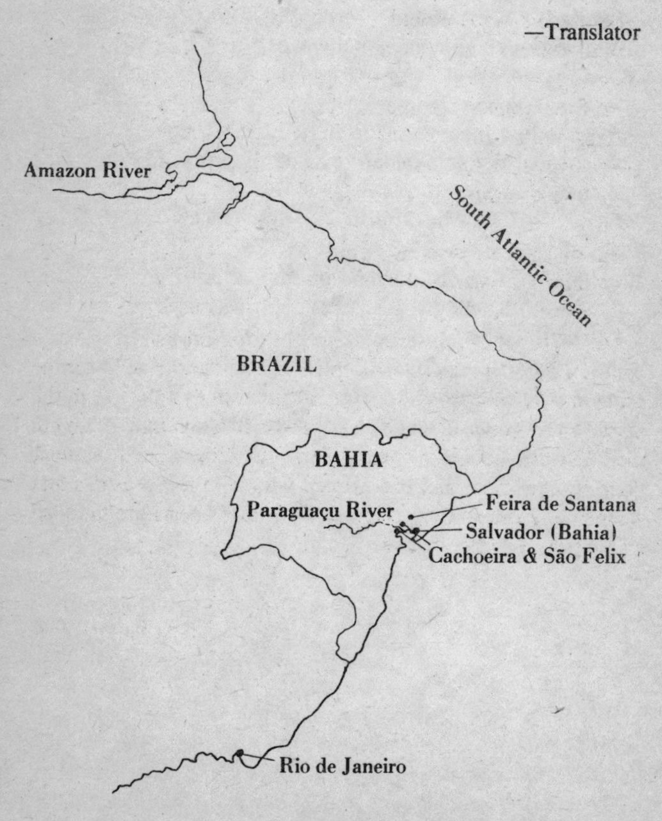

LIST OF UNTRANSLATABLE TERMS

Mingau: A porridge made of sweetened milk thickened by cornstarch, oatmeal, tapioca or another form of starch.

Munguzá: a sweet dish of corn cooked in coconut milk and seasoned with cinnamon and cloves.

Pai-de-santo: an elder or priest in the *candomblé* religious order, a voodoo priest.

Reis: a unit of money used in Brazil; now obsolete. One conto-de-reis was equivalent to 1,000 old cruzeiros, today one new cruzeiro.

Mil-reis: one thousand mil-reis is equivalent to one conto-de-reis.

Capoeira: a folkloric method of combat utilizing movements akin to dancing and acrobatics. It was used among black slaves and still exists.

ABC, Tirana, Coco, Samba: types of folkloric music and song.

Candomblé, Macumba: Afro-Brazilian religious syncretism practiced particularly in Salvador, Bahia.